MY BIG FAT FAKE WEDDING

LAUREN LANDISH

Edited by
VALORIE CLIFTON
Edited by
STACI ETHERIDGE

.

PROLOGUE

VIOLET—FIVE MONTHS AGO

his can't be happening. He can't be leaving me.

Not now.

Not ever.

My heels click across the hospital floor as I race down the hallway. I'm in such a panic, the words blaring over the PA system hardly register from the blood rushing through my ears in a dull roar.

"Code blue, room four! Code blue, room four!"

I nearly trip over my own feet as I break into a shuffling run, boomeranging for the nearest patient room. I swear my heart is going to explode when I spot the correct door and burst inside to see . . .

"Nana!" I exclaim as I see my grandmother, Angela Russo. She looks up from where she's hovering like a hen over my grandfather. The scowl on her face highlights the parentheses of wrinkles around her lips, making her worry immediately apparent.

My grandfather, Stefano, looks up at me, his unusually pale face widening into a huge smile. But even with the happiness blooming, I can tell he's worn out, aged decades in the short time since I last saw him.

"My beautiful little flower, Violet!" he sings, his Italian accent coming through as he holds his arms out to me. "I knew you would come. Come here so I can give you a kiss!"

"Oh, Papa, I was so scared!" I say, rushing into his arms and collapsing into a ball of relief. "I dropped everything and came as soon as I heard."

Papa looks over at Nana with a triumphant wink of his eye as he rubs my shoulders. "See, Angie? This one loves me the most. Do you see any of our other granddaughters here?"

"That's because you've scared them all away with your crazy stories," Nana growls, but there's an undercurrent of affection for the man who is both a thorn in her side and her everything.

Papa laughs and squeezes me with a fierce strength that belies his shrinking frame, raining kisses down upon my forehead. I feel comforted, enveloped in his familiar scent, leather and spicy meats . . . masculine and comforting. For a moment, I forget the direness of the situation as he rocks me back and forth in his arms like I'm a child or the one in need of comfort, though he's the one in the hospital bed.

But the moment is fleeting as reality slams back into me, and I rise to my feet to ask Nana in a rush of words, "What happened? Is he going to be okay? How long has he been like this?"

"The old fool was working out back in the summer heat after I told him he should take it easy and come inside," Nana says with a frosty scowl at Papa, but her voice softens as she speaks, revealing how frightened she really is. "I found him lying face down in the dirt."

"Papa!" I say in admonishment. "You know you're not supposed to be taking on a heavy workload, doctor's orders. Why didn't you listen to Nana?"

Grandpa waves away my worry with a bony hand. "I don't see what the fuss's all about. A man has to work, and I'll do what I need to until the day they put me six feet under. I just tripped and had a little fall, that's all." He says it like he believes that to be the truth.

Nana gives me a sour look that says, 'That's definitely not what happened.' "He passed out—" she begins.

"I fell and was getting up before you came squawking like a worried hen, making things worse," Papa interrupts. "So, I decided to lie back and let you do what you were going to do. You shoulda done the same for me."

"Nonsense!" Nana snaps. "If I hadn't found you, who knows what would've happened?"

"Nothing." Papa dismisses Nana with a nonchalant shrug. "I'd be fine, maybe about to pass out from eating some of your overcooked pasta—"

"Why, you old bast—"

"Bah! Hush, woman, you worry too much. I'm more likely to drop dead from all of your hen clucking than I will from a little heat."

Their bickering is comforting in a twisted way, the camaraderie of being together for decades and knowing which buttons to push to get a rise out of each other but also which ones are entirely off limits.

He pulls a long cigar out from the side of his bed and offers it to her. "Here. Calm yourself and have a stogie." The shit-eating grin on his face says he knows he's poking the bear, and I realize he's giving her something to focus on besides worrying about him. He's a slick old fox, I'll give him that.

Nana snatches the cigar out of his hand, brandishing it as if it's a weapon. "Have you gone *pazzo*? They don't even allow smoking in the hospital. And really? A smoke when you're supposed to be recovering?"

"Sure, why not? I'd rather have a smoke than act like a *pagliaccio*!"

Nana throws her hands up in frustration, the cigar flying from her hands in a perfect arc that ends in the trashcan. If she wasn't so riled up, I'd give her a round of applause, but as it is, I'm staying out of their battle. For now, at least. "Oh, *fanculo tutto*! You're impossible!"

"I know." Grandpa tosses me a mischievous wink meant to lighten the mood. "That's why you married me. You like the challenge."

The two continue to bicker as I look on fondly, feeling a

sense of relief. Whatever happened to land Papa in the ER hasn't robbed him of his feistiness, so it couldn't have been too bad, could it?

It's a particularly hot summer, and it's not uncommon for the elderly to overheat when they underestimate the weather. Maybe he's right and this is all a lot of fuss for nothing. He just needs a slap on the hand to follow the doctor's and Nana's orders a bit better, and everything will be fine.

Even as I tell myself that, I know it's wishful thinking and childish hopes. A girlish desire to deny the mortality of a man who has always seemed larger than life to me. Deep inside, I know he's no more immortal than the rest of us, but even so, I need to know this isn't going to happen again. I love him too much to lose him. Especially not now, and if I had my say, not ever.

After being reassured several times by Papa that he's fine, I excuse myself from the room to let him and Nana bicker themselves out.

In the hall, I run into a man wearing a long white coat and carrying a binder with Papa's name on the spine. His name tag says *Dr. Lee*, and he has an aura of calm control that seems to relax me immediately.

"Are you Violet?" he asks before I can say anything, giving me a warm smile.

I nod. "I am. How'd you know?"

He grins. "Your grandfather wasn't concerned in the least about his health and has been talking about you since the moment he came in, telling anyone who'll listen about his grand-daughter. If you didn't know, he's quite fond of you."

I smile. "That definitely sounds like him. Can you tell me what happened? I'm not sure I trust his version of events."

Dr. Lee's expression turns solemn and the energy around him shifts, making me instantly nervous. "It appears that, due to the heat and overworking himself, your grandfather's blood pressure dropped and he lost consciousness."

"That's what Nana said. So, if we can keep him from over-doing it, he's going to be okay." I say it definitively, like I'm adding tying him to his recliner in the air-conditioned living room to my to-do list.

Dr. Lee tilts his head, his lips pressed together. "Well, as I explained to Angela and Stefano, we're waiting for tests to come back for a more complete picture, but I don't need the tests to tell me that his heart isn't in good shape. It hasn't been in quite some time."

Oh, no.

"But he's stable now . . ." I say, like I'm refuting his medical knowledge with only the power of my hope.

"I'm sorry to be the bearer of bad news, Violet, but . . ."

The growing look of sorrow and despair in Dr. Lee's eyes says everything, and I'm forced to grab ahold of a wall rail to keep from falling.

No.

It can't be.

It just can't.

My worst nightmare come to life.

"How long does he have?" I ask through the lump in my throat. The words sound surreal, like someone else is saying them.

"At his age, it's hard to say," Dr. Lee muses, shrugging his shoulders. "Anything I say is at best an educated guess. Six months? A year, maybe? But he's a stubborn mule who refuses to follow orders, which complicates things. To be honest, he could go at almost any time if we can't get his heart to function properly and him to be compliant."

His words, an awful confirmation of what I feared most, hit me like a sucker punch to the gut, the air leaving my lungs in one forceful gust.

Six months to a year? Or less?

How can Papa, the only father figure I've ever known, the man who practically raised me from a pigtailed toddler to adulthood, the man who could take on anything the world threw at him and live to tell about it . . . have such little time to live?

In that moment, all the should've, could've, and would'ves flash in front of my eyes. It's as if everything I expected to expe-

5

rience with Papa has turned into a puddle that's evaporating quicker than I'd ever considered.

But the worst part is, the one thing he's wanted to see the most is likely to never happen, and that looms like a dark umbrella over my breaking heart.

When's my beautiful little flower getting married so I can walk her down the aisle?

To say marriage is a huge tradition in my family is like saying a tsunami is a little wet. An understatement of such magnitude, it's laughable, especially for my grandparents, who look forward to the next generation of weddings with teary smiles and proclamations of the continuation of their legacy with another branch on the family tree.

Hell, most of the women in my family are married off before they're old enough to drink alcohol. In fact, I'm probably the only woman in my family, at age twenty-six, who isn't married with a wagonload of kids.

Due to my busy career, I've been single for as long as I can remember, although I've always dreamed about having this big fairytale wedding. I used to use Nana's curtains as a makeshift veil and Papa would pretend to walk me down the aisle. I want him to do that for real, hold my hand as I greet my husband-to-be, bless us with a marriage as long and happy as his and Nana's has been, and see that I've finally grown into the woman he always told me I could be. Successful, loved, happy.

Now it's never going to happen.

As if sensing my tormented thoughts, Dr. Lee adds, "If there's anything you need to say or anything important left for you to do with your grandfather, I'd do it very soon. Now if you'll excuse me . . ."

Gee, thanks for the guilt trip, Doc.

Whatever else the doctor says fades off into the background as I watch Nana and Papa bicker through the glass window, happier now and blissfully unaware of the countdown looming.

In that moment, denial surges and I clench my fists.

This can't happen. I won't let it.

Six months to a year?

I can make it work.

Suddenly determined, a feeling of resolution washes over me as a plan formulates in my mind.

Don't worry, Papa. I'm going to find myself a husband so you can walk me down the aisle on my wedding day before you leave this earth . . . if it's the last thing I do.

CHAPTER 1

VIOLET

"*I* still can't believe it!" I squeal, wiggling my fingers and watching my engagement ring flash as the overhead lights reflect on the diamond's faceted surface.

Having already heard this once, or maybe two dozen times, my two best friends sigh but rally with the appropriate oohs and ahhs, even throwing me a bone of another "Congratulations, girl!"

My lifelong bestie, Abigail Andrews, and Archie Hornee, my interior design assistant, are basically saints for putting up with me at this point. "Colin and I are getting married!"

Archie arches one perfectly sculpted eyebrow and presses a palm to his black T-shirt-covered chest, which is most definitely manscaped. Ever the sarcastic ball of sass, he deadpans, "Dear, we know." He continues the performance by pulling a Vanna White, slapping a big fake smile on his face and gesturing widely to the roomful of wedding gowns surrounding us. When he finishes, his face goes right back to his usual blank 'fuck off' mode.

As if we'd be at a wedding dress shop for any other reason. Lord knows, Abigail and Archie aren't looking to get married, and obviously not to each other since Abigail lacks a rather important piece of the perfection that Archie is looking for, a never-ending appreciation of his special brand of hilarious, off-the-cuff, don't-care-about-being-politically-correct, catty-bitchiness.

So nope, not for them, for sure. We're here for me! I can't believe it's really happening.

It's been five months since Papa's diagnosis, and what a busy five months it's been.

Initially, I thought there'd be no way I'd ever get married before his heart gave out. After all, his doctor had painted a grim picture with no happy ending.

But despite the odds, Papa has miraculously held on long enough for me to reconnect with an old high school fling and get engaged after a whirlwind romance where we both said we wanted the whole nine yards—wedding, marriage, kids. Luckily, since Colin and I already had a history, it wasn't starting at ground zero, and instead, we moved quickly after a short get-to-know-you-now phase. He's a really good man, and I think we can be happy together.

Serious relationship, party of two . . . here! I think, adding a shimmy to my ass as I raise my hand, peering at the weighty sparkle resting there again.

But despite my excitement, the rows of gorgeous gowns, and two friends with a sharp eye for fashion, I'm currently trying on what has to be my twentieth wedding dress. Ride or Die Bride, an edgy bridal shop that calls itself the *Number One Bridal Shop for the Modern Badass Chick*, is failing to deliver a dress that is *The One*.

They've got everything from fairy tale princess to woodland nymph to Vegas stripper, mixed in with classic beauties covered in expensive lace and hand-sewn beading. My dress is here, I know it is. But in the three appointments I've made, I haven't found it. Yet.

I need *perfection*.

It has to be. Everything about my wedding has to be perfect in order to do it right for Papa.

"I'm so happy for you!" Abigail declares, rushing forward and pulling me into a fierce hug. A moment later, I feel another set of arms wrap around me, Archie's, and I'm encased in a group hug.

"Hey, guys!" I gasp as I feel my bridal shapewear corset, a marvelous invention that gives me the perfect hourglass figure, squeeze me to within an inch of my life. Any more and I swear it'll crush my ovaries. "I know you're both excited for me, but I can't breathe!"

No one told me trying on wedding dresses and getting the right shape could be this painful. I thought it was come in, try on a few dresses, and after a few twirls and happy tears, be done.

"Shit, sorry!" Abi and Archie exclaim in near unison. As Archie jumps back, Abi tries to loosen my corset but fails as there's too much dress fabric in the way. "I forgot how tight we had to pull it to get you into this thing."

"I'd blame it on the pa-pa-pa-pasta!" Archie sings, doing a not half-bad riff on *Blame It* by Jamie Foxx, while measuring my curves through fingers held in a square like he's a cameraman looking for my good side. His puckered lips and sharp brow remind me of Zoolander, and I'm waiting for him to say something about 'Blue Steel', but it doesn't come.

Still, I can't help but burst into laughter at his antics then gasp as the corset tightens even further. *Shit, is this damn corset alive?* "Hey!" I rasp, leveling a stern finger Archie's way and defending the curves I was blessed with through a particularly short and fierce round of puberty. "I'm half Italian. Pasta, pizza, lasagna, and red wine are a way of life for me, okay?"

With zero apology, he traces my shape reflecting in the mirror, which is admittedly a little fuller looking in this unflattering white taffeta ballgown that's a definite no-go. "No one's commenting on your curvy figure, love. There damn sure ain't nothing wrong with a little a junk in the trunk. Just look at Kim Kardashian." He waits a moment and then adds under his breath, but still loud enough for Abi and me to hear, "Only in America can someone turn an ass and a sex tape into a multi-billion-dollar family empire!"

The next gown is wrong too, and the one after that is even worse.

It's a sparkly number that somehow makes me look like a constipated fairytale princess. Too New Jersey, if that makes any damn sense, and as a half-Italian, avoiding *any* Jersey Shore comparisons is vital to me.

Which probably means I'll have to come back another time to try on even more gowns. Abi and Archie might kill me if I make them sit through this again, but I need their help and want someone to celebrate with when I do find *The One*.

Because I will.

Against all odds, I found a husband-to-be, a venue with an opening for our short-notice ceremony and big reception, and I will find a dress that makes me feel special for my big day.

Abi adjusts my bra straps, beaming at my reflection even though she already told me this dress is ridiculous and Archie made a rather harsh comment about my being ready for Wedding Day: 90s Vegas Style with the amount of bling thrown on this thing.

"When do you want to come check out the invitations?" Abi chirps. She co-owns a local specialty floral boutique and is handling all of my flower arrangements personally. But as my maid of honor, she offered to do the invitations as well.

Shit.

"Oh, yeah, sorry! I've been so busy with work and dress hunting, I totally forgot about that! When do you want me to come by the boutique to see them? Colin and I have a breakfast date tomorrow morning to talk about the wedding, so we could rearrange and come by the shop instead. But Archie and I have a job lined up right after—"

"With Bitch-ella, the Ice Queen," Archie interrupts with a mutter that I can't really disagree with, but I give him a side-eye that begs him to at least try to be professional about the client.

"So, we'd have to be fast," I finish.

Abi purses her lips thoughtfully as she places her hands on my hips, moving my body slightly to the side and staring at my shape in the mirror. "No way. You two do a breakfast date, and we can figure out a time when it's not a rush. Tomorrow's Friday, so maybe we can do it after work and then grab drinks?"

I nod, ignoring the flutters of butterflies in my stomach. I don't know why I'm so nervous all of a sudden. I mean, yes, there's a lot to do and not much time to do it in, but everything's going to plan, just like I hoped.

Papa.

Colin.

The wedding.

I should be on cloud nine. Yet, these butterflies don't feel like good, happy flutters. More like a tornado of responsibility, expectations, and nerves.

Abi turns me, eyeing me thoughtfully. "You good? Everything all right, Vi?"

I don't want to bring down the mood or start examining the questions in my head too closely, so I play pretend, telling myself that slightly cold feet are normal. After all, getting married is a big deal and not one to take lightly.

"I'm fine. It's just this damn corset!" I say with a grimace, grabbing my sides. "After I meet with Colin tomorrow, everything should be good to go." I look between the both of them, spreading my arms out to the side and twirling across the showroom stage in my dress one last time. "Final verdict?"

"Not my favorite," Abi says, shaking her head.

"I agree," Archie co-signs. "It's totally giving me *Tangled*, meets the *Little Mermaid*, meets *Cinderella* vibe, but like they all became dancers on the Vegas strip. Emphasis on the strip."

"Gee, thanks, Arch," I mutter sourly. But funnily enough, I agree with his assessment, although my terms were a little less . . . animated and crude.

Archie winks at me. "You're welcome, sweet cheeks."

"Don't worry, Vi. We're going to keep looking and find the perfect dress that'll knock Colin flat on his ass!" Abigail's assertion settles me slightly, helping me focus on the issue at hand . . . my dress. If I can just find that, everything else will be smooth sailing.

"Yeah, turn that frown upside down!" Archie adds, pushing at my cheeks with two fingers. He looks deep into my eyes, and I'm expecting some sweet words of wisdom, but I should know better with Archie. "Just think, before you know it, Colin won't have to bag it up anymore, and you'll get to feel the *real* thing. How big we talking here?" He holds his fingers a few inches apart, spreading them to indicate a bigger and bigger appendage, but it's seeing the whites of his eyes growing as I don't stop him that does me in.

"Oh, God, you're too much!" I groan, forcing his hand down and chuckling.

Come on, girl. Everything is going to work out. It has to.

"I'M CALLING OFF THE ENGAGEMENT."

The words hit me like a freight train, a grenade launched directly into my heart.

When Colin told me he wanted to meet with me this morning, I was under the impression it was to discuss the details of our wedding, plan who we were inviting, what DJ we were going to use, etc.

Never in a million years did I think it would be to dump me.

"Violet?" Colin asks, noticing that I've gone completely rigid, my latte frozen inches away from my lips and my half-eaten bagel in front of me.

Colin Radcliffe. My fiancé. *My ex-fiancé*, I correct with a wince. *Fucking rat* is what my mind is yelling loudly.

Dressed in a gray, freshly pressed, tailored suit, Colin's blond hair is styled and parted, and he's gazing at me with expectancy, as if I'm supposed to burst into hysterics, crying and making a scene worthy of Hamlet.

But I'm frozen, thinking WTF?

Why?

And . . . why now?

But wondering the whys won't do me any good. Colin's obviously thought this through and wants to end it all.

Doesn't matter that I just spent weeks trying to find the perfect wedding dress.

Doesn't matter how much I want the fairytale wedding.

Doesn't matter that my Papa won't get to walk me down the aisle. Maybe never.

None of it matters to him.

In a hit that's even more impactful than Colin's words, I realize that none of my thoughts on this betrayal have anything to do with us, our relationship, or our love. *Love?*

Do I even love Colin?

Stupid me thought I'd make it work using a checklist for our compatibility.

Both career-oriented people. Check.

Former lovers. Check.

Both matured and ready to settle down. Check and check.

Boy, was I wrong on that last one.

"Violet?" Colin presses again, this time reaching across the table and placing his hands atop mine.

Suddenly, I feel queasy, and I have to fight back the urge to throw up in his lap.

"I know this has to come as a shock to you, but I'll cover the lost deposit on the wedding hall and every other expense associated with our engagement so you don't have to worry."

Just like I thought, he's already planned his exit strategy, as if our wedding, our marriage, was some business transaction. For him, maybe it was. For me? I don't know, I realize. Maybe this is what the buzzing butterflies have been trying to tell me?

"Why?" I ask simply, battling down the surge of nausea.

Colin licks his lips, lips that I once enjoyed on my neck, on my breasts, on my most sacred of places.

"Violet, you know I adore you, and you're beautiful, smart, and kind, but . . . I don't think I'm ready for marriage." He stares at me again, rubbing my hands as if waiting for the crying hysterics he knows must be coming.

He definitely wants a show, just not too much of one. That perfect balance of greedy hunger for drama, tampered with the knowledge that he doesn't want to look bad.

That's why he picked the coffee shop, I realize. Cold and calculated. The Radcliffe way. In public, he knows I'm not going to go fully emotional, batshit crazy or really even make a scene. It's not my style.

But he does want to see me shatter into a million tiny pieces, and he wants an audience while he does his dirty work.

I've been ignoring it, something I could easily do with our quick whirlwind relationship, but I can see it clearly now that he's serving it up on a platter like a Thanksgiving turkey.

Everything is a façade with him. Image and reputation reign supreme.

I bet he thought I'd fit some corporate wife checkbox. Which would be so hurtful, except that I guess I was doing the same thing with my own checkboxes.

This was doomed from the start.

When I don't muster even a single teardrop or argument, he continues, "We're both so young, and hell, we haven't even had sex in over three weeks." His tone is accusatory, like it's my fault we've been so tired that sex has seemed like one more thing on the ever-growing to-do list.

He keeps digging at the wound, pouring salt in a steady stream into the bloody mess of our relationship. "We're both so busy with our jobs. You have that decorating thing you do that you love so much, and it takes up so much of your time, and I'm really busy at Dad's company, kicking ass and making deals. I . . . I just think we're at two different crossroads in our lives."

The decorating thing that I do? Fuck off.

Out of all the things he said, insulting my job pisses me off the most.

And I could argue against so many of his points, letting him know that everything he said was bullshit.

But I'm not going to because, simply put, I don't have time for this shit.

And I realize . . . I don't care. Not about Colin.

I'm such an idiot. But it was all for a good reason.

Sorry, Papa. I tried.

"Fine," I say simply, pulling my hands away from his before

taking off my engagement ring. "Here. You can take this back, too. I don't want it."

I place the ring on the table and slide it across toward him, resisting the urge to throw it in his face or shove it up his nose, not wanting to give him the satisfaction of an emotional outburst. The huge diamond rock in the center sparkles against the light, catching the eye of several women sitting around us.

I swear some of their heads turn like *The Exorcist* to get a better look as they realize what's happening, their eyes as big as saucers as they gawk at the size of the ring.

One of the women even leans so far forward to get a better look that she jostles her steaming hot coffee, spilling it on her hand. But instead of crying out at what I know has to hurt, she quietly blots at it, blowing cool air across her hand so she doesn't miss a single moment of the Colin and Violet Breakup Show.

"You know," I say as I grab my purse and slide on my Gucci shades, ignoring the commotion of googly-eyed stares and growing whispers from women around us, "It was really good to reconnect after so long, Colin. And we tried to make it work. It didn't. Thanks for everything."

My words are clipped and to the point.

If he's going to break off our engagement like this, I see no reason to drag it out with some long ass monologue that'll amount to nothing in the end, anyway.

Finished, I begin to rise from my chair, but Colin grabs my arm, holding me in place, his jaw slack in surprise.

One of the women watching suddenly decides that's her cue and claps her hands sharply, interrupting our scene with one of her own. "Boy, you'd best let that girl's arm go. You had your moment, and a queen like that is better off without a twat-stain like you."

Several people gasp at her language and volume, but Archie has me corrupted to not even blink at that level of crudeness. Thankful for the support, I look over to her and offer a weak smile of appreciation. For his part, Colin scowls but loosens his grip. Still, he's not done.

"Wait a minute now, Vi. You're not even going to try to talk about this? After all we've been through?" His voice has an almost whine to it, confirming what I expected.

He wanted me to break down and beg him not to leave me.

In front of a fucking audience.

Like he's some golden goose prize that I would debase myself to possess.

Well, he can kick rocks.

I won't give him the satisfaction of a show.

I shrug nonchalantly. "Nope."

"Look, Vi, I know how much our getting married means to you. I get it, you're pissed and upset. I would be too, but can we please not end things on bad terms? You don't have to act this way—"

"We're *fine*," I say, disengaging my arm from his grasp and rising to my feet. "Besides, you're right. It's probably for the best."

Colin's lips work for several seconds, at a loss for words. Like he can't believe this didn't turn out how he expected, me in a crying puddle at his feet.

He clenches his jaw, showing that he's actually getting angry. "Violet—"

"'Bye, Colin."

Ruffled, Colin straightens his collar and clears his throat, trying one last tactic, gesturing at my half-eaten food. "Will you just sit down and finish the bagel, at least?"

Turning away, I toss over my shoulder, just as casually as he tossed away our relationship, "No time. I gotta go to work . . . and do that 'decorating thing'."

My single cheerleader stands up, her arm circling in rally. "That's right, girl. Strut it out of here and own the world." She sneers at Colin, more emotionally invested in this than even I am, and isn't that pitiful?

She's my only supporter, though. Every other woman in here is judging me as unworthy of keeping Colin. All they see is a handsome guy in a suit with a flashy diamond ring . . . back on the market.

I imagine Colin will be collecting numbers by the stacks before he even walks out of the coffee shop.

Well, they can have him.

I get into the cab and far down the block before the tears come. Not for Colin, not for the decimation of our relationship, but for Papa and for the little girl I once was, and still am to some degree, who wants to make her grandfather happy.

CHAPTER 2

ROSS—TEN YEARS AGO

I *see her again. Violet Russo.*

The Queen Bee of her little group that includes my sister.

They're watching me. All gathered around Violet's locker, and she's whispering to them behind her hand as if I could read her lips from down the hall.

She's talking shit about me, I bet. Telling them how much of a bastard I am.

I'd be pissed off if it weren't true.

It's become her daily ritual, telling everyone how much she hates me with that wildfire in her eyes. It's become my daily ritual, too, doing things I know will piss her off because it's entertaining to see her explode. I don't even know how the habit got started, but neither of us has any desire to stop the constant warring.

But she's plotting something. Make no doubt about it, some sort of revenge for my relentless teasing is on her mind. I can see it in her eyes, the smug tilt of her smile now that she's dropped her hand, and the way she stands tall like she's unreachable.

Unfortunately for Violet, I have something special for her today . . . courtesy of Bio Lab.

As I reach my locker, Violet furtively glances my way, but as soon as our eyes meet, she quickly averts her gaze. Even the small battles are a victory against her.

But she whispers something into the ear of my little sister, Abigail, who's smiling as if she approves of whatever treachery Violet is planning.

Yep, she's plotting something, all right.

Too bad I'm about to beat her to the punch.

I place my books into my locker and slam it with a loud bang and boldly make my way over.

Halfway there, I hesitate. I'm a cocky son of a bitch, but it's a pack of them and only one of me. And if I know anything, high school girls are like zombies. Easy enough one on one, but in packs, you're nothing but lunch.

But I quickly brush any apprehension aside. I'm the football team captain, for God's sake. I'd be laughed out of the locker room for being scared of a bunch of girls, especially freshmen who look up to me like I'm a god among men.

All except for Violet. Maybe that's why it's fun to tease her. She never takes it easy on me because I'm a big shot at school. She mostly acts like she doesn't give a fuck about any of that stuff and challenges me at every turn to be more creative and strategic with my teasing.

She's gonna regret one-upping me because I've got a good one planned for her this time.

"Hey, ladies," I say as I saunter over, plastering a huge grin on my face. "How's everyone doing today?"

Several of the girls blush and giggle, shooting heart-eyes among each other, but an already tense Violet snaps, "Um, hi. What happened—you lose your asshole hat today? Why are you being so polite?"

I place a hand over my heart, faking a pained expression. "Ouch! Oh, Vi, it gets me right here that you have such a low opinion of me."

I glance to the girl at my right, a blonde whose name I don't even know, and whisper conspiratorially, "She really hates me, huh? I don't understand it. I'm a nice guy." I swear the blonde's eyes widen with my every word, and she's nodding vacantly. I get that reaction a lot, and I hate it.

Violet scowls, not buying my nice guy act for a second, and then growls, "Sure, if that rotted thing you call a heart were capable of feeling emotion."

Abigail peers at me suspiciously, glancing down the hallway to where my teammates are gathering around my locker. "Doesn't our school's resident top jock have better things to do than to harass us?"

"Sure, I do . . . but it's a beautiful day," I say, giving my sister one of my mega-watt smiles before turning my eyes back on Violet. "And I can't think of a better way to spend it than with a sweet girl like Violet." For good measure, I wrap my arm around Violet's shoulders, giving her a gentle squeeze as I pull her to my side. Every jaw drops in shock, jealousy, or some combination of the two. Except for Violet.

"I, uh . . ."

For once, Violet is speechless, caught off guard by my flirting out of nowhere, her mouth opening and closing like a fish as she gawks at me like I've sprouted barbed horns on my forehead. It takes a lot of effort not to laugh. I'm sure she was expecting me to call her chicken legs or one of the other variations we tag each other with, but I like being unpredictable. Keeps her on her toes.

Besides, 'chicken legs' doesn't describe Violet anymore. So, if I'm gonna use it, I have to make it good.

Abigail peers at me suspiciously. "What's got you in such a good mood? Did you get a D- on your biology exam, instead of an F?"

"I came bearing a gift, actually," I say. "For beautiful Violet."

"What the hell —" Violet begins to say as she tries to unsuccessfully pull away from me, totally wary and expecting a punchline any moment. Smart girl.

"How about some frog legs to go along with those chicken legs?" I yell, pulling the not-yet-dissected dead frog I borrowed from Biology from behind my back and stuffing it down the front of Violet's shirt.

Caught off guard, Violet lets out an ear-piercing scream, grabbing at her shirt as she tries to get the frog off her. Between the two of us, her shirt gets more than a little stretched out, and her red lacy bra flashes for a split second.

I'm shocked for a moment, not having expected to expose her. But then she takes off running for the girl's bathroom, still screeching like a banshee, and like the immature asshole I am, I double over in laughter. Nearby, all of my buddies and boys up and down the hall are laughing and pointing as Violet's screams echo through the hallway.

"Dammit, Ross, why do you have to be such an asshole to her? She's my best friend!" Abigail hisses angrily, punching me in the chest. "Why can't you ever just leave Violet alone?"

"*Calm down, Abs. It's just a joke,*" I say defensively, surprised at how angry Abi is.

We play pranks on each other all the time like this, and Abi is usually a good sport about the casual warfare Violet and I have against each other.

But not this time.

It did go a little further than I'd intended, but Violet's cool. She'll be pissed and then come back at me just as hard. I'll have to be on the lookout for her retaliation.

Furious, Abi lets out a disgusted huff. "*Stuffing a frog down her shirt is your idea of a joke? Grow up, Ross! You probably just ruined her favorite shirt, the one her grandpa gave her for Christmas! And half the football team just saw her bra.*"

For the first time in a long time, I feel a pinch of shame. Maybe I took my juvenile antics just a little too far this time. I look back to my boys and see them high-fiving each other and realize that I might've put a target on Violet that I didn't intend.

Some of the guys think the incoming freshmen are 'fresh meat', and I had to put a bounty on both Abigail's and Violet's heads to make sure no one would touch them. Just a big brother looking out, but I might have to refresh the guys' memory about Vi being off limits after that little show.

Shit.

"*Sorry, Abs. I didn't mean —*"

Abigail shakes her head, and I can feel the disappointment coming off her in waves, even as she glares daggers at me. "*You never do, but sometimes, I wonder about you, Ross.*"

I begin to argue. "*I'm just having fun —*"

"*Yo, Ross, that was epic! Get your ass over here!*" My best friend and buddy, Kaede, calls from my locker, laughing.

"*Go and have your little laugh with your friends . . . at Violet's expense.*" The accusation burns, but she's not remotely done. "*But I expect you to give Violet a sincere apology after school . . . or else,*" Abi threatens, letting me know she's going to tell Mom, who can be absolutely ruthless in making me apologize whenever I get too out of line. I might be an asshole to most, but not to my mother.

Once she's sure I understood her threat, Abi walks off in the direction of the girl's bathroom in search of Violet.

As I watch her go, I keep telling myself that Abigail's full of shit.

I didn't take it too far, did I? It was all in fun, and Violet's fine. Hell, she's probably plotting her vengeance right now. She's good like that, exciting, challenging, likes to give as good as she takes. But I'll apologize to keep Abs off my back. Probably have to guard my balls so Violet doesn't rip them off, though. She can be a badass bitch when she wants to be.

For some girls, that'd be an insult. For Violet, it's a compliment.

* * *

Present day

"ANOTHER GOSSIP SPREAD FROM *IN STYLE NEWS* MAGAZINE!" my father, Morgan Andrews, seethes, slapping a glossy tabloid rag down on the board room table and sliding it in front of me. He stabs a hairy finger at words printed across the top while leveling a scowl that could cut through a mountain at me. "When the hell are you going to grow up, Ross?"

"When hell freezes over," my youngest sister, Courtney, who doubles as our father's assistant and my antagonizer, cheerfully supplies. Dressed in a tight black skirt, white dress shirt, and matching glossy heels, she's perched on the edge of the obelisk-like board room table, her arms crossed over her chest and a huge smirk on her face.

I don't have to guess at what's got her so chipper. She never misses an opportunity to witness Dad laying into me. Even in a professional setting.

She calls it karmic revenge for all the hell I gave her as a kid.

I call it Annoying Little Sister Syndrome, even if I was a bit of a shit to her when we were younger. Nothing serious. I'm not a monster.

But I might've convinced her that chicken nuggets were made of zebra meat once upon a time, which wouldn't have been so bad, except she was going through a phase where that was one of the few things she ate. After days of only eating cheese sticks, she finally told Mom what I'd said and I'd been forced to apologize and tell her the truth, and I'd been grounded from chicken nuggets myself for an inordinate amount of time.

25

And that's only one instance of the childish shit I pulled with my sisters.

Fun times, I think fondly. Before everything got so damn serious.

"What am I guilty of doing this time?" I ask my dad wearily, afraid to look down at the page.

Being somewhat of a local celebrity is weird. When I was younger, the media would try to get pictures of our family because my dad is a bigshot in the business world. And then overnight, when I turned eighteen, I went from 'rebellious wild child football star' to 'hottest bachelor on the market', and that's a damn weird thing to hear about yourself when you're barely out of high school and feel like a kid muddling his way through college. My love life, sex life, and private life have become fodder for consumption and it's exhausting. Always on show, always be pulled together, always represent, always be an Andrews . . . like I give a single, solitary fuck about what some past her prime trophy wife in the grocery line thinks about me when I can't even run to the store in grungy jeans because it'd cause some sort of scandal that would hurt my family's company.

Like now.

"Look and see for yourself," Dad growls.

Anxious, I slowly peer down at the attention-grabbing headline.

Notorious Playboy Ross Andrews Nicks out of Nightclub with Wife of Mega Pastor.

The alliterative words are positioned over top of a blown up shot of me and a woman. In the picture, you can see me trying to hide her face, but in doing so, I gave the photographer free reign to take clear pictures of my disheveled mug and wrinkled dress shirt that's got one too many buttons open at the top.

"The hell?" I gawk in disbelief, remembering the night.

I'd met a woman in the club who said she was lonely and wanted someone to talk to. I'm no fool. That's totally code for only wanting one night, and she was hot in a broken doll sort of way. And we had talked. She'd been touch feely, the one to undo that extra button, but that was it. Later, as the night wore on and we both realized that nothing beyond conversation was going to come of the evening, she became adamant that she had to go home and no one could see her at the club, so I snuck her out the back . . . and accidentally into the waiting lens of the press. I'd done my best to help hide her face, though I didn't know why.

"I didn't know who she was or that she was married!"

"It's your business to know!" Dad snorts, pacing the room back and forth like a caged tiger. I can see his mind whirling just as fast as he makes laps from the window to the wall. He turns around to address me once he reaches the front of the table, placing both hands upon it and leaning forward. "What the hell were you thinking, Son? A pastor's wife? Joeden Snow's, no less?"

"Like I said," I say firmly. "I didn't know. She didn't even give me her name, just started talking."

"Sure," Dad says acidly. "Was that before, or after—"

I interrupt him, standing and placing my hands on the table, mirroring his stance because I'm not some intern he can push around. Hell, I'm annoyed that I'm being forced to defend myself about a private matter. "Let me be clear. I didn't sleep with her. She obviously needed someone or something, but all we did was talk, and then I had the driver take her home and then me home."

Dad pauses, brought short by the anger in my voice and the challenge to his authority. He stares at me for a long while, scowling, but then relaxes. Some of the tension eases from my body. "It doesn't matter if you slept with her or not," he finally says with a sigh. "The damage is done. We have shareholders who are members of Pastor Snow's church . . . including the pastor himself. They are not pleased."

"Except nothing happened!"

Dad shakes his head. "Doesn't matter. Bad optics is bad optics. And your track record doesn't help matters." Another dig that stings.

"What I do in my private life is no one's business," I growl. "Our shareholders should concern themselves with what we put in their pockets, not what I choose to do in the bedroom."

"Except for the fact that when we took their money, we made a pact. A pact that stated that we, as a family-run business, would uphold the values of our investors," Dad argues. "Something you're woefully failing at, Ross."

The room grows so silent you can hear a pin drop.

Even Courtney's amused smirk has vanished. There's playing the good daughter and getting jabs in on me. Then there's shit hitting the fan, and this is for sure one of those times.

"Are you for real? Who the fuck are they to dictate what I do with my personal life?"

"They're the people making all of this possible," Dad says, holding his hands out to his sides, encompassing the entire boardroom and the skyline behind him.

"Say whatever you want about me, but I've done a lot for this company, and I'm committed and work hard—"

"You want to know what's really being committed and hard work?" Dad growls swiftly, making me feel as if I walked right into a trap. "Settling down. Being happily married for thirty-five years. All while raising three children and giving them a good life. So, if you want to know what takes *real* commitment and hard work, try standing up, being a man, and finding someone to have a meaningful relationship with."

"So that's what this is really about?" I ask acidly as a conversation we've had multiple times begins playing on automatic loop. "You're using this incident as an excuse to make me fall in line—"

"It breaks your mother's heart to see you strutting around like a cocky, arrogant peacock that endlessly sows his oats," Dad snarls. "You could have any woman you want, and what do you do instead? Carouse around, squandering precious time that could be better used to start a family."

I stare at my Dad like he's lost it. "You're a piece of work."

"Your mother and I aren't getting any younger, Ross," he continues as if I hadn't said anything, "And neither are you. When are you going to grow up? Think about the example you are setting for your younger siblings and this company."

"This is all such bullshit—"

Dad's next words, though quiet and resigned, are like a stab in my gut. "There's a board meeting coming up, and your behavior and its impact on the company have already been added to the agenda. You have two weeks to get your act together and make this storm you've created for our company's image go away. But if you keep this behavior up, even I won't be able to protect you, and they can vote to remove you from the board, demote you, or even force your resignation."

It's a struggle to control the fury emanating from my core. Demoting? Firing? Me?

Never has my father threatened me so boldly, even if he's hiding behind the board. Or maybe he really is as much at their mercy as I apparently am.

Even Courtney, who usually loves when Dad shits on me, is pale faced at his words.

Piling more on the shitshow, Dad proclaims, "Also, it's our anniversary this weekend. We'll be having a family dinner tomorrow night before we celebrate it. I expect you to attend. I'm sure your mother will have something to say about this situation as well."

Is he serious?

The man has a lot of balls telling me what he expects of me after just threatening me.

Out of spite, I want to tell him to shove the dinner up his ass. But eating with my parents on the eve of their anniversary has been family tradition as long as I can remember. Skipping it seems like a toddler throwing a tantrum, even if there's a part of me that wants to do just that.

"Now, if you two will excuse me," Dad says, walking over to the door that leads to his office, "I have the Rosenberg report to go over before I head home to your mother."

The urge to face off with Dad over his bullshit threat is overpowering, but I squash the feeling before it can take root. When my father's done arguing, he'll walk away and won't listen, no matter what you say.

Like father, like son, I suppose. I've been accused of being stubborn a time or two . . . okay, maybe more, as well.

If I want to get in a rebuttal, it'll have to be at another time, because I have other problems to worry about.

"Very well," I say sharply, adjusting my suit and rising to my feet. "Maybe we can further discuss this issue when you're not so . . . frustrated." Dad huffs, knowing I'm just getting the last word in, but as he turns away, I swear I see sad disappointment on his face.

I stalk from the room and head to my office. Behind me, I hear Courtney's heels click across the floor as she hastens to follow me out the doors.

"You know," she says breathlessly as she catches up with my long stride, "normally, I love it when Dad sticks it to you, but that was brutal. Total bloodbath."

"You think?" I ask sourly, stopping to scowl back at the boardroom. "The old man's gone too far . . ."

"But really, a pastor's wife, Ross? A shareholder's wife?" Courtney interrupts, looking at me incredulously. "What in the hell were you thinking?"

"Like I said," I growl, "I had no idea who she was." When I see Courtney's doubtful expression, I add, "and I wasn't lying. I didn't sleep with her. The one time I didn't fuck the woman throwing herself at me, and it's gotten me into more trouble than if I had thrown her the bone she wanted."

Courtney's face screws up. "Firstly, eww. Secondly, are women really throwing themselves at you left and right?"

I lift my brows in answer but feel the need to clarify. "All the time, but don't get the wrong idea. Sleeping with them isn't the norm. I know they're only after me for my last name and bank account. I'm not a saint by any means, but I'm not the playboy the media and Dad think either."

"Okay. I believe you," Courtney says. After a moment, she bites on her lower lip, her expression softening. "Don't be mad at Dad, though. I may be the youngest, but even I can see he only wants what's best for you. He's going about it all wrong, but I don't think he'd really let the board demote you. He's just trying to scare you into the right direction, that's all."

"Easy for you to say. You're Dad's favorite," I grunt. "You're not the one shouldering half the responsibility of the company on your shoulders. I'm starting to think Abi had the right idea and we're the fuckwits."

I like to think Abigail, my middle sister, is the sanest one of us. When she graduated college, she was offered a high-position job at the family company, but much to Dad's dismay, Abi firmly turned down the position and ventured out on her own.

It pissed Dad off, but Abi stood her ground. She'd had enough of him telling her what to do and relished having the freedom away from the drama of running a family business.

Courtney glares at me, balling her fists. "Hey! Speak for yourself. I like my job."

I open my mouth to defuse the growing storm in Courtney's eyes when I hear a familiar voice from behind us ask, "Geez, am I going to have to play sibling referee again?"

I turn to see my assistant and best friend, Kaede McWarren. After high school, we went to college together, him on a football scholarship that helped him get passing grades whether he did the work or not. After graduation, when the pros didn't come calling, he realized that he had no concrete plans and coat-tailed it with me to the family company.

Since then, he's saved my ass countless times since and has really found his niche, keeping me in line, offering advice, and being my partner in crime. It might be my name on the door with the fancy title, but I couldn't do half of what I do without his help.

Courtney blushes, unclenching her fists and ducking her head before she remembers to stand tall. Interesting. "Hello, Kaede."

"Hey, Courtney," Kaede says. "You're not planning to stab your brother with a letter opener or shoot him with a staple gun again, are you?"

Courtney casts a scowl my way. "Not quite . . . but we're getting there."

Kaede chuckles. "I showed up just in time, then."

"And just in time for Courtney to remember she has a long task list to check off before she goes home, lest she end up with one pissed off Daddy CEO," I say pointedly, nodding in the direction of Father's office.

Knowing a dismissal when she hears one, Courtney gives me another look that says, 'We're not finished.' "You two have fun. Nice seeing you, Kaede."

"You too, Courtney." Kaede watches Courtney go for a moment before turning to me. "Meeting didn't go too well, I take it?"

I shake my head, continuing into my office.

"We have a problem," I start as I enter the room, where the city skyline appears before me.

My office is a study in swanky luxury, with floor to ceiling windows that offer a panoramic view, a large dark oak desk positioned in the center of the room, a tufted leather chair that looks like a throne, and a personal wet bar stocked with premium liquor.

Kaede follows me in, closing the door behind him, and walks over to take one of the accented seats in front of my desk.

"Hit me," he says as he leans back, propping his feet on my desk and crossing his hands on his belly. He looks like he could be prepping for a nap, and anyone else who dared defile my desk like that would get a tongue-lashing they wouldn't soon forget, but Kaede and I are casual at work when it's just the two of us. Plus, I know that this pose is his version of a 'thinking hat'. He's ready to tackle whatever problem I've got with focus and scalpel-like precision.

"Remember that night at Club Red?" I ask, walking over to grab a glass from the wet bar and taking out a bottle of whiskey. I normally don't drink at work, the bar is more for show and guests, but this is one of those times that it's needed. Taking a sip, I quickly outline the argument with my dad, the gossip spread, and his threats about how I'll lose my position within the company.

"Fuck, that was the pastor's wife?" Kaede asks in disbelief when I'm done. "What the hell? She was all over you, pouty and sad and damn near begging for you to make it all better. Why would they be pissed at you and not *her*?"

"That's what I'm saying! The rumor isn't true, but still . . ."

Kaede strokes his chin thoughtfully, already in damage control mode. "I'll draft a letter to Joeden Snow," he mutters as if it's a foregone conclusion that I've already agreed to, "conveying your sincerest apologies for not recognizing his wife, a reassurance that nothing untoward happened, and a promise that you'll make a considerable donation to certain acceptable charities."

"I don't like it," I say right away. "It gives that trashy article legitimacy."

The fact of the matter is, I didn't do anything with his wife but offer a listening ear, and such a letter would be an admission of guilt.

And for once, I'm not guilty.

But Kaede is already shaking his head. "What you do or do not like, or did or didn't do, doesn't matter in this situation. Also, I'll suggest that our PR group and Pastor Snow's put out media releases stating that the evening in question was no more than professional acquaintances having a friendly drink and that you wished Pastor Snow and his wife well when you saw her safely home." I glare at him, but he continues before I can say what I'm really thinking. "Look, going the extra mile will be two-fold. You assuage any ill feelings from Joeden, and your father will appreciate that you took steps to rectify any public damage to the company."

It rankles my nerves to have to do anything in this situation.

I do what I want.

When I want.

I don't like people telling me what to do, least of all my father, who's blowing this whole situation out of proportion to get what he wants. Hell, the shareholder part is probably just made up to reinforce his leverage.

But as much as I hate to admit it, Kaede's plan has merit. The man has gotten me out of some very tight situations, and this time will be no different. I trust his judgement, and as much as I don't like his plan, if he thinks it will fix the bad press and heal things with Dad, I'm down with doing it.

I look out at the skyline and make my silent decision. *All right, you win this time, old man. But I'm only doing this so you lose your bull-shit leverage of trying to force me to settle down.*

I down my shot of whiskey but freeze when I hear Kaede add, "But . . ."

"What?" I demand, turning to survey him. He's sitting upright now, both feet on the floor and a tight jaw, a sure sign that I'm not going to like what he's about to say.

"I think maybe you should do what your dad wants."

I don't even have to ask to know what he means.

The truth of the matter is, I'm just not ready to settle down. I'm not the wild child the media thinks, and I've even had several relationships, but something's always missing. When I picture waking up with the same woman day after day, it sounds . . . boring. Monotonous. Predictable.

And I especially can't see myself just finding someone out of the blue to be with just to appease my parents.

"You can't be . . ." I begin to say, but the look on Kaede's face says it all. "Dude!"

"Even if it's not real," Kaede insists. "Just someone to give the illusion that you've changed and are willing to settle down, someone who can help with your image and calm the shareholders. Call it a . . . relationship of appearances."

"The shareholder thing is bullshit to get me to do what he wants, and the letter should be enough—"

"It's not bullshit, actually," Kaede says, shaking his head. "And your parents are not going to stop harping on you now that your dad has you backed into a corner. So, let's pretend for a moment. We know your ego is too big to do something like this after being threatened, but at the same time, you risk losing your seat on the board . . . so, what do you do?"

"Find a fake girlfriend?" I guess.

Kaede snaps his fingers, sitting back in his chair and grinning. "Bingo."

I chuckle at the ridiculous notion, even though I'm kind of intrigued by the idea. It definitely would be the perfect revenge on Dad for having the nerve to threaten me. Wouldn't be so nice for Mom, though, but there's always some collateral damage in war.

The more I think about it, the more I like it, a host of scenarios playing out in my head. Like K said . . . a relationship of convenience. Hell, maybe even convenience with benefits.

The idea is so amusing that I can't help but laugh, thinking about what a fool I could make of Dad for daring to cross me.

But I still have doubts, saying, "That's just crazy."

But Kaede is already mentally scrolling for candidates.

"Got any contenders?" Kaede asks. "I know a small list of trustworthy women who work on this floor who would love to be your girlfriend, even if it's just for show."

I think for a moment, rolling through a Rolodex of faces through my mind. Some of the faces are blurry, some clearer than others. Some of them work under me, and some of them have been under me.

Finally, I shake my head. "No, if we're going to do this, it can't be someone at the office. That'll just be something else for them to bitch about," I tell Kaede firmly, seeing their fear of a harassment lawsuit as clear as day. "And whoever it is, they have to know from the beginning. I'm not willing to play with some poor girl's feelings for my own ends. Whoever we find will know exactly what it's for . . . but will have to sign a very tight-knit NDA that they're not to speak of the details behind our relationship when it ends."

"Agreed," Kaede says, running his hand through his hair, lost in thought. "But NDA . . . that's hard. Law-wise, I mean. Once it's out, you can't get that cat back in the bag. It has to be someone trustworthy. So, where are we going to find this chick?"

"She's out there somewhere," I mutter, turning to look out the windows at the fading sunset and the city skyline. "We just need to find her."

CHAPTER 3

VIOLET

*T*here are three things for sure in life.

Death, taxes . . . and people calling you at the worst possible time.

Like my mom calling me right now to discuss my upcoming nonexistent wedding. But I have to answer. If I don't, Maria Russo will go full mother-mode and call Archie to track me down. No one, least of all me, gets away from her, and Archie takes my mom's side more often than mine any time we have even the slightest difference in opinion.

"Hey, baby girl!" my mom sings as I answer the phone and simultaneously drive to pick up Archie for our big design job meeting. Her voice echoes through my car on the speakerphone, as powerful as she is. My mother is a fifty-four-year-old single woman who's been through the fire and back raising me, and she's only too happy to finally see me getting married off. "How's my soon-to-be-bride feeling this morning? Are you blind from staring at your sparkly engagement ring yet?"

Her words come out in an excited rush, and if I weren't so used to her way of speaking, I wouldn't have understood a word.

Shit.

I can't imagine how she's going to react when I tell her the wedding isn't happening. She wants to see me married almost as much as I do.

37

I do.

Irony at its finest, I think tragically, because I won't be saying that anytime soon.

But it's better I head things off now, before she's too invested in the idea.

Taking a deep breath, I summon all the courage I can muster and say slowly, "Hey, Mom . . . I have some bad news—"

There are times when Mom is already running full-steam ahead and hears only what she wants to hear. And unfortunately, this happens to be one of those times. She ignores my slow-roll lead-in.

"I just got off the phone with your Nana," Mom says right over me, her mouth going a mile a minute, "and she's over the moon at the news . . . and the great part about it all is, she's already invited all of your cousins!"

"My cousins . . ." I groan, feeling like I just got kneed in the stomach. When I told Mom and Nana my wedding date was scheduled, I didn't think they'd preemptively invite my whole family before the wedding invitations were even done.

"Yep!" Mom chirps cheerfully. "Besides your cousins that are here in the US, you have other cousins coming from all over. Italy, France, basically all over Europe. Everyone's so excited for the next Russo to walk that aisle."

"Mom!" I rasp. "I told you not to tell anyone yet! Abi still hasn't even finished printing the wedding invitations!"

I put a hand to my forehead, smacking myself at the useless argument, as if spoiling the surprise of an invite is the biggest deal here. As if 'Hey, there's actually not going to be a wedding.' is just a small detail.

"Vi," Mom says flippantly, and I can imagine her waving a manicured hand as she rolls her eyes, "everyone knew you were getting married, anyway! Nana was on the phone with people at home as soon as you told her. The grapevine moves fast, baby girl."

"But . . . flying in from Europe? What?" I ask in disbelief. I barely remember that I even *have* cousins all over Europe. I haven't seen them since . . . the last Russo wedding, I guess.

"Yes, of course!" my mom growls in exasperation. "You know we have a big family, and everyone wants to celebrate your special day."

"But . . . you . . ." I stammer, the thought of all these people ordering pricey plane tickets on my behalf making me want to vomit.

Still steamrolling, she continues. "Everyone is so happy for you! You should be jumping up and down with joy!" I swear I hear her clapping her hands, and judging by the weird noises coming through the speaker, Mom's jumping for me.

"But, Mom—"

"I can't wait to see my darling little girl in her wedding dress," Mom muses as if I'm already standing before her. Her mood changes in an instant, from giddy happiness to sappy tears. "You're going to look so beautiful. You did find the dress you've been looking for, didn't you?"

No, I didn't find a dress, not like it matters. I realize that the only way to get Mom to listen is to talk louder than she is. I've got to stop this runaway train before the carnage gets any worse.

But it's too late for that because as I'm about to open my mouth to yell out the truth, Mom's next words hit me like a punch in the gut and set my heart racing.

"You know this couldn't have happened at a better time, Vi. Your grandfather isn't doing too well. I wasn't sure he was going to get to see this moment, but you did it, Vi."

"What's going on? Did something else happen?" I demand as guilt snakes up my spine. I'd meant to check on Papa yesterday, but I got so caught up with work and the wedding stuff, I forgot. The thought that something horrible could've happened to him while I was busy with my own stuff is almost enough to break me out in hives.

"Is he okay?"

"He's fine," Mom says reassuringly. "Hasn't passed out since a few weeks ago, but the doctor said a few more of these faints . . . and he's liable to pass out for the last time." Even though we've discussed his mortality, and Papa himself has made

39

all his wishes well-known, it's still hard to hear anyone talk about him dying.

My heart twists in my throat at her words, and I curse Colin for his heartlessness. Couldn't he have waited until we got married to drop me like a hot potato?

And how ridiculous is that? Even knowing what I now see about Colin, I'm still mostly disappointed that I'm going to disappoint Papa. Hell, I might even chance a short marriage and quickie divorce if I could make the old guy happy one last time and bring some peace to his last days.

How can I make this right?

A variety of solutions runs through my mind, one of which is going back to Colin and asking him to reconsider, but I immediately dismiss the idea.

I'm not crawling back on my hands and knees to someone who took joy in hurting me and cruelly wanted to see me cry. Even if I want to give this to Papa and am so desperate that I'm willing to jump through the hoops I have over the past few months, I'm not going to sell out my own self-worth. It'd be disrespecting Papa.

"Vi?" Mom asks, bringing me back to the present. She seems to finally notice something is amiss. "Is there something wrong?"

Before, I was ready to tell her the truth, even if it caused her distress. Now, I'm not so sure. I definitely don't want it to get back to my Papa so soon after his passing out. Yet, at the same time, the people who have booked tickets to fly in need to be told there'll be no wedding so that they don't waste their money.

The stress of having to decide, weighing the truth against my family's expectations and the shock of this morning's unexpected twist, has my head aching.

But what other choice do I have? Honesty is the best policy.

But maybe I can tell her later? I reason. *At the end of the day, after I've given it some thought and figured out how to make the news not hurt so much, I can be honest then.*

But right now, the bad news can wait. Archie is standing on the sidewalk just ahead, two coffees already in his hands and his foot tapping, ready to head to our client meeting. Now is definitely not the time for this conversation with Mom.

Feeling like I'm setting myself up for the biggest letdown of the century, but also feeling like I have no other choice in the moment, I lie. "Everything's fine, Mom."

"JOANNA GAINES AIN'T GOT SHIT ON ME!" I EXCLAIM TO Archie as I finish fluffing out an ivory silk throw pillow and setting it down on the sofa for a finishing touch, then throwing my hands out wide as if to fully envelope the cavernous great room we're standing in. "Ta-da!"

Archie, who initially said I was batshit insane for making such a cheery design for a client he termed 'the handmaiden from hell', gawks in disbelief as he scans the final product. A smile lifts his lips and he offers a quiet golf clap with a head shake.

"Brava! I don't know how you do it, but you weren't lying! It all came together in the end. You are a magician, and I, but your humble assistant. Ta-da, indeed."

His accent sounds like some version of fancy British as he compliments me and bows to my greatness.

"Told ya!" I say with a wink, a surge of satisfaction running through me at a job well done.

The rush I receive completing my creation is the perfect antidote for the terrible news I received from Colin and the extra whammy from Mom this morning.

News I have yet to tell Arch or Abi.

The wound's still too fresh, the shock too potent, and telling them right now after just looking at wedding dresses for ten hours, and still failing to find *The One*, may cause a breakdown.

Mine or theirs? Maybe both?

Which I refuse to do.

Right now, I just need to focus on my work and forget about all the negative things going on in my life. It's admittedly a bit like an ostrich burying its head in the sand, but it's the only way I'll remain sane today. It's one of the things I love most about my job. When I'm creating homes and spaces that uplift the spirit and inspire, I feel centered and at peace.

And I badly need to feel both right now.

I shove my dark thoughts aside and appraise my latest creation with a critical eye.

Fresh cream-colored paint adorns the walls with matching luxuriously welcoming furniture carefully staged around the room, while vibrant pastel colors provide the perfect contrast against the light-colored decor.

The accents are just right—blues, pinks, and yellows.

It gives the room a gorgeous pop.

It's young, feminine, and expressive.

And perfect.

Except for the fact that it might not be what my client wants.

"I'm bored," my client, Lydia Montgomery, said when she hired me for the job. "Surprise me."

And that's all she gave me to go on. No theme ideas. No colors she wanted. No direction.

No nothing.

To be clear, a seventy-year-old multi-millionaire heiress is hard to surprise. She's seen it all, done it all, and from what I can tell, hasn't liked much of anything in her pampered life.

Usually, I can figure out things about a person using cues they don't even know they're sending. Their clothes, their car, or the rest of the spaces in their home says a lot. But Lydia is a blank slate of black designer clothes, architectural but simple, and a chauffeured car that doesn't speak to her likes at all. Her whole house has been piecemealed, room by room, by different designers.

All together, I had nothing but my own instincts to go on.

Given her attitude and what Archie likes to call 'permanent resting bitch face,' I chose to ignore Arch's suggestion that she needed some dick and instead decided she needed a little warmth and softness in her life to temper her sour disposition. And maybe an update of a generation or two.

I think the ultra-light and colorful design is just what Ms. Montgomery needs, if only she likes it.

"How could she not love this?" I ask myself as much as Arch, staring critically at my creation with pride. I *so* love it. The room just seems so alive and vibrant, compared to the dull, gold, overly ornate decor Lydia had before. "We did a terrific job."

Archie dips his chin, his lips pursed. "Let's be honest. *You* did a terrific job. I just looked pretty and did what I was told. You know you're the only one I do that for, right?" His ring-decorated hands on his hips, his tapping boot, and the look of fierceness on his face definitely tell that tale easily.

I laugh, though he's basically right. Archie has a lot of personality, blunt and big and take no prisoners. Why he deigns to work for me, I'll never know, but he certainly never defers to anyone else. Ever.

Truth be told, I'm terrified Lydia's going to trash my design. And maybe I shouldn't have taken a risk with something chic and modern, but my gut said Darth Vader's sister needed some colorfulness in her life.

"Normally, I'd say this room is an easy slam-dunk. But that woman is evil incarnate. I mean, all she's missing is a crapload of Dalmatian puppies and—"

Right then, the giant double doors to the entryway swing open, accompanied by the sound of high-pitched barking.

"Speak of the devil," Arch mutters under his breath. "Bitchella has arrived." I swat at him, but he's too quick, moving a step away and shooting daggers at me from under his arched and slashed brows. "Don't even think about it, Boss Lady."

Dressed in a black pantsuit, her white hair done up into a fashionable French twist, Lydia Montgomery strolls into the room with a small pup balanced on her arm. It's a fuzzy white Pomeranian, not a Dalmatian, thankfully, or I probably would've lost it and started laughing at the moniker that Arch bestowed upon her. The fluffball isn't nearly as cute as the movie dogs, either, and it doesn't know the meaning of *be quiet*, judging by the chorus of constant yips.

Beside me, Arch visibly rearranges his posture, standing up straight and placing his hands respectfully in front of his crotch, which looks a bit odd for someone in ripped jeans and a t-shirt, even if they are vintage 80s and designer. Unconsciously, I almost do the same as Lydia stops in front of us with a frown that could curdle milk as she strokes the head of her yapping puppy.

Damn, you'd think she's the Queen of England. I don't know if I should bow, curtsey, or just roll my eyes.

"Welcome back—" Arch begins to say, and I'm thankful for his attempt at professionalism, but he's silenced by Lydia's frosty glare.

Turning her nose up, Lydia moves away to tour the room, inspecting our work, her militant gaze missing nothing. Her low kitten heels click against the ultra-polished marble floors and somehow manage to sound demanding and ominous.

When she's done, she takes a seat on the gorgeous cream-colored couch I picked out and levels a scowl that could melt lead our way. Meanwhile, pup-inator is growling at us like we stole one of his doggie biscuits.

Arch and I exchange glances, and he mutters under his breath as he begins to slink away. "Okay, you grab all our stuff and I'll go start the getaway vehicle."

Ignoring Arch, I begin blurting out details. "The wall color is Chantilly Lace, the couch is custom in a washed cotton that gives the feel of linen but with better longevity, the art is by . . ." I give her the highlights of the room, making sure she sees the details, though I'm sure her eagle-eyed gaze missed nothing. I think that knowing the pedigree of some of these pieces will make a woman like Lydia Montgomery appreciate them more.

She doesn't so much as look my way as I list out information, though her eyes follow my words around the room.

There's a lot riding on this design. Lydia told me at the outset that this project was a test to see if she'd like to use me to design several more rooms inside her historic estate. And having her on my reference list would get me other clients automatically. As long as she likes it.

Lydia's face morphs into an uncustomary smile in a move that seems almost difficult for her unused facial muscles to pull off, and her words shock me. "It's absolutely gorgeous, elegantly simple but layered and warm. When would you like to start with the rest of the renovations?"

And that's that, I guess. I wouldn't have minded a bit more effusiveness about my work, but I'll take the bare-boned praise happily. Woo-hoo for me!

Twenty minutes later, Arch and I have packed up our work SUV outside and are heading down the road, passing palatial estates and historic mansions. But I don't see any of them as we celebrate our success.

"Can you believe that?" Archie asks, using an unused pillow as a headrest. "I really thought we were going to have to make a run for it before she tried to skin us to make a coat as punishment for fucking up her living room. *It puts the lotion on . . .*" he intones.

"So did I," I say, shaking my head. "For the record, I don't have any fur, though." I smile, waiting a half-beat for Arch's comeback, knowing I lobbed him a good opportunity.

He scoffs and deadpans, "I know. I book your waxing appointments." He looks pointedly at my crotch. "Never fear. I booked you for a full-body removal before the wedding. Don't want Colin flossing with your snatch patch. Should I make it a couple's waxing appointment? Don't want you choking on his dick nest either."

Normally, I'd laugh at that, but my heart stutters at Archie's mention of the wedding, but I try to let it roll off my back. I won't let it dim my flashlight of happiness over a job well done.

Lydia Montgomery is definitely one of those people who are hard to please, and I made her smile with my pure talent.

Eat your heart out, Colin! Decorating thing, my ass!

Attempting to stay on topic, I ask, "Did you see her smile? That's probably the first time she's smiled in weeks. Maybe months."

"No kidding. Her lips stay more puckered than my asshole," Arch agrees, making kissing sounds with his pursed lips. "And did you feel that 'bow down, peasant bitch' aura? I didn't know whether to curtsey or kiss her ring!"

I chuckle, slowing down to give an oncoming Bentley the

right of way in the narrow street. "She does have a way about her for sure."

"Speaking of rings, have you told your family about the wedding date yet?" Arch asks. "Your Papa has to be going mad with anticipation!"

Ugh.

I should've known this was coming. I just don't know if I have the strength to talk about it yet.

I open my mouth to make up some lie when my cell ringtone, Taylor Swift's *Blank Space*, goes off and I see a series of texts go across the screen.

Yay, girly! The wedding invitations are ready!

Can't wait for you to see!

They're so pretty! Perfect, if I say so myself.

Damn it. I'd totally forgotten about those damn invitations. They're totally worthless now, and Abi won't be happy when I reveal that she did all that work in vain.

Not that I could have planned for Colin calling off our engagement.

"Who is that?" Arch asks as I hold in an internal groan. "Your horny fiancé, looking for an after-work booty call? Bow-chicka-wow-wow."

But there's no need to answer him because he dives for my phone and reads the text messages himself. It's part of his role as my assistant, part of his gig as best friend, but mostly just because he's nosy.

"Whoop, whoop!" Archie cheers. "Let's go see these master-pieces Abi thinks she's created so I can fix them the way they should've been done all along." He smirks, and I know he's kidding. Kind of. Maybe. "Let's go, Bridezilla. Take the 305. It's faster."

Sighing at what's to come, I head down the highway back toward the city and resignedly mutter, "Yay. Let's go."

"HERE THEY ARE!" ABI CHIRPS, PRESENTING THE WEDDING

invitations to me, beautifully embossed peach-colored parchment with white vines lining the sides, interlaced with pink-colored roses.

Archie, Abi, and I are standing in the back room of her shop, Sweet Pea Boutique, gathered around a work table stacked with beautiful wedding invitations—around three hundred, to be exact—while Abi's associate, Janey, manages the front of the shop for incoming customers.

My breath catches in my throat as I peer down at the gorgeously designed invitations. They're works of art, rich and creamy card stock, lettering that's flowy without being frilly . . . they're perfection. "Oh, my God, Abi, these are so beautiful!"

Abi beams with pride as a breath I didn't realize she was holding leaves her in a *whoosh* sound. "Oh, sweetie, I'm so relieved you like them! I know you wanted white on white, but when I saw this color, I knew I had to incorporate it."

"You were right," I say breathlessly, a single tear coursing down my cheek, but not for the reason Abi and Arch probably think it is. "These are fantastic."

Archie nods, holding up the invitation to the light, agreeing, "It's definitely a work of art! Pretty in blushing virgin pink! Not that you've been one of those in eons."

He laughs at his own joke as I trace a finger over one of the floral designs, feeling like my heart is going to drop through my chest.

I have to tell Abi and Archie. They're my best friends, but saying it aloud makes it more real, more final, more ridiculous.

Abi, who is always perceptive about my moods, suddenly peers at me closely. "Is something wrong, Vi?" She takes my hands, turning me toward her and holding my arms out wide as she scans me from head to toe. I feel her hands squeeze mine, and then her eyes widen as she grips my left hand and pulls it in front of her face. "Wait a minute. Where's your engagement ring?"

Even though I knew the question was coming, I freeze as Archie and Abi look at me expectantly.

Taking a deep breath, I open my mouth to let it all out.

"I—" Suddenly, a tidal wave of emotion washes over me and I burst into tears. "Colin called off the engagement!" I blurt, sobbing uncontrollably. "We're not getting married!"

"Oh, my God, honey," Abi gasps in horror. "I'm so sorry!"

Immediately, I'm enveloped in the arms of Archie and Abi as they hold my body totally supported while I try to hold back the sobs that won't stop coming. For the next several moments, they both coo and soothe me as the tears I've held back for the entire day flow out of me like a great river.

Girl, stop crying over that asshole! You're gonna scare off Abi's customers with all this caterwauling!

The thought is sobering, and after a few more hiccups, I pull myself together enough to tell Archie and Abi that I'm fine. They let me go hesitantly, eyes ping-ponging from each other then back to me in a silent conversation.

"Did he give a reason?" Abi asks softly, her eyes filled with compassion and fury at seeing me hurt. She's a good friend, and I know that between her and Archie, Colin would be buried in a shallow grave in the woods outside town and we'd all have airtight alibis at the snap of my fingers. Okay, maybe not that drastic for real, but damn close.

I dab at the corner of my eyes with the napkin she produces from her purse that's sitting on a nearby stool, feeling angry with myself for breaking down like this. All day while I worked, I told myself that I'd be strong and I wouldn't do it. But I guess I'm more hurt about it than I'm willing to admit. "He said we both were so busy and that we're at different crossroads in our lives . . . and he just wasn't ready to commit."

"That's code for he wants more pussy," Archie says confidently, and when Abi scowls at him and throws a backhand to his bicep, he protests, "What? It's the truth!"

Abi hisses out of the corner of her mouth like I can't hear her, "I know that, and you know that, but does Vi look like she wants to hear that right now? Shut-ay your mouth-ay."

Archie huffs, his neck swirling. "That's not remotely how pig Latin works, dear. But message received." They face me again like they didn't just have a whole discussion about me right there.

"But seriously, Vi, that's a shitty excuse. You deserve a better explanation than some bullshit that doesn't make any sense."

"But you know what?" I say, blowing my nose. "It actually does. When I really think about it, Colin was right. I don't think we were ever really in love. I don't know why he proposed, but I just got swept up with the idea of love and marriage and having this big fairy tale wedding. Especially because my Papa . . ."

My words trail off as a lump forms in my throat.

Both Arch and Abi give me empathetic looks, knowing how much Papa Stefano means to me.

Just the thought of telling Papa my engagement is over is almost enough to send me over the brink. He was so looking forward to my wedding and walking me down the aisle.

Now he probably never will.

And I know in the deepest, ugliest part of my heart that he was my real reason for rushing with Colin and why I'm not that hurt about losing him, but more about what this all means for Papa. Honestly, it's probably a good thing Colin stopped the whole thing, but that doesn't make it any easier to reconcile that I won't be able to give Papa the one thing he's holding on for.

I feel like a bitch for using Colin that way, but I'd been truly blinded by my own dreams and thought we would be happy. The romanticism of the whole thing was so powerful . . . meeting again, falling in love, the need for a fast development of our relationship. It had felt magical and like my own whirlwind of a Hallmark movie.

Big mistake. Huge.

"I understand," Abi says sadly, understanding my pain.

Archie reaches over and gives my hand a comforting pat. "Don't worry honey. Your granddaddy is gonna be just fine. We're going to find another man who's going to appreciate you for who you are, and you'll get married and have the wedding you always dreamed of with your Papa at your side."

I quiet at Archie's words. He means well, but we all know the odds of that happening are damn near zero. There's no way I'll be able to find another guy I actually like, build a relationship from the ground up, get engaged with him, and then marry before something horrible happens to Papa.

This is the real world, not a Reese Witherspoon rom-com. You don't meet the love of your life and get married over a single weekend, as the shards of my very own fantasy still surrounding me prove quite well.

"But that's just the tip of the iceberg." I sigh. "My mom and Nana went around telling everyone that I was getting married, and cousins I didn't even know I had are going to fly in from all over the world . . . unless I tell them all to cancel their tickets . . . which I have yet to do."

"Holy crap," Archie mutters.

"Yeah," I say. "I'm in deep shit unless I can come up with a magical solution."

At that exact moment, the entry doors to Sweet Pea's open with a tinkling bell, and even from the back, I can see the tall man dressed impeccably in custom-tailored slacks and shirt enter. The soft lighting of the floral boutique makes his dark hair shine and throws his chiseled jawline into shadows and highlights, and a Greek god would be jealous of that physique, broad shoulders and a tapered waist atop long legs.

I recognize him immediately.

Ross Andrews.

Abigail's big brother.

Abigail's *asshole* big brother.

"I know!" Abigail suddenly exclaims with a gasp and a snap of her fingers, her eyes going wide in her dramatic fashion that lets me know Abi's just come up with a crazy idea.

"Oh, no," I say, seeing Abi's face light up as her eyes fall on her brother's face. "Whatever you're thinking, the answer's . . . no way."

But Abi ignores me, waving at Ross and smiling like she's so overjoyed to see him before tossing me a mischievous wink.

"Congratulations, Vi. Looks like we just found your magical solution! You can call me your Fairy Godmother."

Horror strikes me at what Abigail is hinting at. Me and

Ross? But we basically hate each other. Our entire relationship is built on us torturing each other. Definitely no love lost between us. We barely put up with each other because we both care for Abi.

Dimly, I hear Archie argue, "If anyone in this room is going to be the *Fairy* Godmother, it's damn sure not you. It's me."

CHAPTER 4

VIOLET

"*A* fake wedding with my best friend's brother?" I hiss in disbelief as I watch Ross walk up to the counter and laugh at something Janey says. Abi spilled out some hare-brained scheme faster than I would've thought she could, and now I have only seconds to disabuse her of this crazy notion before she calls him over. "The king of all assholes? The guy who made my high school days a living hell, including putting a frog down my blouse in front of the whole football team? Are you crazy?"

"As a whore in church," Archie quips.

"It's perfect!" Abi squeals excitedly, ignoring the insult or my complaints. "Who else, besides Archie, knows you well enough to pull something like this off on short notice? And no offense, but no one's going to believe you flipped Archie."

He shrugs, knowing she's right. "I don't make a very good trade." He's constantly having to explain his lingo to me, but that one I know. A trade is a gay guy who can pass as straight because of his masculinity. Actually, Archie could probably do that in his black jeans, random movie reference T-shirts, combat boots, multiple earrings, and tattoo sleeves. If you only saw him posed against a graffitied wall, you'd think he was a badass punk rocker anarchist. Then he'd open his mouth and sarcastic bitchery would pour out in a tone that would make any gaydar sing like a canary.

Abi's right. Archie's not the man for this job.

Oh, my God, I'm actually considering this. I've lost my mind for sure. Hell, I'd even dismissed a fake wedding with Colin as pathetic.

But as she quickly talks about making Papa happy, having the wedding of my dreams, and then splitting later down the road with no muss, no fuss, it doesn't sound quite as crazy—if the man knew the score from the get-go and was willing to go along and pretend.

But I've known Ross since I was a little girl, and he's not exactly someone I picture as marriage material or being able to make a fake relationship believable.

He's always treated me like I was one of his little sisters, teasing me and making fun of me. Even when I grew up, his recognition of my adulthood never fully transitioned, and he still sometimes treats me like I'm the same little girl who used to look at him with cookie dough eyes in high school. Okay, so I'll admit now that some of my pranks were because I might've had the teeniest, tiniest crush on Ross. But who didn't? He was the big man on campus, hotter than any teenager had the right to be, and I'd soaked up any attention from him I could. Except when he embarrassed me in front of the whole school. It was complicated, a love-hate situation that was purely on my younger side.

All of that's water under the bridge now, though, and we don't see each other that often anymore so we're not as close as we used to be.

And there's the simple fact that he probably won't want to do something as crazy as this.

"Doesn't he have a girlfriend?" I ask, but Abi only notices that I didn't say no and grins big and wide in a 'gotcha' look.

"You're in luck. It was never serious, and he broke it off with her months ago. Mom was devastated when she heard because she's been wanting him to settle down for ages, so this is perfect. Won't she get a kick when she finds out Ross is marrying Violet Russo, the same little girl who was always over at our house for those insane sleepovers! Though we'll have to make sure the eventual breakup doesn't paint either of you in a poor light. I don't want to mess up my own wedding with Mom thinking you're some shrew who broke her baby boy's heart."

She frowns after a moment, tapping her lip thoughtfully. "Hmm . . . Courtney might be a problem, though," she mutters, mentioning her feisty younger sister. "But I can handle her if she tries to start trouble."

Ugh. Why do I have such crazy friends?

But Abi has been the best friend a girl could have . . . despite the occasional bouts of insanity.

"And somehow, you think Ross would agree to something like this?" I demand.

"Sure, why not?" she says with a trademark Abi grin. "I'm his oldest little sister. I should know. Not to mention, he's known you for years. Hell, you're almost just as much his sister as I am. And you've also done stuff for him in the past, remember? He'll have no choice but to agree to our little scheme once we get done with him."

"*Our* little scheme? *We?*" I ask, still reeling in shock. "I never said I was doing this."

Abi smirks. "Sure, you are. I can see it in your eyes."

I shake my head vehemently. "Forget it. It won't work. Besides, we'd end up killing each other before ever making it to the altar."

"Nonsense," Abi says, waving her hand at Ross to get his attention. "Yoo-hoo, Rossy. We're over here."

Ross looks our way and smiles. Then he says something to Janey and moves around the counter, making his way over to us. Even his walk is sexy, confident, and graceful. All things I'm definitely not. I swallow, wishing I could just disappear underneath one of the boutique tables. Or into the center of the Earth to burn up and not have to deal with any of this mess.

Fuck me . . . he's an asshole, but he's a hot *asshole. Why are the bad ones always so pretty on the outside?*

"Hey, Abs. Hello, Violet."

I school my face before my thoughts betray me. *Jesus, I always forget how deep his voice is.* And embarrassingly, I imagine what that rumble would feel like against my skin. Once upon a time, I had foolish dreams of Ross being my first kiss. My fantasies now involve a lot more than just kissing, that's for damn sure. But I've never imagined Ross as that fantasy man . . . until now.

I look up to see Ross standing over me, a fresh batch of stubble shading his chiseled jawline. He's even more impressive close up, looking like he's had a hard day's work, his dress shirt partially opened at the front, his hair slightly disheveled.

How does he manage to look like such an arrogant bastard and so damn handsome all at the same time?

The thought comes from an alien place in my mind, and I dismiss it as my being high-strung in the moment. The days of my crushing on Ross Andrews are long gone.

"What? I don't get a 'hi' too?" Archie pouts. But I can feel his eyes watching the interaction between Ross and me with new interest.

"Hello, Ross," I reply cordially, ignoring Archie's lame attempt for attention. "Nice to see you."

"It's nice to see you too, Chickie. How've you been?"

Ugh. Remind me why I always want to slap you, why don't you?

I used to have chicken legs when I was in middle school, legit pencils attached to a hinge. Ross used to tease me about them relentlessly to the point that I spent a whole summer exercising my ass *on* in order to stop the jokes. And while it stopped all of his chuckleheaded buddies from doing it, Ross still references that first taunt from time to time.

I think it's partly out of habit and partly to annoy me.

"I'm just fine," I say through gritted teeth, biting down on the urge to call him Dumb Ogre, my favorite nickname for him growing up. It's weak, but my middle school brain hadn't been capable of much more than a typical dumb jock joke to bestow a nickname on him. "You?"

Ross grins, noting my irritation. "Peachy." He looks past me to the stacks of peach-colored cardstock.

Abigail gestures at the table. "I just got done making these invitations for Violet's wedding. Aren't they beautiful?"

"Amazing," Ross says, barely giving the invitations a lookover, instead looking over at me. "How's the engagement coming along, Vi?"

I'm not sure, but I think I detect an undercurrent of intensity to his words.

"Uh . . . um . . . it's going . . . okay," I say, not having the guts to tell him I was dumped. But Ross always leaves me this way, with the verbal IQ of a potato when I need to be on my A game around him.

Very frustrating.

Ross's expression is unreadable. "Really? So, you guys have it all figured out?"

Great . . . trapped. I have no idea where to go with this one. "Um we're sort . . . of working on it . . . but I —"

"Have something to ask you," Abi finishes for me cheerfully, elbowing me sharply in the side.

I shoot her murderous look. "Uh, no, I don't."

"Uh, yes, you do," she mimics back.

Ross looks back and forth between us, frowning. "I'm confused."

"Nothing to worry your pretty little head about," Archie interjects, bumping Ross's shoulder in a move that would scream 'bro' if anyone but him did it, but I can see it for the flirtation it is and I can't help but grin a little. Archie's on my side in the ongoing war with Ross and does what he can to set Ross off-kilter. "Bitches be crazy." He says it solemnly, like it's some great insight shared between the males of the human species. "Of course, there's one way to mitigate their impact . . ." He trails off pointedly, his subtlety that of a rampaging wildebeest.

"Vi needs you to marry—ow!" Abi exclaims as I stomp on her foot.

Ross gives us a look like we're all crazy. "The hell's going on over here?"

"Nothing. Didn't you say you needed Ross to stop by for something?" I ask pointedly, glaring murder at Abi.

"Oh, yeah, our parents' anniversary gift. This way, Ross."

Abi takes her brother off to the side where there's a beautiful multi-colored bouquet of flowers sitting on the table, handing him a pen to sign a card.

When he's done signing, they talk for a moment, but I'm close enough to hear that it's not about Abi trying to set up her crazy plan but rather just family drama with the company, before they return.

"Not sure what shenanigans you two girls are up to," Ross says suspiciously, "but we'll talk about it later. Bye, Archie." He winks at me. "Catch you later, Chickie."

Bastard.

He walks back over to the front, says something to Janey, then walks out.

I let out a big sigh of relief when he's gone

"Shiiiit, Abi," Archie says longingly. "Don't take this the wrong way, but your brother is one tall glass of water! I could drink from that spigot allllll day." He makes a *glug-glug* noise that turns into more of a choked *gluck* and I can't help but laugh at what he's implying. The outrageous things he says are funny enough, but when you add his dry delivery, it really sends it over the top.

But my humor dries up when I think about what Abi almost did to me. "You crazy bitch! I can't believe you were about to ask him that!" I hiss angrily, turning on her.

"What?" Abi pouts. "I'm just trying to help. And I already know I'm right." She places a hand to her chest. "Archie already knows I'm right." He nods, though it's with a grimace. "And deep down, you know it too. You were *this close* to agreeing before he came over and gave you a hard time, so just admit it and let's get this deal happening. I don't want you ending up on some therapist's couch crying about your shoulda-coulda-wouldas."

"Gee, thanks for your concern, Mother Teresa," I reply acidly. "But it's not going to work. Even if he did agree to your crazy plan, we'd end up killing each other long before any wedding. You just heard him call me Chickie . . . again. You know how much I hate that!"

Abi waves a dismissive hand. "Oh, stop it. You guys love each other. You're both just too damn stubborn to admit it," she says, holding up a hand when I go to protest. "*And*, there's no one better for the job and you know it. You either get fake married to Ross ASAP or kiss having the memory of the most important man in your life at your wedding goodbye."

Abi's words hit me like a slug to the stomach.

Damn it. As much as I hate to admit it, she's right.

At this point, if I want to get married fast so my Papa has a chance to walk me down the aisle . . . it's either Ross or no one.

But I can't bring myself to ask him something so off the wall.

He'd probably laugh right in my face, right before calling me Chickie, or Chicken Little, or Colonel . . . that one took me awhile to figure out.

Archie grabs my shoulders, making me face him. "Okay, here's the facts, girl. He's single, you're single. He's hot, you're hot. You've gotten along without death or dismemberment for a long time already, so odds are in your favor. He'll probably do it just to have something to tease you about, but weigh that against what I imagine to be some damn good fucking with no strings attached. Sorry, not sorry, for talking about your brother's dick, Abi."

Out of the corner of my eye, I see Abi hold her hands out wide, not offended in the least about the way Arch is talking about her brother.

"Marry him for you and your whole wedding-crazy family, and then fuck him for me and tell me all about it. Slowly and in detail. You owe me that, Violet." He points a finger in my face and I smirk.

"I owe you sex stories?" Why I'm stuck on having sex with Ross when the idea of a fake marriage is on the table is something I'll analyze later. When I'm alone . . . maybe with a vibrator.

Arch crosses his arms over his chest and scowls, looking every bit the rebellious rocker who would rage against the machine of the patriarchy. "I dip-dyed silk by hand for Bitchella's curtains. You owe me a lifetime of sex stories. Good ones, filthy ones, Ross-pressing-you-up-against-a-door-and-fucking-your-brains-out ones."

"You're out of your dirty mind." Archie's sinful thoughts are making me feel uncomfortable . . . if only because they're summoning some very raunchy images of Ross and me together in my head. I've never been fucked against a door, and that's seeming like a shame all of a sudden.

"He will do it, Vi, I'm telling you," Abi presses. "I mean, what's the worst that can happen? Nothing. It's a win-win situation either way you look at it. My mom can stop harping on Ross to settle down, and your grandpa gets to walk you down the aisle."

"Let me think about it," I say slowly, trying to think of a way to get Abi off my back. As much as I want to please Papa and have the wedding, a fake relationship with Ross . . . is just too crazy. "I think I'm going to head home. It's been a long day, a *really* long day."

All of the weirdness hits me at once. Just this morning, a short twelve hours ago, I was happily engaged and dreaming about a life of wedded bliss. Now, I'm alone and considering asking my childhood nightmare to do me a huge solid and pretend to marry me. Whose life is this?

"Veto!" Abi and Archie say in unison, bringing me back out of the hole I'm trying to crawl into.

"You're not going home alone to wallow in a pint of Ben & Jerry's about a douchewaffle like Colin. We're going out. We'll celebrate that near-miss, talk about your new fiancé, Ross, and dance the night away."

I start to shake my head, noticing the bit about Ross she tried to sneak in there, but Archie jumps in.

"Hell, yeah!" Archie chirps, swaying back and forth and air-smacking an imaginary ass in front of him. "I am *so* down for that! Well, I'm pretty much down for *anything*, literally anything, but a night at the club sounds like just what the doctor ordered."

"Hmm," I say, not being able to believe that I'm actually considering the idea—of going out and of asking Ross to be my fake husband. It's all too much, and an escape does sound perfect. Maybe instead of that ice cream I was already thinking of—damn it, Abi, for knowing me so well—I can drown my confusion, frustration, and aggression in a few shots of tequila. "Okay, let's get drunk and dance the night away."

"Yay!" Abi rejoices, rubbing her hands together excitedly.

"But don't let me regret this," I warn. "And don't mention anything about this to Ross. It's none of his business."

"I won't," Abi promises.

"Abi . . ." I give her my best glare, threatening every bad thing I can think of.

"Trust me, your secret is safe with me."

I nod, still not sure I believe her, but I let her and Arch lead me out to the curb where a driver is already pulling up. Archie really is a great assistant when he's not demanding the dirty details of my sex life.

CHAPTER 5

S.*O.S.—GIRL IN DISTRESS.*
I need a HUGE favor.
Meet me at Club Red in one hour . . . we'll have a VIP table ready to discuss.

Looking at the text from Abigail, I can feel my eyebrows start to knit themselves together semi-permanently. She's a bit of a wild card, always rebelling against what Mom and Dad think an Andrews should do, and while it doesn't upset me, her choice of venues doesn't exactly inspire good cheer in my gut.

"What's up?" Kaede asks as he sets his drink on the coffee table. After work, we switched gears from our boss-assistant gig and are just hanging out as friends, watching the fight on pay-per-view at my place. Somehow, we always manage to navigate back and forth without it being weird, a testimony to our long-standing friendship.

"I'm not sure," I reply, holding up my phone. "Abigail."

"Abi?" Kaede says, smiling. He reads the text, and his smile turns into a chuckle. "Any idea as to what this huge favor is? Should I go ahead and alert the PR team to be on standby?"

"Ha-ha, not funny, asswipe. I have no idea," I admit, checking the clock. My head throbs. I've been busting my ass all day, probably subconsciously trying to prove to myself that I deserve my job and not Dad's threatened demotion, and now that the sun's set, I realize I skipped lunch too.

No wonder I've got a headache. I haven't had a thing to eat since about six thirty this morning. I grab a slice of pizza from the box on the table, thankful that Kaede ordered a pie with loads of meat and veggies so it's like a complete meal in five bites.

"Well, regardless of whatever Abi's got on her mind, you probably need to go. Though you should be careful. Another night on the town is the last thing the board needs to hear about. I don't think your reputation could withstand another evening of scandal."

He's busting my chops, knowing full well that nothing happened with the pastor's wife and that I go home to an empty bed more nights than not.

"Yeah . . . she usually has interesting shit happening, which I'm not sure I need," I admit. While I gave her plenty of big brother hassles growing up, my little sister's not that bad. If you put me on the stand, I'd even say she's pretty cool . . . for a little sister.

"And you can use a trip to the club to do some scouting," Kaede points out. When I give him a confused look, he rolls his eyes, sighing. "Fake girlfriend, remember? Get your parents off your ass?"

"Dude, it's Club Red. You don't go to a club to find Miss Right, just Miss Tonight."

Kaede shrugs. "And that's a bad thing this time, why? Remember, short-term, fake?"

"Okay, okay . . . but only if you'll be my wingman," I concede. "This isn't a purely social trip, so having you there to make sure I don't do anything stupid is a good safety net."

Kaede holds his hand up in the Boy Scout salute. "I swear not a drop of the demon rum shall cross these lips tonight, and I'll keep you firmly on this side of the respectability line."

I snort, shaking my head. "Fine . . . let's get ready. But I need another slice. I'm so hungry that I could get shitfaced on light beer right now."

Kaede winces. "Light beer . . . ugh. Okay, so pizza, mouthwash, club. We can pull it off in an hour."

———

It's actually an hour and ten minutes before we pull up in my supercharged Camaro, my own little rebellion against my parents. In a social class of Beamers, Bentleys, and other Euromade cars, my all-American muscle car with a blue collar reputation and an engine that rumbles like an earthquake announces me to the Club Red crowd even before I get out.

Tossing my keys to the valet, I take a moment to look around while Kaede grabs the parking stub. Club Red isn't the biggest club in the city, but it doesn't need to be. It's the club you come to when you've got *it*, and as such, they're picky about who they let in the door.

But that's never a concern for me as an Andrews. Doors magically open with my last name, just like the inner doors of Club Red do tonight. As always, I pause just inside, letting myself adjust to the atmosphere inside.

It's not that Club Red's over the top. If anything, the muted decor and low-key lighting lend a touch of class that elevate Club Red over the grind houses further downtown. Not that the elegance stops the dance floor from being an undulating mass of sexually charged bodies writhing against one another.

"You see your sister?" Kaede asks as we approach the bar. Sure, Abi said she'd get us a spot in the VIP area, but I always stop at the bar first for a 'regular' drink. Just sort of a habit, I guess, to help me get the feel of the place.

"I'm sure she's up there," I assure him, ordering a Rum and Rockstar, my personal weird ass club drink. It's my personal opinion that everyone's got one, even if they don't admit it. "That girl can talk her way into a VIP seat at the White House."

I grab my drink and a club soda for Kaede before we head upstairs. The VIP Lounge at Club Red is perfect, with wide, slightly semi-circular couches that allow you to have privacy while at the same time not jamming you in, and the view overlooking the entire rest of the club allows for great visuals too.

I spy Abi and Archie, the two of them laughing over some private joke as they lean in toward one another. I'm always watchful about whom Abi dates, but Archie's pretty much as gay as you can get on the spectrum without involving glitter rainbows. He's a cool guy and can carry on a conversation about football or music and then turn around and slice and dice you with a well-spoken barb. I like him, and I like Abi being friends with him because I feel like he'd watch out for any assholes who tried to worm their way into my little sister's pants.

On the other side of Abi is a girl, her body half turned away as she talks with a waitress. With the dancing strobe lights, I can't see her face or even her head, really, but from the shoulders down she's a fucking vision. A tight, voluptuous body is practically poured into a skintight red dress that shows off a set of curves just this side of unbelievable.

"Fuck me, that's not an hourglass. That's a day and a half glass," Kaede says quietly, seeing the same girl I'm noticing. "Who is she?"

"Ross!" Abi calls out, seeing me, but before I can answer, I feel like my jaw drops to the floor.

The girl next to Abi . . . *Violet*?

Holy fucking shit on a Ritz. Have I not been paying attention for *that* long? I literally just saw her hours ago, but I feel like maybe I've never really seen her. Not like this.

"A–Abi," I stammer, finding my cool again. "Arch."

"Hey, Ross . . . and Goose," Archie jokes, using his nickname for Kaede. "You still haven't taken me to bed."

"Guess I've lost you forever then," Kaede replies as the two bump fists. Kaede's as straight as I am, but he's chill as Slurpee with Archie, ever since Arch wing-manned for Kaede one night. I still can't pry the full story out of Kaede a year later. I just know he walked into work the following Monday looking like he'd had a holy experience.

"Violet."

The word hangs in the throbbing bass-filled air of the club, and I swear Vi blushes a little as she gives me a nod, but more than likely, that's the pink lights skimming over her skin. "Ross." She seems completely unaffected by me, which unnerves me for some reason.

"Anyway . . . what's the emergency?" I ask as Abi scoots to the side and I find myself wedged beside Violet. Her thigh rubs against mine through my pants, and . . . oh, fuck, *it* moved.

This can't be happening. Violet's my little sister's best friend, to the point that I've heard all of their stupid little girl giggling from the time she was eight years old. She's damn near family, which means off limits.

Nope. Not going to happen.

I am *not allowed* to be attracted to Violet.

Not tonight. Not ever.

What the hell is wrong with me?

But feeling the warmth of her thigh pressed against my leg and the way her lightly tanned skin contrasts with the blood red of her sexy dress, that shade of red I've always thought of as *Fuck Me Scarlet*, is new, and I'm having to fight my own body's desires.

It doesn't care that Violet is Abi's BFF.

It doesn't care that I've known this girl since she had chicken legs.

It only cares that those legs are long, toned, and leading to a body that's erotic in every atom of its being.

It only cares about sheathing myself in one of her body's tight, velvety crevices and emptying itself inside her.

She's a siren calling me to crash on the curves of her shores.

"Hey, Ross? Earth to Ross!"

I blink and look over at Abi, who's giving me a strange look. "What?"

"You drunk already?" Abi asks, grinning. "That's new for you."

"Probably that pizza hasn't digested enough yet," Kaede says with a chuckle. "You know, low blood sugar and all. He hadn't eaten since breakfast." He's good at covering for me, but I can see the questions in his eyes.

What the fuck, man? You okay?

Kaede reaches his hand across the table toward Violet. "Kaede Warren. Good to see you again. It's been a while."

Violet shakes his hand with a firm grip, no wimpy kiss-it greeting from her, and I have to fight the urge to growl at my best friend for touching her. "Violet Russo. I remember you from school, and I've heard a lot about you."

Kaede offers a flirty smile. "I've heard a lot about you too, though it seems not the important things." His eyes drop down, licking over Vi's body, and I cough to cover the kick I throw his way under the table. Luckily, I hit my target and not Arch.

Kaede's eyes snap to mine, humor dancing in their dark depths. The bastard's fucking with me.

Next to me, I can feel Violet fidget, a sort of nervous energy almost vibrating off her body. "So, Abi, what—"

Suddenly, the music changes, and Archie jumps up, grinning like a fool. "Bitches!"

I blink, stunned. "Huh?"

"This is my *jam*!" Archie says, grabbing Abi by the hand. "Come on, Abs. You too, K-dawg. Abigail's gonna need a dance partner while I find one of my own! Unless you're volunteering to be the meat in the sandwich tonight?" He laughs, not remotely serious, but he is pulling Abigail and Kaede out of the booth.

Kaede gives me a raised eyebrow, but I give him a slight tilt of my chin. He's a good guy, and I know he'll be polite enough with my sister that I can trust him. Besides, while he's out on the dance floor, he'll probably be scanning the crowd looking for potential candidates for me.

Knowing him, he'll probably come back upstairs with at least two or three.

The three of them head downstairs, Archie using an intimidating glare and his long arms to make room on the dance floor before breaking out moves that just might put Simone Biles to shame.

"Look at him go."

The quiet words, barely audible over the music, pull my attention back to the person next to me, and I turn to look Violet in the face. I can't decipher her expression . . . shy? Nervous?

68

Pissed? Maybe all of the above at the same time, for some reason?

"He's . . . flexible," I admit. Violet's eyes narrow some, and she looks angrier for some reason. "What's up?"

"Why are you here?" she suddenly asks, and it feels like she's changing the subject. "Did Abi tell you?"

I find myself off-kilter almost instantly. She's the only one who's ever been able to set me off with so few words.

And tonight, firstly, I don't know what Violet's talking about.

Secondly, though . . . she's hot when she's angry.

I never noticed that before. Hot like fire might shoot from her eyes at any moment and burn me up, her frenetic energy surrounding us in a bubble of her making.

"Tell me what?" I ask, sipping my drink to try and regain my composure. I'm starting to wonder if Abi is up to something. But what?

"Don't play stupid," Violet hisses. "She told you, didn't she?"

"I have no idea," I answer honestly. "As in no idea what the hell you're talking about." I can't help the smirk that crosses my face at seeing Violet so worked up. I really don't know what's got her riled up, but I like it. I always do.

But she misreads my smile, thinking I have some insight to whatever she's upset about. "Yeah, she did," Violet says, her fists clenching in her lap. "Goddammit, I'm gonna kick her perky little ass!"

"Whoa, whoa, whoa," I reply, holding up a hand. "First, I don't want to know anyone's opinion of my sister's ass. Second, I swear to you, I really don't know what's going on. Look, here's what Abi sent me."

I reach into my coat pocket and pull out my phone, showing her the text from Abi. "As you can see, I didn't have time after that to hear anything. So, what's going on?"

"You swear?" Violet asks, her lips trembling, and there's a glitter of tears in her eyes. Jesus, she's really shaken up. What's happened to spin her from mad to sad in a blink? "She didn't say anything at her boutique?"

"I don't know anything," I swear. "Vi, I came into the shop to sign the card for my parents' anniversary flowers and told Abi about the old man being an ass lately and making some demands of me that I don't like. That's it. She barely got a word in edgewise about anything else."

"So, *you've* got problems?" Violet asks, a bit bitchy. "I'm surprised Mr. Perfect does anything but shit gold nuggets."

Ouch. But this Violet I know. Cutting, funny, ready to battle and put me in my place. I know this one, *like* this one. The upset, crying version of Violet does odd things to my gut, and I don't like that. But if any time has been the right time to have an actual conversation with Vi, it's now when she's obviously hiding behind our usual status quo.

"Okay, I've done some shit, Vi. But right now, it seems that you've got more on your mind. Come on, what's going on?"

Violet purses her lips for a moment, studying me with an intensity that is actually a little intimidating. Has she always been this way, this . . . intensely magnetic?

Have I not been paying attention at all?

"It's . . . it's about Colin," she finally says, and it takes me a minute to place the name. Oh, yeah . . . Colin Radcliffe. We run in the same circles. His family's got enough money that we don't even really need to measure bank accounts.

When you reach a certain level of wealth, the dollars don't really matter compared to other yardsticks. And the Radcliffe name carries weight.

Still, the little I know about Colin, he's always struck me as a bit of a prick. I guess all young businessmen need to have a healthy dose of asshole in them to be successful, but Colin always seemed to have a bit too much, in my opinion.

"What about him?" I ask, my eyes cutting to Violet's hands. Her fingers are empty, and even before she answers, I know what she's going to say. "Oh, shit. Who broke it off with whom?"

"He . . . he did," Violet says quietly. "This morning."

I snort, shaking my head. "What a dick. I'm sorry, Violet."

Maybe it's the sincerity in my words, or maybe it's that I called her by her given name, something I don't do all that frequently, I realize. But a torrent of words unleashes from Violet.

In a stumbling, somewhat confusing stream of consciousness rant that lasts all the way through two club remixes, she tells me everything.

Her Papa.

His health.

Her going into a relationship with blinders on because of it.

Her family going just a little insane.

Everything.

"So . . . I know it's crazy, my wanting to get married just for Papa," she says finally, tossing back the last of my Rum and Rockstar to wet her throat, "but it wasn't until Colin was breaking it off that I realized that's all I was doing. Colin was waiting for this big breakdown and I was just 'meh' about it." She shrugs like getting dumped was no big deal, but I know it had to sting a bit. "I was 'meh' about him." She sounds sincere, not like a woman bereft after a painful loss.

Not that Colin is much of a catch, anyway.

"But it would have meant so much to Papa. And then, when I told Abi, she said that I should have a fake wedding, a fake husband . . . at least until after Papa's passed away."

Violet rolls her eyes so hard I'm surprised she doesn't see her own brain on the top of the roll, and it hits me.

Abi planned this. She didn't tell Vi anything about my problem, and vice versa.

But Abi's smart, and she put two and two together.

"She even said I should ask you," Violet says, laughing lightly. "How insane is that? We'd kill each other. Probably literally."

I take a deep breath and catch the attention of a passing waitress. "You aren't going to believe this," I tell her, leaning back, "but not all that insane at all."

"What?"

I nod, swallowing. "Order yourself another drink. You just might need it."

CHAPTER 6

ROSS

I keep my silence until the waitress returns with a mimosa for Violet, who downs half of it in a single gulp. "Whoa," I counsel her as she immediately orders another. "Slow down. It's a long night."

She ticks off on her fingers, emphasizing each point. "My fiancé dumped me, my best friend seems intent on hooking me up with *you*, of all people, and I'm wearing the most daring dress I own." Pointing directly at me and daring me to disagree, she finishes with, "I'm gonna drink what I wanna drink." I'm reminded that despite her soft amber eyes, she's definitely half Italian.

So, if she wants to toss back mimosas like Powerade . . . she's gonna toss back mimosas like Powerade. Since I don't really know how well she handles her alcohol, I can't criticize her. Besides, they're mostly juice, right?

"Okay," I concede. "So . . . you've got a problem. And Abi thinks I can help you."

"Which is insane," she interrupts.

I tilt my head, trying to figure out the best way to go about this. Violet is fiery and has taken me to my knees more than once. If she does that this time because I go in too hard, it could be to both of our detriment.

"Have you been keeping your eye on the news?" I ask, and

Violet shrugs, not questioning the random direction I'm leading us in. "What's that mean?"

"It means I read the style section to keep up," Violet admits. "But if you want to ask me who's in first place in the National League, I couldn't even tell you the teams."

"Fair enough," I reply, silently admitting to myself that I've never read the style section of the news. "Let's just say I've had a few scandals. I told Abi that Dad's throwing his weight around, and it would help me personally and professionally to have a . . . steady plus one."

"A steady plus one?" Violet asks, not putting one and one together to make two yet. Fuck, how strong are those drinks? She's usually quick on the uptake.

Finally, her eyes narrow, flicking past me to Abi, who's spinning herself dizzy at Kaede's direction.

"Oh, my God! Abi set this up! That bitch. I'm going to kill her."

I place my hand on her thigh, keeping her in her seat, but I damn near hiss at the heat coming off her skin and wonder if she's that hot all over. "Wait. You're right, but think this through. You need a fake husband. I need a fake girlfriend. Maybe we can meet in the middle and somehow make this work for both of us."

"I need to get *married*, Ross, and you're looking for arm candy. That isn't equal at all. There's no middle ground there."

She's not lying. Those are light years apart. And if we go with the bigger of the two, a wedding and short-term marriage, there's the issue of the fallout when we split. There won't be any quiet and easy way to do that, not with my parents who'll nuclear fucking bomb the whole thing and probably end up hating either Violet or me. The long-term repercussions could be catastrophic since she's been like another daughter to them.

And there's the whole issue of actually faking a relationship with Violet. I try to imagine what that looks like, feels like, and I hate to admit it, but parts of me think it sounds pretty damn good given the way she looks in this red dress. Still, I'm uncomfortable with the whole idea because I definitely had no plans to get married anytime soon.

"Still, maybe we can work something out?" I ask suddenly. "Let's be honest, Vi. You'd be the perfect fake girlfriend."

"And you'd make a *decent* fake husband," Violet retorts with a sudden laugh. "Talk about damning with faint praise. Fake girlfriend . . . thought you were smooth, Ross."

The dig feels normal, just like we always tease even though things might never be the same after this conversation, whether we go through with the craziness or not.

The waitress comes back with another mimosa and takes Vi's now empty glass. "I'm just trying to keep it clear, Vi. If I brought some rando home, there'd be so many questions. Us? We can tell the truth . . . mostly. Friends for years and then one night, everything changed." I gesture to the club around us, implying that this is that night.

"Friends for years is a stretch. We're frenemies at best," Violet replies, but she leans back and turns her body toward me, letting me know that she's at least considering this. "So, what does being your arm candy entail? And I'm warning you, if you say one word about a ball gag to keep me quiet, I'll rip your balls from your body."

She says it with a smile, like it's a sweet promise. If it didn't sound so violent, I'd probably be picturing her touching me, fondling me, teasing me, sucking me . . .

But this is Violet, so I shut that shit down.

I chuckle, leaning in closer to her. She's wearing some light perfume, nothing heavy or cloying, but this close, it's spicy and floral. "Well, a few family dinners, a few public appearances at company events, maybe a date or two where the paps can snap a few shots . . . should be able to make it fit right in with a whirlwind engagement before the wedding and right afterward. Hell, we could probably even spin it that I was comforting you after your breakup with Colin, because you know that's going to get social page coverage, and things between us unexpectedly ignited."

"You want to be my rebound guy?" She smirks, and I shrug.

"If that's what it takes to sell this, sure."

"Well, aren't you the gentleman?" Violet says with a teasing light in her eyes. It's partly alcoholic courage and partly her own big brass balls to make light of something so serious.

I laugh softly, my eyes stealing to the valley of her cleavage in her dress. "You have no idea whether I'm a gentle man, Vi."

Violet's eyes go wide, and I can almost see the flutter of her pulse in the curve of her neck. I pull back, licking my lips as she downs another half a mimosa, side-eyeing me the whole time.

What the hell am I doing? This is supposed to be a *business* negotiation, and here I am putting moves on her.

She sets her glass on the table, staring into its empty depths like it contains the secrets of the world. Or at least an answer to our current question of whether this is a good idea or absolute lunacy.

She takes a large breath and pulls her shoulders back as if she's preparing for war. I almost do the same, ready for her to slay me with her verbal barbs. "Okay," she says on an exhale. "Let's do this. Come on."

She stands and grabs my hand, trying to pull me out of the booth, but I don't budge. "Where are we going?"

"If people are going to believe this, we might as well get started now. So, let's go dance, stare into each other's eyes lovingly, and look all sweet and cuddly. You can fake that, right? Side note, I'll be judging your dancing because we will be dancing at our wedding. I need to know if you can cut a rug or if you're going to spend the whole time doing The Carlton. No pressure, though."

Lies. There's so much pressure on us both, from every angle.

But she's right. A public display at Club Red will be the perfect jumpstart for our story. And at least I can adjust myself as we go downstairs because if Vi's going to grind on me in that dress, I need to be prepared with a mental list of baseball stats to keep things as unawkward as possible. But still I resist, lifting an eyebrow.

"You haven't asked yet."

Violet laughs, then stops when she sees I'm dead serious. "Are you fucking kidding me?" she bites out.

I know my smirk lights her up, probably not in a good way,

but I can't help it. This is the game we always play, and it's so easy to fall into the habit of poking her buttons.

"Fine." She turns to me, bending at the waist and unintentionally giving me a view of two of the most delicious, mouth-watering breasts I've ever seen. "Ross Andrews, will you fake-marry me?" It's the most venom-filled proposal in the history of the world. It's perfect.

I grin, nodding. "How twenty-first century of you to do the asking. Of course, I will."

I finally stand, ready to head to the dance floor, but the waitress appears with another drink for Violet. I guess Abi told them to keep them coming all night. I expect Vi to leave it on the table, but she downs it in a single gulp before leading me down the steps. As I watch her heart-shaped ass flex dangerously in her tight dress, my mind fills with ideas.

I'm going to have *fun* with this.

Violet needs me a lot more than I need her, which in business is called leverage. I might just indulge a little. I won't go too far, but we need to sell this relationship to the public, to the media, and to our families. Getting sassy spitfire Violet to act all lovey-dovey and doting toward me, maybe even fawn over me a bit in front of my parents, might be my biggest and best prank yet.

We hit the dance floor, and out of the corner of my eye I see Kaede, who's left Abi dancing with Archie. "Ross?"

"Can you drive the car home?" I ask Kaede, cutting my eyes to Violet. It's code for us, saying everything's cool, and Kaede nods. He knows I'll fill him in on the details later.

The music changes, another club remix, although this one I at least recognize. Nikki Minaj and Arianna Grande work together to sing about goin' side to side as Violet starts to move to the beat, her ass hypnotic as I dance right with her.

As I do, I'm more and more aware that whatever temporary relief my dick got from moving down the stairs is quickly evaporating as Violet dances. She can move, everything swaying in different directions and bouncing in ways that have my head spinning.

"Not bad." She giggles, turning around and suddenly

pressing her curvy ass up against my crotch. Her arm drifts up, pulling my head forward so she can speak hotly into my ear, "Mmm . . . not bad at all. You've got moves, Mr. Andrews."

"Vi—" I start but stop.

This might not be the best idea, but fuck it. I grab her hips, grinding into her through her tight dress, and she moans, the two of us practically dry humping on the dance floor as the throbbing beat pulses through the soles of our feet. I tell myself it's for the show, just a way to make appearances and start chatter about us, but my dick says differently.

I wrap my arms around her, laying my palms on her flat stomach to hold her to me. In response, Violet presses back against me, her head falling back to my shoulder, and she looks up at me, her eyes cloudy with lust and more than a few mimosas as the song keeps going. I can feel her lush body pressed against mine, making me want to pull the tight hem of her dress up and see if the smooth firmness I feel cradling my throbbing cock is satin, silk . . . or just toned ass.

Before I get too carried away, the music stops and Violet does too, her eyes a little confused at the interruption. She tries to step away, and I hold her close for a half second, getting one last feel of her against my cock. When I let her go, she stumbles in her heels slightly and I have to steady her.

Damn, she's plastered. How many drinks did she put down before she started telling me about Colin and his bullshit?

"Ross," Abi says from next to me, her right eyebrow lifted about three-quarters of the way up her forehead. Fuck, she's been watching, and by the little upturn on the corners of her lips, she's happy with what she's seen, for some reason.

I love my little sister, but damn if she doesn't gloat when one of her schemes goes off without a hitch. I guess she figures her little plan to solve both of our problems is already a success.

"I'm gonna take Violet home," I declare, taking Violet by the hand. "Come on, Vi. I think you've had enough."

"Drinks!" Violet yells, giggling. "Mimosas for everyone! I'm getting married!"

Vi pats my chest a bit too hard, and a group of girls on the dance floor drunkenly slurs out, "Con-grash-u-lashuns!" Well, I guess that's that. We're public.

I sigh as Abi grins hugely, waving her off and dragging Violet to the door. I grab a taxi and out of habit tell the driver to take me back to my place.

It's not a long ride, and Violet's still as bubbly as the champagne she's been drinking when we get there. I lead her out and to the elevator. Violet gapes as the doors close, giggling again as she eyes me with a girlish smile. "What?" I ask, curious about what has her acting so silly.

She pushes her body against me. "Are you taking me to the penthouse?" Her voice lowers, like there's a deeper meaning, but my brain's too fuzzy from her closeness to figure out what she means.

I nod, trying to resist the luscious plumpness of her glossy lips, but when she stands up on her tiptoes to reach toward me, I can't hold back anymore. I crush her to me, kissing her hard as the elevator quietly hums its way up the twenty-seven floors.

Vi's lips are silk, warm and tender, electric in every touch against me. I press for entrance with my tongue, and she opens up, as much taking me in as I am invading her mouth. She moans against me and I swallow the sexy sound.

As the elevator door opens and we half twirl, half stumble our way to the door of my penthouse, all I know is I want her and she wants me.

Reality hits, though, when Violet stumbles on the single step that leads down to my living room area, and I remember that she's drunk. I'm tipsy, for sure, but she's drunk-drunk . . . and I'm not going to take advantage. Certainly not of Violet.

"Where are you taking me?" Violet says as I help her up and lead her to my bedroom. "Ooh . . . I've wanted to see this for awhile." Her eyes are glassy as they bounce around the room, and I wonder what she thinks of my space. Does she think it suits me? Does she like the décor?

"I'm sure you have. Probably want to tell me that the color's atrocious or the Feng Shui is all wrong," I tell her, holding myself back as I pull the comforter and sheets down. "Need help with the heels?"

Violet shakes her head, which seems to disorient her because she tumbles down to the mattress before rolling onto her back. She sticks her long legs up straight in the air and giggles as she pushes off one of her heels with her toes. It falls to the bed and bounces off, hitting the floor. "Boom . . . missile launched. Preparing missile two, Captain." She repeats the move, her other shoe clattering to the floor.

Violet is definitely a happy drunk, looser and less biting than her usual self. I wonder if this is how she is with people other than me.

Her legs flail, bending and opening, which gives me an unexpectedly spectacular view.

Holy shit, she went commando tonight. Beneath the short hem of her dress is nothing but the same soft caramel skin of her honeyed thighs, leading up to a cleft that has my cock leaking precum into my pants before I can do anything about it.

Shiiiiit.

Violet is stunning, and I'm a total asshole for never noticing. But I'm sure as fuck noticing now.

"Now you . . . no ssshoes on the bed." She pats the mattress next to her, and I realize that she thinks I brought her to my bed to fuck her. And in the surprise of the century, I want to. I want to fuck Violet Russo, the annoying pain in my teenage ass whom I honestly haven't given a moment's thought about until tonight.

But not like this. Not so drunk she doesn't even know what she's doing.

Someone should nominate me for sainthood.

Instead of doing what every instinct in my body says it wants me to do, I pull the sheet up over her body and she starts shimmying underneath the sheet.

"What are you doing?" I ask, my brow furrowing. She grunts a little, her pink tongue sticking out in concentration. "You need a drink? Some water?" I clarify.

She doesn't answer, but getting a bit of space seems like a good plan right now because Violet's writhing around in my bed is looking better than I would've thought it ever could. "I'll be right back."

Before I can even get to the door, her dress hits me in the back of the head. I glance back to see her triumphant face and hurry to the bathroom, where I stick my face underneath the cold water of the sink until I can actually think.

Violet Russo is in my bed. Naked. Lusting for me. Me? And I want her?

How did this happen?

My cock's rock hard at seeing even a quick peek of her pussy, and I force myself to focus and play memory games, an old trick that I used back in my college days, reciting Super Bowl champions going backward until my brain's able to take hold again.

It takes me all the way back to the Miami Dolphins before I feel the pressure in my balls subside enough that I don't think I could crack a brick with my dick, and I quickly flush the toilet for my cover story. I splash my face again, looking at the confused, haunted eyes in the mirror when I'm done.

Holy Shit. Leaving my thoughts of naked Violet for a moment, I'm struck with the bigger reality of the night.

I said I'd *marry* her.

Not a silly flirtation we could play off as a one-time thing. Not a drunken night we could both ignore. Not even a short-term fling to get people off my back.

But I said I'd walk down the aisle with her, fake or not, in front of her friends and family. In front of *my* family.

What the fuck was I thinking?

The devil on my shoulder laughs, knowing exactly what I was thinking. That she's sexy . . . and kissed me . . . and needs me.

And doesn't knowing ball-buster Violet Russo needs me do something squirmy to my insides? Just yesterday, I would've said it was glee at getting one over on her. Tonight, I'm not so sure that's what this warmth is. It feels bigger, deeper, hotter than our . . . what did she call it? Frenemies? Yeah, this feels like more than a frenemy-ship.

What the fuck am I going to do?

This is such a bad idea. I know it. She knows it. Hell, Abi set us both up, and even she's gotta know it. Even if it would solve some problems temporarily, I don't think anyone would actually believe that our bickering and teasing caught fire and led to insta-love and marriage. Would they?

Taking a deep breath, I head back to my bedroom. I need to break this off before it goes too far because this is so many types of mistake that I can't even list them all in my foggy brain. And when Violet's not desperate and drunk, she'll see that I'm right.

But what I see at the doorway stops me in my tracks.

She's an angel, sleeping peacefully on a cloud of high-thread-count cotton in my bed. Her eyes are closed as she snores softly. With each exhale, her lips poof out just a little bit, and as I watch, she hums softly before squirming and getting more comfortable. She hugs one of my pillows to her chest before sighing happily in her sleep.

I can't.

I can't what?

Fake marry her? Or *not* fake marry her?

Yeah. Both of those, at the same time. Which makes no sense, but there it is, swirling in my head and my heart. And okay, in my pants.

A fake wedding is truly crazy on some epic level, but I can't say no to her, either. Not to that innocent face, those hungry eyes, that surprisingly tender heart . . . I can't.

I press my lips together, my hands on my hips as I search the ceiling for some divine intervention and realize that I can only hope that she was so drunk before asking me that she doesn't remember in the morning. That'd give us both an out.

CHAPTER 7

VIOLET—14 DAYS UNTIL THE WEDDING

"*Mm* . . . so, then the red velvet ottoman goes over there—" I murmur, but the disembodied client voice says they want it in orange juice—no, ice with a hint of whiskey. *That's not right*, I think, and the discordance rouses me slightly.

I blink, soft light warming my eyelids, and I realize that it was all a dream.

I open my eyes more, fighting the gritty feeling, and see a silky-smooth comforter, an eggshell white wall . . .

Wait.

This isn't my bedroom.

Oh, shit. This is bad.

In surprise, I jerk back, stopping when I feel a warm, thick, *hard* presence nestle against my ass.

Ohmyfuckinggawd. What did I do last night?

I sit up in the bed, my head swirling dangerously, and try not to scream when I turn around and see Ross lying on the other half of the bed. He's damn near naked as the day he was born, every inch of tempting flesh on display except for a decidedly skin-tight pair of boxer briefs that don't hide a damn thing.

He's carved out of wood, and I'm not just talking about his bulging boxers, which are barely containing a cock so large and thick that I can literally see the head start to push the waistband outward, like a snake ready to climb out of its cave.

"What the fuck?" I rasp, only it comes out a lot louder than I expect. I flinch, my head pounding and begging me to keep the volume down. I look down, and I'm stitchless, only the sheet puddling in my lap giving me any slight modesty. I see my red dress and bra hung up on a hanger next to the door, my heels almost carefully placed underneath them.

Ross groans and stretches, opening his eyes and smiling at me, making my heart skip a beat. How is it that I wake up naked, in bed with Ross Andrews, with no real memory of how I got here, but the first thing I can think of is that I want to jump back in and drown in those sexy blue eyes of his?

"Good morning," Ross says quietly, his smile widening into a grin as his eyes obviously trace a path along my bared breasts and belly.

"Oh, my God," I gasp, looking around. I see a bathrobe hanging off a very expensive modernistic German armoire, and I hop up and snatch it, ignoring the tilt-a-whirl floor that threatens to take me down. I pull it on as if it's armor that can protect me against the awkwardness of waking up with my best friend's brother, my archenemy. As if it can protect me from my body's reaction to his.

I tighten the belt and tuck the bows just to make sure it stays tied, but I have to admit it's a very, very nice robe . . . and it smells like Ross. Which isn't doing anything to help my embarrassment or my arousal.

"Okay," I tell him finally, feeling my eyes pulse in my skull and the beginning of a headache coming on. "Let me guess . . . I got drunk?"

"You ordered mimosas for everyone in Club Red," Ross says. He seems ridiculously at ease and not at all freaked out about our current situation, stretching out on the bed and displaying his sexy, leanly muscled body for me.

I can't help but look on in appreciation. I'm stupid, not dead. He grins, seeing my expression. "Like what you see?" He traces his hand over his chest and down his abs, cupping himself. My hands itch to shove his hands out of the way and make the journey themselves.

But this is *Ross*.

"Ugh!" I protest, turning around to give him my back even as sinful thoughts of the six-foot-one-inch of man in bed behind me fill my brain.

Oh, shit . . . wait, did we —

I whirl back around, which is a big mistake for my precarious balance, but my shock and fear keep me vertical. He must read the horror on my face because he answers my unspoken question.

"Don't worry," Ross says as he gets out of bed and walks easily and comfortably across the room. I can't stop my eyes from following him. "I was a gentleman, and even though you showed me quite an eyeful . . . we didn't have sex."

That's good. Really good, but there's a hint of disappointment coursing through me too.

Out of the corner of my eye, I see him go over to a door, disappearing into what looks like a pretty big walk-in closet before coming out in a pair of workout shorts and a tank top that, while hiding a little more of his skin, still has the temperature in my borrowed robe a few degrees this side of warm.

I'm not sure if I'm happy or upset about that.

Physically, I've wanted to fuck Ross since about the time I knew what sex was. And then he basically tortured me through middle and high school, squashing any crush I'd had on him. Well, most of it, anyway.

What's that saying? He's pretty packaging on an ugly inside. Okay, there's nothing remotely ugly about Ross, except how he can zing me good and embarrass the fuck out of me, and somehow, I still enjoy it and live for that bright smile of his that marks his victory over me. But that speaks more to my weirdness, probably, not his.

He's always seen me as an annoying little sister, so emotionally, I'd rather go celibate the rest of my life than sleep with Ross Andrews.

And that's that. Problem, meet solution.

I'm just going to pretend last night never happened. And he's going to do the same.

"Come on," Ross says, stepping aside and gesturing toward the door. "We can talk over some breakfast. You've probably got a hangover the size of Australia brewing inside your head, and I can see the hamster spinning in his wheel with the lightning-fast speed of your thoughts crossing your face."

I nod slowly, following a barefoot Ross out of the bedroom and down a hallway. As he walks, he calls out, "Geoffrey, dim the windows to twenty percent, please."

Oh, no! Is there someone here? A witness to my embarrassment this morning?

Before I can ask if Ross has a butler or something, a masculine computer voice replies, "Of course, Mr. Andrews. Shall I start coffee?"

"Full pot," Ross says before glancing back over his shoulder with a huge grin. "Geoffrey's the electronic assistant. Basically, Alexa, but a thousand percent better."

"A thousand . . . *percent*?" The snarky challenge rolls off my tongue unbidden.

"Give or take a few hundred percent," Ross quips back, unperturbed at continuing our usual banter in such a weird situation.

I'm at a loss for words as I pad into the main room of the penthouse. It's huge, semicircular, and slightly tech-modern, with lots of blacks and brushed steel that strike me as Ross's natural style. Not my personal choices . . . but it fits him.

The curved exterior wall is dominated by huge, two-story-tall windows that are tinted to a dark smoke right now, and the interior designer part of me loves it. High-tech windows that can change at a voice command? Talk about eliminating the need for drapes! I've heard of this technology, even saw it at a conference once, but I haven't had a client who wanted something that high-tech yet. Usually, my clients want their estates updated, like Ms. Montgomery, so high-rise style is out of my wheelhouse, and even hungover, I'm tempted to play with it to see what all Geoffrey and those windows can do.

"When did you get the *Starship Enterprise* as your penthouse?" I weakly joke as he leads me over to the far side of the room to a high-tech chef's kitchen. While you couldn't put a restaurant in here, it's fully equipped, everything in tasteful matte dark colors and black marble countertops. Ross opens the built-in fridge and pulls out a blender cup, swirling the contents before studying it carefully.

"Cover your ears," he says right before slapping the cup on a blender base and pulsing it a few seconds. Even with my hands over my ears, it's painfully loud, but the shock of it is helping to clear my head. When it's ready, he pulls out a huge glass from a cabinet and pours me a light green smoothie. "Here. My patented hangover cure, just this side of hair of the dog in terms of effectiveness. Drink up."

He eyes me, daring me to disobey, and when I lift the glass for a sniff, he smiles like he knows he's already won. Answering my previous question, he says, "I had this place renovated three years ago. If I'd known how good you were going to get with interior design, I'd have hired you." The compliment warms me inside. I am good, and I know it, as does half of the city's upper crust, but somehow, Ross saying it so casually is different from those accolades.

He takes the other half of the smoothie mixture and downs most of it, his throat working in a way that has me staring at him with decidedly non-breakfast thoughts in my head, and I have to remind myself to take a sip. I'm worried. Usually, people who drink green smoothies in the morning tend to be those who live on Vitamin Shoppe supplements alone, and I am not that girl. My breakfast usually consists of copious amounts of coffee darker than Satan's soul and a single small, buttered croissant, just like Nana taught me. But before I know it, the glass is empty.

"Wow . . . this is delicious," I comment. "What's in it?"

"Mostly fruit. Apples, cherries . . . a little spinach for the vitamins, and willow bark. It's a natural aspirin."

"Willow bark?" I ask, and Ross nods, going over to the far

end of the counter. He picks up some papers and taps them carefully into order. "What's that?"

He doesn't answer directly but instead takes a roundabout way I'm not used to with him. He's usually so decisive and direct, but I can feel him hemming and hawing.

"Do you remember asking me to marry you last night?" He stares directly at me with the question.

Flashes of the night come back to me. Talking. Drinks. Dancing.

I swallow, nodding. That part, asking him to be my fake husband, I totally remember now. I remember right up to the dance floor, and then turning around to show him my moves . . . but not much else until this morning. "I remember."

"Did you mean it?"

I can feel the heat creeping up my chest, my cheeks flaming hot as I try to decide how to answer that.

Yes? No? Maybe? It depends on how much fun you're going to make of me for losing a fiancé I didn't even love and how hard you'll judge me for wanting to get married for my Papa.

He sighs and his eyes soften. "It's crazy, I know. I spent the better part of last night hoping you would forget and that we could just pretend that conversation never happened. But you know what? It really does solve both of our problems." He pauses to let that sink in. "That's why I called Kaede last night and had him draw these papers up."

"What are they?" I ask again, hoping for an answer this time.

"What you wanted," he says, handing me the papers. "A non-disclosure agreement."

"An . . . NDA?" I ask, my brows furrowing together as he nods and hands the stack of papers over.

It's not that I haven't had non-disclosure agreements before. A lot of my clients are very private, and they know inviting me into their homes or businesses means that I might be privy to things that they don't want anyone to know. It's professional courtesy to keep your mouth shut, but to put clients at ease, I have a standard NDA I offer which states that I'm allowed to boast that I redid their decor, but that's it.

This isn't one of those standard agreements.

"Come on, Ross. Is this really necessary?" I reply, my voice rising before my brain reminds me that loud noises are a really, really bad idea right now.

I read the NDA over, expecting some standard verbiage about sticking to our story and not throwing each other under the bus with the media and our families. But then I notice the rules on page two. "What's this shit? I'm to *obey* you at events where your parents or members of the company might be present? You're out of your damn mind. *Oh-bay?*" I lengthen the word, tasting its uncomfortable restraint. I'm not a woman who obeys anyone or anything, and Ross damn well knows it.

"Obey," Ross repeats, smirking. "My folks are a little . . . traditional. I need to show that I'm strong and in charge. Looks better for me, you know? Don't get caught up on the label. Just stick with the intent of it and we'll be fine."

I growl, rubbing at my temples. "And if I want to give you a heaping service of attitude?"

"Maybe I'll spank that curvy ass of yours," Ross teases, but his voice has a dark undercurrent through it that I've never heard from him before. It says that he might actually try it, and in my head, I wonder if I might like it, too.

Still, a girl's gotta have her pride. "You don't know Italian women very well. We rule the house by rolling pin, *capiche?*"

"I'm sure we can agree on *some* limits to what I'll demand," Ross replies smoothly. "Never fear, Chickie. Though I'll never admit it and will deny having said so, I like your sass."

And doesn't that stop my arguments in their tracks. *What? Ross likes when I give him shit?* I always thought I was annoying the fuck out of him. *Huh, who'd have thought?*

"I'll even toss you this bone. I'll sign an NDA too. I'm not going to hurt you, Violet." Soft, sweet, weighted words that mean more than he could possibly know.

"And when this . . . marriage is over?" I ask, and Ross simply shrugs. "What's that mean?"

"If we're really going through with this, I think it'll be best for both of us if we go with the 'too young, too quick, irreconcilable differences' excuse and not say a damn thing otherwise. We both walk away with the least damage to our reps from it, and the most benefit. I'd like for us to still be friends after all of this is over, or else my parents and sister are going to kill me."

That actually sounds . . . not bad. I can tell he thought about this last night while I was passed out. Oh, God, did I snore? When I'm drunk, I sometimes snore like Godzilla having an asthma attack.

Back to the issue at hand, though. I consider his proposal. Vaguely, I remember being the one who proposed, and I groan internally.

"That's fine . . . sounds good, even." I flip through the continuing stack of papers. "But what about the rest of these?" I ask, reading over each rule. With each one, my irritation grows. "Seriously? I'll answer the phone whenever you call? Even if I'm at work and with a client?"

"It shows that you're head over heels with the love of your life. But I respect your work, and I'm a busy man. It's not like I'm going to call for baby talk every half hour, *Shnookums*."

"Okay, agreed. If you never call me that again. It's worse than Chickie." I see a shadow cross his face, but it's gone too fast for me to decipher it.

"Take the blame if the story comes to light outside of one of us breaking the NDA? Are you crazy? It'd ruin me professionally."

"Like the Million Dollar Man used to say, 'Everyone's got a price.'"

"Well, this one I'm not willing to pay," I declare. Ross shrugs and sips at the rest of his smoothie. I know what he's doing, playing the hard silence and making me sweat.

But it's damned effective. He knows what I've got on the line with all of this. Papa's happiness is first and foremost in my mind. Finally, I crack and concede. "Fine. If the shit hits the fan, it's probably a better angle to say we were trying to make a dying old man's last wish come true than to say your Dad was blackmailing you into settling down. But we need to circle the wagons to be sure nothing gets out. Who already knows about this?"

"Kaede. Abigail. Archie?" I nod, and he finishes, "And you and me. No one else, deal?"

"Deal. You do know it's two weeks until the wedding, right?"

"Of course. You told me approximately halfway through your second mimosa . . . at least, the second I saw you drink," Ross says.

We've reached a stalemate. This is it . . . do it or don't do it. I'm not sure how it all got so carried away with such a crazy-ass idea. But here I am. And here Ross is.

I swallow thickly, still tasting the sweetly fruity smoothie and thinking the bitterness of coffee seems better suited for the moment. "Are you sure you want to do this? With me?"

In answer, Ross opens what I assume is his junk drawer and pulls out a pen. He signs on the last page with a flourish, initialing each of the other pages before turning it around to me. "I already called Kaede and told him I had personal biz to deal with today. I figure we can get you a proper engagement ring. Something that suits you better than that gaudy as fuck monstrosity Colin gave you. So . . . you in?"

I pick up the pen and slash my signature at the bottom. "Fine. But our relationship will be on my terms."

"Fine," Ross says with a chuckle as I initial the last page and shove the NDA back to him. "Let's pretend this is on your terms."

He's got a huge grin on his face, and I hold in a groan, knowing better than to doubt him. He's going to make me pay for this scheme. We might be friends afterward, but damn if he isn't going to have some good ammunition to hit me with after a fake marriage.

I ROLL INTO WORK JUST AFTER THREE IN THE AFTERNOON, thankful that Archie can keep the train chugging in my unscheduled absence. We don't always work weekends, but this is an industry where we meet when clients are available and source when stores are open, so a Saturday in the office isn't unusual.

He's on the phone when I come in. "I'm so sorry. She's with a client today. Can I help you with something or give her a message?"

God, he's good. He even sounds sincere, which is a feat, considering the hairy eyeball he's giving me as he looks me up and down suspiciously.

I set my bag down on our communal worktable, and unburdened, I feel the heaviness of my new engagement ring in my pocket.

I'll hand this to Ross. At least he was polite enough to not make me go ring shopping in the same hoochie-mama dress and heels I wore to Club Red last night. That would've been one hell of a walk of shame, even if it was to a fancy jewelry store. Instead, he calmly lent me one of his T-shirts, some sweatpants, and even a pair of flip-flops before he drove me back to my place. Fifteen minutes later, we were on the road to do ring shopping, and after quick success with a fawning shop assistant, Ross dropped me at work so I can get some things done today.

Of course, as soon as I open the door to my office, I'm greeted by none other than Abi, who's got the world's biggest shit-eating grin on her face as she shoves her laptop onto the table. Guess she was getting some work done while stalking, I mean waiting, for me. "Whoo . . . Russo, last time I came into work at three in the afternoon after a drunk and disorderly night, I was walking like that cowboy on TV, James Bennett, when he took a flyer off a bull's back and did the splits in the dirt. *Hee-hee*." Her voice pitches painfully high for the sound effect.

"When'd you start watching rodeo?" I grumble behind my sunglasses, wishing that somehow, my hangover would magically go away. Even with a chaser of two Midol with lunch, my brain's hurting . . . although that could be the situation I'm in.

Archie, of course, overhears us. "Girl, you don't need to be into rodeo. That video went viral, making everyone *into* James Bennett," he says, making hungry sounds. "Which I could be . . . balls deep, if he played for my team. Too bad he got himself married. Lucky bitch to ride that cock every night. I wonder if the bull-riding made him a bit . . ." He holds his bent finger up, looking at it contemplatively.

I shrug, not digesting anything they just said and too exhausted to give Archie a rebuttal for his dirty comments. "Please tell me that the world hasn't burned down while I've been out."

"Out?" Abi asks, giving me that damn Vulcan eyebrow of hers again. "Is that what the kids are calling it these days?" I don't respond to the hook and she continues. "Last time I saw you, you were literally hanging on my brother as Ross was leading you out of Club Red, and you didn't answer your phone this morning. Soooo . . . can you give me the PG edited version? He's my brother, so I don't need all the gory details."

Archie slaps Abi's arm, psshawing. "Then gee-tee-eff-oh if you don't wanna hear. I live for this shit, and Virgin Violet ain't usually got any good stories to tell. Something tells me that's not the case today. So spill all of those filthy, dirty details to Daddy Archie, girl. You owe me good sex stories, remember?"

"Nothing to edit," I reply, pinching the bridge of my nose as I start tapping that spot behind my ear I read helps with headaches. "I was drunk, and he took me back to his place and put me to bed. And before you say it, there's no double meaning in that."

Even though I'm telling the truth, it's hard not to blush as I think of what I saw and some of the thoughts that have been running through my head all day. Because, damn it all, Ross is sexy as hell. And not just in that cute, older guy way I used to think. No, he's all grown up now . . . all over.

Yeah, he demanded my 'obedience,' saying that we might need to practice that part of our arrangement since I'm such a ball-buster, but he did it with such a roguish charm, a sort of gentlemanly imperiousness, that I still felt like he was doting over me. Deep inside, I liked that he thought I was tough too, not some vapid little girl chasing after him but rather a challenge, an equal, with thoughts and opinions of my own.

Like shopping for my engagement ring. At first, I was going to pick out the simplest ring that I could see not embarrassing him, but when I tried, he took my hand and looked me in the eyes. "This is going to be the only engagement ring I'm ever going to give you," he said to me while the salesgirl practically drooled over him and silently begged him to seed her ovaries. "I want our ring to reflect that . . . so pick out your dream ring."

I'm still not sure what to make of that, but how could I refuse?

"So?" Abi asks, pulling my attention back to the office. "Did you tell him about your problem?"

"Yes," I reply, cutting my eyes to Archie. "Can you get me a coffee? As black and thick as possible."

He snaps, "One Lizzo special, coming right up."

"Thanks," I tell him as he disappears through the doorway, but I know he's still listening. "And he told me about his problem too. For the record, we're both going to kick your ass for scheming like that."

"It'd be worth it," Abi says with the sort of brutal honesty that makes her my best friend. "So, what's the plan?"

My answer's simple as I pull out my engagement ring and show it to her, her squeal jacking my headache up by a few notches. "Goddamn, girl, it's beautiful!"

Her excitement has Archie hustling back with a half-full coffee cup that he basically drops in front of me so his hands are free to grab at the ring. He holds it up to the light. "Nice ice, ice, baby."

"You know my head feels like I've been skull fucked all night, right?" I reply, cringing at their volume before regretting my words. "And again, no fucking went on between us." I point back and forth from Abi to Archie to make sure they have that clear.

"Well, guess I'll need to get those invitations reworked and ready, then," Abi says. "So put the ring on!"

"We agreed to wait, make it a public proposal," I answer, putting the ring away. "Don't know when, but it'll have to be fast. Two weeks and all."

"Whirlwind romances can be the best, though," Abi says hopefully.

Archie's lips curl. "So, Boss Lady, speaking of public . . . in your whirlwind of an unexpected day off, did you see the paper, by any chance?"

I shake my head, confused. "No, why?"

He intones, "Dun-dun-dun-duuuuuuun . . ." He disappears back out to his desk for a split second and then slaps it open in front of me.

The gossip column headline blares out at me. *Playboy Ross Andrews Has Another One on the Hook.*

There's a picture, and I wonder just how shitfaced I got last night based on my relaxed facial expression and unfocused eyes. Reluctantly, I read the copy, anger pulsing behind my eyeballs as I do. "*A low-level interior designer wannabe?*" I ask, seething. "I'm going to kick this bitch's ass!"

"Relax," Abi says soothingly. "Seriously, that writer always rips on whoever Ross gets photographed with. We think she has a crush on him, but we can handle that. Lord knows, Dad has had to call the paper before to threaten lawsuits if they don't cease and desist."

"But my reputation—" I start, groaning when my phone rings and I see the name. *Mom.* "Nope, not answering that."

As soon as it stops, the office phone starts to ring, and Abi reaches for it and I try to stop her. "Uh-uh! Leave that damn thing down!"

"Why? It's not like anything's official yet," Abi says, and before I know it, we're struggling over the cordless phone.

Archie, unperturbed, sips at the coffee he got for me. That thief. "Two girls, one phone . . . so not my thing."

"Dammit, Abi, please!" I beg, finally snatching the phone from her. "Let me think!"

"What do you need to think about?" Abi asks, grinning in confusion. "You are linked to Ross now. He's agreed to be your husband and you're going to be his wife. Now, I know he's an asshole sometimes, but he's got a good side to him. He just . . . needs to be cajoled to show it a little more."

"Yeah, well, I don't know how to do that!" I seethe, putting the phone back down and silently vowing to call my mother later.

"We're going to kill each other before we even get down the aisle!"

The big picture of walking down the aisle with Papa and Ross standing there to greet me hits me all at once and I blanch. "Oh, my God, I'm marrying Ross Andrews!"

Abi is still smiling, though, even as I have a minor mental breakdown. "You two always fight like cats and dogs, but that'll just make the makeup sex better."

I'm starting to wonder about my best friend's sanity because she seems to think this is no biggie. And shouldn't she be weirded out to talk about her big brother's sex life? Like, a few minutes ago, she was saying she wanted an edited version of the night and now she's telling me to have crazy, wild makeup sex with Ross. Her brother.

Or is that just what I'm picturing?

"I'll help you with Ross. I know he drives you nuts sometimes," she says patiently.

"And half of the state's going to think I'm some social-climbing gold digger," I grumble, regretting signing that damn NDA more and more each minute. "I'm going to be ruined."

"Nonsense. This will all blow over before you know it. Especially when the papers start reporting that you and Ross are dating, meeting the family, and engaged. A few starry-eyed pictures where you two look like lovebirds, and maybe some well-designed PDAs, and you'll be the romance story of the millennials. The childhood friends who finally ignite in fiery passion that can't be stopped long enough to plan a proper wedding. Oh, no, the way this story goes . . . you two are ready for your forever, right now."

She makes it sound plausible and easy. Maybe she's right and I'm overreacting?

Seeing that I'm calming somewhat, she starts handing out instructions. "For now, you're going to get a few hours of work in, send a few emails, and then . . . Paradise Burgers," Abi says, grinning. "The big ones, with tomato, those four types of cheese you like, and . . ."

"You're evil. You know I've been dieting to get into *the dress*. The dress I haven't even found yet," I remind us all sharply.

" And the garlic aioli you adore, with milkshakes," Abi continues, ignoring my interruption. "Come on, their milkshake brings all us girls to the—"

"Stop!" I finally laugh, shaking my head. "You know if you keep it up, Archie's going to start twerking!"

"Won't ever happen," he says dryly, but we all know he was popping his shoulders left and right a bit and I can see the song lyrics running through his head. Hell, if Abi kept singing, he'd probably hop up and do a little whacking for us, the arm-twirling dancing kind, not the 'call HR type', and finish with a death drop.

But before he can, Abi's and my phones both buzz, and I look at mine to see a text from Ross.

Dinner tonight with family. 8 PM. Dress nice . . . honey.

There's a wink emoji after 'honey' and I know it's in reference to our discussion to not call me *Shnookums*. I guess he's trying out terms of endearment. "Ooh, that son of a . . ." I hiss, showing Abi my phone. She holds hers up too, showing me a much nicer, much more polite text from Ross inviting her to the family home for 'an important family dinner'. "I'm so gonna get him."

"Good," Abi says, taking her phone back and slipping it into her pocket. "In the meantime, I'll help you learn how to get under Ross's skin, how to cajole him to be nice. When we're done with him, he'll be eating out of the palm of your hand. I've got a few years' experience in driving guys crazy, especially my brother. And coupled with your track record, we should be golden. Let the games begin."

I hold my breath and count to ten, gathering myself. "Okay . . . so how do I twist Ross around my little finger and make this whole thing not so ridiculous?"

CHAPTER 8

ROSS

I'm able to hold off until I get to the office, but finally, my primal brain takes over. I barely drop my briefcase in my office, thankful that Kaede's not at his desk to see my desperation, before I'm bolting for my private bathroom, locking the door behind me as images flash through my mind.

Last night, the feeling of that lush, delicious body pressed against me.

Her lips against mine, her moans when I cupped her ass in the elevator and squeezed.

Waking up to see her nude in all her glory, heavy teardrop breasts succulently swaying with every word.

Her face lighting up with joy when I took her ring shopping. I wonder if she knew she was hugging my arm, pressing her body against mine when I was being a gentleman to her, and if she was purposefully showing me the challenging fire in the dark depths of her eyes when I wasn't.

But most of all, the sight of her gleaming wet pussy, wanting me to press her into the mattress and fuck her as hard as I could. I'd never even considered what Violet's pussy might look like, but now it's all I can imagine.

I've been with her all night and all day, a patient saint who didn't want the delicious torture to end. But I can't hold back anymore. I drop my pants and wrap my hand around my aching hard cock.

This is wrong, so wrong, but I can't help it as another image of her soft pink pussy lips and caramel colored nipples floods my overtaxed mind.

In my head, a fantasy Violet drops to her knees, running her hands up my legs and over my thighs, her pink tongue licking her lush lips before taking my balls into her mouth.

I stroke hard, rough, as I give myself over to my lust and my need for her.

Violet Russo. The pest I childishly tortured who grew into the vixen I never noticed and is now the beauty I'm going to marry.

In less than a dozen strokes, my climax hits me like a shotgun blast to the balls, and thick, ropy streams shoot out of the purplish head of my cock to splatter against the toilet and into the water below.

"Fuck," I rasp, grabbing a handful of toilet paper and wiping up the mess. I can't believe how fast I came, so fast I didn't even get to her sucking me or climbing into my lap . . .

I need to stop, or I'm going to walk out of the washroom just as hard as when I walked in. Flushing the toilet, I take a good two minutes to wash my hands and splash water on my face, getting myself under some semblance of control before heading back into my office.

The door's open and Kaede's waiting for me, sitting in one of my chairs and tapping away at his tablet so fast and hard that I suspect I'm going to be buying him a new one within a few months. I'm just hoping he was distracted enough by whatever he's working on to not have heard what I was doing in the bathroom.

He looks up when I sit down and judging by the concern and not smirking judgement, I think I'm in the clear.

"How's the headache?" And what warrants calling me in on a weekend?"

Straight to the point, I like that about him.

"Barely there," I reply, opening my laptop. "Listen, I need you to—"

"Wait," Kaede says, holding up a hand. He does that sometimes, and while most executive assistants would probably lose their jobs for interrupting their executive VP bosses, I've come to trust his judgement. He clicks around on his tablet, muttering, "Password protected and off the servers, just to be careful while I'm taking notes. Okay, so about Violet . . ."

He eyes me expectantly. Of course he knows who Violet is. He went to school with us and knows enough of my social life and family life to recognize the name, even if he hadn't seen her in years before last night. And I'm sure Abi probably gave him a full earful of her dastardly plan.

He shows it by quickly ticking off the benefits. "Well . . . explaining the relationship is easy. And she's certainly good-looking and smart, her rep in the design world is top-notch, so she's believable as your girlfriend—"

Maybe Abi didn't give him all the details of her plan after all?

"I'm marrying her."

In the entire time Kaede's worked for me, I've only once seen him drop his tablet to the floor, and that required a clumsy UPS delivery girl, three boxes, and his shoe being untied by accident.

This time, though, it only takes three words and his tablet slips from his fingers to bounce off the carpet of my office, his face so slack that he doesn't notice it at all. "You're *what*?"

"I'm marrying her," I repeat, pulling up my email and starting to type. "In fact, I'm going to hold a dinner at my parents' house tonight to announce it to my family. We need to get in front of the gossip hounds that I'm sure are already jumping on this story. We went ring shopping this morning."

"Dude . . . Ross, are you sure you want to take it this far?" Kaede asks. "I mean, when I said fake girlfriend, that's one thing. But married? That's a bit much, don't you think?"

"No," I immediately reply. "Listen, Violet has her reasons too. It's a win-win for both of us."

"And she's not going to try and fuck you?"

I blink, my cock surging in my pants at the idea Kaede's question plants. As weird as it seems, my body certainly wants Violet to fuck me. "Excuse me?"

"When it's over," Kaede explains. "You know, big public divorce, get a settlement . . . ?"

I laugh, relieved at what he means. "No. Not that I think I need it, but that's what the NDA I had you pull together was about. Not for her to be my girlfriend but to be my wife. And I'm sure my dad will want her to sign a pre-nup. No getting around that, so the aftermath should be easy."

"Easy?" he says, not looking like he believes that for a second. But he recovers enough to pick up his tablet. "You're the boss. So, you're really doing this?"

I nod and quickly type out a pair of messages, the first to my family, the other to Violet. I could have copy-pasted and sent her the same thing I sent my family, but the idea of calling her 'honey' sarcastically is just too delicious. It's so much fun to get under Vi's skin, wind her up, and see how she comes back at me.

After hitting *Send*, I lean back.

"Okay, I'm going to need you to cover my ass professionally a little here," I tell Kaede honestly. "This engagement's going to be at warp speed. Violet needs to be married in two weeks. And there's going to be a lot to do. I'm sure my parents are both going to be stunned and hopefully back off a little on the pressure cooker, but there are a lot of irons in the fire that I need you to put out."

"You know I'm on it," Kaede says simply, checking his tablet.

"Okay, I'll send you Violet's contact info so you can check in with her on what needs to be done. I'm sure Archie and Abi have that under control, but backup couldn't hurt. We've got the Johnston meeting in three days. Everything prepped there?" He nods, and I know I could do that presentation in my sleep, which is a good thing because my schedule just blew up with all the additional tasks.

"Need to book a honeymoon. It's a sham, but no reason we can't have some fun. Hawaii, maybe? Clear my schedule for those days too."

Kaede is tapping away, and I trust that he's got everything. He's that good.

Before Kaede can comment, my phone rings and I pick it up

to see Abi calling. "Go on . . . you do your stuff and I'll do my end of things. And get yourself a better tablet. On me!"

Kaede smirks and gets up, heading out of the office while I pick up Abi's call. "Hey, little sister. See you got my text?"

"What's all this about a family dinner?" Abi asks sweetly. I can hear the bomb about to drop in her butter-wouldn't-melt-in-my-mouth tone. "It wouldn't have anything to do with an announcement, would it?"

"You're a scheming little chess master, you know that?" I growl, but Abi's laugh still makes me smile.

"I do what I can," she says, and I can almost imagine her humbly curtseying at the compliment.

"I can only assume you and Vi talked?"

"Of course."

In the back of my head, I wonder just how much Violet's told Abi, and more importantly . . . what's Abi's angle on all of this?

I'm not exactly the best fake husband for Violet. I've got too much baggage and too public a profile to really play a fake role.

Meanwhile, for me, Violet's need for the marriage isn't exactly ideal, either. What would be best would be a six-month, no-stress social thing that never gets too serious. Truly, just regular arm candy for show like Violet said.

So this isn't a perfect match for either of us. But at the same time, a niggling little voice that's been going off in my head since I saw her curled up in my bed says it's totally right, too.

But what is Abi's role in all of this? She's the fly in the ointment right now, but I have to trust her somewhat.

"And?" I prompt.

"And what?" she snaps back. "You might not believe me, Ross . . . but I'm doing this for both of you."

I hum, not sure about that. Abi always has a master plan. I'm just not sure what it is right now. Though I guess covering both her brother's and her best friend's asses with this crazy idea might be the entirety of her scheme. Lord knows, it's not something either Vi or I would've come up with on our own.

"Have you told Courtney about this?" I ask, a little worried. I love my youngest sister, but Courtney wants to be the good girl

103

in the family way too much. There's no way she'd understand what I'm doing or why.

"Hell, no!" Abi says, her opinion of Courtney totally lining up with mine. "You remember the number of times she ratted on me to Mom and Dad when I was in high school? Getting out of the house to go on dates with Danny Reeves was damn near like *Prison Break* with her around."

"He was a douche," I point out, something Abi found out for herself before she went to college. "So, this is just between us? No one else can know, for both Vi's sake and mine."

"Already discussed and agreed upon, big brother."

"So, you'll be there tonight and help me not blow the whole thing before we even get it started?"

Her chuckle does nothing to soothe my nerves at making this play in front of my family. What if we can't pull this off? What if they can tell that Violet would rather kick me than kiss me? What if they know we're not compatible at all, with the constant teasing and bickering?

"Oh, it's already started, Ross. But I'll be there. It'll be fine. Vi'll be ready. I'll be ready. Just make sure *you're* ready."

She's trying to calm me, but something about her words makes it sound like I need to be ready for just about anything. When Abi and Vi get together, I guess that's usually true, which is terrifying.

"All right, Sis. See you at Mom and Dad's tonight."

The click severing the connection feels like a sign of what's to come. I'm dead, so fucking dead if this goes wrong.

THE ANDREWS ESTATE ISN'T QUITE THE HISTORICAL FAMILY heirloom that the name implies. My family's wealth is too new. In fact, I can remember living in an upper middle-class home before my father's hard work paid off. If anything, those memories are part of why I'm busting my ass so much to prove myself to Dad.

He built the company with his hard work . . . but I'm going

to be the one to make it multi-generational. He built a kingdom. I'm going to turn that kingdom into an empire.

But first, I need to get past this hurdle.

The estate is certainly beautiful, an anniversary present from Dad to Mom, and in many ways, it does seem to have a bit of a fairytale castle vibe to it, with its sand-colored stone and big windows that look out over twenty manicured acres. It's got all the usual toys of the rich, including an Olympic-sized pool, a rose garden, and a lawn roughly the size of a football field.

But in a nod to just how good a set of parents I've got, there are a lot of things that you wouldn't expect. Like a huge wooden playset with slides, swings, and more, and a tree house with chairs in both little girl size and older brother size.

There's a full gym in one wing of the basement, installed so that a son who wanted to be a high school football player could bring his friends over and make sure his team was fully prepared for the gridiron.

And a game room where we actually sat at the table and played cards on rainy nights. It was there I first discovered a love of business when I beat my dad at Monopoly. He'd been proud at my win and encouraged me to learn strategies that I later delved deeper into in business school.

Yeah . . . I owe a lot to my parents.

Which is why I didn't tell Dad to fuck off with his ultimatum. He's right to a small degree, as much as I absolutely hate to admit it. He has been a great example for me, as a loving husband and father and as a businessman. But he's also a lot to live up to.

Which is also why I don't gun my Camaro's engine as I pull up out front, parking in the crushed gravel semi-circle driveway. At a glance, I'd say I'm the first to arrive, but it's all good.

"Mister Ross," Karl, the butler, says. "How is Geoffrey?"

I swear Karl gets a kick out of my 'digital assistant,' or maybe it's professional jealousy. Either way, he always makes a note to ask. "Currently having dinner with Cortana," I joke. "He just stole her from some plumber named Mario."

"Very funny, sir. Your parents should be home soon. Your

mother had a charity meeting she needed to clear this afternoon. The caterers are already here, and dinner will be ready promptly at eight."

"Excellent. Thank you for coordinating dinner tonight on the fly." He nods deferentially. Leaving the foyer, I make a quick check of the dining room where I see the extra place laid out, then the kitchen, where the caterers are doing fine. I went all out, with Dad's favorite of beef Wellington, Mom's favorite Shiraz wine, and sides that reflect everyone's favorites. I even had Abi send me Violet's favorite dessert, which of course, is tiramisu.

Everything's ready.

"Miss Abigail Andrews and Miss Violet Russo," Karl announces from the foyer, and I turn around, only to stop short when I see Violet.

How can this be? She's even more beautiful than she was last night, dressed in a midnight blue dress with white accents, slightly demure while still being so sexy that I immediately feel bad about jacking off in the bathroom a few hours ago.

Not because my cock isn't swelling—it's already threatening to strain the compression boxers I'm wearing for just this purpose—but because all I can think of is all that wasted cream that could be coating the twin swells of her breasts.

"Violet—" I begin, but before I can say more, the rumble of Dad's classic Jag comes through the door, and Karl steps out again. "Okay, show time."

Dad shows up with Mom on his arm, the two of them casually chatting about their day when Karl announces them. "Well now, Ross, I do hope . . . Violet?"

"Hello, Mr. Andrews," Violet says politely, offering her hand. True to form, Dad ignores the hand to give her a quick but warm embrace before stepping back for Mom to do the same, this time with a kiss on both cheeks.

"Oh, hush with that 'mister' stuff," Mom says, smiling. "You've slept over here enough times, and I've made you enough cocoa, that you don't need it. Please, just Morgan and Kimberly?"

"I'll try . . . Kimberly," Violet says, glancing at me out of the corner of her eye. "How are you doing?"

"Just fine, dear. I heard about your newest design success. Apparently, you got through to Lydia Montgomery? She's been positively raving about you. Well done, dealing with her. She can be a bit of a battle axe . . . sharp and lethal."

Violet chuckles, saying conspiratorially, "Good to hear. Although, please don't call her that. I don't want to have a slip of the tongue at work."

"There are much better uses for tongues," I interject, making Violet blush and Mom and Dad give me withering looks. They probably think I'm trying to make fun of her, and I guess I am . . . but not in the way they expect.

"I must say, Violet, while it has been too long since you've been to the house, your coming to dinner is unexpected," Dad finally says as we all leave the foyer and head toward the living room. "What brings you by?"

"A surprise," Abi says, saving me with an innocent smile. I swear, she's looking forward to this . . . which is all the more reason not to trust her.

We settle into the comfortable chairs and sofas that ring the living room, and I spring my first little 'test' on Violet. When she goes to sit down next to Abi, I clear my throat and pat my own knee. "Violet?"

I love the way her eyes flash fire, her tanned skin flushing just a little as I basically silently order her to perch on my knee, something I know she'd never do willingly. I'm on edge, so curious whether she's going to obey. Mom and Dad both give us confused looks while Abi looks about ready to spit nails at me.

Violet debates internally, her eyes scanning me, and I know I'm going to pay for this. Funny thing is, I'm looking forward to it. Seeing what she can come up with to keep me on my toes is an exciting change of pace from my work-sleep-fuck-repeat life cycle.

Finally, she tosses her head, flipping her hair in a dark ebony wave over her shoulder before starting to sit down . . . only to slide past my knee and onto the cushion of the loveseat next to me. Her smile is pure saccharin.

Ooh . . . so close. That was a good one, leading me to think she was going to actually obey and then doing exactly whatever the fuck she wants at the last second.

The funny thing is, I like this attitude from Violet. If I were actually looking for a wife, I'd want one who could match me strength for strength, who'll give as good as she gets.

The thought is unsettling, something I've never really considered in my work-focused life. A wife, a marriage, and especially a family, have always seemed like far-off, long-term goals. Not something to worry about now. And even if I had imagined it late at night, I'd always pictured being married to a debutante-socialite type. Not because that's my preference but because they're easy and everyone knows the score. Keep them well-kept and go on with life while they go on with theirs. But that's not a marriage. It's a contract.

Somehow, this arrangement with Violet already seems more personal than a gold-digging wife ever would be, though.

"Why, thank you, Ross," Violet says, resting her hand on my thigh just a little higher than is friendly.

"Violet? Ross?" Dad asks as Mom looks on with equal parts surprise, hope, and glee in her eyes. "Is there something going on?"

"You know we should wait until dinner, Dad," I reply. "You taught me that lesson. You don't strike until the right moment." It sounds like a compliment, but my gaze is hard. I respect him, look up to him—hell, I love him—but that doesn't mean that I'm not still furious with him for throwing his weight around, threatening me, and putting us all in this position.

"Well," Mom says, trying to interrupt the tension, "how are things with Colin, Violet? The last I heard from Abigail, you were going to get married soon?" She asks it lightly, but her eyes are definitely laser-locked on where Violet's hand rests on my thigh. To make a point, I lay my own hand over Violet's, interweaving our fingers.

I swear my mother is going to have a conniption fit. Only her years of keeping up appearances hold her back from peppering us with the questions I know she has.

Violet tries to remove her hand, but I hold her steady, and she blushes, a pink tone that I want to see flushing her entire body as I bring her to the edge of coming and then make her wait for my command to fall into the pleasure. I mentally smack the shit out of myself. Seriously, what is it about Violet the past twenty-four hours that has me as horny as a fourteen-year-old boy seeing tits for the first time?

"Miss Courtney Andrews," Karl announces, and Court comes in, looking like a million bucks. I swear, if she wasn't intent on making her own path in the family corporation, she'd be able to pull seven figures as a fashion model.

"Hey, guys, what's up?" she asks, smiling when she sees Violet. Violet stands and gives Court a quick hello hug. "Hey, Vi. How's the wedding prep?"

"Uhm . . ." Violet says, glancing at me to take the lead on this one as she sits back down at my side.

Courtney's looking from Violet to me, and I can see in her expression that she saw the newspaper article about Vi and me this morning. Dad might've missed it if he had a busy day, but Court always reads the gossip pages first.

"I'm not with Colin anymore," Violet blurts out.

Courtney and Mom gasp, and I can see that Mom wants to comfort Vi as she tuts out, "Oh, my dear, I'm sorry." But Violet doesn't need comforting. She's fine—more than fine—at the loss of an ass like Colin. *Especially now that she has me*, I think cockily.

"What?" Courtney says. She knows Colin's family better than I do. One of her sorority sisters in college actually dated Colin's brother, so I can see she feels a little closer to this. "What happened?"

"Doesn't matter," I reply, holding out my hand to Violet, thankful when she takes it easily. "Last night, Violet and I met up, and well . . . one thing led to another, and we realized something we should've realized a long time ago."

A pregnant pause stretches out, and I rub at Violet's bare finger, suddenly wanting my ring there as a sign that we're doing this, that we're in this thing together. I can't wait until dinner, don't want to play the strategy game with Dad. I need to mark her somehow, if only a little.

"Hey, Abs, a little help here?" I raise a brow at her and her mouth opens into an O before she jumps up and runs to the foyer.

She reappears a moment later with a small velvet box in her hand. "Here you go, Ross," she says at volume. Under her breath, I swear she whispers, "Don't fuck this up." But her face is frozen in a sweet smile so maybe I imagined that.

Courtney, Mom, and Dad all look like they just got dropped into one of those off the wall British sitcoms that Mom used to watch on BBC America.

"N–F–W," Courtney says, pronouncing each letter out loud as I open the box and reveal Violet's ring. "No effin' way!"

"Way," I reply, taking the ring and getting down on a knee. "It took me too long to see what I should've seen all along, and for that I'm sorry. But I promise, if you'll let me, I'll make it up to you each and every day for the rest of our lives. Violet Russo, will you marry me?"

CHAPTER 9

VIOLET

I stare at the ring, the entire world slowing to a stop.

I know I shouldn't be reacting this way . . . I mean, we just went shopping for this ring fewer than eight hours ago. But looking down at the band of platinum and diamond with pink rubies dotted around it, I can barely breathe.

It's gorgeous, but more important is the look in Ross's eyes.

I was so ready to smack him when he patted his knee earlier, silently ordering me to sit like some obedient little Barbie doll. And I could tell he was enjoying the uncomfortable silence as Abi fetched the ring, the cocky smirk on his lips making me sweat bullets while his parents and Courtney stared at us like goldfish in a bowl.

But now, there's no laughter in his eyes. There's no teasing, no deception. He's looking into my eyes, just me and him as the rest of the room disappears. And in this instant, I can almost imagine that this charade is real, that I'm actually marrying the boy I had a crush on a decade ago.

I'm so in shock that I can't think, and silence stretches, my heart pounding like a war hammer. I only remember myself when Ross nudges me with his thumb on my kneecap and the world starts up again.

"Yes!" I shriek, forcing the word out, and them more quietly, "Yes."

Ross's smile is genuine again as he slips the big rock on my finger, and the way his eyes twinkle in the light of the living room makes my head swim. His handsome face is filled with emotion, forcing my heart into a double-twisting triple-backflip.

Real. This feels real, and that's weird and dangerous as fuck.

He surges toward me, standing to clasp a powerful hand on each side of my face, and then we're kissing again, his mouth powerful and claiming me with a single touch. I give in to him, kissing him back just as hard, and this time, I'm the one pressing on his lips to wrap my tongue around his, invading his mouth and claiming him right back.

In just a second, we've gone from a polite post-yes kiss to full-on tonsil hockey mouth snogging, and it's only our need for oxygen that forces us to pull back. He presses his forehead to mine, his eyes gleaming as they fill my field of vision. His cheeks puff up as he grins, and suddenly, I'm reminded of that same grin ten years ago.

My stomach drops. This isn't real. No matter how much of a roller coaster ride this has been in the last twenty-four hours, it's all a front.

He's not like Colin, not at all, but Ross is all about the image, at least right now. The image I just helped him present.

And the real Ross is triumphantly laughing inside, maybe not at me but at his own family, at Morgan and Kimberly and Courtney. Hell, maybe even at Abi some, although she's obviously a partner in all of this.

Ross is still the same asshole you've always known.

There's an audible dramatic gasp from Courtney, followed by momentary shocked silence. Morgan and Kimberly both look absolutely gobsmacked, the first time I've legitimately been able to use that word since reading it back in junior high school. They all look back and forth at each other with wide eyes and open mouths.

Before anyone can say anything, though, Karl comes in, clearing his throat. "Excuse me, but dinner is served."

Oh, great. *Now* the fun starts.

———

COURTNEY IS THE FIRST ONE TO BREAK THE SILENCE WHEN WE sit down around the dining room table, her face pinching when Ross takes my left hand, showing off the ring even more.

"But, Ross . . . Violet?" she asks in disbelief, her nose wrinkling like someone unleashed rotten eggs. "Isn't this the same girl you held down against the grass and then farted in her face because she called you a big hulking ogre in front of your friends when you guys were in middle school?"

OMG, I think, almost choking on a piece of my salad, *I'd almost forgotten about that!*

Just remembering it brings the annoyance I felt with Ross during our youth, and without even thinking, I nudge him in the ribs with my elbow.

Not to be undone, he nudges me right back, except his is so powerful I almost fall out of my seat.

Luckily, no one notices.

"Courtney!" Mrs. Andrews—Kimberly, gotta remember to call her Kimberly—scolds. "Please, let's not dredge up ancient history!"

Courtney doesn't back down. "What, Mom? It's true! I spent my entire childhood listening to Abi and Ross fighting like cats and dogs, and more often than not, it was over how Ross treated Violet. I really don't see how this could happen. I mean, seriously?"

"I guess opposites attract," I say as I pinch Ross's thigh underneath the table while maintaining a fraudulent smile. "And when we looked at each other with fresh eyes, we realized that there was something there the whole time." I look at him lovingly, which is somewhere between easy and hard. Too easy to be real, too hard to be fake.

"All of my antics were apparently because I wanted her so badly," Ross adds, grinning at me in a picture of happiness. In contrast, his returning pinch is so sharp I nearly gasp out loud.

Courtney scowls. "You must really love the smell of his farts then."

113

"Courtney!" Kimberly scolds again. "No more, please!"

"It's fine, Mom. Court . . . it's like that old cartoon I saw on TV when we were kids," Ross says, turning to her with a placating plea on his face. "It was an old Looney Tunes, I think. But in it, there was this bear."

"Oh, great, a love story with a bear," Courtney groans, but Ross chuckles and looks at me in such a way that I'm suddenly enraptured by him again. He's damn near magnetic when he wants to be.

"Yeah, so there's a bear who was raised in the circus. And one day, the bear gets released into the wild, I forget how. But he meets this girl bear, and at first, he tries to be nice to her. The girl bear ignores him for a few days, but he doesn't give up."

"I bet," Abi says sarcastically, one eyebrow lifting up her forehead. "So, what happened?"

"Well, the boy bear approaches the girl bear with a bouquet of flowers like he saw the humans at the circus do," Ross continues, "but the girl bear hauls off and just smacks him across the face, sending him flying backward."

Courtney shrugs. "And?"

"So, the boy bear tries again," Ross says, still looking at me, "and again he gets smacked. The boy bear thinks the girl hates him, so he goes off to sulk . . . and one of the other animals fills him in on the deal. In the wild, bears would smack each other when they like each other! So the boy bear, realizing the truth, runs over to the girl bear, and when she smacks him, he hauls off and smacks her right back. Boom! Happily ever after."

"So, you've been *flirting* all this time? How stupid are you, brother bear?" Courtney asks, but if she's teasing him, she must be at least starting to believe us.

It's my turn to nod, looking over at Ross's eyes a little dreamily. Is he serious? He's explaining *us* using bears and flowers and the circus? "Stupid enough," I quip. The barb doesn't seem as funny as it would've just a few short days ago, though.

"This is ridiculous," Morgan says, his voice tight with anger. "What are you trying to pull, Ross? And how did he get you tied up in his mess, Violet?"

"Morgan!" Kimberly says, but apparently, nobody is listening to her admonishments about the rules as Morgan continues.

"No, Kimberly," he says, making the barest effort to soothe her before turning back to Ross. "How can you two be engaged when just a few days ago, she was set to marry Radcliffe and you were splashed all over the papers with Joeden Snow's wife?"

"Because things change, Dad. Isn't that what you wanted? Me to grow up and settle down? Well, I am. *With Violet.*" He gives my hand a little squeeze that reminds of the band on my finger. "As for Colin, he didn't see what was right in front of him, and I'm damned lucky he didn't. I was near blind myself. It took me so long, and I'm going to make up for that lost time."

Morgan's about to reply when Kimberly reaches out, putting her hand on her husband's forearm. "Morgan . . . please, let's enjoy dinner?"

He glares at Ross for a moment, then shakes his head in obvious disbelief and confusion. "This isn't over."

Ross glances at me, but I don't need to reply to feel the burning ember in my chest. "Dad . . . it's like I just said," he finally replies, making one more attempt. His voice is softer, more vulnerable than at any point in our conversation. "The fact of the matter is, we've always been in love. We just were too caught up in our heads to admit it."

My heart skips a beat at the seeming sincerity in Ross's eyes. He looks a hundred percent genuine, and I have to keep repeating a mantra in my head.

This isn't real, this isn't real, this isn't real.

It only partially works because Ross's fingers are woven through mine as he fidgets with my ring.

"Yeah, right," Courtney hisses, looking down at her plate as Karl and the caterers bring out platters of beef Wellington and vegetables. "I'm with Dad. You can't be in love, either of you. Violet was just engaged to someone else, and now she's marrying Ross. It doesn't work like that, just turning it on and off like a faucet."

Ross, who looked so genuine and heartfelt just a moment ago, shrugs and snaps at Courtney. "Oh, and you know so much about love? Remind me, how many serious relationships have you had?"

That seems to be a sore spot because she shuts right up, though she's eyeing Ross with fury and hurt. I tell myself to ask Abi what that's all about later.

"And you're such an expert?" she fires back.

"One, that's how many. One serious relationship, and she's sitting right here next to me," Ross tells Courtney.

Morgan stabs at his beef with his fork so hard that I'm surprised he doesn't put the silverware through the china. "This is just such a surprise." Morgan is trying to backtrack, but only slightly, still keeping everything on his terms.

"You'd better get used to it fast," Ross says, raising his voice for the first time and taking over the room, "because the wedding's in two weeks."

Everyone stops in shock, except Abigail, who still looks like the cat who got the cream. She's loving this, for some reason. The whole damn thing.

"Is this your way of testing us, Ross?" Kimberly asks, her voice half choked with emotion. My heart aches for her, and I realize that regardless of why we're doing this for Ross, it's going to play with people's emotions.

We're going to have to tightrope this as carefully as we do with my own family to avoid hurt feelings on both sides.

Ross turns on his mom, his eyes wide. "You know what Dad said to me?" She nods, though it looks like it's painful. "Testing you? I think it's the two of you testing *me*! Well, never fear, you got your way. I'm just lucky that it's with someone I love, Violet, because this could've backfired on us all, Mom."

I can sense that Ross is even more hurt that his mother knew about his Dad's ultimatum than he was about his Dad's part in the whole argument. They've always been such a tight family, one I envied, so seeing them at odds this way is setting me on edge.

"Enough," Morgan growls, his eyes blazing. "Fine, Ross, you're engaged. Congratulations, Violet. Or condolences. I'm not sure which."

"Morgan," Kimberly says, trying to soothe her husband. "Give them a chance."

Morgan growls, getting up. "Excuse me. I'll take my dinner in my study."

Morgan disappears, and a tense, ugly silence drops over the remaining five of us. I look at Ross, who sighs and gives me a supportive pat on my thigh.

"Well, that could've gone better," he says dryly.

How the hell are we supposed to make this work? And we still have *my* family to tell. The folks flying in I'm not worried about, but Papa, Nana, and Mom?

Boom. Like that, my headache's back, and I haven't even touched the wine after my boozy behavior last night.

"Really? I thought that went well," Abi says cheerily, downing the rest of her glass of Shiraz.

The rest of us stare at her, and she just grins, shrugging. "What?"

CHAPTER 10

VIOLET

*T*he trip to my place after dinner is awkward as fuck.

Actually, if you'd asked me two days ago, this ride probably would've ranked up there with the most uncomfortable things I've ever done—riding along in Ross's growly muscle car as he works his jaw and gear shifter with thinly corralled fury coursing through his veins. Veins I can literally see flexing in his forearms where his shirt sleeves are rolled back.

But that awkwardness ranking would've been *before* that dinner.

Now, I'm not sure much of anything will outrank that. Ever.

After Morgan's outburst and abandonment of the family dinner, it didn't get any better. Kimberly made some initial admonishments, but Courtney expertly sidestepped her mother and continued asking question after question. Ultimately, Kimberly had defected to Court's side, her curiosity getting the better of her.

It'd started out easy enough, and I suspect Courtney had been lulling us into a false sense of security with her inquiries about the wedding. Venue? Of course, we have that. Date? Yep, have that too. Invitations? Abi had fielded that one and tried to help by saying she was updating them to reflect the new groom information and that they'd be ready to mail within twenty-four hours.

Kimberly had literally clutched her pearls and clarified, "You mean all the wedding plans are the ones you had with Colin? You're just removing one groom and . . . inserting another?" Her distaste was heavy with judgement. Of me.

I'd swallowed a too-big piece of beef and looked to Ross for help because that's exactly what we're doing.

He'd laid his arm over the back of my chair possessively and grinned, apparently enjoying this a little too much. "Of course we are. That seems most efficient, and I do know how much of a hurry you've been in for me to get married and start popping out grandbabies."

If I'd thought the death grip on her necklace was bad, it was nothing compared to the way Kimberly's mouth had dropped open and her eyes had shot to mine, then to my table-hidden belly, and back up at Ross's proclamation. The question was unspoken, but I'd answered it anyway. "No, of course not. And we're not looking to start a family anytime soon. Right, dear?"

To hurry Ross's answer, I smacked the back of my hand against his chest, telling myself that purple-nurples are a no-no at the dinner table while somehow simultaneously reminding my hoo-ha to ignore the hard expanse of muscle there. And I definitely refused to imagine Ross pumping iron to get those pecs of steel. Nope, didn't think of that at all. "Tell your mother this isn't some shotgun wedding. We haven't even had a chance to discuss babies yet, much less *be* pregnant."

Courtney had leaned forward, both elbows on the table at that little tidbit. I had been able to read the 'gotcha' loud and clear in her eyes, the delight dancing there and making me squirm in my seat like a caffeinated preschooler. Ross had cupped the back of my neck firmly, forcing me still, and my instinct was to shake him off. But I couldn't without it looking bad to his family, and oddly, his grip had settled me.

"So you haven't discussed babies, but you are suddenly so in love that you're getting married in two weeks? That's the story you're going with?" Court said.

And things had devolved from there. They smelled blood in the water, and like sharks, Kimberly and Courtney had started asking more questions. Ones we should've had answers to, but because we're flying by the seat of our pants here, neither Ross nor I had any idea.

So that had been the number-one most awkward moment in my life so far—getting grilled by a family that I once considered a close backup to my own. But this car ride was gaining ground on that frontrunner by the second.

"So, that went to hell in a handbasket faster than a speeding bullet. Now what?" I ask.

Ross downshifts, buzzing past a slower driver on the highway. His jaw clenches again . . . once, twice, three times that muscle pops in his jaw, and I wish I could read his mind. Is he regretting this already? This is such a complicated web of lies when all he really needed was a steady plus-one for a few society page appearances to get his parents off his back. The messy factor is all me—my family, my needs, my lie.

Guilt hits me full-throttle and I turn to Ross. "If it's too much, it's fine. I understand if you want to back out, because that was a bloodbath. Babies and weddings and where your birthmark is?" I shake my head. "I can't believe Courtney actually asked me that!"

Ross's lips tilt up ever so slightly. "But you knew. How did you know the answer to that, anyway?"

I can feel the heat coloring my cheeks, so I answer back with fire to cover the embarrassing truth. "Look, it's a brown patch the size of a half-dollar on your lower back. I saw you in swim trunks basically every summer of my life. How could I not know?" I roll my eyes and hope he believes me.

He cuts his eyes over to me, and I smile, hoping it sells that this is no big deal. His answering smirk says I failed big time. "It is just a small spot that happens to be right above my ass. If you weren't looking at my butt, you'd probably never even notice it. So tell me, Vi . . .were you looking at my ass?"

I bite my lip and shake my head, refusing to answer, but the lady doth protest too much.

"I get it. It's a nice ass. Can definitely bounce a quarter on it.

I'll show you sometime," Ross offers. A tease or a promise? I'm not sure which I'm hoping for.

He didn't answer my question, though, and as much as I'd like to keep with the distraction of his ass, I need to know. "Do you want to back out? It's fine. I understand."

His hand leaves the ergonomic comfort of the gear shifter to rest on my thigh. It's broad, covering a swath of my skin, and even through the fabric of my dress, I can feel his heat. He could burn me up in a flash if I'm not careful. I've never had his hands on me like this, at least not sober, and because I don't remember a lot of last night, this feels new and dangerous. So fucking stupidly dangerous.

Because this is Ross. The guy who made my life hell for so long. The guy who is still mid-prank on his family, which shows he hasn't really grown up all that much. The guy I really want to slide my dress up and grip my thigh the way he held my neck earlier.

He licks his lips, and I wonder if he tastes like the wine he had at dinner. I'd skipped it entirely, keeping to my short-term promise of water only after last night's overindulgence. "I think I have an idea," he says finally, a hitch in his voice that worries me.

"What?" I ask, not sure if I want to hear this.

"So our story is a warp-speed wedding so we can make up for lost time, yeah?" I nod slowly, agreeing with him. "So we need to *make up for lost time*, quite literally. By spending all of our time together." He smirks, smug and proud like he just solved the global climate crisis, but I didn't hear anything ground-breaking in that little plan.

"So, we do daily dates? We'd already agreed to that. Make sure the paparazzi see us eating fancy dinners out, stop by each other's offices, stuff like that. What else?" I say, trying to read what he's thinking.

He shakes his head, and I can tell I'm not going to like this. "No, I mean *all* of our time together. You're moving in with me. Tonight."

Shock washes through me in an electric jolt. "No, I'm not!" I yell, my ears ringing in the tight cabin of Ross's Camaro.

"Moving in? That's crazy . . . I mean, even crazier than what we're already doing!"

"Vi, we're about to get married. Don't people these days usually cohabitate *before* getting married?" Ross argues. "It only makes sense for us to do it too, especially given the speed demon pace we're setting. If we're so all-fired up in a hurry to get married, we would be just as in a hurry to be together every second we can."

Shit. That makes sense. Convoluted sense, but it's pretty realistic sounding. Or at least as realistic as an overnight engagement.

"And after the wedding, we'd have to live together for a few months anyway to keep the charade up. So, what's the difference if we bump that up a couple of weeks?"

The difference is I'm not sure if I'm ready for this. This crazy idea is starting to have a life of its own, and I'm feeling severely out of control. I can't imagine that walking around Ross's place for weeks—no, months—on end is going to be good for us.

I'm going to kill him.

I'm going to fuck him.

I'm not sure which is the worse option.

But he's right. I was going to have to do this after the wedding, so what's a couple of weeks to really sell the story? I can do this.

It's just Ross. He'll probably put a rubber snake in my bed or Nair in my shampoo. It won't be weird, it won't be awkward, it won't be a dream come true to see him walking around half-naked every day.

No, not that last one. Scratch that. Because any crush I used to have on Ross is long gone, burned to ashes in the years of growing up I've done. This will just be two frenemies cohabitating for a good cause. That's it.

I can feel his eyes weighing on me and realize I've had an entire conversation with myself in my head that he hasn't been privy to. I kinda like that he can't read me, though, so I don't share any of my thoughts. Instead, I just sigh heavily and say dramatically, "Okay, fine. I'll move in with you. You're such a needy bitch." I hold back the smile for a split second and then can't contain it anymore.

The smile is accompanied by a snort of a laugh, completely unladylike, and if Ross was someone I was actually dating, I'd be covering my face and pinching my nose to get it to stop. But he's not, so I don't. I let the piggy-snorting laughs go, enjoying the shocked horror on Ross's face.

"Oh, my God, never do that again, Vi. That's worse than fingernails on a chalkboard!" I snort big and loud on purpose at that and then giggle when he cringes. He shakes his head. "Well, I guess we'd better pack your shit."

And that's that. I'm moving in with Ross. My fiancé.

A FEW SUITCASES TURN INTO ABOUT HALF THE STUFF I OWN, and that's just for the first 'essentials only' run we do tonight. I just couldn't choose which of my work clothes to pack for this. And there were my favorite pajamas, and of course, my shampoo and conditioner. This hair of mine needs salon-quality conditioner, or else I end up with a rat's nest on my head.

What was supposed to be an hour's work tops stretches out to nearly one in the morning before we take the elevator up to Ross's—I mean, our—penthouse.

The elevator dings and the door opens, and my heart starts racing against my will. This is real. I'm moving in with Ross Andrews right now.

He picks up my heaviest suitcase from the floor and leads me to the living area, carrying the bag like it's nothing. "You know, you could have just packed an overnight bag."

"That was kind of the plan at first," I reply, following with my two rolling bags. "We can unpack it all tomorrow, though. I'm beat and have an early morning tomorrow."

"Early tomorrow? It's Sunday. Isn't that a day of rest, even for the wicked?" Ross questions me, the implication of my wickedness apparently both an insult and a compliment if I'm correctly decoding the twinkle in his eyes.

I force my shoulders back, challenging him. "Well, normally, yes. But since I'm moving with absolutely zero notice and you rushed me to get my butt in gear tonight, I figured I'd go back for the rest of what I need tomorrow after I unpack this stuff. I want to get this all done before Monday when I'm back in the office."

See? Reasonable reasons I can't just laze around the house all day tomorrow with a loungewear-clothed Ross.

Oh, God! I bet he wears grey sweatpants and nothing else when he's sitting around. He's definitely the type to do that.

And again, my girly bits try to tell me that's not so bad. But it is. So bad . . . so, so very bad.

"All right, then. If we're getting up early, I guess we'd better call it a night." He disappears down the hallway with two of my bags, assuming I'll follow him along like a dog. I root my feet to the floor and call after him.

"Where are you taking my things? Guest bedroom?" I cross my fingers on both hands and wish I could cross my toes, but they're too short and stubby to do that.

I hear his answer, but it's too mumbled to figure out what he said. Steeling my nerves, I decide this isn't the battle to die on and trace his steps down the hall . . . to his bedroom.

He's already in the walk-in closet, setting my bag along the back wall. He turns, taking the one remaining bag from my hand. "Why are you putting my stuff here? Don't you have a guest bedroom?"

He rolls his eyes. "Of course I do. But I also have a family who questions the validity of this relationship, and each of them has a key to the front door. If you think Courtney isn't going to 'pop by' within twenty-four hours of finding out we're living together to check the status of my closet and where your toothbrush is, you're an idiot. And I know for a fact that you're not."

Huh, that was almost a compliment. I guess we're making progress. I walk back out to the bedroom and he follows me this time.

"Okay, I concede that Courtney is nosy as fuck and will definitely do some spying, but I think we need some ground rules for this to work."

Ross opens his hands wide. 'Ladies first,' he seems to be saying.

"I'm not sleeping with you,' I blurt out. Ross's eyebrows jump up his forehead. "No, I mean literally . . . I'm not sleeping in the same bed with you." I pause, "And also, I'm not *sleeping* with you."

His lips spread wide, showing off that cocky smirk. "Funny that as far as ground rules go, the first thing to come to your mind is fucking me. Maybe you still have a little bit of that crush after all?"

"No." I can feel the embarrassment burning bright and hot in my belly because I know he caught me. He's right, one hundred percent. There might be a spark of that crush left, but it's buried under years of experience with players like Ross, both my own and my friends', and I won't make that mistake.

"Counter. I'm sleeping in my bed because it's my bed. If you choose to sleep on the couch over there" —he points across the room to a tufted leather sofa— "that's your choice. Personally, couch sleeping for months on end wouldn't appeal to me much when there's a perfectly good bed right there."

I look from the couch to the bed to Ross. His face is straight as can be, no hint of a bluff, and I realize this is his business face. Because this is a business negotiation.

The silence draws out, tense on my part and apparently cool as a cucumber on Ross's part. Seriously, sleeping next to this man, again? How am I supposed to get any sleep at all when half the time I'm in his presence, my ovaries seem to be dancing to *Mi Gente* on repeat?

I roll my eyes. "Fine. We can sleep in the same bed. Probably better if anyone asks questions about your snoring, anyway. But you'd better stay on your side. No midnight snuggles or morning wood grinding." I make circles in the air around my butt, indicating that no part of him should be touching me while we sleep.

He dips his chin in agreement. "To your second point, we are going to be married, Vi. And no wife of mine, fake or real, is going to cheat on me. Nor am I a cheater. So for the duration of this arrangement, we will not date other people or fuck other people."

"Agree," I say easily because neither of us wants to be made a fool of by the paparazzi catching us with someone else. That'd ruin the whole arrangement and definitely leave us unable to end this gracefully.

"So I'm open to casual sex if you are." I start to argue and he holds up a hand to silence me. "But if not, we're adults and we have needs. Needs that we can meet on our own." His voice is deeper, gravelly, and it's hitting me in all the right places.

Wrong! I mean, the wrong places!

"So what do you suggest? We make a schedule for our 'alone times'?" I do the air-quote thing with my fingers. "Or do we use a signal like in college? Like if there's a sock on the bathroom door, leave me alone?"

Fire burns in his eyes. "Vi, if you put a sock on that doorknob, I don't know if there's a lock in existence that'd keep me on the other side of that door. And if I did manage to stay out, you can trust that I'd be jacking off while I strain my ears for even the slightest moan from you."

Well, holy shit. Ross isn't exactly dirty talking, but damn if that doesn't sound sexy as hell. I can picture us on either side of the door, only the inch of solid wood separating us as we both pleasure ourselves.

I swallow thickly to wet my dry throat and lick my lips. Ross's eyes follow the movement. "Okay, so we'll just go discreet on that. No schedule, no signal, just whenever you need to . . ." My voice is too quiet, too weak, and trails off as he reaches up to push a lock of hair behind my ear.

He's touching me, not as a show for someone to see us but seemingly just because he wanted to.

He smiles, and I look for the arrogance, the assuredness that he got me, but it's missing. It seems like a genuine smile, maybe? "I'm going to get ready for bed, Chickie."

The nickname kills any kind thoughts I might've been having about his improved teasing nature.

He likes fucking with your head as much as anything else.

He disappears into the bathroom, though I swear I see him adjusting himself as he turns away from me. Maybe I'm not the only one being affected by that sexy teasing he was doing.

I wander back into the huge closet and dig around in my suitcases to find my PJs. These are my favorites, silky and luxurious. They were a treat to myself after a particularly successful and stressful design install. As an additional bonus, they're sexy without being overt. Just a spaghetti-strapped cami and flutter-leg boy shorts. If Ross is going to tease me, I'm going to tease him right back. It's what we've always done, so why would it be any different now?

You're playing with fire, the angel on my shoulder warns. But the adjacent devil is dancing a jig. *Show him who's got chicken legs now!*

The bathroom door opens and Ross appears in black pajama pants . . . and nothing else. The wide, chiseled pecs I woke up against are back, covered in a light dusting of dark curls that highlight the hills and valleys of his muscles. His arms are ripped, and through the thin material, I can see a long, thick bulge running down his left thigh.

Shit. Looks like I wasn't the only one with the idea of sexy pajamas. But two can play that game.

"Bathroom's all yours," Ross offers as he walks to the bed. I can't help but study the flex of his ass in the pants, but I catch myself doing it and make a run for the bathroom, closing the door a little too hard.

I look at the girl in the mirror. My eyes are bright, my cheeks flushed, and my hair a little messy from whipping my head back and forth at dinner from the verbal warfare we endured.

How did I end up here?

But I know the answer to that one. Papa. This is all for him, and to make him happy, I can get through this night and many more with Ross. It's not even that bad. It's not like he's some ugly monster or a jerk who expects me to wait on him hand and foot.

He did do that whole 'sit' thing before dinner, though, I remind myself. But honestly, it was a test, a prank like we've pulled a thousand times, so I'm going to let that go as nothing more than an attempt at a point in his favor. I turned it around, though. And there will be plenty more chances for us both to goad each other like old times, but also to make everyone believe this is real.

Resolved, I pull my clothes off, folding them neatly. I pull the pink cami over my head, refusing to admit, even to myself, that my nipples are stiff and tender because of Ross. I repeat the same denial when I realize that my arousal has soaked through my panties. Guess I'll have to go commando because fresh undies are in my suitcase, and I'm not walking back in there to get them because that would be way too obvious.

I pee, wash my hands, and brush my teeth. Before I open the door, I take a deep, steadying breath. And then another.

This is not real. I can do this. This is not real. I can do this.

In the bedroom, Ross is sprawled out on one side of the bed. His side, which I guess makes the other side mine. He's stretched out in all his masculine glory, his bare feet crossed casually and his cute outie belly button topping the thicker happy trail of hair that runs down past his waistband.

Not that I'm looking.

"Well, you certainly know how to pack for moving into a new home," Ross says, and in his pajama pants I see a heavy twitch. "I'm looking forward to this more and more by the moment." He switches to a dry, documentary-style voice. "Night one. Subject is combative initially but quickly sees reason. Forecast for future successful interactions seems likely." His report of our evening makes me realize that he's right. This is night one of *many* to come.

I pretend like I don't know what he's talking about with the commentary on my PJs and ignore the attempt at a joke, too caught up in his proximity to come up with a comeback. "Goodnight, Ross," I force myself to say, my body pulsing with need as I cover myself with the sheet.

He pulls the sheet the rest of the way over my shoulders, his hand resting like a burning warmth on top of the sheet when he's done, and I can feel his intense gaze staring at the side of my face.

Steeling myself inside even as my pussy starts to throb, I turn my face to look up at him. "Yes?"

"We're going to get through this, Violet. It's going to be okay . . . for your family and mine, for you and me. I promise." I wasn't expecting him to say that. Not at all. He's vowing this to me on pure faith and willingness to do whatever it takes. Some tiny worry I didn't even know I had because I'd been suppressing it eases.

"Thanks, Ross." I roll back over, settling in to sleep. "Good-night," I repeat, and this time, he answers in kind.

He lies down, his back toward mine but a solid foot of space between us in the king-size bed. "Geoffrey . . . lights out."

"Goodnight, sir," the computer voice says, and the lights fade to darkness. In that inky blackness, I can hear him shift and try to get comfortable, obviously aroused by what he saw and prob-ably as confused as I am by the roller coaster of the night.

For my part, I lie still, forcing myself to breathe deeply and not think of what's right behind me. Because the more I do, the more I wonder how I'm going to survive this fake engagement without either killing Ross . . . or fucking him into a coma.

It's all going to depend on which comes first. Or *who*.

That damned devil on my shoulder smugly answers, "Me. I come first."

The crazy thing is, I bet that's true. I bet Ross would be gentlemanly enough to make me come first. And that's exactly what I'm thinking about as sleep finally takes me under.

CHAPTER 11

ROSS—MONDAY—12 DAYS UNTIL THE
WEDDING

"*I* want to talk to you."

Looking up from my computer, where I've been pounding away at my keyboard, I see Courtney standing in my office doorway in her 'power stance', her eyes fiery and set so fiercely she could melt a lesser man.

Thankfully, I'm tougher than most so her gaze doesn't faze me in the least. In fact, it looks like the bell ringing on round two with my littlest sister.

Let the games begin . . . again. She's nothing if not persistent, though I guess she'd have to be to make it as the baby in a family like ours.

"Come on in," I reply nonchalantly, shaking out my hands. "I haven't typed this fast since the two hours before my junior year poli-sci paper was due. Kaede's out picking up his new tablet, so if you need to coordinate something with him, I'd say the best idea is to send him an email."

It's a calculated move to set her on edge. I'm well aware she's not here to schedule a meeting and doesn't need to see my assistant, but in making it look like there's nothing unusual going on, I reiterate that my relationship with Violet is the new status quo. Nothing to see here, just two lovebirds in love.

"I'm not here to talk to K-dawg," Courtney says, her voice just barely softening when she uses Kaede's nickname. I've suspected for awhile that she's had a bit of a schoolgirl crush on my best friend. Luckily for them both, she's never made a move on him, and he would never. Bro code all the way between us.

She shuts the door behind her, giving us some privacy, and I know she's come armed for war. I'm curious whether she's going to pull out the tears like she did when she was younger or if she'll go with the cutting comments she's learned at Dad's elbow since she started working for him.

"I'm here to talk to you. What the hell is going on? Dad damn near chops your balls off because you're gallivanting all over town with random pussy, and days later, you show up with a fiancée. That'd be suspicious enough, but then the fiancée happens to be Violet Russo, the girl you literally tortured for half her life. Something's rank in Denmark, and it's not hard to figure out that, as usual, it's you."

Can I get cutting comments for one hundred, Alex?

"Court, we've already gone through this. Yes, Violet and I have a rather checkered past, but things are different now. *We* are different now, all grown up and whatnot. I need you to just be happy for me because she makes me happy."

Her eyes narrow, and I can almost feel the x-ray scan she's subjecting me to. I need to wrap this up because it's too risky to rehash the same shit over and over. Too many reruns of *Law & Order* have taught me that. Courtney might as well be the police asking me to repeat myself again, and then again, so she can look for holes, things that don't line up, and any small changes in my story. "If that's everything, I need to get this proposal ready for the board meeting before Violet arrives. I'm going to be too distracted once she shows up."

Courtney sighs but at least abandons her hardline attack enough to sit down in a chair opposite my desk. She might be shorter than me, but she's got one hell of a looming presence when she wants to be a pit bull. "Fine. Why is she coming here? You going to parade her around the office and introduce her to all the alphabet suits?"

It's not fine, and I know it. She's only rope-a-doping, not

surrendering, but I'll take that for now. I ignore just how right she is about my main motives at having Violet stop by too.

"She offered to give my office a little refresh, so she's coming by to see my space and take some measurements," I say airily.

Truth be told, this was one of our rather genius ideas yesterday as we unpacked and moved the rest of Violet's things to the penthouse. We need time together in public to sell this, and we're both busy people. She can't just start stopping by for lunch randomly and keep up her work-hard pace, nor can I cut out of the office and meet her all over the city while she's seeing clients. A minor update to my space gives her the chance to literally put her mark on me, my home, my office, my life, and no one can refute the importance of that.

Plus, she can stop by morning, noon, and night with a cover story beyond a booty call. Though I hadn't been averse to everyone thinking she was coming by for her daily dose of my dick, but I could also understand her resistance to developing that reputation.

Courtney looks around, seeing the same industrial cold décor that my home possesses. Black leather, gleaming metals, everything simple and luxurious. "What's wrong with your office?"

I'd been surprised at what a couple of throw pillows and a fuzzy blanket had done for my living room, and I'm interested to see what Violet will do with this space. "Nothing, but Violet's a magician with her designs so I'm going to let her work her magic. She already did great things at home."

"Home?" Court says, her perfectly sculpted eyebrow raising.

I smirk. "Yeah, when we moved her in this weekend. We're engaged, Sis. It only makes sense for us to live together." I use the same logic on her that I did on Violet, hoping it works just as well.

"You moved in together?" She screeches in shock.

Yep, pretty much the same reaction.

Courtney composes herself, uncrossing and then re-crossing her legs before smoothing her skirt. I can see her take a calming breath too. She's going in for the kill.

Is it weird that a twisted part of me can't wait? I live for this shit—the verbal debate, the battle of wills—and I'm glad Court's finally grown up and skilled enough to be a worthy adversary. She keeps it interesting at the office, at least.

"Seriously, Ross? How can you be in love with her? I mean, seriously, she was just engaged days before you two hooked up!" Evidentiary point, Courtney.

"But I wasn't engaged," I point out. "I was single. And what I feel for Violet means I don't care about before that. I'm just glad we finally found each other." Rebuttal point, me. Bonus point for using emotions as a tactic because Courtney can't refute those.

She rolls her eyes. "How do you know it's not just a rebound? From what I'm hearing, it's not even a rebound. She was so freshly broken up with Colin, the ball hadn't even hit the rim yet!" Her eyes widened. "Oh, shit, did Colin break up with her because of you?"

We'd wondered when someone was going to question the timeline of our getting together. I'd expected it to be the media painting Violet as a cheating man chaser, not my sister.

"They broke up because Colin is a dumbass who didn't appreciate what he had. Abi and Archie took Vi out to comfort her. Kaede and I saw them at Club Red, and one thing led to another. We talked all night, and things changed." It's the truth, one hundred percent, just not the whole truth.

"You're getting played, Ross," Courtney reiterates. "I'm not saying Violet's doing it on purpose. She's Abi's best friend, and I think she's pretty damn cool, personally. But her head's gotta be all sorts of messed up after Colin, and now this. Seriously, it's been days and I still can't wrap my head around it. It's fast, too fast."

"Don't care," I reply with a calculated laugh. "Courtney, have you ever been in love?"

Courtney blushes, her eyes narrowing. "Don't be a dick, Ross. You know I've had my heart broken."

"Of course I do. I distinctly remember throwing Eric Butterfield off our boat into the middle of the lake during your senior year of high school for just that reason," I remind her. Not that I minded. He fucking deserved that and more. "But think back to those moments before it all went to shit. Did you ever just feel it in your gut, in your heart, in your soul that he was it?" She bites her lip and I know I have her. Reminding her of the guy who broke her heart is a shitty thing to do, but it's the only way I can get her to remember what love feels like and let this go.

"Courtney, I can't really explain it, but it's real. There was just this moment when I looked in her eyes and I saw . . . I saw the two paths my life could take. On one hand, I could keep going the way I have been, and in some ways, it looked good. I was happy, carefree, and adventurous. But then, I saw this other path with Violet. A houseful of kids, a dad bod, the picket fence, the whole nine. And I could see that life without her was empty. I picked her, knowing it would be messy and hard and that people would doubt us. But it just happened. We fell. Hard."

It's bullshit, but at the same time, as the words tumble out of my mouth, I find myself liking what I'm saying. Having a few kids and a home with a woman like Violet . . . okay, I could do without the beer gut, but the rest doesn't sound half bad.

Shit, maybe my parents were right . . . just a tiny little bit. Not that I'd admit it to them, ever.

Maybe after this pretend relationship is over and Violet and I have had our respectable breakup, I should think about actually settling down. This could be like a trial run to see if I'm cut out for that lifestyle. The thought surprises me but might be worth a bit of consideration.

I'm about to continue when there's a knock on my door, and I look up to see Violet opening it slowly, Archie peeking over her shoulder. "Hey, honey," she says with the practiced ease we worked on over the weekend. "Is this a bad time?"

"Not at all, babe," I reply, getting up and going over to the door. I pull her in close, my hands clasping around her waist before I kiss her hard. This is one part I don't mind at all. Violet's lips are delicious, and as she moans against me, I reach down to cup her ass, squeezing lightly and causing her to whimper into my mouth.

"Honey . . . we have an audience." Violet gasps as she pulls back, blushing even as she scolds me.

"I don't mind one damn bit," Archie answers for himself, hip-bumping his way past us and into my office. He sits down in the chair next to Courtney. "By all means, feel free to carry on." He waves his hand like he's the queen, encouraging us to kiss again. I wink at him and press one more chaste kiss to Vi's lips as Archie grins evilly.

He looks to Courtney, whispering conspiratorially. "Ain't love grand?" Her brows shoot together and he laughs. "You should see your face. Speaking of face, I can see the resemblance. You must be Courtney, the sister? I'm Archie Hornee, the one tasked with keeping Violet in line—no easy task, mind you." He shoots Violet a glare, but it seems to be in jest.

Courtney looks gobsmacked. Whether it's by Violet's appearance in the office, our steamy kiss hello, or Archie's over-the-top comfort with basically everything and everyone, I don't know.

I take advantage of her momentary silence and look Violet up and down, virtually salivating. She's stunning, her work pants sexy but professional, her blouse hugging her curves perfectly. And now . . . she's all mine. Or at least, I get to pretend she is.

"Courtney, I'll have to cut this short," I comment over my shoulder as I stare into Violet's eyes and feel my head start to spin. "But I'll see you at the meeting today?"

"Meeting?" Violet asks, and I nod. "I didn't know you had a meeting. Is this a bad time?"

"Sorry, babe. I was so caught up in . . . well, *you,* that I forgot about the weekly Monday meeting," I tell her, linking my arms around her waist to keep us as close as possible. I stare into her eyes deeply, wondering what's going through her head, what she thinks of my office, and what she thinks of me.

There's a small piece of me that worried she would freak out once we separated this morning to go to our respective offices. But if she did, she's got the part of dutiful fiancée down pat now, and she looks lovingly back at me as if she missed me in the few hours we've been apart. I realize with a start that I did miss her.

Courtney hums under her breath as she walks past us, and I know the war's not over, just this round. "I'll see you there, Ross. Nice to see you again, Violet, and to meet you, Archie."

I shut the door behind her, giving us the room. "It's fine. The meeting's no big deal, more of a weekly informal pow-wow. Normally pretty cut and dry because we hash everything out via email beforehand. But Dad likes to do things old school and look people in the eyes so he doesn't miss anything. Speaking of which . . . I missed you this morning, you know that?" A truth I didn't intend to share, but it came tumbling off my tongue before I could stop it.

I don't want to think about the whys of that, nor do I want Violet to, so I lower my lips to hers. There's no Courtney, Kaede's still going to be gone for a little while, and Archie doesn't matter because he's in on the whole ruse.

But I do it anyway, kissing Violet simply because I want to. She's a beautiful woman, she's in my arms, and kissing her makes us both feel good.

Behind us, Archie makes a pretty good wolf whistle, and I pull back, both of us flushed and feeling the heat in the small space between us. "Wow," Violet whispers quietly, looking up at me before shaking her head, seemingly to clear it. I fight back the victorious grin at having made her lose herself for a moment.

"So, your office?"

For the next hour, we talk ideas for my office suite. Violet's spent the past two days living in my penthouse. She knows my style well enough, so her suggestions are on point. Archie adds ideas here and there and takes copious notes. I can see that Violet and he are a great team, built on creative genius and respect, much like Kaede and I are.

"So, a basic update, nothing major," Violet summarizes. "We'll add some warmth for a more welcoming feel, using wood and brass instead of the blacks and steels of the penthouse. Silk drapes on both ends of the window, even though you'll probably never close them with a view like that. It'll frame it nicely and draw attention to the main feature of the space. New chairs for guests in a subtle pattern, and a casual seating area with a couch and coffee table for less formal meetings."

"Isn't that going to be a lot of unnecessary clutter?" I ask, looking around the sparse space. I'm one for function and efficiency—desk, chair, bar, and a chair or two for guests. I don't need much else, and honestly, I only got the guest chairs because Kaede refused to continue rolling his chair into my office to have a place to sit.

"No, it'll still be clean and simple, but more . . ." She pauses, eyeing me, and I can feel her relax viscerally. "Look, I'm going to ditch the professional speech and tell you straight out, 'kay?" I spread my hands, open to an unfiltered version of Violet. "You have impeccable taste. Each piece is top-notch and gorgeous, but the fact that you keep your office like the rich boy's version of a bachelor pad, i.e. transient and empty, tells everyone from your Dad to the board that you're not all in. They see you as temporary because you're telling them you're not putting down roots."

Well, fuck. Guess the gloves are off. And ouch.

I look around my office, the one I've worked in for years and that feels like a symbol that I've made it. But I can see her point. I could move out of here in one truckload, a small truckload at that. And that's if I was taking the furniture with me. Realistically, I could walk out today and never return. There's not a single picture, no artwork other than the generic modern art canvases that are unemotional filler. Hell, I don't even have a plant for Kaede to water.

"And you think putting a couch and some pillows is going to solve that?" I ask, my lip curling with recognition that she's right.

She nods. "Yes. A couch, some pictures, some trinkets, some personality. Partner that with settling down with a wife, and you're a whole new Ross Andrews, aren't ya?"

Archie clears his throat, garnering my attention, and I realize he's enjoying watching Violet take me down a notch or two. "This is the part where you say 'yes, ma'am' and let her do her thing, man."

I cut my eyes back to Violet. "Yes, ma'am." There must be a god somewhere with a soft spot for me because I'm saved from her gloating by a beep from my computer.

"You have a call? Need us to step out?" Archie says as Violet and I eye each other.

"Meeting," I correct. I stand up, going around my desk, and

offer Violet my hand. She slips hers into mine and I pull her to stand with me. Her eyes search mine, looking for what, I'm not sure.

I don't think about what I'm doing. I just press my lips to hers and she gasps. I take advantage and sip at her deeply. She pushes against my chest, but it's a split second too late and I know, could feel, that she sank into me for a moment. "Have at my office. Have at the penthouse. Show me what you can do."

I stride toward the door, but she calls my name and I stop, wondering if she's going to filet me for taking liberties. The anticipation has me on edge, a sensation I like where she's concerned. "What's your favorite color?" she asks, but I can see her lips twitching, and I wonder what she was going to say.

"Violet. My favorite color is violet."

Just outside, I can hear Archie's voice carry. "I've never been that close to actual porn before. You two were this close to combustion, and you know I was keeping my mouth shut so maybe you'd forget I was here and just go on and get underneath that man. Fuck, Vi."

I smile to myself, walking away before I hear her answer, not sure if I want to hear the protests I know she'll throw out.

———

THE MEETING TAKES PLACE IN THE BIG CONFERENCE ROOM, Dad sitting at the head of the table. He's looking pretty good for a workday, all smiles and congeniality, until I come in and his face immediately goes to stone. Paul Washington, the head of the R&D department, says something and catches his attention, pulling his assessing glare from me.

The meeting's just like normal, everyone basically saying that their divisions are clicking along and no major updates from Friday's email dumps.

Dad asks a few questions, pointedly avoiding me until the end. "Okay, if there's nothing else—"

"I have something," I reply, sticking my hand up and rising. I glance around the table, meeting each member's eyes like my dad taught me to, and then settle on Courtney, who sits to Dad's right, taking notes. "Courtney, could you bring the guest from my office, please?"

Her eyes widen and her jaw drops. "Ross?" I give her a nod, letting her know that I have a plan and know exactly what I'm doing. She shakes her head but does as I request, heading down to fetch Violet.

The rest of the board members look at me in confusion. But they're the ones who started this, either by pressuring my father to get me in line or by going along with him. At this point, it doesn't matter which came first, the chicken or the egg, because the scheme's hatched and has a life of its own. My life with Violet.

"I'm sure you've all read the papers, heard the rumors, and seen the scandals," I start, stepping back and starting to circle the room. "Some of them are true, and some of them aren't."

I reach the end of the table, opposite Dad and nearest to the door, and stop to turn and face the room. "But I understand your concerns. Each and every one of us is a representative of this company, twenty-four seven, in the office, in public, and even in the privacy of our own homes."

I let that sink in because while I might be a bit too loose around town, all of us have things we'd prefer to not have splashed across the society pages of the paper. And if these people are going to judge me, threaten me, I feel quite all right returning the favor. I am giving in to their ultimatum in some ways, but it's on my own terms, at least. Some of them wouldn't be able to say the same if their dirty little secrets were to be exposed as liabilities for the company.

"Even so, I'd like to apologize for any negative publicity I might have unintentionally created by my actions with an acquaintance." The words drop with a heavy silence, and I can see a few people looking at me in shock. I get it. Apologies from me are about as rare as four-leaf clovers. But the reality is, this one is heartfelt.

"And while I can promise until I'm blue in the face about how things are going to improve, the fact is, my metrics are solid," I continue in what is perhaps the understatement of the century. Even Dad can't argue with that, and I'll beat anyone to death with my numbers if they want to challenge me. "But this isn't about metrics. It's about leadership, respect, and image. That's the reason I wanted you all to know right away about some changes in my life."

"Ross—" Dad starts, half getting up, but Courtney appears in the doorway with Violet, who looks a little flustered. But she composes herself quickly when she sees the people in the room, her professional demeanor taking over.

I plan on shaking her from that. "This is Violet Russo," I announce, going over and taking her hand. "I've known her since she was . . . well, just about as tall as the table you all are sitting around right now. And I'm going to be honest. I was pretty damn terrible to her a lot of the time. More than once, Violet told me she hated me when we were in high school."

Violet blushes, nodding in agreement, but she smiles softly. "He deserved it."

I smile back, basking in the glow surrounding her right now and helping to spread it throughout the room of nay-sayers. "Recently, Violet and I reconnected, and something was different. I think I was different, finally seeing the truth that had been right in front of me all along. And for some reason, Violet saw something in me too." I press a soft kiss to her lips, right there in front of everyone, and then tuck her to my side, wrapping my arm around her shoulders as we face the board.

"I've asked Violet to marry me, and she's accepted."

There's a beat of silence, and then another as the bomb ticks before detonating. As what I said sinks in, Violet holds up her hand, showing off her ring. That's when it becomes reality and people start to react.

"Congratulations, Ross. Violet," everyone echoes. There's even a small golf-style smattering of applause in celebration of the news.

People get up from their chairs, coming over to shake my hand and introduce themselves to Violet. A couple of them even ooh and ahh over the ring.

141

I don't know what I was expecting, but it wasn't this easy acceptance and support. It feels like a solid victory, especially as even Courtney looks a bit more convinced. That is until I look over at my dad, who's sitting in his chair at the head of the table.

He looks like he could chew glass and spit lightning as he stands up. He knows that I've maneuvered him into a corner. I've gotten the support of my peers. The noise has garnered the attention of the assistants walking up and down the hallway, and they make the grapevine in the company work even faster than email, and if he refutes Violet and me now . . . he comes off looking like the world's biggest bastard of a father.

"Thank you, Ross. But do you think you could give us a little more warning on the baby announcement?" he lamely jokes, still earning a few smiles. "Okay, then, I can't think of a higher note to end this on, so we'll end it here."

Success.

When we get back to my office, Violet turns to me, her eyes sparkling for a whole new reason. "You could have told me!"

"I could have," I admit, refusing to apologize, "but I wanted to hit you with the surprise. I figured it'd be a more authentic reaction."

"Yeah, well, next time, you're getting an authentic knee in the balls," Violet whispers, her cheeks flushing again.

I grab her and spin her around, then growl into her ear. "Please, keep talking about my balls. I like it when you talk dirty, Vi."

She huffs, acting put out, but I can see the front for what it is now, even as she steps away and says firmly, "If you're done with the whole stage production, I've got to get back to the office. Archie is already whipping together some digital picture magic."

"No rush," I assure her, liking this sass. "You think it worked?"

"I think your father looked like he wished his last name was Lannister when he stood up," Violet replies. "Courtney looked better, though."

I nod. "Doesn't really matter at this point if Dad's happy or not," I concede. "Everyone else bought it."

Violet nods, but her face looks a little sad, or maybe wistful. She's got thoughts she's not sharing with me, and that worries me. Ironically, this fake engagement means we need to be even more open and honest with each other than a lot of real couples are.

"What's on your mind?" I ask quietly, stepping closer to her. "You feeling bad for my dad?"

"No . . . it's nothing," she reassures me, but I know she's not being completely honest. I think it's with herself, though, so I let it go for now. "But I'm worried. You see, my family, they're not . . . well . . ."

"What?"

Violet clears her throat. "They're not into the big over the top stuff. Once you're family and accepted, sure, they'll rant and rave. But Papa, Nana . . . to outsiders, they're wary. And the more showboating you do, the more they're going to freeze on you. And somehow, I've got to introduce you to my family and explain how I'm already engaged after Colin dumped me. Oh, and they don't even know that happened because I couldn't bring myself to tell my mom that."

I take the opportunity to grab Violet's hands and pull her closer, kissing her. The line is blurry and getting blurrier by the second. We said this would be for show, but I find myself wanting to comfort her, touch her, know her, whether there's anyone around or it's just the two of us. But I can't analyze that right now, not when she's scared. Because that's the label she's looking for as she sinks against me, letting me support her.

Big, badass of a fighter Violet Russo is scared to introduce me to her family. And I'm a catch, so I know it's because she doesn't want to disappoint them or hurt them. She doesn't like lying to them, and I get that.

"Don't worry. Everything's going to be fine, Violet. You're my fiancée, my woman, Violet Russo."

I don't know where the words come from, not all of them . . . but they don't help with Violet's look. If anything, she looks even more confused and concerned.

CHAPTER 12

VIOLET —TUESDAY—11 DAYS UNTIL THE WEDDING

I knead the dough beneath my hands, confident in the one job Nana has let me do for years. There are certain dishes she still teaches me . . . *Violet, we only use the best olive oil . . . not like that. It's not a race. Be gentle, dear . . . now add the sauce. Perfecto.*

But kneading dough is one of the first jobs she gave me, and I've been a pro since I was ten. The mindlessly repetitive work — and it is *work* —lets my mind wander. Right back to Ross.

The moments keep flashing in my head. The way he looks at me. The way he pulls me close to kiss me even when nobody is around. The way he talked me down after the meeting. The way I catch him following me with his eyes as we get ready for bed. The way I feel more relaxed with him by my side, even when my body is begging for more each night.

I want to believe it's real. All of it.

Yes, I know the physical attraction is there. Which is surprising after a lifetime of calling each other names. But I know if I so much as make a hint of a gesture that I'm open to that, Ross would be on me. And I secretly want that.

If only it were that easy.

But it's not. Mixed in with all that chemistry and desire is a heaping load of emotional baggage and drama. Because he's good at this . . . at flirting with me, at making me feel like I'm the only thing that matters in his life, at being in a relationship with me. The big gestures and the little ones, like bringing me coffee in bed in the morning.

And *that* I know is fake. Or at least it doesn't hold the meaning that some small part of me wishes it did.

But Ross is a good guy, so playing house and being nice isn't a hardship for him. It's just never been our MO, and having him be his usual self to me is doing weird things to my heart. Things I can't trust.

This is just pretend, I remind myself. *A means to an end.*

And right now, in the kitchen with three generations of Russo women, I need that reminder of why I'm doing this.

"For the love of Susan Lucci, I'm telling you for your own good . . . Sofia, you put too much salt in with the tomatoes!" Nana says in an argument with her sister that can be traced all the way back to . . . well, before I was born, that's for sure.

"Don't you dare invoke the great Susan Lucci on me! Bah! You know nothing about how to make the sauce," my great aunt, Sofia, shoots back as she points a red-tipped, arthritic hand toward Nana. She glares as she tosses another sprinkle of salt into the bubbling pot of tomato sauce on the stove. "It's why your marinara is as bland as boiled potatoes!"

Oh, hell, it's on now. You can call Nana a lot of things, but if you criticize her housekeeping or her cooking, you're in for it.

"Did she invoke *Susan Lucci*?" Mom whispers, her brows clenched together. "Never thought about it, but I think I prefer Sophia Loren." She smiles like I'm in on a secret joke between the two of us and bumps my shoulder. "I think we should just hang back and roll out the pasta," Mom says under her breath as her mother and aunt go at it, forgetting their English to start with spicy, liquid Italian. I'm quite certain that it's one advantage of the Latin languages over English. You can argue and curse at someone a whole lot faster and with a lot more imagination.

"Mom, about tonight's dinner." I try to sidestep my way in to telling her about Colin and Ross as we start rolling out the dough and slicing the fresh pasta sheets into the right shape for Nana's big cast iron pan, but before I can, Mom looks up and sighs dramatically.

"Mama! Sofia! Come on, now, this is supposed to be a night of *amore*, not war! Violet's bringing her man for dinner, not WrestleMania!"

Sofia, who lived in New York's Little Italy until her husband Giuseppe died a decade ago, turns to us with a dreamy sparkle in her eyes. "WrestleMania? Child, you know nothing of wrestling. Giuseppe used to take me on dates to the Garden where we'd watch a real wrestler, Bruno Sammartino! Now if Bruno had asked me out . . . well, you'd have had a different uncle, that's for sure." She winks, or at least I think that's what she's trying to do, but both eyes close at the same time, so it's more of a saucy blink. "God bless my Giuseppe's soul," she finishes as if she didn't just say she would've picked another man over her beloved husband of forty years.

"About that—" I start, but Nana and Sofia are back at each other in Italian, half arguing, half reminiscing. I catch some of it, honestly. While I've tried to keep up with my Italian, I'm nowhere near fluent.

I sigh, glancing at Mom, who's got stars dancing in her eyes. "The dress. Did you find the dress?"

My face falls. "Mom . . ."

She bumps my shoulder again, smiling broadly. "Oh, don't you worry, baby girl. You'll find it. And no more apologies about going with your friends. I completely understand that if you invited me, those two would want to tag along." She tilts her head toward Nana and Aunt Sofia. "And then Colin's mom would want to go. It's a domino effect and we're a lot to handle. It's right that you go with your friends, and I know you'll look beautiful in whatever you choose. I got my dress! Did I tell you?"

She rambles on about the mauve pleated gown she chose, not letting me get a word in edgewise, though I try several times.

Somewhere after the third time I try to interject, Mom tsks. "But Violet, we must send the invitations out immediately. At this point, they're nothing more than a formality since everyone already knows the day and time, but it is still the proper thing to do."

"Mom, about that . . ."

"Violet, finish browning the sausage, will you?" Nana says to me, pointing to a skillet on the stove. "And Maria, lay out the first layer of pasta and cheese while we get this sauce right. I need to fix what this *nincompoop* has done."

"*Nincompoop?* I'll show you a nincompoop!" Aunt Sofia shoots back, which is almost funny coming from a gray-haired woman who goes to Mass three times a week. Especially because, to them, nincompoop is apparently the utmost in insults when it's not even close. Not that I can imagine my Nana or Aunt Sofia busting out with some of today's barbs.

Though that might trigger the silence I need to spill my guts about the bomb about to go off in this house.

Nana and Aunt Sofia start back up again, the battle of tomato versus salt, round one hundred and three, going full-throttle in the small kitchen. Which gives me zero opportunity to say anything. I know I need to, can feel the sand running out in the hourglass, but one more minute of relative peace is so much . . . easier.

Mom looks over at me. "Come on. If we don't get this done soon, your man's going to arrive and be sitting around waiting on dinner. That can't happen!"

"He's . . . Mom . . ." I try one more time, but she shushes me, literally putting a finger to her mouth.

I HEAR ROSS LONG BEFORE HE ARRIVES, MY BLOOD TURNING to ice in my veins.

It's too soon. I haven't told them yet! Shit!

This isn't downtown, where Ross has his penthouse and big noise is normal. This isn't the Hills, where the Andrews Estate rests separated from their neighbors by huge stretches of land.

This is Oakridge, the planned neighborhood of the city where you can reach out your kitchen window and smack a fly on your neighbor's wall if you've got a fly swatter. It's a subdivision of wooden privacy fences and prefab swing sets jammed into back yards so tightly that you stop playing on them by the time you're eight or so.

Not that it's a bad place. Far from it. The neighbors are nice, and every July Fourth there's the Oakridge Independence Barbecue, with a dozen grills going, games, and fireworks in the cul-de-sacs, the whole shebang.

But it's quiet and quaint. Things that Ross's loud Camaro are decidedly not. Hell, half the neighborhood is probably peeking out their windows to see who this interloper is, because sure as Nana's lasagna is going to be delicious regardless of any salting issues, Ross is an outsider.

Mom looks to me. "Did Colin get a new car? I thought he had a Mercedes."

I bite my lip, shaking my head as I plead with her with my eyes. "I tried to tell you, but you kept cutting me off."

Mom's face has gone straight and strict, and her voice is tight. "Tell me what?" I can feel Nana, Papa, and Aunt Sofia looking at me expectantly too.

I steel my back and force confidence into my voice. "Colin and I broke up."

"*Dio Mio!*" someone says as pandemonium breaks out, everyone asking me questions at once.

Mom claps sharp and quick, corralling the craziness into a hushed anticipation. "Violet Antonia Carlotta Russo, who is coming to dinner?" she asks but doesn't wait for an answer, running to the window to peek out. Nana and Aunt Sofia follow suit, and after a quick heartbeat, I do too.

Out the window, Ross's blue sportscar is parked against the curb. He gets out and walks around the back bumper, his eyes scanning the address and then landing on the window where four female faces peer out.

He looks good. He's changed from the custom suit I saw him leave in this morning, replacing it with navy slacks and a pale blue button-down shirt that's open at the neck. Cognac dress shoes and a matching belt complete the outfit. I wonder for a second if he chose the outfit after listening to me say his black and steel office was cold and sterile, because right now, he looks warm and friendly and sexy as hell.

He does that hot-boy two-finger wave, and I feel like my very own Jack Ryan is coming to get me. God, if only he could rescue me out of this mess.

But in a way, I guess he is. After all, it's my crazy plan. Well, Abi's, really, but it's my neediness that prompted the whole thing.

"Is that Ross Andrews?" Mom says as recognition dawns.

"He's got good taste in cars," Papa says conversationally from the window on the other side of the room as my heart hammers. "Not Italian, but an American classic will do. Who's the guy?"

I run to the door, ignoring their questions, and rip it open. "Ross . . . uhm, hey. I haven't had a chance to explain . . ."

The congenial smile on his face falters for just a second, but I see it and feel that I've hurt him somehow by not coming clean with my family yet. He did it with flair and ease, and I'm stumbling and freaking out.

"Oh," he starts, scanning the lot of us because everyone has piled in around me. "Well, hello. I'm Ross Andrews, Violet's fiancé. *Signor* and *Signora* Russo, this is for you." He holds up a bottle of wine, presenting it to Nana. "And Mrs. Russo, these are for you." Like a magician, he holds out a small bouquet of flowers. "And Violet, this is for you."

He kisses me right on the mouth, right there in front of my family, God, and the whole freaking neighborhood, who are obviously still watching out their windows.

Over my shoulder, I hear Aunt Sofia. "What'd you bring for me?" She laughs as Ross offers a handshake, which she takes. "I guess it's a start, but I think I want the story of this whole thing instead."

Papa clears his throat, his voice stern, but there's almost a thread of amusement in it. "Inside, please. Let's not do this on the front steps."

Mom nods, giving me the stink eye as Papa, Nana, and Aunt Sofia head into the house. "I thought that ring looked different."

I feel frozen, stapled to the ground as my family goes inside, and Ross gives me a grin. Finally, I find my voice and whisper to Ross. "Oh, my God, we're doing this, aren't we?"

He looks at me like I grew a second head on my left shoulder, the one where the devil always sits, which makes sense because only he could talk me into something this absurd.

"Violet," he says so quietly it's only for me, his voice steady as he takes my hands and bends over me, creating a cocoon for the two of us. "Are you having second thoughts? I thought we'd already settled this. We've told my family and the board, Abi's updating the invitations, and it's a done deal. Right? This is what you wanted."

I nod absently. "It is. I just hadn't realized how it would feel to sit at my Nana's table and lie to them."

I see a flash in his eyes, there and gone so quickly I can't decipher it. "We can do this. For your Papa. For you, Vi."

From behind me, my mother's voice chimes out. "Excuse me, *piccioncini*. If you'd like to sit down, dinner's ready. And you've got some explaining to do."

Piccioncini. Love birds.

To Mom, it probably looks like we're having a quick, private lovey-dovey moment, not Ross helping me chill the fuck out as I freak. I start to turn, and Ross murmurs by my ear, "Breathe, Violet."

And I mean to, I swear I do. But right that second, he lays his hand on my ass and squeezes ever so slightly. And I gasp, jumping a bit. Mom can't see the reason since Ross's hand is behind me, but at my reaction, she guesses. "Now, Violet." Her lips are pressed into a thin line.

"Now what?" I hiss at him.

"Now, I'm going to be my usual charming self and you'll be . . . *you*." He's got that cocky smirk stretching his full lips again, but somehow, this time, it doesn't seem so mean. It's like this is just what we do . . . banter and bark, but there's no bite. Not anymore.

And doesn't that make me think of biting Ross's shoulder as he ploughs into me, his mouth buried in my neck, nibbling the tender skin there. I know I'm as red as Nana's sauce as we sit down at the table, all eyes on us.

Papa takes charge. "Okay, Violet . . . explain."

"Actually, if you'd let me, Mr. Russo," Ross says quickly, looking chagrined as he pats my hand but not all that chagrined. "You see, Violet had a really bad Friday. It seems that Colin Radcliffe . . ." he looks at me with fake concern. "Well, he broke off the engagement."

"What?" Mom asks, outraged. "He did that, and you didn't tell me? Violet, what has—"

"And when I ran into Violet later . . ." He pauses and looks around. "Wait, backstory for your grandparents, honey. As Ms. Russo knows, I've known Violet for a very long time. She's best friends with my little sister, Abigail."

"Ah, Abigail!" Nana says, smiling a little. "Such a lovely girl. And you . . . you are her older brother?"

"Yes, ma'am," Ross confirms, suddenly all manners and politeness. If he wasn't doing my dirty work for me, I'd tease him about suddenly turning into Eddie Haskell. "More importantly, I was pretty insufferable in my younger days. I teased Violet a little too harshly, and I'll be honest with you, sir. I won't repeat the things I said back then for fear of catching three or four rolling pins in the head, and then you'd rightfully start in on me. But never fear, Violet held her own and got me back time and time again."

He smiles at me like the awful things we used to do each other were cutesy and flirty. To be clear, they weren't. Not even a little bit. But it seems to be playing well to my family.

Papa hums while Nana smirks a little. "So, how did you end up here, then?"

"It seems that all those bad acts, and again, I am sorry," he says, kissing my knuckles, "were an immature teenage me not being able to recognize that I was head over heels for Violet. And Friday night, seeing her and hearing what she said, it felt like everything just clicked into place and I had a second chance with her that I never even knew I wanted. Even before I drove Violet home that night, I knew I wanted to marry her . . . and by some miracle, she saw me the same way."

Nana looks unconvinced as her suspicious eyes flick from Ross to me, but it's Mom who speaks first. "Oh, Violet, why didn't you tell us? I mean, for Colin to break it off so quickly after getting engaged —"

"I know, Mom," I say, feeling Ross squeeze my hand. "I guess I was so shocked when Colin broke it off, and then when Ross and I saw each other and things . . . well, like he said, clicked so hard . . . everything's been happening so fast, but I'm so happy. I'm sorry, Mom. I just didn't know how to put it in words."

"You could have told us," Aunt Sofia scoffs, making me laugh. "What, girl?"

"Aunt Sofia, I tried to tell you guys today. Several times, in fact. But every time I tried to say something, you and Nana would start cursing at each other in Italian and invoking Susan Lucci. You know how hard it is to get a word in edgewise with you Italian women when you're arguing over cooking?"

Papa laughs. "Eh, *benvenuto nel mio mondo,*" he says. "I've been trying to get a word in for over fifty years without much success." He leans over and places a liver-spotted hand on Ross's shoulder. "You will learn, son. Best to keep your mouth shut until it is time to say 'Dinner is delicious.' and 'Thank you.'"

"Oh, hush, Papa," Nana admonishes him, but she's smiling. "I guess we did sort of talk over you the whole time, Violet."

"Please," Ross says in a voice dripping with sincerity, "I know this is sudden. And it might just be a little crazy on the surface. But Violet and I . . . just give us a chance?"

It's just right, and Nana nods, getting up. "I'll give you enough of a chance to eat some of my lasagna . . . provided Sofia didn't ruin it with her salt."

"Don't make me say *her* name again. I swear I'll do it . . ." But then she looks over at our new dinner guest and makes the decision to behave, for once. "Never mind," Sofia says, following Nana into the kitchen.

As Nana plates the lasagna, the inquisition really starts. "So, Ross, what do you do?" Nana asks. "You have a good job?"

153

Ross grins, nodding. "Yes, ma'am. I'm an executive vice president at my family's company."

Nana nods, and while her voice remains pleasant, I see the glance she exchanges with Sofia. They might fight like a couple of drunken Marines and they may say absolutely vile things about each other . . . but they've been sisters for seventy years. They're a unit. They're family.

And more importantly, when they want to, they can unleash a torrent of questions that would break a Mafia boss on the stand. Frankly, the Supreme Court's got nothing on my Nana and Aunt Sofia.

It's not that they ever raise their voices or that they're insulting or intimidating. It's just that their questions are confusing, bouncing around from subject to subject seemingly randomly. But it's not random, not at all. It's calculated and strategic.

I've faced this from Nana alone, and it's both comforting and confusing. You're answering questions about your favorite cookies when *BAM!* you've got a seemingly innocent question about a college experience you'd rather not share with your grandmother on your hands.

If you're lying, or bullshitting, or just trying to get one over on Nana, she's going to catch you. Why? Because she never, ever forgets a detail.

And with Aunt Sofia backing her up . . . my stomach twists into a cold lump of clay in my gut even as the lasagna-filled plates are passed out.

"So, Ross, I remember you were a football player. Why'd you go into business instead?" Nana asks. "I would have thought that a big, strong athlete like you would want to stay on the field." See? Memory like an elephant, and it sounds almost complimentary, but she's just getting him to relax and play along before she zings him.

"Well, football was a passion and taught me so much. If an NFL contract had come my way, I would've been on cloud nine. But the reality was, that wasn't going to happen. The plan was always to go into the family business, and I love my work there."

He drops his voice low. "Maybe even more than football, but don't tell my old coaches I said that or they'd probably still make me run drills. I don't doubt they could."

Nana smiles, completely charmed. Sofia picks up the baton.

"So, what are your plans for our Violet? One-, five-, and ten-year, please."

"*Dio Mio*! Aunt Sofia! Please, we're already moving at break-neck speed. Could you give us a minute?" I beg a little too loudly.

And I just spilled way more about our new relationship than I intended. Damn, I walked right into that, and I know better.

Nana holds up her hand, and Aunt Sofia gives her a soft high-five. But it's Mom that does the follow-up. "Okay, so maybe not all that." She waves at Sofia, who's grinning like the cat that ate the canary. "But something, Violet. Tell us your plans."

I swallow and look to Ross. "Well, we're getting married. And I moved in with him over the weekend. Abi's done with the invitations, I think. I tried on dresses over lunch and found a possible contender, but I'm not certain yet, and Ross has a tuxedo already." Luckily, that I know because I saw it in his closet.

Ross runs a thumb along my cheekbone, looking at me rever-ently, and I swear Mom sags in relaxation as he caresses me. He speaks to my mom and everyone else at the table, but his eyes never waver from mine. "We're getting married, and from there, we'll figure it out. Whatever Violet wants—kids, house, puppies, white picket fence—whatever it is, I'll get it for her. We'll get it together. That's the one-, five-, ten-, and forever-year plans."

It's that moment that I melt into a big puddle of goo under Ross's weighty stare. That sounds good, so temptingly good. It's not the specifics. I don't even have time for a dog or kids right now. It's that overriding sense of teamwork and happiness. The potential of a life filled with good things.

He licks his lips, and I press a kiss to them. Sweet, appropri-ate, but meaningful. I realize that's the first time I've kissed him, and the smile on his face says he knows that too.

"Ross," Papa says, finally getting in on this. He's been

watching the show, quiet and unobtrusive until now. "I had a question. This other man, Colin Radcliffe," Papa asks. "Have you spoken with him since you and my Violet came together?"

Came together? Oh, dear God, my head starts to fill with images, and I'm distracted by the beginning of Ross's answer. I can't help it. I've been sleeping in the same bed as Ross for days now but haven't touched him . . . and my body has needs. I've even been too shy to handle things myself, afraid he'd hear me or somehow just *know* even though I haven't heard him. Not that I've been listening at the door . . . much.

"And so I'm celebrating his stupidity," Ross finishes, pulling me back to reality as he takes my hand on top of the table. "His loss."

"I see . . . and if he tries to disrespect Violet?"

Ross smiles, but it's a predatory smile. "Mr. Russo, my littlest sister reminded me of something I did a few years ago. When I was still a bit of hellion, you understand, but it stands. A boyfriend of hers disrespected her . . . the details aren't important. But it ended with my taking that boy, hauling him out into the middle of a lake, and throwing him overboard to swim a half mile back to shore. What my sister left out of the story, since she never knew, is that before throwing him overboard, I taught him a few lessons about disrespecting my family, and he left my family's boat *sans* trunks. My last words to him were if he ever said anything to my sister other than apologizing, there'd be more serious consequences."

Ross looks to me, grinning. "Don't tell Courtney that, 'kay, honey?" I nod, surprised at the twist to the story I never knew. I remember the guy he's talking about, Eric something or other. He was a total jerk who thought he was *so* bad. I was glad he'd prompted Abi's little sister to grow out of her short-lived bad-boy phase.

Papa laughs, nodding as he takes a bite. "You are the one. I'll be honest with you now, Violet. I never liked that Colin, anyway. He always struck me as someone who . . . thought his shit didn't stink. Those are the ones who are always worse than an outhouse baked in the sun."

Ross chuckles while Nana looks sufficiently outraged. "Stefano! Don't cuss at my dinner table." He raises an eyebrow at Nana and she purses her lips. "Well, fine, but don't do it in English in front of our guest." She lowers her voice, like it's private between her and Papa, though we can all hear, and singsongs out of the side of her mouth. "You have to baby step him into the craziness of the family or he'll run."

"Pshaw, woman. I am who I am. You ain't gonna change it now. Too late for an old dog like this to learn new tricks, and I ain't got enough time left to even try," Papa says jovially.

And that's the brunt of it. All of this is because of his age and health, the impending doom of his passing that I can't imagine weathering. I look to Nana and can see the cracks in her strong wall, and then to Mom, whose eyes are glittery. Sofia puts a hand over Nana's, and I know that she's thinking they'll be back together soon. Just the two sisters, both widowed by the men they love with all their hearts.

Even more than WrestleMania.

Nana gets up. "Let me get dessert."

"So, let's talk about this wedding!" Nana says bravely as she and Mom come back in with bowls of gelato for everyone. "We've got everyone flying in. There are cousins Stefano and I haven't seen in decades, and their kids, and maybe a few grandkids. I already had to talk to Father O'Flannigan at the church, and he assured me the sanctuary will be big enough."

"We may just put his boast to the test," Sofia boasts. "This will be a Russo family reunion that won't be matched for a generation, at least. The perfect sendoff for Stefano!"

"My husband isn't dead yet, *vacca!*"

"No, but you said you wished I was when I said I didn't like your gnocchi," Papa teases, making Nana turn pink with anger. The teasing bickering is comforting, the soundtrack of their lives together.

"I did not! And you should count yourself lucky to eat my gnocchi!"

Papa grins. "I've been eating your gnocchi for decades, and you never complain."

That bad metaphor has both Mom and me groaning, and Ross laughs. Leaning over, he whispers in my ear, "Just wait, honey. Before you know it, I'll be nibbling on your gnocchi, and maybe I'll let you taste my cannoli."

I blush deeply but can't help but take advantage of the golden opportunity Ross has presented me with. "Do you know what *cannoli* means?"

Ross nods, his eyebrow quirked. "The pastry tube things with cream inside?"

"Papa, could you tell Ross what cannoli translates to, literally?"

He can read the teasing smirk on my face and can follow the thread from his teasing with Nana. He grins widely, holding his fingers a couple inches apart.

"Little tubes. I think you might want a different metaphor . . . éclair, maybe?"

The moment of silence is broken by raucous laughter by everyone at the table. And the firing squad seems to have called a momentary truce.

Conversation returns to the family members who are traveling in for the wedding and the festivities to come. I glance at Ross, who is smiling and glibly mixing into the conversation, and finally, I put my spoon down.

This feels comfortable. But the stab in my heart reminds me that it's fake, and that hurts most of all because it does feel so right.

If only, my guilty heart reminds me.

CHAPTER 13

ROSS —WEDNESDAY—10 DAYS UNTIL THE
WEDDING

*S*omething's wrong. I thought last night with the Russos went fantastically, better than we'd hoped. But toward the end of the night, I could feel the tension weaving through Violet, even though she kept the warm smile on her face.

When we got home, she claimed exhaustion and went to bed immediately. When I'd lain down next to her, she hadn't so much as made a peep, and I'd slept fitfully, worried about what was worrying her. This morning, she'd been all smiles, thanking me for her smoothie but swirling out the door for a client meeting before I could ask her a thing or we could talk about the dinner.

But I can read her like an open book. She's hiding something, nerves and second thoughts and probably a fair amount of stress at our rushed timeline.

All things I can help with. I wish she'd ask me for help, but that's not who Violet is. She's independent, likes to handle her own shit, and is used to taking care of herself.

But I'm here for her now. Not to do it for her, but to do it with her. Because fake or real, we're in this together, and we need to be able to lean on each other, for the wedding and for however long we decide the marriage needs to last.

So after a long day at the office, I escape home early to make some preparations. First up, my Versa Climber.

I slip my headphones in, listening to my workout mix as I

159

pound my way up imaginary stairs. My record for a half hour workout is just short of a mile, but I'm expecting to do a little extra cardio tonight so I take it a bit easier.

As my arms grasp the main handles and my legs pump up and down, I try to mentally go over my checklist. My mind returns to all the things to do for the wedding and then to Violet. I try to imagine what it will feel like to stand at the front of her family's church and see her walking down the aisle to me, taking my hand, and repeating vows to me in front of everyone.

I'm not a dreamer type of guy. This is the first time I've ever imagined what my wedding might be like, and I'm not surprised that the image Violet's created in my head is what plays out. Perfect and beautiful and . . . us.

As I reach the fabled 1776 feet, I'm not thinking of how my body's covered in sweat or that my arm and calf muscles are pumped. I'm thinking about Violet and the look in her eyes when she said yes to my proposal. I think we'd both felt a bit of something in that overwhelming moment.

But tonight is about not being overwhelmed. Not by deadlines, not by families, not by pressure. Not by anything.

Tonight's about us. Two frenemies in a really weird situation who are going to make the absolute best of it. *'Embrace the crazy'* is going to be our new motto.

I rinse off and pull on grey sweat shorts and a tank top, comfy and casual so she doesn't suspect a thing when she gets home.

And then I get to work.

THE PHONE RINGS AND THEN HANGS UP, THE SIGNAL I WORKED out with the doorman to warn me that Violet's home. I light the candles and slide the plate and glass onto the small table.

"Ross?" I hear her call as she opens the door.

"In here," I bellow down the hallway.

"Did you just get home? What are you doing . . . ?" Her voice trails off as she sees what I've been up to.

The bath is drawn, fresh rose petals floating on the surface and scenting the air. There are several candles on the vanity, giving the marbled room a soft blurriness it usually lacks. And there's fresh, hot pizza and wine on the side table by the tub.

Her mouth drops open and her hands rise to cover the O of surprise. Behind her hands, I can hear the muffled, "Oh, my God! Ross!"

I smile, glad that she's pleased. "I know last night was a lot, and planning the wedding is stressing you out. I thought you could use a bit of a break. Take a bath, eat dinner and drink wine, then get comfy. I've got a surprise for you when you're done, but no rush. Take your time and relax."

She shakes her head, and I think her eyes are bit glassy. "I can't believe you did all this." The shock seems to give way just a bit because she looks at me with that spark I know so well. "Did Kaede help you?"

I let my jaw fall open, feigning insult. "Of course not. The only help I had was the pizza place on 4th. They make the best fresh mozzarella, and their thin crust is crispy perfection. Oh, and I bought the roses from Abi. But don't tell her I mutilated them for your bath or she'll probably kill me. She was talking about heirloom this and boutique that. I just wanted some roses, so I nodded and took what she recommended. Long story short, those roses are some fancy-bougie stuff, so you should probably get in."

She bites her lip and says gently, "Thank you."

"You're welcome, Violet," I say simply and then leave her to it. In the living room, I sit down and wait for her. She doesn't take nearly as long as I expect. After less than an hour, I can hear the water draining and her soft footsteps around the bedroom.

She appears in a spaghetti-strap nightgown that hits mid-thigh, nothing too risqué, but seeing her soft-skinned and bare-faced is one of the sexiest visions I've ever seen. I don't think I'll ever get used to seeing her with her guard of power suits and icy glares gone. This softer side of her, with no barriers, calls to me and makes me feel like a lucky bastard to see her with her hair down, literally and metaphorically.

I pat the couch next to me, and she willingly comes over and sits beside me. *Progress*, I think, but I don't dare tease her about it.

"Okay, now what? I feel like you're buttering me up to rip the rug out from underneath me." So distrustful and suspicious, especially of me, and that needs to change, starting now.

"No buttering. Just teamwork. Like my old football coach said, 'Alone, we can do little. Together, we can do much.' So that's what we're doing." She tilts her head, not sure at all what I'm talking about.

I hand her my next offering, Cherry Garcia ice cream and a spoon. Violet smiles a little, her eyes clearing as she undoes the plastic seal and takes off the lid. "You know, Ross, you're not always an asshole."

"Thanks." I admit with a chuckle, "I try not to be." I shrug. "Well, *sometimes*, I try not to be, if we're being honest."

She laughs at my self-deprecation.

I watch with amusement as she stabs the ice cream with her spoon. I've learned from watching Abigail that there are two kinds of ice cream eating. If she's running her spoon along the top, sort of gathering a layer of softer ice cream, things are good.

If she's stabbing the ice cream like a villain in a horror movie . . . "So, what happened at dinner last night?"

She shrugs one shoulder but says, "You were there. You know."

"Denial and avoidance? C'mon, Vi. You can do better than that. Talk to me. In for an ounce, in for a pound, so lay it on me."

She eats another bite, flipping the spoon upside down onto her tongue to eat the creamy goodness as she thinks. "It was just a lot. I wasn't ready when you got there and had planned to tell them first. And then it was this whole out-of-control scene, and then dinner was going so well, which was great. But it was just . . . a lot."

I nudge her knee with mine. "Why, Violet Russo, it sounds like you're a control freak or something. I planned . . . out of control . . ." I throw my voice into a high falsetto that sounds nothing like her, and she grins. In my own tenor, I reassure her.

"Vi, it was fine. They loved me, and by the time we left, they were naming our children. They totally bought it and are looking forward to the wedding. That's what you wanted."

Violet pauses her ice cream eating. "I know. But it's like they're all ready, all settled about it, and this is all just one big party, a family event. Come see Violet get hitched and Stefano get planted. Two for one!"

Her lip trembles, but the fire in her eyes says she's not done fighting yet. She won't be curling up in a ball and giving up on Papa just yet. And if she's not, I'm not.

"Violet, in some ways, I think your grandparents are being incredibly brave with it. Too many people hang on for no other reason than they're afraid of what's on the other side, or maybe they're just too stubborn to give up. If there's a reason, like your grandfather has, that makes sense, but . . . I think most of us hope to reach that point where we've done all we wanted with our life, every item on that bucket list checked off. And it can be a blessing to leave on our own terms, happy and secure in the legacy we leave behind."

"But he's still got so much to live for!" Violet pleads. "And now . . . everyone acting like this is going to be some big party . . . Ross, I know what the Russo clan's like. Even the ones I've never met and only heard about. And when I say a big party, I mean if we're not careful, it's going to end up one police call short of Spring Break in Cabo."

"Sounds like fun."

Violet stops and gives me a double-take. "What?"

"I said it sounds like fun," I repeat. "Violet, in talking with your grandparents, I get why you want to do this. And if they want to turn this into a big party, so what? I mean, if you're going to go out, go out with the biggest, happiest bash you can. Go out in style. You're giving him style."

"The party alone is probably going to be enough to give him a heart attack," she says gruffly, and then her eyes widen in horror. "Oh, God, I didn't mean that." She looks up to the ceiling. "If there's anyone listening, please, I'm begging you with everything I've got, don't let Papa have a heart attack at my wedding." She

163

crosses herself, something I've never seen her do, so that must mean it's a serious prayer.

"Violet, no one can control what happens. Not even you, Control Freak Russo. But there are some things you can control. Would that make you feel better?"

She eats another bite but nods. "Probably," she mumbles around a mouthful of cherry fudge.

I pull out a notepad and pen. "All right, hit me. What's on your to-do list? Wedding dress, bridesmaid dress, decorations, flowers, invitations? Tell me everything."

"Why?" she asks, shoveling in another bite, and I smile, surprised at how adorable she looks curled up on the couch, open and talking with me as she messily eats ice cream. I'm so not going to tell her about the tiny dribble of ice cream on her chest, even though it's driving me mad. I want to lick it off so badly.

"So I can help you," I answer, the *duh* barely held back.

"Archie and Abi are already helping me, and Kaede and Archie talked for over an hour the other day. I think at least half of it was about the wedding. I hope it was, at least," she offers as protest.

"Right, but that's them. And I'll coordinate with them, of course, to help where they need me because sometimes, I can grease wheels they can't." I rub my index finger and thumb together, knowing that money talks, especially when we're talking a big event in fast order. "But it's my wedding too, might I remind you, and I want to be involved. So tell me your vision because I know you have one. Lay out the whole Pinterest board, Instagram-worthy dream on me."

And like the magic elixir I knew it would be, the ice cream loosens her lips.

She tells me about her dress search and then describes what she's looking for as I take notes. I vow to myself to call every bridal shop in the city and have them bring similar dresses to Vi's office as soon as possible. That way, she can try them on and barely miss a beat at work.

She talks about Abi doing the invitations and how they need

to be mailed out immediately, likely with priority postage. I volunteer the mailroom clerk at the office to handle that, knowing that a bonus and some genuine appreciation will go a long way in checking that off quickly.

She goes on and on. Venue . . . booked, but needs updated payment info, which I can do over the phone. Food . . . I'll rent out the finest Italian restaurant for the day so they can cater the wedding. Decorations . . . totally an Archie job, but if he needs a spare pair of hands, Kaede can help. Flowers . . . Abi, of course.

Beyond her family, a lot of her stress is in the length of the to-do list and the short time frame. And I'm not too proud to throw money at it if it'll help, and for so many things on the list, it will. If that's all it takes to make this the wedding of Violet's dreams, I'm happy to do it.

As she wraps up, I can tell that some of the weight is lifting off her shoulders. "You'll really help with all that, Ross?" she asks uncertainly.

"Of course," I reassure her. "Also, I think we should hire a wedding planner." Her mouth is already arguing against it, but I steamroll right over her. "Not because you can't do it all, but because you need someone to delegate to so you can keep all the balls juggling. And on our wedding day, while you're getting ready, you need someone who knows your vision inside and out to keep it running smoothly. They will do exactly what you tell them to, Control Freak."

She pinkens but shakes her head finally, agreeing. "Fine."

That was easier than I expected. We're doing better. "But there is one thing."

I take the ice cream and spoon from her hands, setting them on the coffee table as she protests. "What are you—"

I set my notepad down too and reach to the floor beside the couch, coming back with an elegantly wrapped box, complete with a fluffy bow, which I hand to her.

"What's this?" she asks. I don't answer, instead getting up to take her ice cream to the kitchen. She opens it slowly, like she's afraid snakes are going to jump out of the box and scare her.

But when she spreads the layers of white tissue apart and

sees what's inside the box, her brows knit together in confusion. "What?" she asks again, her eyes jumping to me.

"You seemed uptight. Thought you could use a little bit of fun," I explain.

And then, faster than a flash, I pull out my own Nerf gun and blast off a round her way. "Gotcha," I yell before the soft bullet even lands. "Bullseye!" It hit her right in the cheek next to her gaping mouth.

"Are you serious right now?" she shouts.

I'm off, ducking around the kitchen counter and hiding behind the dining room table, definitely signaling that I'm deadly serious. This is war . . . Nerf war.

"Oh, it's on like Donkey Kong!" Her voice is already lighter, brighter than the overwhelmed and stressed Violet she was just a moment ago. Those issues are still looming, her Papa and the wedding, but that doesn't mean we can't take a break to just let loose a bit.

And we do, foam bullets flying as we talk smack to each other, running and diving to hide from incoming blasts, and taunting as shots go wide and miss completely.

It's ridiculous, it's hilarious, it's . . . fun.

From somewhere in the foyer, I hear her call out. "Where'd you get this idea, Andrews?"

Oh, we're going for last names now, are we? "Saw it on YouTube and it looked good, so here we are, Russo. With you about to lose to me all over again! Just like old times!"

That's the truth. It was just a silly video I saw on YouTube after watching a TED Talk, but it had sparked an idea in me. That I needed this, that Violet needed this, that we needed this. A silliness reminiscent of our younger days, but without the hurtfulness of the way we used to interact.

"All right, all right. I'm out of bullets and don't have any close by to scavenge. I surrender. You win," she says, but now it sounds like she's back in the living room.

Victorious, I come out of my hiding spot, cockily swaggering toward her. "Guess that makes me the champ —" I start to say, but as I get close, a bullet hits me squarely between the eyes.

"Bullseye! Can't believe you fell for that!" Violet taunts.

I see red. Not the angry kind, but the flash of her cotton nightgown, and I give chase. She screams, scrambling to run from me, laughing the whole time. I think I even hear one of her cute snorts.

I tackle her, turning so I land on my back to take the brunt of it but quickly rolling her over and pinning her. I toss her now-truly-empty gun away and trap her hands above her head. She's breathing heavy, pink with giddiness at getting one over on me, and squirming beneath me.

She's never looked more beautiful than she does in this moment. Silly, girly, daring me at every opportunity, challenging me in every way.

Fuck. I want Violet Russo.

And in her eyes, I can see it. She wants me too.

I kiss her, passionate fire igniting and burning up any thoughts I might have of whether this is a good idea or not. In this moment, I don't care. I just want. I just need.

Her mouth is hot, greedy, and she moans against me, her tongue finding mine and her legs parting as I press down between them, feeling the heat from her pussy. Again and again, I kiss her, delving deeper into her mouth, tasting the candy sweetness she usually hides from me with her sour coating of barbs.

"Ross . . ." she moans breathlessly. Her hands tear at my shirt, yanking it over my head as I move her to the sofa and pull her nightgown off.

"Spread your legs for me," I growl, hitting my knees and sliding down her body to lick her belly button.

Violet eagerly obeys, biting her lip as I kiss from her left knee to the soft skin of her inner thigh before repeating the process on the other side. "So good. More."

I grin at the order, and though she pushes at my head, guiding me where she wants me, I hover my mouth just over her pussy lips, close enough that I know she can feel my breath but not get the release that she wants. "Say please."

Violet trembles, knowing what I'm demanding. Strong

LAUREN LANDISH

woman, always resisting any restraints, always refusing any rules but her own, especially the ones we agreed to in our contract. This is my opportunity to get back at her, but it's not out of spite, not to be a cocky winner this time. It's for her own good. By giving in to me, I'll reward her. Greatly and enthusiastically. She just has to say please.

She swallows and bites her lip. "Please."

I know what it cost her to give me that. I'm going to show her that she can let go of her tight grip on control sometimes and can trust others, namely me, to do what's right and even what's best for her.

I slide my tongue deep inside her while keeping my eyes fastened on her. Deep inside me, a little voice says I need to claim her, to learn every nuance of her body and what makes her scream in pleasure, so I study her carefully.

With every lick, every nibble on her skin, every broad stroke of my tongue over her lips and to the wonderful bump of her clit, I memorize her every movement, every expression and reaction.

Violet wraps her legs around my head as I pleasure her, her heels digging into my back as I bring her to the edge before backing off, drawing my tongue up and down her lips, easing them open as she whimpers and squirms. "Ross, please. I . . . I need . . ."

The *please* came easier that time, but giving Violet exactly what she needs is my focus now.

"Need what?" I tease, licking again and causing her to gasp. "Do you want to come?"

"Yes," she cries softly as I suck on one of her pussy lips. "I need to come."

"Tell me," I command, reaching down and freeing my cock.

"Please, Ross, make me come," Violet whimpers, shuddering as I flick her clit once.

She reads my mind and swings her legs off my shoulders, getting onto her knees on the sofa. She leans forward, her hands going to the couch back, and presents her pussy to me. "Please?"

Oh, my naughty little minx. Begging, saying please like I demanded . . . but at the same time, she is totally in control, knowing she already has me addicted to her sweet pussy. And now that curvy peach-shaped ass wiggles in my face, her wetness gleaming in the light.

I jump to my feet, shoving my shorts the rest of the way down and off before grabbing a handful of Violet's hair and pulling her close to me. "This has been so long coming, Violet. I'm gonna fill you with my cock, split you in half so all you can feel is me at your core. I want you to shatter into a thousand pieces knowing it's me who did that to you. Ready?"

Before she can answer, I thrust my cock into her slowly, desperately wanting to go hard but at the same time relishing the feeling of her giving way to me. Her pussy's so tight, hot velvet that grips my head and shaft even as she pushes back into me.

I have to stop halfway and pull back, letting Violet adjust as I let go of her hair and reach around her, cupping her teardrop-shaped breasts. "Mmm," she moans as I squeeze and tug on her nipples, pushing in with my cock as I do. "Fuck, you're killing me. More."

"You feel so good, honey," I rasp in her ear, knowing it's as much an admission as her pleas. In this moment, she fucking owns me. As my cock nestles all the way inside her, she hisses, and I pause, holding totally still. "You okay?"

She bucks, and I can feel her body adjust. I ease up on her breasts, massaging lightly and letting her feel me, knowing she's safe until she hums in pleasure. "Give it to me."

I pull back, thrusting again and letting my body take over as I listen to her. Every time she cries out, I hear nothing but plea-sure, her breasts swaying and shaking in my hands as I stroke deep and hard, in and out of her body.

For at least this moment, we aren't adversaries, aren't frene-mies. We're two souls tangled up into one big knot of past, present, and future.

Finally, I can't hold on and let go of the grip I have on my control, grabbing her waist to pull her tight as I speed up.

Violet pushes back into me as we start fucking each other, meeting stroke for stroke and leaving me breathless. The deep well of sexual passion inside her thrills me. She matches me, challenges me, both of us driving the other higher and higher until we're trembling. Sweat drips down our bodies as we balance on the knife edge of ecstasy, not wanting to tumble over because it feels so good but at the same time, unable to stop ourselves.

Violet's fingers dig into the cushion, and she screams, her pussy clamping tightly around me, and I unleash myself in a mighty roar, slamming deep inside her to release the torrent of heat that's been building inside me. My balls pump again and again into her while she cries out, screaming her orgasm in tandem with mine until we're both spent and my legs can't hold me up any longer.

CHAPTER 14

VIOLET —THURSDAY—9 DAYS UNTIL THE WEDDING

Despite getting only a few hours of sleep, I wake up with the dawn, and immediately, I feel like things are never going to be the same again.

I'm lying with my head on his chest . . . on the sofa. Despite Ross's protests that sleeping on the too-small surface is impossible, after last night's torrid sexual poundings, we were both out like lights. And I have to admit, I'm incredibly comfortable naked atop him, listening to his soft snores, his arm thrown over his eyes as he lies with his other leg falling to the floor.

With him laid back and unaware, I can't help but take advantage and look down to the thick cock lying between his legs. Even now, soft in his sleep, I can't believe he was able to fit it all inside me. Oh, yes . . . yes, he did, and if my lust-clouded memory serves me correctly, I gave as good as I got. I pushed back into him and begged him to pound me harder by the end.

Now we've crossed a line I never, ever thought I'd cross with Ross. And while, yeah, teenage me is jumping up and down for ticking the biggest box off her bucket list, adult me is drowning in doubt.

I just slept with my best friend's big brother. The tormentor I hated. The boy I lusted after before I even really knew what desire was. The fake fiancé that I'm going to marry.

So I just jumped pussy-first into a whole new world of trouble. This was supposed to be a business arrangement only, not a 'tear a hole in the sofa cushion with your fingernails as he sends the third orgasm exploding through your body while you fake being in love' sort of arrangement. That's just cray-cray.

But the craziest thing of all? I like it. I like it a lot.

It's like before this wasn't serious, but now it's gotten real. Very real.

For me, at least. And isn't that the million-dollar question? I'm not a casual sex person, usually, but with at least six months with Ross looming on the horizon, I wonder if I can be. Can I have sex, fake being in love, get married, and then walk away when the time is right without being broken? Can he?

Though questions are still rolling through my head, my bladder is telling me that regardless of any moral boundaries I might have obliterated, I've got some physical needs to take care of. I quietly slip off the sofa and hurry to the bathroom, where I freshen up.

"Good morning," Ross says quietly behind me, wrapping his arms around my waist and kissing my neck. I arch my back, pushing my bare ass back against another part of him that's woken up as he slides his right hand up to cup my breast and pinch my nipple lightly. "Mmm . . . so that wasn't a ridiculously vivid sex dream last night."

"No," I say with a small smile, turning my head to look up into his eyes. "But thanks for confessing that you wanted me first." I can't help the tease as it slips from my tongue.

With a grin, I tell him, "We can't right now . . . I've got an early client, and it's just luck I woke up in time."

Part of me, a big part of me, wants Ross to ignore what I just said and bend me over the sink so we can watch in the mirror as he gives me a very big good morning. And though I hate to admit it, I want him to make me say 'please' again because damn if he didn't make it worth it.

But instead, he pulls back, a smirk on his face as he nods and heads over to the toilet cubicle, closing the frosted glass door behind him. It's a nice customization and allows us to both be in the bathroom without actually having to watch anyone 'do their business'. A little mystery is a good thing, especially when I'm not sure what side of the real-fake line we're leaning toward.

"You know, I never really thought this would happen," Ross says, broaching the subject while I start washing my face. "You know, us . . . sleeping together. I figured we had better odds of killing each other."

I chuckle, though some small gash in my teenage heart heals a little bit at the longed-for recognition, and then we're both quiet for a moment, our eyes locked on one another in the mirror as he stands behind me.

Ross laughs, and a moment later, the toilet flushes and he comes out and washes his hands. "Okay, point taken. But you're Abi's best friend, the same girl I taunted for years." Seems his thoughts this morning are in line with my own. I wonder if they diverge from my wishy-washy uncertainty, though.

"That you did."

Ross hums, then quickly bends down and literally kisses my ass. "Well, those chicken legs of yours have become finger lickin' good!" His finger traces up the back of my thigh.

I shiver, gasping when he smacks my ass playfully. "Bastard! Do you know how much I hated that? You were the sole reason I learned how to do a proper squat and lunge. I did supersets every night for years."

"I didn't know that," Ross says, stepping back, his smile fading a little. But then the teasing light comes back, though a little dimmer. "I'd say I'm sorry, but have you seen your ass? Whatever you did worked and was worth it, honey."

I chuckle, and then we're both quiet for a moment, our eyes locked on one another in the mirror as he stands behind me.

"I don't regret what we did." His voice is rough, like he's talking over gravel.

"I don't, either," I reply, grabbing my toothbrush and green Colgate toothpaste. I prep my brush, then look up at him. "Look, we've crossed that bridge, and it was nice, ten out of ten, would ride that ride again. But I know the drill. Fake marriage, fake relationship, no strings attached. But there's nothing wrong with us getting a little something extra out of the deal, I guess."

"Rebel, you're breaking your own rules," he says, but instead of a tease, it sounds like a compliment. The way his eyes trace over the reflection of my naked body feels like a compliment too. Then he straightens, everything I just said apparently hitting him on delay. "Did you just say that last night was 'nice'?"

I smirk, giving him a version of his own cocky grin, and nod. "Yep," I say, popping the P.

"I'll show you nice," he growls, turning me to lean my ass against the cold marble and dropping to his knees.

I try to protest, really, I do. "Ross, I have to go to work. I'm going to be late."

He looks up at me, feral and possessive. "Brush your teeth. I'll make this pussy come before you're even done."

And though it was his own words, he gets to it and I can almost hear the 'challenge accepted' resonating in his mind.

He licks me fast and hard, fluttering his tongue over my clit as he slips two fingers inside my already wet slit. His other hand jacks himself in tempo with his thrusts. It's the slowest tooth-brushing session of my life. It's the fastest orgasm I've ever had. He's lucky I don't choke on the toothpaste.

As I float back to Earth, white foam running down my chin, he grins at me from the V of my legs, evidence of his own orgasm on the floor beneath him. "Was that nice, Vi?"

I purse my lips. "Okay, it was better than nice. It was good." And with a squeal, I jump up and make a run for the bedroom closet. He chases me and pins me up against the wall, handing me a towel to wipe my mouth on. "I really do have to get ready for work."

"I know, but we deserve better than nice or good. Seems like we've got some work to do."

He knows as well as I do that nothing about last night or this morning was ho-hum 'good'. It was mind-blowing, life-altering epicness. But he's letting me hide, letting our teasing game continue, and I appreciate that. I need that buffer for my heart to remember who he is, who I am, and that this is fake and casual.

He smacks my ass and presses a kiss to my still overly minty mouth. "Go to work, Chickie."

YOU ARE LOVINGLY INVITED
Together with their families,
Ross Andrews & Violet Russo
Request the honor of your presence at the celebration of their love
At St. Luke's Church of the Hills
Saturday, June twenty-sixth, at six in the evening
Reception To Follow

"IT'S GORGEOUS," I WHISPER AS TEARS SPRING TO MY EYES. They're beautiful, the same peach and white embossed paper that she bought for my wedding with Colin, but now that it's printed out with Ross's name next to mine, there's a hitch in my throat.

She also added some subtle metallic glitter or something so the whole thing feels dreamy.

"How did you do that?" I ask, tilting the paper one way and then another.

"Shimmer spray," she answers with a shrug. "I'll lay them out and do them in batches. Dries instantly, so it'll be quick, but I think it adds a little something extra."

It absolutely does.

"So this is the prototype. Do I have your approval?" Abi asks.

I nod. "Of course. Absolutely. They're everything. Too bad they're for a wedding that's—"

She cuts me off. "A wedding I've been looking forward to since we were about ten years old and I saw you go gaga over Ross," Abi says, hugging me. "However it's come about, it's happening. My best friend is marrying my best brother. I'm happy about that, regardless of the circumstances. Which you can thank me for later."

"Abi, he's your *only* brother," I point out, but I still smile a little.

"So everyone keeps saying, but I keep surprising them," Abi says with a grin, giving me another squeeze before stepping back. "So, let me punch in the print order here . . . and by the time you get done telling me about work and the wedding preparations, everything will be ready to go to the mailroom clerk."

"How'd you know about that?" I ask.

"Well, my one and best brother might have spilled a little bit of his plans to make this whole thing easier on you when he stopped by for roses. Did you like them? They're a special heirloom variety with a Dutch history going back centuries." She smiles like I know what she's talking about, but I have no idea beyond roses are pretty and smell good.

"I loved them," I tell her honestly. I do remember to leave out the part where Ross tore the fancy flowers down to their petals for my bath, but I can feel my face heat at the memory of last night.

Abi grins big and wide, wolfishly devouring my reaction. "That look right there," she says, pointing to my cheeks. "What's that all about? You're blushing, Vi, which means something happened. Spill it, girl!"

"Nothing. The flowers were just a really nice surprise, and he offered to help with a lot of the wedding prep that's stressing me out." Even to my own ears, it's a weak explanation of the continually growing redness, which is creeping down to my chest now.

Abi narrows her eyes, searching mine. "You slept with him, didn't you?"

My heart stutters and then stops. "I'm so sorry, Abi. You know I would never do anything to risk our friendship. We just got carried away and . . ."

My tumble of words dies out as she bursts out in laughter. "Fina-fucking-ly. Took you long enough. I figured you two would've boned that night after Club Red, but then you got pretty sloshed, so maybe my brother's not a total Neanderthal, after all."

My face blanks. "You're . . . not mad? Isn't that like some red-line girl-code thing? You shall not pass?" I intone.

Her quirked brow communicates quite easily that she thinks I'm a dolt. Droll and sarcastic, she summarizes, "Yeah, Vi. I totally hooked you up with my brother, the one I know you had a schoolgirl crush on for years . . . and the guy who quickly gets bored of vapid bank account chasers . . . for a fake wedding and at least a six-month relationship where you live together twenty-four seven . . . and thought you two would never bump uglies."

She rolls her eyes. "What kind of moron do you think I am? More importantly, what took you so long? Is he still being an asshole to you? I'll kill him if he is because he needs to get his head out of his ass and wake up to the awesomeness that is you staring him right in the face and figure out how to make you love him for real, forever, so we can actually be sisters."

That's a lot to process. Abi's not mad. She assumed we'd have sex. She wants us to get together? For real?

Oh, my God. She is such a schemer!

"I . . . I don't know what to say," I stammer.

Abi is having no such tongue-tied problems, though. "So, are we talking casual, no-strings sex, or are we talking 'I love you, you're my sun and moon' sex? What step are we at so I can advise accordingly?"

"Casual?" I say it as a question even though it's what Ross and I agreed on just hours ago. What step? She thinks there are steps from casual to sun-and-moon? "That's all this is, Abs. There's nothing serious between us, I mean, other than the fake marriage. This is still Ross and me."

As if that's explanation enough.

She smiles knowingly. "Yeah, but you've been living together for days now, have already weathered battles against both of your families, and are planning the event of the season in less than two weeks now. And you know what?" She pauses and I shrug. "You haven't killed each other. Oh, wait, unless you killed him with sex. Did you fuck my brother to death, Violet Russo?" she accuses.

I can't. I don't know what to do with her. She's acting like this is no big deal. And that's putting ideas in my head. Ones I don't know what to do with, like how his smoothies are just the right blend for my sweet tooth, how he stopped at the store and picked up an industrial-sized bottle of my favorite conditioner 'just because', and a dozen other little things. And last night, the bath and nerf war silliness that I didn't even know I needed. And the way he knows how to hug me, or to kiss me, or . . .

"Oh, God, Abi. I'm falling for Ross Andrews," I say, horror-stricken.

She smiles victoriously and does a little shimmy shake of happiness. "Okay, so now that my work there is done . . ." She reaches behind herself, literally patting herself on the back. "Let's talk wedding preparation. Hit me."

My mind is running in a thousand different directions. How in the fuck did this happen? How do I stop it? I cannot allow my heart to get tangled up in this mess, especially when we agreed hours ago to be cool and casual. We're basically fuck-buddy roommates with some messy paperwork attached, but it's not supposed to be emotional.

It's not supposed to be real.

Abigail snaps her fingers in front of my face. "Okay, you're panicking, so I'll go. Archie and I went shopping last night while you were doing dinner with the fam. I picked out my dress and he got a matching suit, so your bridesmaids are ready to go. Wanna see?"

I blink at least three times but nod. She grabs her phone, flipping through pictures until she finds the one she wants. She's posing on a pedestal at Ride or Die Bride in a frothy peach chiffon dress with the tiniest spaghetti straps, a cinched-in waist, and a flowy bottom that swirls around her calves. She looks gorgeous, slightly vintage but modern at the same time. "It matches the invitations and the flowers I've ordered, so it'll all look seamless. I think I'm going to do nude heels, something bare, with just a couple of skinny straps."

I'm still nodding mindlessly, only part of what she's saying sinking in. "Archie actually found a suit in the same peach color, too. I was afraid it'd look like a 1970s prom picture with him standing next to me, but it was actually divine against his dark skin. He did say that he's wearing a black shirt, no tie, and his combat boots with it, if you're okay with that? The black will go with the groom and groomsmen tuxedos, but it's still Archie, you know? He's not going to get all monkey-suited up unless you make him, and I'll admit, he looked pretty cool. The edge kinda toned down the peachiness a bit."

"That's fine. Sounds great," I reply, having no idea what I just agreed to. But if Abi and Archie think it'll look good, right now, I'll take their expertise as gospel. Because my brain is a bowlful of Jell-O mush.

Ross. Me. Ross. Me.

The loop plays on, images superimposed over one another from our misspent childhood antics to just this morning. But not in a continuous line. Oh, no. The pictures in my mind are mixed up, old and new taking on unexpected meanings with every flip through my mental scrapbook.

Abi plows on as if I'm not a zombie in the middle of an existential crisis. "Okay, so we're doing great. Invites and flowers are spectacular, courtesy of *moi*. Venue is all set. Kaede told me he called today to update their info and direct everything to him. And he is meeting with Luciano's owner this afternoon." She looks at her watch and amends, "Right now, to get the food squared away. Bridesmaid outfits are done, and Ross and Kaede have tuxedoes. I sent Kaede a color swatch so he can do ties and handkerchiefs to match me and Archie. We do need to decide who else Ross is going to have stand with him so that it's balanced, two on your side and two on Ross's."

"Does Luciano's make cake?" I ask woodenly. I don't know why that stuck out in the laundry list she just rattled off, especially when I couldn't tell you half of what she said. But I forgot the cake, even when I was talking to Ross last night.

Who forgets the cake at a wedding? See, this is doomed from the start.

"They do, Italian cream, if I remember correctly."

Well, I guess that's one problem solved at least.

"My dress. I still don't have a dress. Do you know what he did?" I ask, not needing to specify who 'he' is.

Abi shakes her head, hope on her face now that I'm reasonably coherent.

"He sent gowns to my office," I say quietly, the shock of seeing racks of white gowns returning anew as I tell Abi. "Archie was at Bitch-ella's." I sigh, getting my haywire brain to focus. "I mean, Archie was at Mrs. Montgomery's, working on her ball-room. It's coming along quickly since it's designed to be a mostly empty space, good for event-specific setup. He's supervising the painters today." I shake my head again, focused but completely off track from where I'd intended to go with what I'm telling Abi.

"Archie was gone, and the office door opened. I went out to greet the visitor, and there was a bridal shop associate there. With a rack of gowns for me to try on right then and there. She said my fiancé made it clear how busy I was, so she was ready to help me try on the ones that interested me quickly so I could return to my schedule." My eyes bug out as I look at Abi. "Who does that?"

Her smile is pure triumph. "Ross does, apparently, though I've never known him to make even a fraction of this effort for anyone before."

Her words give me pause, and hope tries to bloom. Maybe he's feeling some of what I'm feeling too? Could it be?

But no. Not Ross, and not for me. This is a big deal, a production to fool everyone. We can't go at it half-assed or everyone will know it's fake. That's why he's doing this. It has to be.

"So, did you find the dress?" she asks, hands clasped below her chin.

I shake my head. "No, not in that batch. But the associate said another batch—maybe even another store—would stop by tomorrow. I tried to argue about my schedule, but she said it'd already been arranged with my assistant and that he'd blocked out the time. Can you believe Archie?"

Even as I say it, I know it's ridiculous. Archie will do what-ever the hell he wants, and there's nothing I can say or do to change it. I might be his boss, but he's a man of his own wills and wants. It's one of the things I love about him . . . usually.

Before Abi can answer, the bells jingle, signaling a customer up front. She turns to go help them, but a voice calls out. "Violet, where are you, baby?"

Abigail and I meet eyes, both of us with pinched brows and animated horror marring our faces.

"What the fuck?" I whisper as I go out front to see . . .

Colin.

He's wearing his usual workday suit, spit-shined shoes, and slicked back hair. He looks . . . boring.

"Oh, there you are, Vi. I saw your car on the street and knew it was the sign I was looking for." He smiles like any of that made sense.

"What are you doing here, Colin?" I say, not mad, exactly, more just confused with what's going on.

Abi is flailing her arms wide, waving him off. "No way, mister. You can spin on your thumb and get the hell out of my store."

"I wanted to talk," Colin says to me, ignoring Abi. "I . . . I wanted to say I'm sorry, and I've been thinking. I was wrong."

Unable to deal with Abi's act, which had evolved into something like a manic dance at this point, I step around her. "You said you wanted it to end, Colin. So it's over. I haven't looked back"

"I overreacted!" Colin says, his voice touched with anger. "You were pressuring me, neutering me half the time, and—"

"Neutering?" I scoff, trying not to laugh. Neutering is the last thing I want from a husband, especially after the way Ross fucked me rough and hard. Nope, give me a fully functioning set of balls, thank you very much. But those balls have to come with respect. "Colin, I never neutered you. I wanted you to be you and for me to be everything you could ever want in a woman. In fact, I still hope you find someone and have a good life. But as for you and me . . . it's over."

"Woman, you don't tell me when things are over!" Colin thunders, his entitled brattiness at having his toy taken away making him have what equates to a grown-man temper tantrum. But newsflash, I'm not a toy. And also, what did I ever see in him? Was he always this . . . childishly annoying?

"Except that I just did. As much as I hate to say it, you were right. We weren't meant for each other—"

He interrupts me, a sneer twisting his lips. "So I've seen in the papers. You think you're suddenly *meant* for Ross Andrews? I'm sure you do. You think you're marrying better, don't you? Hooked you a sucker with a bigger bank account than mine. But he'll see you for the gold-digging whore you are."

Of course, he'd think this is about money and status, as if those are the only reasons to get married. It's like he thinks I'm some shiny toy. He doesn't want me, but he damn sure doesn't want anyone else to have me either.

Fighting hard for the high road, I say neutrally, "For so many reasons, I'm happier without you. Just leave."

I turn my back on him, walking through the doorway to the back. As I pass her, Abi is glaring at Colin, shooting daggers with her eyes that could accurately pin a bug to the wall. "You heard her. Get out."

She puts her arm around me, ushering me into the depths of the workroom. A moment later, I hear the jingle of the bells again.

"He's gone," Abi says, rubbing my back. "What the hell was that?"

I shake my head. "No idea. I haven't heard a single word from him since the coffee shop, and now this."

"What a douche canoe! No offense, but how did you ever love him? Oh, God, how did you fuck him? Please say it was missionary with the lights out. Wham, bam, thank you, ma'am is the only way I think a woman could handle a guy like that. Just get it over with."

Her outrageousness helps dry up the tears trailing down my face. I'm not sad, not even mad at Colin. It's just ridiculous, and I feel stupid for wasting my time with him, blind for not seeing who he really is. And getting called a gold-digging whore is bound to do a number on even Lizzo-sized self-confidence.

"Is everyone saying I'm a gold-digger? I know that one article did, but is that what everyone thinks?" I ask Abi, not sure if I want her to tell me the truth.

"Who cares what they say?" she responds, and I know she's

giving me the kindness of not saying out loud what the grapevine is calling me. 'Gold-digging whore' is probably the kindest of it.

"I'm scared, Abs," I confide. "I'm scared everyone's going to find out this is all fake and it's all going to fall apart in flames of glory. I'll be the laughingstock of the city, and Ross will be a pariah, any hopes he has of improving his reputation at work dashed by our secret arrangement."

There's so much more to this now, but on the surface, that's my fear. Fear of being found out. Because the rest of this, the emotional questions playing below that surface, are too much to face right now. I can't consider that I might be a fool in front of Ross . . . again. And this time, it would be a devastating blow I might never recover from.

Because I've fallen for him. Slowly, over years, and then fast, all at once. But I have.

She traces comforting circles on my back, speaking clearly and certainly, daring the universe to not obey her commands. "No one is going to find out that it's a fake marriage so you can both save face. You're going to walk down that aisle and make your Papa proud for his last days, and Ross is going to get Dad off his back and kick ass at work. And in six months, when the dust is settled, you'll see where you land. Maybe it's together. Maybe it's not. But you'll at least have had the dream."

"I hope you're right," is all I can say, because it's the absolute truth. *Universe, if you're listening, please let her be right.*

CHAPTER 15

ROSS

I stare out the windows overlooking the city, mentally reciting my presentation. This is a big one, important to the company and to my career. I need it to go well, and it will. I'm prepared, the numbers are great, and it'll be a boon for the company.

As long as Dad can see that.

A knock on the door interrupts my speech. I look over to see Kaede in the doorway, his brand-new 'armored' tablet in his left hand. "It's time."

I nod, and we stride off down the hallway together. Knights to the battle, updated from the medieval brand of warfare to a battlefield of conference tables surrounded by the old guard.

We walk into the meeting room, where the only member of the board not yet present is Dad. It gives me a minute to review my meeting notes behind the podium while Kaede gets the display set up, him giving me the thumbs-up just as Dad and Courtney walk in.

Subtle, Dad. I know by his being tardy, he's sending a signal to the rest of the board that I'm unimportant, that this presentation is unimportant. Everything with him is a multi-layered power play of strategy. Always.

"Thank you for coming, everyone," Dad says before taking his place at the head of the table. "Ross?"

LAUREN LANDISH

"Thank you, Dad, board members. I know a lot of things have been happening recently," I start, getting a few chuckles from the more sympathetic board members, "and if I sound a little sleep deprived, my apologies."

"Hell, it's understandable. We were once young and in love too," someone says, earning a chuckle from almost the entire room.

"Oh, good. I'm so glad to hear that planning a wedding wore you all out too," I continue the joke before sobering. "Today, I'm here to propose a new venture for your consideration. I truly feel, and think you will too, after seeing the numbers, that this'll set the company on a generational path of growth, making certain that we're leading the cutting edge for the next decade and beyond."

For the next half hour I go through my proposal, Kaede helping from time to time with his computer magic. He's got the amazing knack of taking a hundred pages of scientific gobbledy-gook and turning it all into something that someone who received their MBA from Harvard back in the Reagan administration can understand.

By the end, even Dad looks a little less hostile, and as the lights come up, I know that I've made some headway. I bust my ass to deserve my spot in this company, and I'm even going so far as to get married under his directive. He has to see that and recognize the potential this deal has too.

"Ross, I'll be honest," Dad says as the board looks at him, "I understood about a quarter of that speech. Not that you or Kaede didn't do a good job of dumbing it down for us geezers."

There are a few laughs around the room, and even Courtney smiles a little. "If you'd like, Dad, I can start over?"

"No!" Dad protests, holding up his hands and smiling congenially. "I think you could spend a year trying to explain it to me and I still wouldn't get some of it. That's fine. I know the cutting edge keeps marching on and sometimes, we're left watching it go. The part I did understand was the finances. And that told me everything I needed to know. We need accounting and R&D to double-check your figures, of course, but if everything looks

186

good . . . well, I'd say we might have a new Andrews venture. We'll reconvene on this when you're ready."

A thrill goes through me, so electrifying that I float for the rest of the meeting. A few board members do ask questions about my presentation, and I have answers at the ready, able to speak to any concerns they might have and even pump up the interest a bit more. After that, Dad talks about quarterly statements, and before I know it, the meeting is over.

Before leaving, Paul Washington, the head of R&D, comes up. "Impressive, Ross."

"Thanks, Paul. I assume your guys are going to tear it apart?"

"Oh, we won't give you a quick shine-on," Paul says with a grin. "But just from my perspective, you nailed it. Your new young lady must really have gotten you grounded over the past few days. She must be something special to tame you so quickly." Something about the way he says that lets me know he's heard the rumors of my painting the town red, which is what started this whole ultimatum. But at least he can see the difference in me and is saying positive things now.

"She's . . . amazing, Paul," I tell him honestly. "And she does have a way with people, especially me."

Paul leaves as the rest of the board files out, and I turn to look at the head of the table. Worry trickles through me when I see Dad sitting in his seat still, a scowl on his face.

Dammit. I thought he'd been behind me, that I'd knocked his socks off. But it was all a charade to him. He was smiling because the rest of the board was smiling, and he didn't want to make a scene.

I'd busted my ass to give him what he says he wants, and still, he isn't happy.

"What?" I say sternly, readying myself for verbal warfare with him.

"I don't get you, Ross. You are so brilliant, could do so much, but you persist in wasting your time, your life, with pie-in-the-sky dreams and transient pleasures. This venture won't happen. It's not sustainable, nor is this relationship with Violet." He slams his hands on the table, fierce eyes boring into me for a moment before he puts his head in his hands.

He's shaking his head, mumbling toward the table, but I can hear him perfectly well. "We gave you everything. Education, support, opportunity. Maybe that's where we went wrong. You never had to work for anything, and now you're distracted by every shiny new thing that flits in front of you."

"Ouch," I deadpan. "And fuck off, Dad."

I don't talk to him like that, crass and combative. It's not our way, and his jerk of reaction shows that he didn't expect it.

"Don't you dare speak to me like that, Son."

Not this time. "I have worked my ass off. I earned every grade I ever got, earned my spot on every football team, and earned my degree. Yes, obviously, I got my position here because of my last name, but that's more of a hardship than a boon because every day, I have to prove that I deserve it. And I do. You know that. You watch my numbers. I know you do. Maybe my personal life hasn't been the picture-perfect fantasy you envisioned, but I'm working on it. I love Violet, and she loves me, and we're getting married."

So much of what I just said is the truth. A tiny voice in the back of my head whispers . . . *maybe all of it?* But that's not true. Violet and I are making progress, big strides toward a healthier relationship, but it's not love. There's no way after just a few days.

Dad takes a big breath in and then slowly lets it out. His eyes look out the window and then back to me. "She'll sign a prenup."

I huff. "She's not a gold-digger. She could care less about my last name, but yes, she'll sign a pre-nup. She knew you would require one, and she's fine with that because she's not marrying me for my money."

He hums, like he's tasting that statement for truth but still profoundly doubts it.

I'm done with this.

Let Dad suspect. Let Dad feel a bit emasculated as I lay the foundations for the future. This isn't exactly corporate warfare. We're on the same team. It's more like a pro football team. He's the old star quarterback, and I'm the young lion coming up.

Dad wants to hang onto the starting job. He wants the accolades.

But this isn't college any longer. I'm not going on a four-year time limit like I was back then. And this isn't football, where I was good, but not top-flight.

No. No, this time, I've got the skills, the insight, and the ability to be not just the starter, but an All-Star. Before my career's over, I'm going to be hoisting a few championships and MVP awards of my own.

And he won't stop me.

I don't think there's any way to make him happy, to make him see that I'm doing everything I can for this company, for him, for mom, for our family.

For Violet. For yourself.

I get up and walk down the hall, leaving him at the head of his empty table.

In my office, Courtney is perched on my desk like she owns the place, her phone in hand.

"I don't have the time or the patience for this right now, Court. Get out," I snap.

Courtney lifts one brow, talking into the phone. "Yeah, Mom. He's right here. Let me put you on speaker."

Fuck, just what I don't need. More family pressure and drama.

"Ross, dear!" Mom's chirpy voice comes through the speaker. "So glad to catch you!" I eyeball Courtney, promising revenge for whatever she's pulling right now.

"Sure, Mom. What's up?"

"Well, the Community Freedom Gala is this weekend, and I know you don't usually like to attend, but I've been talking to everyone about my lovely daughter-in-law to be, and everyone can't wait to meet her. You two simply have to come," she says like that wouldn't be the equivalent of lining us up in front of a firing squad.

"Mom, we're pretty busy with wedding prep stuff, you know.

189

I'm not sure we can fit that into the schedule," I say, injecting regret into my voice even though there's no way in hell I want to go to this shindig.

It's one of the almost quarterly events where all the state's rich and charitable get together to celebrate life, liberty, and patting yourself on the back for donating while drinking Moet. No, thank you.

"Nonsense. You'll come and play nice." There's no room for argument in her tone this time. The gloves are off. "Also, we'd like to make Violet's family our special guests. It's been so many years since I saw Maria. I think it's time we reunite if you kids are getting married."

My mouth drops open and Courtney reaches forward to push it closed with one manicured finger. The smile on her face says she's enjoying every bit of this.

This could be a disaster.

While Abi's cool, and Mom seems happy . . . there are going to be plenty of people at the Gala who'll take one look at Nana Russo and give *the look*, pretending to be charmed while being sanctimonious and looking down their noses at the working-class family.

Knowing what I know of Nana and Aunt Sofia, they might end up snatching a few wigs and causing a scene . . . which is exactly what Violet would want to avoid. She's nervous enough about her family starting to show up and the craziness the wedding might devolve into.

"Fine, Violet and I will come, but her family can't exactly drop everything and attend a *gala*, Mom. I'm not even sure if Papa can get around that well right now."

"Well, whoever can come, they should." It should be a welcoming thing to say, but it sounds like a directive. "I'll have Karl schedule them for a fun day of relaxation—manicures and hair treatments and dress shopping, our treat, of course. Goodness knows, they deserve it with everything going on with Maria's dad."

"I'll see and let you know." It's the best I can do for right now. Maybe I can get them out of this later, somehow? I'll tell

Mom that I asked and they couldn't come because . . . of something. I'll figure it out.

But fuck, I committed Violet and me to going. There's no getting out of that.

She's won either way.

"I gotta go, Mom," I say wearily. Between Dad and Mom, I've got whiplash so hard, my brain's spinning. Dad wishes Violet would just go away, and Mom is trying to bring her whole family into the fold.

"Oh, of course, dear. Thank you for your help, Courtney!" she calls out as she hangs up. Court grins, knowing full well what she helped Mom do.

"Why are you doing this?" I ask Courtney, almost as mad at her as I am Mom and Dad.

Her face falls. "Look, Ross. I like Violet, and I don't know what you two are up to. Hell, maybe you really are in love. I don't know, really. But you need to do this. It's how our family works, within our walls, within the society pages, and within the upper crust. You get engaged, you show each other off, parading around like show ponies for Mom and Dad. By *not* doing that, you're raising more eyebrows."

I hadn't realized just how sharply perceptive she is. Nor that I hadn't considered that by hiding away, we would be more suspicious. I was hoping for a bit of 'Out of sight, out of mind.' Honestly, I was hoping to just rush headlong through any barriers and get to the finish line of the altar.

She gets up and struts to the door but pauses and looks back. "Don't hurt her, Ross. Violet's a good person. Just don't hurt her."

I can't stop the bitterness that flies off my tongue. "And what does that make me?"

Her answering smile is sad. "Just unaware, big brother. Maybe a bit immature, still, but that's okay. It's one of the reasons we love you."

I close my eyes and start rubbing at my temples as she leaves. After meeting the Russos, I know Violet's going to have a fit over this. It's the last thing she'd want, and to be honest, the last thing

I'd want too. Papa and Nana Russo are good people, and I don't want them to be embarrassed by some stuck-up society rich bitch because he still talks a bit like a *paisan*.

I'm gonna have to do some pretty major convincing to get her to go along with this latest development.

EVERYTHING'S PERFECT, WITH THE SCENT FROM THE INCENSE wafting through the air as I double-check that the outdoor table's been laid out just the way I want.

"You got everything?" I ask the chef, who nods. "Double-check with me. The wine—"

"Lodovico Blend," the chef confirms for me. "Are you sure, though, sir? There are much finer wines available."

I nod, knowing that for the chef, fine basically means expensive. But I noticed three empty bottles of Lodovico on a shelf at the Russos', and while I'm no sommelier, I know enough about wine to know a working-class family like that doesn't drink a thousand dollars of wine on a regular basis, so the name means something to them.

"I'm sure. And the garlic bread?"

"Personally prepared by me, sir," the chef assures me. "And the lamb ravioli will pair perfectly with the wine."

"Excellent," I comment, checking my watch. I had to hurry to get everything prepared. Thankfully, building security is used to letting workers in if I call ahead. "Okay, my fiancée should be home in just a few minutes, so let's make sure we're on time."

In fact, Violet's a minute early, opening the door to the penthouse with a groan. "Oh, God, Ross, I still haven't found a dress, and you wouldn't believe how much my ribs hurt from the corsets. What's all this?"

I smile, my crisp white shirt unbuttoned just enough to let her get a hint of my skin as I offer her my arm. "I thought something other than pizza and ice cream might be in order tonight," I say lightly.

Violet looks at me suspiciously, her eyes clouded, and I

wonder if she's thinking about all the times I pulled shit on her when we were kids, sweet talking her one minute, only to humiliate her the next. "Where's the frog?"

"I swear, not a frog in sight . . . although I must admit a certain mischievous side of me did think of putting frog legs on the menu for tonight. But in the end, the non-asshole side of me won out. I'd like to say I've grown up since high school, but I think it's just your positive influence." She rolls her eyes at my over-the-top flattery.

I lead Violet outside, where Chef awaits at a fully set table, dishes under cloches to stay warm, twin candles burning in silver candlesticks while a single red rose rests in a vase.

"What . . . you really shouldn't have," Violet tells me as I hold her chair for her.

"Of course, I should. You deserve it." Chef goes to pour the wine, but I wave him off and pour the wine for Violet myself. "If I thought you wouldn't have laughed at me, I'd have cooked myself, but unfortunately, my repertoire is pretty limited."

"You make me happy with those smoothies," Violet says quietly, and it's my turn to feel the warmth flush my neck.

I make her happy. Somehow, those little words mean a lot to me.

"Give me some time, and I'll figure out how to make a decent grilled cheese," I say, unveiling dinner. "Here you go . . . lamb ravioli in a proper tomato sauce, garlic bread, and—"

"Lodovico wine!" Violet nearly squeals, seeing the bottle. "Oh, Ross! How'd you know?"

"Saw it in the kitchen," I answer her, proud of myself. "What's the story?"

"Lodovico is very special to Papa," Violet explains. "It's too expensive for any but the most special occasions. So the three bottles are for Nana and Papa's wedding, Mama's birth, and my birth. I'm almost afraid to ask, but—"

"We'll put it on the menu at our reception," I immediately answer her, raising my glass. "For now, to Violet Russo, who hurt her ribs today for love."

Violet blushes, tapping her glass against mine. "Thanks. I'll

193

keep looking, but I do think I decided today that I don't care how gorgeous the dress is. If I can't breathe in it, it's not the one."

"Sounds reasonable," I tell her.

We dig into our dishes, Violet moaning at the first bite. "Oh, my. Don't tell Nana, but this is better than hers!"

"Don't worry," I reply with a chuckle. "She can't hear you."

"That's good. You should have heard her and Aunt Sofia go at it before you showed up. She'd have my hide if I dared to compliment someone else's cooking over hers."

She tells me about her family, how Nana and Sofia go at it like cats and dogs half the time, while Papa catches his fair share of yelling too . . . but it's all in love.

We move on to discussing our days, and she cheers for me when I tell her about the meeting going well. Her eyes turn to molten fire when I tell her about Dad's private reaction, though, and the way she has my back warms me.

She shows me a glittery invitation, raving about Abi's genius, and I have to agree with her. "Something else did happen today, though."

Her tone is stilted, hesitant to share. I lay my hand over hers. "You can tell me anything, Violet."

"Colin came by the flower shop. He saw my car outside and came in. He told me he wanted to get back together."

My heart stops as cold fury lights its way from my gut to my fists, which clench unconsciously. "And?"

She tilts her head, reading me. "You're mad?"

I spit out, "He comes chasing after my fiancée and I'm just supposed to be okay with that?"

Well, if that didn't toss kerosene on an already confusing fire. She's not mine, not really. But fuck if I don't feel possessive of her, possessed by her.

"Would you lose the pissed off look if I said I kicked him out on his ass and told him to have a good life?" Her smile is one of sass and confidence.

"Actually . . . yes," I admit, sighing in insane relief. "Was I that obvious?"

"If he'd been here, you'd have thrown him off the balcony without a parachute."

"Perhaps," I reply, troubled, relieved, and gladdened by her news. "But simply because Radcliffe's a douche who doesn't deserve you."

"We both didn't deserve each other. I was never in love with him. I just wanted to have the fairy tale wedding . . . and wanted Papa to have that memory."

Again, my heart leaps in my chest hearing she was never in love with him. This is getting heady, and it's not the wine that's making it happen.

"And he will," I vow. "We'll make his dreams come true. Yours and mine too."

My voice is husky, promising so much more than a fantasy wedding. Hearing her talk about Colin, thinking about how easily she could've gone back to him, because at one point, she believed what they had was real. Even if she knows better now, it's more than what our initial relationship is built on.

But where we started is not where we are now. Not by a long shot.

I set my napkin down and step around the table to stand beside her. She looks up at me through her lashes, feeling that the mood has shifted.

"Violet," I say, not sure what I mean to say.

"I know," she says, confusing me because how can she know if I don't?

I take her hand and lead her down the hallway. From behind me, I hear the front door close with a small click and know the chef has left discreetly.

I lay her down on the king-sized mattress, crushing her underneath me as I kiss her hard. Trailing my lips down her neck, I kiss to the V of her blouse before unbuttoning the silk.

"Mmm . . ." she moans, losing herself in the sensations as I expose more and more of her silky soft skin to my mouth. I'm raging hard in my pants, but this isn't about me. This is about her.

For the first time in my life, it's about *her*.

Letting her gasps of pleasure guide me, I open her blouse to uncover the lacy edges of her bra. I lick where it meets her skin, teasing her until I see her delicious nipples harden to stiff little nuggets for my tongue.

Thankfully, she's wearing one of those front-closure bras, and seconds later, I'm devouring her breasts, nibbling and sucking while my hands roam over her legs, squeezing her ass until she's arching to my touch, begging for more.

"Ross," she moans, guiding me lower as hunger and desire sweep through her body. I follow, unbuttoning and kissing my way down her stomach to the hem of her shirt.

She's a work of sensual art, bra and shirt wide open, tits on display for me, her skirt working its way higher as she bucks. Her hair's getting fluffier as she writhes, and her skin is flushed with desire.

"Watch," I tell her, unhooking her skirt and peeling it off her legs before rolling her soaked panties down and off. Her eyes take me in silently, her chest rising and falling in deep breaths as I hook her knees over my shoulders and lift her up slightly, just enough to let her see as I drag my tongue between her pussy lips.

She gasps, grabbing my hair as I part her lips again, scooping up her wetness before circling her clit with the tip of my tongue.

I lick her.

I nibble on her.

I suck her.

I *worship* her.

With every sweep of my tongue, my grin grows until I'm wolfish, consuming her even as Violet bucks and grinds her hips against my ravenous lips. The only word that leaves her lips the entire time is my name, repeated again and again as her body is pushed into overload.

But my name is all I need. I can hear the differences, when she wants me to go faster, when she wants me to slow down, and when I find a spot that has her seeing stars. Each time is pure pleasure for me as this woman, who is transforming in front of my very eyes minute by minute, relishes the pleasure I give her and offers back my name in supplication.

I wrap my hands around her thighs, holding her tight for the final plunge. Finding her clit, I circle my tongue quickly, lapping at her firm little button until Violet's thighs quiver and her back arches unconsciously.

"Ross!" She screams as she comes, covering my face in her sweet juices as the waves sweeps through her. I don't let her get carried away. Instead, I'm her rock, holding her safe and secure in my powerful arms.

Violet moans deeply, her legs and hips turning to jelly before she sags and I pull back, rearranging her on the bed. I rip my clothes off and cover her with my naked body in a second, not letting her come down fully from her orgasm before I shove inside, filling her.

"Fuck, Vi," I groan out, relishing the hot silk feel of her pussy as she grips me tightly. "You feel like . . . heaven," I grit out.

Home. I almost said she feels like home, and that's the truth. But now isn't the time for that conversation. There might never be a time for that, so I'm going to enjoy this for whatever she wants it to be right now.

I fuck her hard, holding her hips and moving her in time with my thrusts as I kneel between her legs. I want to watch her face lost in pleasure, want to see her tits bounce, want to enjoy the look of her pussy stretching around me. I want it all . . . all of her.

In and out, over and over, I make my mark on her. She is mine. And whether she wants it or not, she's holding my heart and all the cards.

She spasms anew, crying out my name, and I fall over her, one elbow on either side of her head. I want to be closer, in her face as she comes from our fucking. Her quivering walls trigger my own orgasm, and I explode violently, painting her with my cum as I kiss her passionately, sharing breath the way we share pleasure.

I relax, barely able to hold my weight off her as I get my bearings. "Holy shit, Ross." Her voice is hazy and breathless.

"I know, me too," I say, turning her onto her side before wrapping her up in my arms.

"Ross," she says, taking my hand and kissing my knuckles. "You—"

"Are going to take care of you, whatever that means," I tell her, kissing the ebony waves of her hair. "So don't worry. We'll make it together, Violet."

She sighs and snuggles against me. "Thank you."

I hold her tighter, not ready to sleep but not wanting to be anywhere else right this moment.

CHAPTER 16

VIOLET—FRIDAY—8 DAYS UNTIL THE WEDDING

*I*t's barely light outside when I stir. I slide my eyes open, stretching luxuriously to find Ross awake and watching me.

"Good morning, Sleeping Beauty," he says as he leans over and plants a sweet kiss to my mouth, zero cares given to my morning breath.

I smile, teasing, "Why are you watching me like a creeper?"

"I have something to tell you," he says, his expression serious.

I shuffle in the bed, sitting up and leaning against the pillows. I take a big breath, steeling myself. "How bad is it?"

He ducks his head. "Remember how you asked if I was buttering you up with the bath?" I nod, and he says, "Well, I wasn't. But dinner last night was supposed to butter you up, but I got sidetracked." He cuts his eyes to the side, scanning down my body hungrily even though I'm mostly covered by the blankets.

I smack his shoulder, scolding, "Get it to it. I'm dying here!"

It's telling that I'm not worried he's backing out. That thought never even enters my mind because I know we're a team, but I am worried if whatever this is requires easing me into it.

"My mom called yesterday," he says. He goes on to tell me about the gala and his mom wanting to invite my family. "I tried to tell her that there was no way it'd work. I knew you wouldn't want the stress with everything we're trying to get accomplished, but—"

"But it's hard to tell your parents no," I say, clenching my teeth. "I'm worried about getting our families getting together at all. But at a fancy charity event?"

"I know. I told Mom it wouldn't be good for Papa's health, so we could probably get a pass for him and maybe Nana, but we're roped pretty hard into it."

I growl. "I don't want to be in any more paparazzi shots, and knowing our luck, there's going to be some crazed Ross Andrews fan who reports every faux pas I make."

We've managed to stay out of the society pages for the last few days, and I'd really like to keep it that way after the initial article that painted me so poorly, especially after the fresh burn of Colin echoing the same insult. It's not that I care what he thinks at all, but I know he's repeating the gossip about me and Ross that's circulating through that entire crowd.

He reaches over, taking my hand. "If it helps, I'm right there with you. I try to avoid these galas and events because Mom does them all the time, and I spent years as her golden child show pony. She meant well, was just proud of me, but it only gets more awkward the older you get."

"But we have to go?" I ask, wishing there were a way out of this.

His lips screw up, and he nods. "We do. Mom and Courtney tag-teamed to get me to agree on the phone, which means Dad definitely knows by now. If we don't show up, I'm afraid it'll raise red flags."

I pale, knowing that'd be the kiss of death for us right now. Morgan doesn't believe us already. Refusing to show our faces to his cronies would only demonstrate that he's right to have doubts.

"Okay, so we're stuck, but we'll handle it. What about our families?" I shake my head. "Fuck, Ross. I really didn't think about how our *families* are supposed to get along. I mean, your Mom and Dad are okay, but Papa and Morgan? Talk about polar opposites. Or Nana and Morgan? Though that one might be fun."

Okay, it might be a little evil to take some sick joy in the thought of Nana verbally fileting Morgan to shreds, but I'm not going to admit that out loud.

"Those two? What about Nana and Mom?" he asks, both of us smiling at the image of Kimberly trying to converse with Nana or Aunt Sofia. Kimberly probably wouldn't be able to get a word in edgewise. "Although I do think our mothers could get along decently. They used to be okay when Abi and you were going back and forth between houses. Maybe they can build on that?"

"So we've got one possible match and several landmines. What could go wrong?" I say, throwing my hands wide and scooting back under the covers. Maybe I can just hide out and not have to deal with any of this. That'd be okay, right?

Ross leans over me, searching my soul with his eyes. "So, we're all in?"

I bite my lip but nod. "Okay . . . but I'm still worried. I want it on the record that I think this is a bad idea."

He boops my nose, and I shake my head, refusing the tease. "Noted."

* * *

"MOM?" I ASK AS SOON AS I HIT MY OFFICE, WANTING TO GET this out of the way. "I've got good news."

Okay, well good news isn't quite the word I'd use for this, but dammit, I'm going to try and see this from Mom's point of view.

"Hey, honey, I was just about to call you. What's up?" Mom asks. Even as she asks, she sounds distracted, but I dive in to get this over with.

"There's a charity event, and Mrs. Andrews was hoping to turn it into a family affair to give everyone a chance to meet before the wedding."

"Really?" Mom asks before her voice fades and she yells from a distance, "Yes, Mama! I'm telling her now! I know I need to get to work!"

"What's going on, Mom?" I ask, confused. She should be at work, but it sounds like she's at Nana's. Terror shoots through me. "Oh, God, is Papa okay?"

"What? Oh, yeah, the old goat is fine. It's just that . . ." she sighs, and I know she's only half talking to me because I can hear her shuffling and moving around on her end of the line. "Three of your cousins are scheduled to arrive today. You know . . . Vanessa, Estella, and Marissa?"

"Which Marissa?" I ask, grinning. There are a lot of *M*s in my family.

"The Triplets. They just finished their first year of college," Mom replies. "Which is why I'm heading out now. Seems they found one of those last-minute ticket deals, so they're coming in a few days early for the wedding. I don't begrudge the tight budget and bargain hunting. Really, I'm just glad they can come, but . . ." her voice drops, and I wonder if Nana's in the same room with her. "I'm glad they're staying with Mama so I don't have to listen to their constant singing."

"That's great, Mom. I'm glad they're coming too," I say, also relieved that they're staying with Nana. Being college students means they're broke as a joke, I'm sure, so it's a real gift that they're coming for the big family affair of my wedding. And I know they want to see Papa one last time. But I've heard them sing, though it was years ago, and Little Mix doesn't have to worry about the triplets taking over their sales, that's for sure.

"That's what I was going to call you about, Violet. They land in about ninety minutes, and I have got to go work. If I call out today, my boss is going to crap himself."

I can hear the direction she's going with this and glance down to my planner's to-do list and appointments. Another dress shop is coming by, I need to finalize the velvet for Ms. Montgomery's drapes and prepare for the next room in her never-ending renovation, order Ross's couch for his office, and now I need to get ready for this gala. I pencil that in and scribble a Post-It note to remind myself to fill Archie in when he gets here.

"Okay, I'll send a car to pick up the triplets. Don't worry, Mom." There. See? I can do it all and not miss a beat.

"Violet," Mom draws out my name in disappointment. "You cannot send an impersonal car to pick up your family. That would be disrespectful. You need to go pick them up, please?"

That should be a question. We both know full-well that's it's not. It's an order, a directive I can't and won't ignore.

I sigh, drawing an arrow through the couch ordering and moving it to tomorrow. Ross won't mind, not when he's the one who added the gala to my to-do list, anyway. "Fine, I'll get the triplets and take them to Nana's. What's their plan from there? Do I need to play hostess with the mostest?" I pray that's not what Mom wants me to do.

I hear her car start up, and she switches me over to the speakerphone. "No, nothing like that. Just pick them up, go to Nana's and politely excuse yourself for wedding things. They'll understand. Beyond the wedding, they're mostly here for sight-seeing, free food, and laundry services. Nana will take good care of them and enjoy doing it."

"Okay, I'm on it."

"I've got to go, baby girl. Can't drive and talk, you know. Can you text me the information about this charity event thing Kimberly wants us to go to? I'm happy to do whatever you need me to do, Violet. I'm just so proud of you." There's a moment of hitched breathing, but then she lets out a big exhale. "Sorry, I really have to go. Love you, bye!"

And with a click, she's gone. "Fuck me!"

"Intriguing, Boss Bitch, but I think that job's already taken," Archie says, sticking his head in my door. "What's up?"

I give him the full rundown on everything's that's happened as he takes notes, and then I summarize. "I need you to go onsite and handle the ballroom for a few hours," I tell him, grabbing my purse and keys. "Apparently, I've gotta pick up some cousins and drop them at Nana's. I'll text my mom about the charity gala, and achieve world peace, which would probably be easier than integrating my family and Ross's. Then I need to pull off the miracle of finding the right wedding dress. So my, you know, actual career I need to leave in your capable, manicured hands."

Archie checks out his black-polished, stubbed nails,

humming. "Speaking of which, I really do need to take some time off for a mani-pedi—"

"You'd better be joking."

Archie grins and smacks me on the hip. "Of course I am. Go. Chill the fuck out. I got this shit." He looks cool as a cucumber, reclining back in my guest chair with one booted ankle resting on his other knee. "Oh, I'll coordinate with Jeeves to get you and your family all scheduled for a fluff and polish before the gala."

I blink, his words taking a moment to sink in. "His name is Karl, Archie. He's the Andrews' butler. Butler? Is that the right word now? Assistant? Home Manager?"

Archie's eyes twinkle as he drolly says, "House elf? *Dobby is free. Master gave Dobby a sock.*" The high-pitched squeal and fake British accent sound odd out of his mouth, which only makes me grin more.

"Thanks, I needed that. You really are the best!" I lay a quick kiss on his cheek and then head for the door. "Oh, Abi told me about your suit. It sounds awesome! Can't wait to see it."

At least the drive out to the airport is easy. Traffic's pretty good at this time of day, and I'm even able to sit in the baggage pickup lounge for twenty minutes, typing out emails and sending them.

I just hit *Send* on my message to Mom, giving her the details of the Gala and letting her know that Karl and/or Archie will be in touch with our appointment times to get ready, when I'm interrupted by a harmonic squeal. "Violet!"

I look up as Estella, Vanessa, and Marissa come up, practically bouncing along and making a young guy who's wheeling his bag out the door stumble as he does a legitimate triple-take. I'll give it to the triplets . . . they're lookers, all of them.

"It's been too long," I tell them honestly, group hugging and exchanging cheek kisses all around. "What, ten years, at least?"

"At least!" Marissa says with a grin. "You look great, Vi. Damn, girl, I hope your man likes boobs!"

Uhm, wow. That was loud, judging by the looks of the folks around the baggage area. I forgot just how bold and brash and unfiltered my extended family can be. My blush answers everything for them, and Estella laughs.

"Just messing with you, girl. Last time I saw you, you were looking a bit twiggy. Good to see that those puberty glow-ups really do happen to us mere mortals because you look great! It really is good to see you! I've been stuck indoors too much between studying, practicing, and performing. In fact, what is that burning ball of fire in the sky, anyway?" Marissa holds her hands in front of her face, cringing away from the sunlight coming in the airport windows.

"Whatever," Estella teases. "You've just been spending too much time with Mark Brierson on top of you to see the sun." Vanessa holds up a fist which Estella bumps back. They even do the finger-waggle explosion thing, and I suddenly feel ridiculously old.

"Green with envy is not your color, Sis," Marissa taunts back, and all three of them devolve into silly giggles.

We get their bags loaded, and they pile in. Driving back to Nana and Papa's, they fill me in on college life and trying to get noticed for their singing, but it's hard to keep all the details in place.

I mean, they are triplets, and while not identical, they're close enough that I have a hard time telling them apart after ten years of not hanging out together. It's especially hard because they tend to talk over each other constantly and finish each other's sentences.

"So, tell us about your man," Vanessa says. "Do you love him?"

"Is he hot?"

"Is he loaded?"

"Yes, yes, and yes," I answer easily, laughing.

"Whoo-hoo!" Estella cheers, almost punching the roof of my car in her excitement. "Girl, we are so happy for you! We were all getting nervous that you were never going to get married, or if you did, it wouldn't be in time." Her eyes widen, "I mean, shit . . . sorry. It's just . . . you know how old school the family is, and you've always been the closest to Papa, his favorite. I'm glad he's going to walk you down the aisle."

"It's a dream come true," I agree, but I feel like shit saying it. Tack three more onto the list of people Ross and I are lying to. It's enough to make me certain that Lucifer's warming up my own little corner of hell.

We reach Nana's house, and as soon as I pull up, the door opens with Nana and Sofia and Papa all coming out to hug the girls, making a huge fuss. "Oh, babies, you've gotten so grown, so beautiful!" Papa says, smiling hugely. "A vision for this old man."

"Sing for us!" Aunt Sofia demands as if they're performing bears for her entertainment, but her smile softens the order. "I've been hearing so much about your talent, but I can't use the damn YouTube properly!"

The triplets smile, obviously basking in the praise, though Vanessa blushes as she answers. "Uhm, most of our songs are . . . you know, sort of mature?"

"And what am I, the Mickey Mouse Club?" Sofia asks, grinning. "What, you think your generation's the first to discover songs about your hoo-hah? Child, I know a few Italian songs that would make that Cardi B blush!"

The triplets laugh, knowing they're not going to get out of doing a little bit. "Okay," Estella finally says, looking at her sisters. "This is one of our standards. It's a little old and *clean* because I do not want to think of your old lady hoo-ha, Aunt Sofia, but maybe you know it."

The girls start humming, and I'm shocked at how much they've improved. Maybe it's reaching maturity, maybe it's just that they understand the emotions behind the lyrics, but as Estella sings a contralto lead at first before Vanessa and Marissa join in with alto and soprano for a new spin on *Fly Me To The Moon,* I'd say Frank Sinatra would be proud.

"Whoo, you girls had better save that for the wedding!" Nana says. "You girls do that, Violet here's going to have a bun in her oven by Sunday night!" She sways her hips so far left and right, I'm surprised she doesn't pop one out of socket, but Papa doesn't seem to mind because he's watching transfixed. I can't decide if that's gross or sweet.

Wait, what? Singing at the wedding. "Nana—"

"We'd love to! It'll be our gift to you and Ross!" Vanessa exclaims, grinning. "Oh, Vi, thank you!"

I know what I should do. I should just say no. I should say we've hired someone. I should say that Morgan Andrews goes into violent flashbacks if he hears anything but acoustic smooth jazz, PTSD from a torrid youth spent in the seventies.

Instead, I clear my throat. "Maybe a song or two?" It's the only way to corral this and not look like a bitch.

Please say you can't, please say you can't, please—

"We'll give you a list of choices that'd be perfect, and you can pick, and then just point us in the direction of the mics," Marissa says with a laugh.

Shit.

Guess I'll add that to my to-do list . . . telling Ross and the wedding planner and then picking a song. Or two?

"Hey, Nana," I say, changing the subject before the triplets start auditioning songs right here and now. "Ross's mom extended an invitation for a charity gala at their estate tomorrow night. I sent Mom a text about it, but it's for us all."

"A bake sale!" Nana says, her eyes twinkling as she totally misses the point. "Perfect! Sofia and I can make cannoli. They did great at the last charity sale at the church, and—"

"No, no, Nana, it's not like that!" I half yell before I jerk myself back. "It's a . . . well, I guess you could say a ball. Like a super-fancy thing. It'll be catered. You don't have to cook anything, but we'll need to get you ready. Hair, makeup, and a dress. Archie is getting everything arranged for us to have a day out tomorrow, okay?"

She claps her hands and then looks at Sofia, whose eyes are wide and bright. "A fancy ball? Like we're Cinderella?"

Sofia scoffs. "You think you're Cinderella? Guess that makes me the evil sister? Pshaw, I don't think so."

Nana grins. "Or . . . since it's pretend, we can both be Cinderella?"

Some agreement must be silently reached between the two of them because they begin dancing and twirling around the kitchen. I'm not sure who's leading who, but I have a bigger concern as they bump into the refrigerator.

"Could you two knock it off? You're going to break a hip if you keep it up in here. There's no room for dancing," I say, half-scolding and half-laughing at their antics.

Papa laughs hard enough that it makes him cough a bit, but he manages to choke out, "I've danced Angela around this kitchen more times than I can count. She's just fine. As for that one over there" —he points at Sofia— "she's trouble no matter where she is."

They glare at each other, but it's good-naturedly.

Papa turns to me. "Violet, dear, I'd love to attend this gala with you, but I just don't know that I can get this old body to dance the night away two weekends in a row. And if it's all the same to you, I'd rather save what soft-stepping I've got for your wedding." He looks at me so sweetly, love radiating from his eyes to mine.

Guilt slams into me, but that's what I'm doing all of this for. To give this man, the only father figure I've ever known, the dream he's always wanted. The dream I've always wanted too.

"Of course, Papa. Stay home and rest. You can meet the Andrewses next weekend at the wedding," I tell him, patting his hand.

MOM HOLDS UP HER MIMOSA, THE ONE I MADE SURE WAS more orange juice than champagne, and toasts. "To my baby girl. It might have taken you a while, but I think good things comes to those who wait. And Ross is a very good thing." She giggles as she sips at the drink, but the oddly girly quality to her speech has me thinking that maybe even the weak version of her drink is too strong. I pass her another mini quiche and then hold my own up, cheering with them so she'll down some protein in the form of egg and bacon yumminess.

"Thank you, Mom. Ross is great," I agree.

The dress shop assistants—yes, there are two of them for our small group—swirl back in with a rolling rack of dresses, sections separated by plastic tags with our names written on them. They carefully carry the dresses into fitting rooms and then turn to us with congenial smiles.

"Ready?" Britnay asks. That's not a typo or a misspeak. She'd told us quite clearly that her name wasn't the usual Brittney, *'No Brittney bitch jokes here,' she'd pleaded, but 'Brit-nay' with the long a sound. My mom apparently wanted me to suffer,'* she'd said with a shrug and a wink.

As they roll call each of us, and I say a silent thanks for my rather unusual but normal name, we enter our assigned rooms. "Look through the ones we've selected and choose your favorite. We'll have everyone come out at once, like a show and tell moment. We're happy to help with any buttons or zippers." She looks to Nana and Aunt Sofia, obviously thinking they might need a little assistance.

I appreciate the top-notch level of customer service, especially since neither Britnay nor her assistant, whose name I never caught because I was so stuck on Britnay's, are stuffy and formal. Their casualness makes this whirlwind seem not-so-crazy.

We spend the next hour trying on dresses and coming out to see each other. Estella, who volunteered to stay home with Papa and doesn't need a dress, gives critique and applause as we swish in front of the mirror.

Finally, I try on a beautiful red number. It's short, which I definitely didn't expect for a gala, but Britnay assures me that it's very on-point for the season with the heat coming in for the summer.

When I step out, my eyes jump to everyone else. We all look so fancy! "I love that one, Mom!" I tell her truthfully and smile as she turns this way and that, checking herself out in the mirror.

"I think I'm done," she says happily.

I look to the mirror, checking myself out. "I don't know about this one. It's a lot of leg and so bright." I turn sideways, pushing the small pooch of my belly out and lamenting, "I need to cut back on the pasta before the wedding."

Britnay chuckles. "No need to get that drastic, dear. I can help with that." She disappears for a moment and returns with a swatch of nude spandex. "Put this on."

I pop back into the fitting room and take the red dress off, hanging it up temporarily. I eye the spandex, which looks ridiculously small. "Uhm, Britnay? Are you sure this is my size? It's literally the width of my thigh, not my waist."

Her affirmative answer doesn't reassure me in the least. "Yes, step into it and pull it up a little at a time, working up your left leg an inch, then right, back and forth. Do you need me to come in and help?"

That sounds like the embarrassment of the century, so I decline and take a deep breath, telling myself that I can do this. I survived the corsets for the wedding dresses. I can survive this.

I step into the undergarment, and I'm doing okay until it's mid-thigh, at which point I suddenly become hilariously knock-kneed. With my knees pressed together, my hips look ginormous compared to the tiny opening I'm trying to squeeze them into. I grunt and jump a bit, instinctively wishing that gravity would somehow make the too-much of me slip into the too-little of the spandex. To no one's surprise, especially not physics, it doesn't work that way.

I grunt and pause, needing a breather. God, I'm sweating and I still don't have this damn thing on.

"How's that coming, Violet? Would you like some help?" Britnay says from the other side of the door. To her credit, her voice is nothing but kind, but I know she must be able to hear my struggles.

I look in the mirror, having finally gotten the torture device up enough to create an even worse spare tire than I naturally have. Guess all that excess has to go somewhere. I look ridiculous and definitely don't want anyone to see me like this, especially not barely-past twenty and barely-over-extra-small Britnay. "I'm fine. Just deciding if I like it," I call out.

That's a lie. I don't like it. I hate it . . . a lot.

But I finish wiggling it on, repeating to myself, "It'll be worth it. It'll be worth it." Lastly, I slip the red dress back on over the undergarment and step back out. "What do you think?"

Mom eyes me critically. "You look uncomfortable. Can you walk in that thing?" We both know she's not talking about the dress.

I take a few laps around the small area in front of the mirror. I raise one eyebrow, looking at Britnay who promised miracles and magic. "The legs are rolling up, the waist is rolling down, and I can't breathe at all. But that's probably a good thing because if this were any tighter, it'd be giving me a wedgie so bad I could smell my own ass." I turn, looking at the ass in question. Admittedly, it does look . . . smooth, I guess would be the word. But even as I shift from one foot to the other, it doesn't move at all. It looks unnatural.

Nature . . . that reminds me. "How do you pee in this thing, anyway? Am I supposed to go through the hell I just endured every time? In a public bathroom, or worse in this case, the bathroom of my in-laws-to-be?"

Britnay shakes her head, smiling like I'm ridiculous. "No, of course not." My relief is short-lived, though. "You pee before you get dressed and then when you get undressed. You just, you know, hold it in between."

Nana screeches. "That's not healthy! A girl will get an infection if she holds it that long. The things you young 'uns come up with, so unnecessary. Violet, go take that ridiculous contraption off and wear that dress the way God and my pasta dinners made you. Perfect."

Usually, I think Nana's overreacting and even overly dramatic, but in this case, I'm taking her advice to heart. I go back in the fitting room, wiggle out of the spandex contraption with a lot of difficulty, including some very unladylike grunts, and slip back into the red dress with just my usual bra and panty set on.

I turn to the side, examining my belly again. It's not flat, but it's not exactly round either. But if going au natural or going squeezed to death by a spandex boa constrictor are my choices, au natural it is.

"I think this is the one for me. Do you think the length is okay?" I ask, still worried about the amount of leg sticking out of the hem. I mean, Ross called me *Chicken Legs* for so many years that even now, knowing I'm worlds away from the twiggy pubescent I used to be, I'm still sensitive about my legs.

Britnay's assistant comes to the rescue. "Here, how about this?" He's holding a large patterned scarf, which he does some magician trick with and then ties it around my waist in a fluffy knot. It has the effect of an overskirt, flowing out behind me like a train. Britnay high-fives him and then adds a brooch pin to the center of the knot.

I look in the mirror and smile. "It's perfect. Classy but sassy, appropriate but creative. Thank you so much!"

Once everyone has made their dress selection, Britnay brings over shoes and jewelry to complete our looks. We look stunning, each and every one of us . . . from the neck down.

Estella claps. "*Bella*! But please tell me we can move on to the spa now. I'm ready to get pampered!"

I grin as I think that while she might not have been trying on dresses, she's been plenty pampered with champagne and the fancy brunch. But a facial and haircut do seem to be in order, so after changing back into our regular clothes and handing off our dresses to be delivered, we hit the spa.

CHAPTER 17

ROSS—SATURDAY—7 DAYS UNTIL THE WEDDING

I look out the window of the bedroom, high over the city below, which is full of activity. Cars jetting this way and that, people walking to destinations unknown, and tall buildings of glass that hide the chaos of work, even on a Saturday afternoon.

It's hard to believe that one week from today, I'll be getting married. The fact that I don't collapse into a ball of blubbering drunken nervousness speaks to just how far I've come already in the short time with Violet. I think about where I was a week ago —going out at night to random clubs, coming home alone, usually, but occasionally with women whose names I barely knew for one night of pleasure, and getting that ultimatum from Dad.

Now, in a blink of time, I spend my nights in bed with Violet, my days with thoughts of her running through my head, and my cock only hardens for her. For something that started out so fake, this feels so very real. And so very right.

I glance at the clock, putting a little fire in my pace. Violet should be back from her day of pampering any minute, and I need to be ready to go. I hope she had fun today. She certainly deserves it.

Not just because she works her ass off with her interior design work, her passion so readily apparent in her attention to

213

detail and the beautiful spaces she creates, but because this whole relationship has taken on a life of its own. And I know I'm not an easy man to be connected to. Tonight's gala is proof of that, and my primary hope is that we can get through the gauntlet of paparazzi unscathed. Though a very close second hope is that my family and Violet's family get along without bloodshed.

Family. Both a blessing and a curse.

Dad has still been distant and judgy, Mom has moved on to excited acceptance, Court seems resigned to my being my apparently asshole self, and Abi keeps giving me scouring looks as if she can sense the true progress Vi and I have made with each other and is thrilled by it.

Violet's family is over-the-moon blissful about us, zero concerns given to the speed of our courtship or that it came so hot on the heels of her breakup with Colin.

Her family is just that loving and supportive, their only wish to see her happy. Violet told me more about her mom and Nana and Papa over breakfast one day, and it'd only increased my respect for the entire Russo family. When a young and single Maria had gotten pregnant, her boyfriend had bailed, leaving not just her but the city, with no forwarding information. Alone and broke, she'd turned to her parents, and Nana and Papa had welcomed her back into their home, supporting Maria while she went to school and worked full-time and taking care of baby Violet. Those years only strengthened their bonds, so that even when Maria finished school and moved out into her own place with Violet, they got together frequently.

Somewhere in there is when Violet and Abi became friends, at dance class, of all places. I try to remember what they looked like, all gangly limbs and tight buns, but the memories are lost to time and too foggy. Because of Abi, Violet tagged along on a dozen different activities. She was able to get introduced to the right people, to get the right opportunities to show just how special she is.

And somehow, years later, here we are . . . about to get married.

I hear the front door open and then close as the click of heels across the foyer lands on my ears. She's home.

I pull my tuxedo jacket on as I walk out. "We need to go. Mom asked that we get there early—" My voice dies as I see her.

She's gorgeous in the deep red gown she's chosen for tonight. Its short and bright, both daring choices, but she looks confident and comfortable. Her dark hair cascades down her back in waves, and her long, shapely legs end in red high heels that show the arch of her elegant feet.

"Holy fuck, Violet," I stutter.

She grins and does a little walk in a circle, the patterned fabric of the overskirt flying out behind her like a cape. "You like?" she sasses.

I wolf whistle for her. "I fucking love it. Goddamn, I want to bend you over the table right now, fist those curls in my hand, and slip that skirt over your ass to get at you." Crude, but true, and Violet doesn't seem to mind, judging by the flush covering her cheeks now.

"Don't you dare mess me up. You have no idea how many people and how many hours it took to get me to look like this," she says lightly, and I can tell she had fun today. "You sure the short length is okay for the gala? The sales associate swore that it's seasonally appropriate, especially since the gala is an outside event. But . . ." she looks down, turning her leg back and forth. I can read her mind and hate the voice of doubt that I helped to put there with my thoughtless teasing when we were younger.

"It's perfect and you look stunning. An absolutely ravishing lady in red." Her sweet smile means more to me that her flush from my dirty talk . . .almost. Okay, maybe important in equal measures. But it's enough to make me sway toward my gentlemanly side, for now. When we get home, all bets are off and that dress will be on the floor.

But for now, I offer her my arm, which she takes elegantly. "Shall we?"

We take my Camaro to the mansion, pulling up a little early, but that's what Mom wanted. "When did you arrange for my family to arrive?"

"They'll be here soon," I remind her, thinking of the chauffeured limo I sent for them. I'm sure their whole block is going to be on their front porches, watching them leave this evening, and the image of Nana and Sofia waving to their neighbors like they're queens makes me smile.

The grounds of the mansion have been turned into a fantasy, with twinkling lights hung from the branches of the trees in Mom's manicured garden, round dining tables arranged in one area and lush couches for lounging set up on the rich, lush lawn.

The *piece de resistance*, however, has to be the flagstone patio, which has been transformed into a dance floor. It's surrounded by floodlights that light up the patio itself and even the façade of the mansion, bathing them in a colorful glow.

"It's beautiful," Violet says, looking around. "Really summery, but classy. Whoever did the decor really highlighted the best of the space, both the gardens and the mansion."

"Too bad we had to take down Abi's tree house," I reply, pointing to the left of the garden where an old maple used to stand before a lightning strike took it down three years ago. "I actually used it myself from time to time."

"Huh, and I thought I was hallucinating when I told Abi it smelled like stinky boy," Violet teases. "And it was a nice tree. We had a lot of really great sleepovers there."

Even though we're still early, there are still plenty of people here, early partygoers who represent the big money in the state. With them, of course, are plenty of media, with photographers and even a couple of TV crews set up to cover what is one of the biggest charity events of the year.

We make our way around, exchanging pleasantries, and I introduce Violet to everyone. So far, they seem pretty chill about her being my fiancée, though I see a few eagle-eyes notice her ring and raise an eyebrow. Well, metaphorically speaking. The truth is, I'm not sure many of these people, male or female, can move their foreheads enough to actually raise their brows anymore. But the same evaluating vibe is there. I suspect it would be more harshly judgmental if they knew the wedding was in one week, but no one asks us that, seeing it as improper and invitation-digging.

Finally, we find Abi, who has arrived early as instructed too. She's a bit of a rebel, but she knows when to fight her battles and when to acquiesce. Violet and her hug like they haven't seen each other in ages, though I know they saw each other two days ago.

I'm standing quietly by, listening to their girl talk when Karl comes up, dipping his head once. "Excuse me, sir, but your father would like to speak with you."

"Of course . . . excuse me, ladies," I tell them, giving Violet a peck on the cheek and whispering in her ear, "Relax, have fun. Trust me, after the champagne starts flowing, nobody's going to notice a damn thing." A saucy wink seems to put her at ease, and I trust that Abi won't leave her to the wolves.

I follow Karl into the house and up to Dad's study. The huge glass doors are open, and Dad stands on the balcony that overlooks the garden, looking pleased as he sips a gin. "Well, now, Ross, seems things are getting interesting."

I walk over to his side, following his sight line. A black limo is parked in the drive, the driver helping Violet's family exit. Two young women, who must be part of the triplets Vi told me about, look around in awe, clutching each other's hands. Next comes Maria, and then Sofia and Nana get out last, the driver smiling and laughing at something Sofia says. Honestly, there's no telling what just came out of her mouth to have an experienced never-show-a-reaction driver behaving so . . . normally.

Nana turns back, ducking into the limousine, and returns with a foil-covered dish before pinching the driver's cheek. He waves and walks back around, getting in to pull away.

"Is that . . . did they . . . bring food to a catered affair?" Dad asks with a soft laugh. But as Karl runs up to greet the group of ladies, offering to take the dish, Dad turns to me. "Ross, tonight is important. To your mother and to the company." I can feel the heat of his embarrassment, the fear that the Russos are going to make him look bad.

I smile wryly. "For the people you're raising money for? Because let's be real. They're just the poster children for the real purpose of this party—to see and be seen, to negotiate back room deals and rub elbows with other people just like you. There's just enough humanity left in that crowd out there to want a sad-eyed kid as the bow on top so you don't seem like heartless Scrooges rolling around in your money."

The muscle under Dad's eye ticks. "You make it sound as if you're not one of us. As if you didn't grow up right here with this privilege. At least we're trying to make a difference in the world, yes, by hobnobbing with the wealthy, but that's how change happens on a large scale. It costs money, Ross. And if money offends your delicate sensibilities, when was the last time you made a difference on a personal level? I have three MBA candidates I'm mentoring this year through the university, and your mother reads at the homeless shelter four times a month." Dad shakes his head, utterly disappointed . . . in me.

But he's not done. The hits keep coming. "This is what I was saying. You're nothing but an entitled brat who's stomping his foot at any rules or expectations outside the boardroom, no matter how reasonable they may be. But this time, you're going to hurt a lovely young woman in the process. Violet doesn't deserve this, Son. She deserves better than to be used."

I gape, incredulous.

It's not that Dad doesn't believe that this is real, not because of the speed or convenient timing. It's because he thinks I'm not worthy of Violet, that she's too good for me and could never actually love me. In a lot of ways, he's one hundred percent right. She deserves the sun and the moon and everything she could ever wish for. But for my own father to say that I'm lacking somehow stings more than I would've ever thought it would.

"I love her, Dad. And I will do everything in my power to provide anything and everything she could ever need or want." The words ring true, even to my own ears and heart, which doesn't surprise me in the least.

He shakes his head like I'm missing the point, and I realize he thinks I intend to buy Violet's affection. He couldn't be more wrong. She isn't with me for the money, is maybe the only woman who ever wasn't, but for her own reasons.

Reasons that are changing, growing, morphing into something different, better. Just like my reasons . . . just like me.

But he doesn't see that. Not yet. But I'll show him and show Violet. Most importantly, I'll show myself just how much I can grow.

I never considered myself a brat, even though my younger days were plagued by pranks and a devil-may-care attitude. But even with everything I've been given, I have worked hard to get to where I am. Maybe I just played a little too hard too, I realize. Could Dad's ultimatum be for my own good like Courtney said? A way to force me to grow up personally, not just professionally?

That idea sits uncomfortably on my shoulders, weighing me down and reframing so much of my childhood, my adulthood, my life.

"I need to go back to Violet. I'll see you at the party," I say neutrally, not belying any of the swirling thoughts racing through my head. Dad's a shark, and if he thinks for one second that he's making headway in whatever this battle is between us, he'll go in for the kill to drive his point home. To be honest, I think I need to do a little self-reflection instead, not be beaten over the head with his take on my successes and failures.

Dad takes a sip of his gin. "Don't . . ."

But I'm already out the door, not wanting to hear the rest of his decree. Don't embarrass him? Don't hurt Violet? Don't be an immature asshole? All of the above?

I swear, I'll show him . . . what?

What do I want to show him? Because the truth is that Dad's right. This engagement's a sham. I never would've done this if he hadn't forced my hand. And Violet never would've dated me, much less planned to marry me, if she didn't have a time clock pushing her pace. She's doing this out of love, as weird as it is.

But that's the thing. Dad doesn't even know why Violet's doing this, but he already knows what I'm just discovering. Her heart's beautiful, as beautiful as anything I've ever encountered in my life.

I'm tempted to just load everyone back into the limo and leave, but when I reach Violet's side again, she's smiling. "Nana's over the moon. The band leader here knows Sinatra. She's made him promise . . . hey, what's wrong?"

There must still be something in my eyes, but I shake my head, forcing myself to smile. There's no way that I'm going to let Violet know the comments my father just made about me and her. "Nothing. Just Dad had some business news. Nothing I can do about it until Monday, though."

"Honey!" Mom says, her smile lighting up her face as she comes up. Dad's words put a pall over her easy delight, though, making me question whether she thinks Violet's too good for me too. Maybe she's just this happy because she thinks Vi will finally get me to grow up. "Maria," she says when she exchanges kisses with Violet's mom, "it really has been too long. You look . . . you're going to make a few trophy wives jealous tonight!"

"Oh, hush," Maria says, still grinning. "Just make sure you only point me to the single men, okay?"

"Too bad you can't show off your *torta*," Sofia interjects, grinning. "Best way to a man's heart is to let him nibble your pie!"

"Uhh . . . excuse me?" Mom says while I try not to laugh.

Leave it to Sofia's blunt craziness to get me out of my head and into the moment. There will be time enough for self-recriminations later. For now, I need to remember that we are midshow, the flashes of cameras reminding me that everyone's watching.

"Mom, this is Violet's Aunt Sofia," I say, introducing the two. "She'll tell it to you like it is, and she's one of the best cooks I've ever met."

"Knew Violet picked right," Sofia says, giving me an almost starry-eyed smile. "Ross, if I were forty years younger—"

"You'd still be too old for him!" Nana teases, making everyone laugh.

Mom shows us to our table before someone calls her away for more duties. Pretty soon, all the guests have arrived and dinner is served. I'm encouraged when Mom, Abigail, and

Courtney all join us at the same table, although when Dad joins us, his look is best described as stony.

"They got Taylor Richardson to speak this year," I tell everyone for distraction, nodding toward the VIP table nearby, where the city's most famous face sits next to the lieutenant governor and his wife.

Taylor gets up to make a speech, and while it's cookie-cutter, pretty much fitting any charity event from ASPCA to the YMCA, he delivers it well, and there's plenty of applause when he's done.

"You know, Morgan, you have quite the son," Nana says, trying yet again to strike up a conversation with Dad. Unfortunately for her, most of his replies have been grunts or one-word answers, to the point he's damn near come off as a caveman. "He's been so kind. And the children he and Violet will have . . . oh, my, you're going to have to hire security to keep them in line and safe. Did Violet tell you that twins and triplets run in the family?" She winks and laughs, like she's letting us in on a big family secret.

Violet half chokes on her white wine, spraying her plate a little as she tries to control herself. "Nana, it's a bit early for that talk, don't you think?"

Dad's eyes cut to me, hot fire burning in their depths. Once upon a time, that look would've terrified me, gotten me to stop doing just about anything in my desire to please him. Now, I throw my arm over the back of Violet's chair and pull her closer to me. He grunts, which Nana takes as a response to her joke.

The band strikes up a tune, and I decide maybe a little dancing is just what we need. It's a lot better than encouraging them to keep on about me and Violet making babies.

"I'll save mine until they play Sinatra," Nana says when I offer her my hand. "Go on, now. Show your woman there some fun."

I nod, holding my hand out to Violet, who takes it almost shyly. I chuckle a little when a couple of young men come over to ask Vanessa and Marissa for dances, but I lose track as I pull Violet into my arms and we start to move.

I make a show of it, doing my best to pull up everything that I can remember from the social dancing classes Mom insisted I take in junior high school, what I can think of from being forced to watch *DWTS* with Abi, and whatever my mind can come up with to distract Violet from the tension in the air.

I twirl her, I swing her, and we practically parade around the dance floor as the bandleader plays some up-tempo jazzy music, downshifting only when I've got Violet leaned back, her hair thrown back and her body stretched out in my arms. "Now that's how you finish a dance," I say against the skin of her neck before pressing a soft kiss there to test her pulse. It's beating almost as fast as mine.

"Whoa," Violet says, smiling and a bit hazy-eyed as I straighten her up and pull her closer for a slower song, a sultry instrumental version of *Waiting For A Girl Like You* by Foreigner. "Look at you with all the moves."

I drop my voice, whispering hotly in her ear. "I'll show you some moves when we get home." Flirting with her is easy, comfortable ground, and desire works its way through me in a flash.

Violet chuckles ruefully. "Even if it means twins? Or triplets?"

"Let them enjoy their fantasy. I've got a few of my own, too," I tell her, remembering my earlier plans to lean her over the dining table in this dress. "They'll talk either way."

"Except for your dad," Violet answers, biting her lip. My flirtiness drops away as she says, "The way he was with my family . . . it was damn near hostile."

"I know, and I'm sorry. I swear it's not about them, though. It's me," I try to explain. But Violet looks unconvinced.

"Baby girl, mind if I cut in?" Maria asks her daughter. "You know, for some practice for the reception?"

"Of course, Mom," Violet says. "I think I need a drink, anyway."

Maria and I start to dance, and as we do, she gives me a smile. "You're doing pretty well, *amico*."

"Friends now, are we?" I tease. "Should I start calling you *Madre*?"

"Only if you want my high heel in your butt," Maria says with a laugh. "But seriously . . . I'm no fool, Ross. I can see your father doesn't approve. I got that look a lot of times after I got pregnant, people thinking they could judge me when they couldn't."

These Russo women are killing me tonight with their perceptiveness.

I repeat the same thing I just told Violet. "It's not about you or Violet. It's about me. Dad doesn't think *I'm* good enough for *her*, not the other way around."

It's hard to say, and probably a stupid thing to say to your future-mother-in-law, but it seems fitting to tell her the truth about this, if nothing else.

Maria purses her lips, looking at me in surprise, and then her eyes glance over to where my dad and mom are swaying on the floor. When she looks back at me, I feel like a guilty man about to hear his sentence from the harshest judge in the county. "I had my doubts. It was so fast, and I remember her rants about that 'annoying boy'. But I see the way you look at Violet and the way she looks at you. For her to find love and be happy is all I've ever wanted for my daughter, Ross. And I believe you are the right man for her. It's all going to be okay. Eventually, he will see what I do."

"Thanks, Maria."

The dance ends, and Maria steps back, punching me in the chest and grinning. "But that's for calling her Chicken Legs for all those years."

There's a tapping at the microphone, and I look up to see Mom and Dad at the main podium with the lieutenant governor's wife, Delilah, who's the MC tonight. "I hate to interrupt the dancing, folks," she says, grinning the newscasters' smile that got her on cable news commentary quite a lot in her pre-lady-who-lunches days, "but I just had such amazing news."

"I think we should have a seat," Maria says, looking around at the clearing floor, and I nod. We head back to the table where

Violet's already waiting, and I sit down next to her, taking her hand and holding it on my thigh.

"As most of you know, this is Morgan and Kimberly Andrews," Delilah continues, "our hosts tonight. But in addition to offering their lovely manor for tonight's festivities, Morgan just approached me and said he's making a hundred-thousand-dollar donation to the Gala Fund!"

The applause is huge, and even I'm shocked enough to clap as people rise to their feet for a standing ovation and Dad is passed the microphone. "Thank you, Delilah," Dad says, his most professional smile on his face. "Honestly, I spent all night feeling the need to say thank you. This organization does such great work for our community, and I'm so proud to be a part of that."

His eyes find mine in the crowd. "Can I let you in on a secret confession as well?" Delilah nods like a bobblehead, and I swear she leans forward far enough that she's in danger of faceplanting. Dad takes Mom's hand and she smiles. "I had an ulterior motive for wanting the microphone for a moment tonight. You see, my oldest child, my only son, recently got engaged, and their time-line didn't allow for the usual engagement announcements, wedding showers, and whatnot. So . . . surprise, multi-purpose party! Seriously, though, we just wanted to brag for a moment."

The applause sounds out again, smaller this time, but interested eyes turn to me and Violet before going back to Dad.

What is he doing? Why is he calling me out like this?

"We weren't sure he was ever going to grow up," Dad says lightly, and chuckles sprinkle through the garden. "But the power of a good woman is a miraculous thing. Welcome to the family, Violet. He's your problem now." Dad raises his glass with a big smile, and everyone cheers, thinking the toast is meant to be a silly roast between a loving father and son.

I don't realize how hard I'm clenching Violet's hand until she lays her other hand over mine and taps me. I let her hand go abruptly, and we pick up our glasses, saluting with fake smiles, and then drink. Violet takes a small sip. I toss the whole thing back in one go, even though it's champagne.

"You okay?" she asks quietly.

"Yeah, just unexpected," I say in the understatement of the century. "I'm not sure what his play is with that, but there's a reason. There's always a reason."

Delilah takes the microphone back and raises her glass our way. "Congratulations, Ross and Violet."

Looking back over the audience, she confides, "Kimberly spilled the beans to me about the upcoming nuptials and the quick timeline, and I felt called to help you two have the wedding day of your dreams. As many of you know, I'm the chairperson for the City Philharmonic, who have played so beautifully this evening." She holds up a hand, gesturing to the group of strings players off to the side of the dining area, and everyone claps politely. "So I called in a favor or two, and my husband, John, and I would like to offer a wedding gift to the bride and groom. We've secured a strings ensemble to play at your wedding." Delilah is so pleased with herself that she grins hugely, so big and open-mouthed that I can see her back teeth.

The crowd gasps, and I can sense Violet's jerk of response.

What? Oh, shit, that's so nice, but so overwhelmingly not needed. And what are we talking, here? Like a small quartet or the whole string section of the City Philharmonic?

But Delilah's not done. "I also talked to my friends at KMBP." She pauses dramatically to let everyone remember her days on the daily news. "And they offered a crew to do your videography. Personal, of course, not for the news."

"Seriously? A news crew following us around all day?" Violet sounds as horrified as I feel.

But somehow, I stand and pull her up beside me, a fake smile plastered on my face because I've been trained my whole life for weird shit like this and know that mission one is to save face gracefully. I squeeze Violet's hand until she smiles too. "My goodness, Delilah. That is so generous." I want to refuse it. Fuck, how can I get out of this? One look at Dad tells me the bottom line on the situation and I straighten my spine. "Thank you so much. We'd be delighted to accept."

CHAPTER 18

"*And in society news over the weekend, the normally mundane Community Freedom Gala was shaken up last night as, apparently, love was in the air in addition to charitable goodwill.*"

The video then cuts to Ross and me dancing as the reporter does a voiceover.

"*That's right, ladies. Playboy bachelor, Ross Andrews, is apparently off the market. Aww.*" *Her sadness and smile are both as fake as her bottle-blonde hair.* "*He's been snatched up by up and coming local interior designer, Violet Russo, according to Morgan Andrews, the father of the groom-to-be. It seems everyone was feeling the love, too. Check out the generous support Mr. Andrews, Lieutenant Governor John Border, and Mrs. Delilah Border gave at the evening's festivities.*"

The video cuts again to clips of Morgan's donation to the Gala Fund, and the offer for the orchestra and camera crew, before cutting back to the anchor in the studio. "*So with the nuptials less than a week away, many, many eyes will be watching to see if this Cinderella story really can have a happily ever after.*"

I hit the *Pause* button on my laptop and close the clip. I've seen it before. It premiered on the *Sunday Local Wrap-Up* first thing this morning, and Ross's Google alert had notified him that his name was in the press again, but it seems that the clip's gone a little viral since someone dubbed *I Had The Time Of My Life* from *Dirty Dancing* over it.

Archie sent it to me an hour ago, excitedly proclaiming that it had ten thousand views. The counter in the corner says it's at more than triple that now, though more than a handful of those views are mine.

The bathroom door opens, and a naked Ross comes swaggering back into the bedroom "Vi, stop torturing yourself and don't watch it again."

Firstly, he looks good. Downright lickable, in fact. But I can't even focus on the amazing specimen of man in front of me because . . .

Secondly, our engagement and rush-order wedding are splashed all over the news, we've got a who-knows-how-big orchestra slated to play, a news crew coming, my cousins are singing, more family showing up any day now, and I don't have a dress.

Oh, yeah, and it's all *fake*.

"What are we going to do?" I say, shaking my head. "I thought this would be easy, just a quiet ceremony and we'd be all set. This is nuts." My eyes bore into him. He has to see that, right? Maybe we should cancel it? But that would do more harm than good at this point, I think.

"Violet, have you met your family? I mean, really? You thought you were going to have some quiet little countryside wedding, and it'd all be idyllic and sweet. And most importantly, under your control." His tone is even, but the sarcasm is heavily implied and virtually dripping from his raised brows.

I freeze. God, I hate that he knows me so well sometimes. True confession—I love it at other times. This is not one of those times. Right now, I want to pretend that this over-the-top craziness is all someone else's fault and that something, anything, can be done about it.

I cross my arms but glare when Ross looks newly intrigued at the way it pushes my breasts up. I'm as naked as Ross is, but we'd collapsed last night when we got home, both of us quietly letting the wild roller coaster of the evening play out on repeat in our minds.

Remembering one of the earlier oddities of the evening, I ask him, "What was really up with your dad? I know it wasn't a work thing he wanted to talk to you about. It was about us, wasn't it? Did you know he was going to make that speech?"

Ross shakes his head and sits down on the side of the bed. His elbows on his knees, he buries his hands into his hair and growls. "No, I definitely did not know he was planning that. Maybe I should've seen it coming, though? He definitely increased the pressure on us and put a big old target on our backs with the press. Not sure how he thinks that's going to play out in his favor."

I'm quiet, just waiting for Ross to decide whether he wants to tell me about his private conversation with his dad. I know it must've been important or it wouldn't still be eating at him.

After a long minute where I can virtually see his mind tracing steps and possible outcomes, I almost tease him about calling me a control freak. But before I can say a word, he finally speaks. "He doesn't think I'm good enough for you."

It takes a moment for the words to sink in. "You mean he doesn't think I'm good enough for you," I say, making the obvious correction.

Ross huffs a humorless laugh, "No, really. He basically told me that you've always been a lovely girl, hardworking and honest, and that he and Mom love you. I, on the other hand, am an immature asshole of a brat who fucks up everything in my personal life to the point where my only redeeming quality is my work. He basically said that I had to be paying you or black-mailing you or something because there's no way you'd actually like me, much less love me, just for me."

My jaw drops. That's not at all what I was expecting to hear.

I scoot over to sit behind Ross, my butt on my heels with my legs bent beneath me. I scratch lazy circles along his back, tracing each muscle. "I am so sorry. That's ridiculous."

He shudders beneath my hands. "It was definitely not the conversation I was expecting to have with him."

"What did he say? Like word for word. Maybe you misunderstood or something? Because the obvious outlier here is me, not you. I mean, my family brought a cheesecake to a catered gala affair, and then Sofia basically propositioned the lieutenant governor."

Ross looks at me, horror and humor in equal measure. "She did not."

I nod vehemently, "Oh, yes, she did. Told him he was 'quite handsome for a man of his age' and then offered to teach him a few things she'd bet he's never tried. When he politely declined, she tried to play it off that she was going to teach him pinochle, but we all know she's shit for card games."

"Oh, my God, how did I miss that? I needed that laugh last night." He starts to chuckle a little. "Hell, I need that laugh now."

I laugh too, hesitantly, before dipping my toe into the deep water of his relationship with his dad. "Look, Ross, I don't know what it is your dad wants from you or sees in you, but to me, you're a . . ." I pause, narrowing my eyes at him, "I want you to know how much it pains me to say this, but you're a . . . good guy."

His smile is soft, just one corner of his lips, really, but it feels like it's an important step so I keep confessing.

"Once upon a time, you were a jerk. An immature asshole of a brat, as you said — "

He interrupts, rolling his eyes and shoving me back toward the pillows. "Oh, please, stop with the flattery."

I smirk, returning that cocky one he so likes to toss my way. "Seriously, we were both little shits to each other. But I think we've both grown up, moved past a lot of that. You're a good man, doing amazing things at work, taking care of your family legacy, and doing a ridiculously kind thing for me with this wedding. A selfish bastard wouldn't go this far for someone, especially not someone you didn't even really like, unless you're either a masochist, a brilliant strategist who's going to do something awful like leave me at the altar, or an actual good person. I think it's the last one, myself."

He's quiet for a minute, letting my words sink in. I hope they help because I mean them. Once upon a time, I both hated and loved Ross in equal measure. He was the big shot on campus to my invisible nothingness, and I railed against him because I doubted myself. Plus, it was fun.

But we're both different people now, not entirely, but enough has changed that there's no hate in the equation any longer.

"Do you remember homecoming my senior year?" he says quietly.

I nod slowly, the memories coming back, though I'm not sure what they have to do with our current conversation. But if he needs to bob and weave to avoid the deep talk, I can follow. "Yeah, that was mine and Abi's freshman year. We won because you got the game-winning touchdown."

"Do you remember what I bought you and Abi that night?" he says, looking at me from the side of his eye.

"Chicken, of course," I answer with an eyeroll. "I was pissed as hell because you came into the after-party, dragged Abi and me out, and took us to dinner, but it was adding insult to injury with the chicken legs dig. Our reputation never recovered from being the babies physically removed from that party, I'll have you know." I kick out at him, poking his hard bicep with a red-painted toe. "Asshole." But there's no venom in the word.

He grabs my foot and begins to massage it lightly. I can't help but groan, my emotions going crazy. On one hand, the old memories of him ruining my life piss me off, but on the other hand, he's doing amazing things to the arch of my foot, which is sore from those heels last night.

"Before that, at the game. It was raining, and you and Abi were sitting in the fresh meat section of the stands with all the other freshmen, looking like drowned kittens. And we were getting our asses kicked. Down three touchdowns before the rain stopped, half the stands empty because no one believed we could come back from that and they weren't willing to sit in the downpour to find out. But as I jogged out for the second half, I heard something—"

I smile, repeating what I'd said on that night so long ago. "Hey, Ogre, you'd better get your butt in gear and win this

231

game, or I'm gonna stick my Kentucky fried foot up your ass!" I laugh at the memory. "Oh, God, Abi dared me to insult you, said it would fire you up. I got in so much trouble from old Mrs. Henderson for cussing at the game. 'That language does not befit a young lady, Miss Russo!' she told me."

"Well, Abi was right. It pissed me off and fired me up. It was ugly, and I hurt for three days after that game with all the hard hits I had to take, all the tackles I had to smash through, but we won. Although to be honest, that last two-point conversion shouldn't have counted. I hit the turf at the one-yard line and slid into the endzone on my chest and facemask."

I think back, laughing when the memory surfaces. "I remember. You were running around the outside and jumped, and then . . . sploosh!" I say, using my hands to imitate the huge spray that I remember seeing. "But when you got up . . . you were the winner."

He smiles. "We were. And then I went to the after party. People were clapping me on the back and taking pictures with me. It was a riot. Until I overheard a couple of guys talking about you and Abi." His jaw clenches and his eyes narrow as if it's happening right now, not years ago. "The football team all knew you two were off-limits, but I guess word hadn't spread all over yet. So I set those guys right, made sure the whole damn school knew not to mess with you, that only I could do that. And then I got both of you out of there. It was mostly luck that KFC was the closest place open that late." He shrugs.

Something clicks into focus that I never knew was blurry. "You were looking out for us even then. You were taking care of me," I say, choking. "I didn't realize, just thought you were being your usual overbearing, chest-thumping, 'little girls do what I say', asshole self. It honestly never occurred to me that you were . . . nice back then. I thought I was just annoying and weak, an easy target."

His face falls. "Oh, no, not at all, Vi. I think that's why I gave you such a hard time, because you were the only one strong enough to give it back to me. Everyone else would just follow me around like a puppy, guys and girls both, but not you. Not Violet

Antonia Carlotta Russo. You pushed me, challenged me, dared me at every opportunity, and I secretly loved it. You were never invisible to me. I just didn't know what to do about it, any of it." He closes his eyes like he's remembering everything so differently now too. "That night, at homecoming, there was a scout there. How I played in that second quarter is what got me the university offer. Your threatening to kick my ass got me into the college of my dreams."

Ho-lee shit. What?

I never knew that. I guess I just figured Ross was a sure-fire admission to the college of his choice based on his last name, and doesn't that make the younger me a catty bitch for thinking that way? I know he got great grades and was a stellar football player, but I never dreamed he would've been nervous about being good enough to get that invitation to the next step.

"I had no idea, Ross. I'm just glad it all worked out, I guess," I say, not having more words to describe how this feels.

"We're going to have to be tough to get through this. Just like that homecoming game and high school. You, as Little Ms. Badass, fierce enough to stand up to even an asshole like me. And me, as a grown-up who handles the drama with grace and elegance. I'll admit, I like your chances better than mine, so you're going to have to help me here."

I take his hand. "We'll get through this together. We can do it."

He leans over me, pressing one fist to the mattress by my hip and caging me in. "Sealed with a kiss," he says softly before pressing his lips to mine. As the kiss heats, he says in stilted words, "Thank you for not hating me back then, and thank you for helping me now."

I return the words. "Thank you for helping me. But to be clear, I did hate you just a little in high school." I hold my finger and thumb up an inch apart with a flirty smile. "But I thought you hated me too."

But the sentiment is lost to the fire as everything we've been through to get to this point fades away—all the silly insults, all the ridiculous pranks, all the life we've lived apart, all the promises we've made together.

"Never," Ross growls against the tender skin of my neck.

I turn my head, giving him better access. "So since we're playing true confessions, I have one too."

"Later," he says, not stopping his progress toward my bare breast.

"You'll want to hear this one, I think. You see, I didn't always hate you. I did have a bit of a crush on you . . . sometimes. And teenage me heard things about you from Abi, and then the gossip from every girl in the school as they gushed over the *gorgeous* Ross Andrews." I can feel the lift of his lips as he smiles, and even though I can't see it, I know it's his cocky grin.

"One of the girls, Savannah DeMiles, said she gave you a blowjob under the bleachers after a game. She described it in rather intimate detail. To my innocent mind, I was stockpiling the details away like a tips and tricks to-do list." I drop my voice down, making it slow and sultry and full of heated promise.

Ross looks up, a question in his eyes. "What are you saying?"

I bite my lip and look at him hungrily. "Stand up."

He moves curiously but quickly, standing with his feet spread wide and his arms at his sides beside the bed. I climb out too, dropping to my knees in front of him. "Violet?" he says, but his voice sounds choked.

I look up at him through my lashes. "Back then, I imagined it was me under the bleachers, your cock in my mouth and your hands in my hair, guiding and taking me. I imagined you losing control because of little old me. Back then, I was nervous and figured I could spit it out discretely so it wouldn't be weird. But now, when you come, I want to swallow you. I want it all . . . all of you."

"Fuck, Violet,' he says, nodding, though I don't think he even realizes he's doing it.

I lay a sweet kiss, soft as a butterfly's kiss, to his crown, and he hisses as his hips surge forward. I lick a swirl of a loop around the mushroom head and murmur appreciatively, "I can't believe I got all this inside me. Finally, Ross Andrews fucked me, Violet

Russo." It may have happened within the last week, hell, within the last days, but I'm talking about who we used to be. Back then, I don't think either of us would've ever predicted this degree of chemistry between us. Maybe in high school, we wouldn't have even had chemistry, too young and not ready for whatever this is.

I'm still not sure of what label to slap on this because we've moved well beyond fuck buddies and no strings attached, and I know there's something bigger growing in my heart, but I'm not sure Ross is feeling that at all. And with everything on the line, I won't risk asking. But this right here, the fireworks that ignite between us, doesn't feel like a gamble at all because this part, at least, is a certainty.

Ross chuckles a bit at my disbelieving brag at being one of his conquests, but it turns into a gaspy moan of pleasure as I swallow him inch by inch. I wrap my fist around the base of his shaft, pumping him with my hand as I suck his cock in and out of my mouth, worshipping him but also controlling this sexy man with my power.

He slides his hands into my hair, gripping but not forcing me. No, he lets me take him, drive him wild, and I delight in the way he loses control, his hips starting to thrust gently, helping me work him.

"Mmm . . . that's it, honey. Your mouth feels so good. Reach down. Play with yourself for me. I want to see you on your knees, coming apart as you suck me down." His voice is gravelly, the image he paints powerful.

I whimper around him in answer, spreading my knees and sliding my middle finger through my folds to gather the wetness there. I hold my hand up for him, and he leans forward to suck my finger clean, his tongue swirling over my finger mimicking what I'm doing to his cock.

My fingers and my mouth move together as I bob up and down on Ross's cock and stroke between my lips and over my clit.

"I can't," he groans. His fingers tighten in my hair, holding me still as he takes over and starts to fuck my mouth. He thrusts deeper and deeper, edging into my throat as I slide first one, then two fingers in my molten pussy. He's powerful but restrained, our eyes locked on each other the whole time.

I moan around him as a mini-orgasm, a precursor of what's to come, sweeps through me, and he groans at the vibration, gifting my tongue with a sweet dollop of his precum.

"You sure?" he grits out, and I suck harder, my fingers a blur across my pussy.

He plunges hard into me, and any thoughts, doubts, or words I have are obliterated as he shatters me. I gasp and spasm around him, my whole body quivering as I rise up to get more and more of him.

He freezes deep in my throat, and I feel the hot jets as he comes with a bellow. I swallow reflexively, not wanting to lose a drop, but there's no risk of that because Ross holds me there, filled with him to the point I can't even breathe.

But for this quick moment, at least, it feels like he's all I need. Oxygen be damned. The wedding be fucked. Our families and past are meaningless. It all washes away, and all I can feel is . . . Ross.

I wanted him, and now I have him.

I need him, and he's given himself to me and keeps giving more and more.

I can't name it, am scared to, honestly, but I feel it.

I sag to the floor, leaning into his touch as he cups my face. His thumb runs over my lips and I press a kiss to the pad. "We're in this together, Vi. I swear, we'll take care of everything and we're going to pull this off. I promise."

I nod, taking his hand and placing it on my breast, over my heart. "I know. Together." It's all I can give him because he's got all of me, including my heart. I just hope he'll protect that too.

Sassy to a fault, I look up once more. "So, better than Savannah DeMiles?"

Ross laughs. "I don't even know who that is, but I can tell you I never got a blowjob under the bleachers. Not once."

My bottom lip pouts out. "Well, hell, there went my fantasy."

Ross flashes me that cocky smile I love now, and I get ready for the zinger. "Too bad for you, because I just had one of mine come true. One I didn't even know I had, but I will never forget what we just did."

Sweet, so very sweet. But also, he's reminding me that whatever this is, it has an expiration date and then all we'll have are these memories. And my heart cracks just a little.

Stupid, silly heart and stupid, silly girl, I chastise myself.

CHAPTER 19

ROSS—MONDAY—5 DAYS UNTIL THE
WEDDING

"*S*o, what machinations are you up to now, dear sister? How scared should I be here?" I ask Abi. She called Kaede yesterday, on his day off, he'd reminded me, and had him add an appointment with the tailor to this morning's schedule. "You know I have a tuxedo already and I need to get into the office."

She claps, the smile on her face bordering maniacal. "I know, but that one is black. So outdated."

My brows dart together. "Outdated? More like classic, I think." I look to Kaede to back me up, but he throws his hands wide and shakes his head, communicating quite clearly that I'm on my own with my crazy sister and her even crazier plans.

"No," she says simply.

Deciding it's better to hear her out before saying no, which I will be doing, I give her the floor. "All right, Sis. Whatcha got in mind?"

She paces as Kaede and I sit, taking full advantage of the dramatics she's prone to as she paints a picture for us less creatively gifted people.

"You saw the invitations? Peach and white, and Vi's dress will be white, obviously. I've been working my magic with the flowers" —she wiggles her fingers in front of our faces— "and that's when it hit me. What goes perfect with that pale peachy-blush color?"

Kaede and I glance at each other and shrug. Abi rolls her eyes at our boorishness. "Green," she declares, as if it's the obvious answer.

"Green," I repeat dully. "Okay, so like some greenery or something mixed in with the flowers? I think Vi would be fine with that, but you should probably just ask her." I start to stand, thinking my work here is done, but I sit back down slowly when Abi glares daggers at me.

Shit, she's really good at that. Must've learned from Dad.

"For the tuxedos."

My jaw drops. "Uhm, what? You want me to wear a green tuxedo?" I'm already shaking my head. "No way, nope, nuh-uh," I say, just to make sure my thoughts on the matter are clear.

Abi's visual daggers get bigger, sharper. She's basically tossing out eye-swords at me now, and Kaede crosses his legs, protecting his family jewels in case he's collateral damage.

"Mason, we're ready for you now," Abi calls out, ignoring my protests completely. I love my sister, but sometimes, she's a real . . . something I would never call her and live to speak again.

Mason has been our family tailor for about ten years. He's young for the industry, only in his mid-forties, but he's skilled and his work is impeccable. "Would you like to see the fabric choices now?" he asks politely.

"No," I answer.

"Yes," Abi answers at the same time.

Mason's eyes jump from mine to Abi as he tries to decide who the high-ranking person is. I'd love to say it's me, as the oldest and only brother. However, I'm quite certain it's Abi, though I'd die before admitting to anyone, most of all, her.

"Perhaps if you told him your vision?" Mason says to Abi gently.

She rolls her eyes. "Why are you making this difficult, Ross? Show up and look pretty, that's all I'm asking." I don't bother to tell her that if I told her that, she'd chop my balls off and fricassee them before feeding them to her dog. She doesn't even have a dog, but she'd get one just to torture me.

I raise one eyebrow and she relents. "Fine. Picture this . . . you and Kaede in tuxedos of the deepest, darkest green with white shirts and black shoes. Your choice of matte or patent," she says, as if that's a big concession on her part. "Your ties will be a floral pattern on a peach background. My dress is peach chiffon and Archie's suit is peach too. We told Vi that he was wearing a black shirt under his suit, but instead, he's going to wear one that's the same dark green as your tuxedos. The archway over the ceremony space will be full of lush greenery, blushy peach roses, and white baby's breath. It'll be elegant and lavish but simple because the rich colors will be so enchanting."

I have basically no idea what Abi just said, but she's excited about it. "You're sure Violet wants this? It's not your dream wedding, it's hers?" Abi nods but looks insulted that I even asked.

Kaede holds up his phone. "I texted Archie and he said he's in. Apparently, this little scheme is both his and Abi's this time." He lowers his voice so only I can hear. "She's branching out, man. Getting minions. We should take her head while she's still weak, before she takes over the world. Muahaha."

He's probably right. But I can't kill my sister until after the wedding, even if she is turning into a brilliantly evil 'villain'. For now, we need her, and if green tuxedos are what Vi would want, then green tuxedoes, it is.

"Okay, I guess we're in," I answer for both Kaede and myself.

Mason nods, gesturing to the platform for me to stand for measurements. "If you would, Ross."

I step up and Mason gets to work, efficient and graceful as he stretches his tape measure from my waist to the floor, talking the whole time in reassuring tones about having the custom pieces completed in plenty of time for a customer like me. Pretty sure it's not me, per se, but rather my last name and the media coverage his work is going to get, but whatever makes it happen is fine by me.

"Oh, just one more thing," Abi says, clicking away on her phone. She doesn't even glance up as she drops a bomb. "Don't tell Violet. It's a surprise."

I chuckle, and Mason 'accidentally' sticks me with a pin. "Be still, please."

"Abi, I can't *not* tell her. It's our wedding, for fuck's sake."

"This is a good surprise, Ross. She told me I had free reign with the flowers, and everything else is based on those. Don't stress her out any more than she already is. Do you know she still doesn't have a dress? The wedding is in five days!" Her voice pitches a little high at the end, scaring all three of the men in the room.

Kaede begs me with his eyes to go along and save us from the impending explosion of a pissed-off Abigail Andrews.

I'm not sure about this, but Abi does have a point. Violet has so much on her plate, and it's not like the color of my tuxedo is some major thing. All eyes are going to be on her, the beautiful bride. I'll just show up and look pretty, as Abi said.

"Okay, we won't tell Violet."

Abi nods and makes a few clicks on her phone.

"Next order of business, your groomsmen."

I look to Kaede, who holds his hands wide again, his eyes telling me he's innocent of whatever shit Abi is about to say he did. 'Fraidy cat asshole, scared of my sister. "What about him?"

"He's fine. I mean that Violet has both me and Archie standing up, and you only have Kaede. No offense, but you need more. Who else do you want to stand with you so that it's even?"

I quickly flip through college buddies and work friends in my head. I even consider that once upon a time, I'd dreamed of having my dad stand up with me when I finally got married. That's definitely not happening.

I shrug. "I don't know. It's pretty last-minute to hit up some guy from college, right?" I hold my hand up to my ear, mimicking a phone. "Hey, buddy, haven't seen you in years. Wanna be a groomsman?"

Mason snorts. "You'd be surprised. I've heard worse."

Abi smiles that grin that tells me she's already worked out the solution to this too and was just baby stepping me to it. "Who?"

"Courtney! It's perfect! Me and Archie on one side and Kaede and Courtney on the other. It'll look balanced, and really, she's your next best friend . . . after Kaede, me, and Violet, of course."

I twist my lips, "Is that weird to have my sister as a grooms-man? I mean, groomswoman? I mean, groomsperson?" I shake my head, not knowing the proper term but figuring it doesn't matter right now.

"Uh, no weirder than the rest of this circus," Abi answers cryptically. But when she lifts her chin to the window of the shop, my gut drops.

Culture vultures.

Or at least that's what my mom has always called them in the privacy of our home. She wouldn't dare say something so crude in public.

There's a small group of paparazzi outside on the sidewalk, their cameras shoved up against the glass as they try to get a shot of me. I've never understood this. I'm no one important, so why can't they just leave me alone?

Kaede gets up to chase them away, but it's a pointless and futile mission. They'll just circle around the block and be right back, ready to follow us to our cars with flashbulbs going off so quickly that they could induce a seizure.

Abi goes back to boss-mode. "Court's your best bet. Both personally close to you, and I know it'd mean something to her, especially since it'd be in poor taste to have two-thirds of the Andrews children up there and one sitting in the front row." I hadn't considered that, but Abi's right. "Plus, I can get her in for dress measurements today so that it'd be ready for Saturday."

Nodding, I tell Abi, "Okay, I'll talk to her as soon as I get to the office. Anything else?"

She scans her phone, clicking away, and then looks up at me. "Nope, mission accomplished for today. I'm off to meet with Violet next."

I stop her. "Abs?'

She turns back. "Yeah?"

"Thank you for everything. Is the shop okay while you're doing all of this? I know how hard you work, and I don't want to mess that up with *this*."

I mean to imply the fake wedding, but with everything feeling so real right now, it doesn't sound right.

Abi smiles. "Everything's fine. Janey is helping out more, and she's loving the publicity we're getting for doing *The Wedding of Ross Andrews and Violet Russo*." She moves her hands through the air like she's reading off a marquee of lights, which I'm afraid to mention lest she decide that's a good idea. "And I'm happy to help, Brother, with anything you need, even if it's a kick in the pants to get your head out of your ass."

Something about the way she says it makes me think Abi knows I'm feeling some very real emotions for Violet, but at least in this, she's letting me find my own way. For now.

"HEY, COURT, THANKS FOR COMING DOWN," I SAY AS MY youngest sister sits down across from me.

I'll admit it. I should've gone to her office, but I'm a chicken shit who didn't relish the idea of going toe-to-toe with my dad today. And since Courtney office is right outside Dad's, I took the coward's way out and asked her to come to me.

"No problem. What's up?" she asks casually, but I can see the weariness in her eyes. I wonder what Dad's been saying to her about me, about Violet, about us. But I don't ask because I feel like I already know the answer.

"About the wedding on Saturday . . . Violet has Abi and Archie standing up with her as bridesmaids. Bridespeople?" I shake my head, again unsure of the correct verbiage, but it still doesn't matter. "And Kaede is standing up with me. I was wondering if you would stand up there with me too. As a . . . groomsperson?"

I smile, thinking I finally got it right.

Courtney frowns. "Ross, I need to ask you something, just between you and me. I swear it won't go any further than these four walls. Sister to brother, okay?"

I smile, trying to tease her a bit because I'm scared of what she's about to say. "That's what Mom and Dad said when they brought you home from the hospital. 'Here's your *sister*, Rossie! Isn't she adorable?' Honestly, I thought you looked like a wrinkly old man, but look at you now!"

Her lips don't so much as twitch. "I know you and Abi are hiding something from me. What is it? It's about the wedding, isn't it? This about-face with Violet out of nowhere . . . I just don't get it."

"I love her, Court. That's it."

She doesn't look convinced, but I don't care at this point. Fact is, three days ago I struggled to even say the 'L-word.' I'd say married, committed, together, or some other poetic dance-around.

Now, though . . . even I'm not sure if my feelings are true or fake. I just know my feelings for Violet have grown.

"Dad is furious with you," Courtney finally says. "And I feel like I'm being ripped in half. Because I understand his point. This is so *out of character* for you, and the timing is just too fucking convenient, Ross."

Her turn of phrase is an obvious kindness, a softening of Dad's version of 'immature brat'.

"So, what's the ripped in half part?"

Courtney blushes a little, and she looks down before meeting my eyes once again. "Because I want to believe that my brother cannot seriously be pulling everyone's chain and playing with a nice girl like Violet's feelings. So I'm trying to give you the benefit of the doubt. But it's damn hard."

I consider telling her the truth for a moment, wanting to trust that in the same way I've grown up, she has too. And that she wouldn't go running to Mom and Dad the same way she once would.

But I can't take the risk. Not with Violet at stake.

So I just repeat my earlier words. "I love her, Courtney."

She smiles. "Okay, then yes. I'll be your groomsperson." She tilts her head. "Is that even a word?"

I shrug. "No idea. Thanks, though."

CHAPTER 20

VIOLET—MONDAY—5 DAYS UNTIL THE WEDDING

"*H*ey, Honey, did you see the news?"

I groan, wishing there was a way to *not* see the news. "Yes, Mom. Archie made sure that I got a full-on replay of it in stereo as soon as I got to work this morning."

Maybe it's the phone connection, maybe it's just Mom's excitement, but she doesn't hear the frustration in my voice. Instead, I wince as she squeals like she did at her first Marky Mark concert way back in the day, which she demonstrates every time his songs come on the radio, much to the displeasure of my ears and any surrounding dogs' hearing. "My baby's having a dream wedding! Like the princess I always knew you were."

I don't bother correcting her that I'm so far from a princess, it's comical. We grew up struggling, and even now that we're all comfortable financially, I'm not a fussy, prissy type. Nope, not a princess, Mom.

But she's still talking as I'm having a mental dissection of *Princess vs. Violet*. I don't compare to Diana, Caroline, Kate, Cinderella . . . wait, that last one's not real. "I'm so happy for you, and I gotta say, the triplets are furiously practicing their asses off. They know this'll be huge exposure for them!"

"Mom, about that. With the orchestra and all—"

"Oh, don't worry, honey. Vanessa called the orchestra this

morning," Mom says gleefully. "She explained it all to them, and get this . . . the director's really big into cross-genre stuff. His comment to 'Nessa was that if Guns N' Roses, Queen, and Toni Braxton can do songs with symphonies, then why not do the same for your wedding? The girls are already over there talking songs and arrangements. It's going to be great!"

Shit . . . what next, pyro and laser lights?

I pinch myself as punishment for even thinking that, not wanting to tempt the universe into delivering that level of craziness.

I hear a commotion outside the office, and I look out to see a small group of paparazzi surrounding a man who's marching with a purpose as he pushes a rack of garment bags. Seems my next dress appointment is here.

I open the door and yell out, "Please leave him alone." Thankfully, I managed to hold the phone away from my ear so I didn't deafen my mother with my shout.

The paps turn toward my voice and I think, for one second, that they're going to comply. Instead, their cameras all point at me and start clicking away as they call out questions.

"Where are you going for the honeymoon?"

"Are you marrying Ross for his money?"

"When's the baby due?"

"How'd you snag the city's hottest bachelor?"

"You still haven't found a dress?"

"Ugh, no comment. No comment," I tell the vultures. To the stone-faced bridal assistant, I wave a hand, hurrying him. "Come on before they eat you alive." He tosses a withering look over his shoulder like there might actually be zombie monsters coming after him but that he'd gladly take them on.

Putting the phone back to my ear, I say, "Mom, you there? This is crazy. I've worked with clients who have paparazzi following them everywhere, but it's never been me. How do celebrities do this? I just want to be left alone."

"Oh, hush!" Mom crows, giggling. "Just sit back and take it all in. Use it to your advantage."

That might be wise advice if I had any idea how to do that.

As it is, I just feel like the increased visibility is going to come back and bite me in the ass because there's no way we can pull off a fake wedding with their constant scrutiny and sneaking around.

"I'll try, Mom. I need to go, though. I've got dress trying-on to do."

We hang up and I turn to the bridal assistant who's been waiting patiently.

He sticks out his hand. "Weston Worthington, Ms. Russo. Considering our timeline, are you ready to get to it?" I like him instantly, all business and professional, not a word said or a care given about the circus outside my office.

"Yes, that'd be perfect."

"If you're comfortable, perhaps you can change into your foundational garments and let me evaluate your shape. I find that to be most efficient so that we can focus on gowns that will flatter you personally."

I know an order when I hear one, so I turn to head back into my office, which we've been using as a makeshift dressing room. "Certainly. If you wouldn't mind, could you close the curtains? They're one-way visibility, but I don't want to risk anyone getting a shot of me in my underwear."

I swear I see Weston's lips twitch like he's holding back a laugh. See? Obviously, not a princess, and barely fit for polite company with this sassy mouth.

I strip and wiggle into the bodysuit I've been using as my mainstay for the wedding gowns. It's nothing crazy like the Spanx that almost killed me under my red gala dress. This set is more smoothing than compression, so it's comfortable and all one piece, which makes it easy.

I open the door slowly, making sure the front room is fluores-cent-lit only before coming out in what equates to a flesh-toned colored swimsuit. Archie's droll voice greets me. "That one. You should absolutely wear that and nothing else." He points my way, making a spinning motion, which I answer with a middle finger.

I know he's exhausted with doing all the dress shopping and

wedding stuff on top of our full schedule of actual work. He's been a saint, doing so much at Mrs. Montgomery's while we both keep all the juggling balls in the air. I did at least get Ross's couch ordered yesterday, making the most of our 'lazy' Sunday by working diligently on my laptop all afternoon.

Abi interjects, apparently having arrived with Archie while I was changing. "Okay, let's get to work. Snap, snap, people."

She's in boss mode, which makes me worry she's got too much on her plate with all she's doing to help with the wedding, but then she smiles at me and I can see the joy she's taking in planning this. I know she loves working with flowers, but I think she really loves weddings.

Weston walks a full circle around me, then holds my arms out wide in a T-shape and eyes my chest, waist, and hips critically. He doesn't seem deterred by my rather curvy figure but rather seems to be visually measuring me. I'd bet he'd be able to get with a quarter-inch if he guessed my measurements.

"Okay, let's begin," he says, letting my arms go and turning to his rack of bagged garments. Like a magician, he opens one and pulls out a white fluff of fabric. "This one will highlight your small waist and give adequate support for your breasts. The bottom is a full ballgown silhouette, perfect for the grandeur of the church."

It looks like a stunningly bedazzled cupcake, but at this point, I'm willing to try anything.

Weston helps me into the gown, and I turn, facing the large mirror leaning against the wall. It is beautiful and dramatic, but it doesn't feel right. Weston can see it on my face and quickly suggests that we move on.

I like that he's not offended by my lack of gushing because I know he's worked hard to hand-select these gowns for me. He just pulls out the next, and then another. And then one more.

None of them are it.

"If you'd not been so picky before, we wouldn't be dealing with this now," Archie mutters, but he smiles when I look at him. "I'm sure you'll find something." His tone implies that's not remotely true at all, and we both know it.

Weston opens a bag, shoving it aside, but something catches my eye. "Oh, my God, that's it!" I exclaim.

Three sets of eyes follow my pointing finger.

Weston hums. "If you'd like to try it on, ma'am, then of course. However, I will caution you that it's a silhouette designed for a willowier body type." He eyes my full breasts with concern.

I clap and say definitively, "I want to try it."

He pulls it out of the bag with a flourish. It's beautiful, with a flared crystal-encrusted skirt and a pinched waist, but best of all, lace shoulders and sleeves that will let me look both sexy and classy. "It's called The Fairy Tale, an inspired blend of Kate Middleton's dress and Grace Kelly's iconic gown." Weston's voice is wistful, as if this gown is his favorite too.

Hesitantly, he helps me step into the gown and then slowly, he pulls it up my thighs. I slip my arms into the delicate sleeves and he fastens the tiny buttons at my back.

I turn to look in the mirror. It's . . . *not perfect*, I think with a sigh. But I so wanted it to be. My face falls.

"I thought this was it, but I look like a sausage stuffed into a too-small casing. And my boobs are flatter than pancakes." I can feel the tears hot in my eyes. I haven't cried in so long, it seems, not truly. Not since Papa's last spell, but this dress not fitting me the way I want it to has done me in.

Weston hops to my side, biting his lip. "Perhaps something could be done?" He looks me up and down. "Your foundational garments are not compression. They make significantly more powerful pieces that could help because you are not that far off from it fitting properly. But unfortunately, there's no room in the seams to get added inches." He's being kind by saying I'm not far off, but it's a good size, maybe more, too small.

Archie snorts. "Compression? I think you need ratchet straps." I glare at him.

"I could do that, I guess," I say about the hated spandex of death, nodding even as I remember being stuck in them before. "They almost killed me when I tried them for the gala, but for this dress, I'll do it."

Weston lowers his voice as if he's imparting secret wisdom,

LAUREN LANDISH

"If you'd rather not, have you heard of the keto egg fast? It's hardcore, at least six eggs per day, plus a little cheese or butter, coffee and water, but that's it. Definitely not sustainable, but you should read up on it and see if it might be a very short-term fix."

Archie's already clicking away on his laptop. "Got it. You should try this *and* the Spanx. Uh-oh." He stops reading and looks up. His lips are tilted up at the corners. "This says that one of the side effects of the egg fast is hellacious farts. Guess you'll be blowing the mystery wide-open there with lover boy." He pitches his voice high, "Happy wedding day . . . brrrrrupt . . . oops, was that me? Tee-hee-hee." His dry delivery makes it even funnier, but I don't dare stroke his ego and let him know that.

I roll my eyes. "Eggs and Spanx I can do for the waistline. But I can't exactly change my boobs." I rub my hand over my chest, accustomed to the soft flaring out, and then back up my chest. In this dress, it's just one smooshed-flat surface.

Weston smiles. "I can definitely fix that." He moves closer and gestures to the lace at the top. "I'll alter this part so that it's more of a portrait-style neckline. That'll show off your collarbones and give you and your breasts room to breathe."

My heart soars, and I look in the mirror once again. Abi steps to my right, Archie to my left. "Violet, are you saying yes to the dress?"

I can feel the tears rolling, because of this dress, because of this moment, because of the wedding. It all feels like what I'd dreamed it would really be like. But I choke the tears down with a reminder once again . . . fake, fake, fake.

So I force a big ,toothy grin and say, "Yes to the dress. And eggs and Spanx, I guess, too."

Archie and Abi's smiling faces match mine in the mirror, and I wonder if they're faking it too.

Archie pulls his tablet up from his side and starts clicking away. "Okay, ordered Spanx to be here tomorrow. Ordered eggs, and some good-smelling candles, to be delivered to your place so you can start tonight. Sent Ross a warning about your incoming flatulence, and last but not least, marked the wedding dress hunt as complete on the to-do list. That'll go to Kaede, Abi, me, and the wedding planner."

I turn to him, grabbing him in a hug. He balks at first, so not a touchy-feely person, but he relents. "Thank you so much, Arch. What would I do without you? Wait, did you say you told Ross I was going to be gassy? What the hell?"

He ignores my outburst. "Without me, you'd still be small potatoes, just a one-woman shop, running yourself ragged as you tried to do it all. At least with me, you're free to be your creative genius self and leave the details to *moi*."

"Humble brag, much?" I tease, knowing he's one hundred percent right.

"No reason to be humble when it's true," he answers. "Just call me Kanye."

I hug Abi and then Weston. "We did it, guys. This is actually happening!"

Wednesday — 3 Days Until the Wedding

Ross . . . is a saint.

I'm sure of it. I'm on day two and a half of not eating anything but eggs, the thought of which now makes me nauseous. I know I'm snappy, and Archie's been walking on eggshells since yesterday afternoon around three o'clock when I went full Hungry Girl Crazy. Metaphorical eggshells, not literally. I'm not that much of a mess.

Ross, though, has been there beside me the entire time. Even when the gas hit me like Arch's research said it would. I tried to leave the room before I let loose, pink with embarrassment, but he'd followed me and laughingly told me that I 'broke the farting barrier first' as he let one rip too. Between the two of us, we'd made the whole room smell like sulfur and had generously sprayed some Febreze and burned down three candles to cover the stench.

It'd actually been oddly funny and even cute in a weirdly gross way, but I had drawn the line at a farting competition, even when Ross tried to egg me on. 'Get it? Egg?' he'd prodded as I'd groaned at the bad puns he kept coming up with.

But I have lost three pounds, so hopefully, it'll be worth it. I did make Abi promise to make sure I don't inhale my dinner at the wedding. I'm afraid that when presented with actual food, delicious food from one of the best Italian restaurants in the city, I'll succumb and go into ravenous caveman mode and start shoveling it in. At first, she'd said she'd pay money to see me do that in my fancy white gown. But when I reminded her that it'd be all captured on video for posterity and forever linked to her brother, she'd relented and agreed that it would definitely not be funny, after all.

Oh, God . . . the video crew. *I still can't believe this is my life*, I think as I watch the vultures following me. Ross has another crew of his own tracking his every step, but he seems to mostly take it in stride, going on with his business as if they're not there.

But I take sweet glee in watching the gates close behind me, effectively locking the paps out and giving me a moment's peace.

Today is our final walkthrough and stamp of approval on Mrs. Montgomery's ballroom. I'm nervous, but not nearly as much as I was for her living room project. I feel like we have a steady grip on the style and look she's going for now, and I'm looking forward to beginning on her formal dining room after the honeymoon. It's got this great twelve-inch-thick crown molding that's still the original walnut stain, and Mrs. Montgomery wants the room to be dark and dramatic. I think I'm going to paint the walls a deep forest green.

The maid shows us into the ballroom, as usual, and Archie and I examine our work one last time before Mrs. Montgomery shows up.

"Don't stress, Vi. It's gorgeous and Lydia's going to love it," Archie says quietly.

I smile and tease, "Oh! Lydia is it, now? What happened to Bitch-ella?"

He shrugs. "So maybe she's not so bad after all. She kept coming through to check on the ballroom, and at first, I thought it was because she didn't trust me. I mean, I know I'm not the usual guy you just invite into your house when you're someone like her." He motions to his combat boots, ripped jeans, anarchy logoed shirt, and his fluff of hair that is currently covered by a jaunty ball cap. "I figured she thought I was going to steal the silverware. But then she just talked and watched me work and even had the cook bring lemonade to the paint crew one day."

My jaw drops. "You didn't tell me that!"

He smiles wryly. "You've been a bit busy, Boss. It's fine, but she's just . . . not so bad. Lonely, maybe, and I think her resting bitch face is just a bit too much Botox." He stretches the skin of his face back and opens his eyes wide, and I laugh.

But I stop myself before I get too loud or jostle my belly too much. The last thing I need to do is fart in Mrs. Montgomery's ballroom moments before she walks in.

Luckily, we get our faces back to their professional blandness as she walks in. "Mrs. Montgomery, thank you for taking time to meet with us today."

"Of course, Violet. Good to see you again, Archie. Please, do show me about."

We move around the room, discussing details and high-lighting features. I show how the room can be arranged in a multitude of ways for different events and moods, from formal to more intimate.

True to Arch's call, Mrs. Montgomery's face barely moves as she nods along with my presentation. But when I'm done, she offers warm praise. "Well done. I like the functionality as well as the finery. So, the formal dining is next?"

I nod. "Yes, ma'am. As we discussed, I'm out of town next week for my honeymoon, but we've already taken measurements and discussed what you'd like for the space. As soon as I return, we'll begin the first phase."

Mrs. Montgomery turns to me, a sparkle in her eyes I haven't seen before. "Oh, yes, you are marrying Ross Andrews this weekend, aren't you?" She's intentionally trying to make it seem like a small, forgettable thing but failing spectacularly. "Mind a little advice from an old lady?"

I respond the way I'm expected to. "Oh, Mrs. Montgomery, you're not the least bit old. Why, you don't look a day over fifty!" Lies, lies, lies. But she pats her white, coiffed hair proudly.

"Thank you. Even so, I have some experience with marrying well, dear." She lowers her voice. "Read the prenuptial agreement, every single word, and have a lawyer read over it too. Do not walk down that aisle without doing that. Take it from me." She gestures around her, and I wonder how it is that a widowed Mrs. Montgomery came to live in this large house. I'd never even thought about it, but now, I do.

"Thank you for the advice. I'll definitely take it under advisement," I say politely. "Archie will work with your house manager to schedule our appointments for the dining room after I get back."

"That sounds lovely, dear," she says as she shakes my hand. She offers a cheek to Archie, and he presses his to hers, both of them making an air kissing sound. "Don't be a stranger, Archie."

Outside, I give him an incredulous look as we get in the car. "Are you two BFFs now?"

He points a finger at me. "Don't you dare say a word. We actually have a few things in common."

"Such as?" I say, not able to think of a single thing Archie, a twenty-something, sarcastic, gay punk rocker might have in common with Lydia Montgomery, a seventy-something, old-school wealthy socialite.

He mumbles the answer, but I hear him clearly. "Real Housewives of Monte Carlo."

I laugh a bit too hard at that, and before Archie can complain, I roll the windows down and shut my mouth, trying not to breathe too much.

CHAPTER 21

ROSS—FRIDAY—1 DAY UNTIL THE WEDDING

I don't think either of us imagined, in our happiest dreams or our scariest nightmares, that our wedding would be like this.

But today, the eve of our wedding is putting any hopes we'd had of a simple ceremony firmly to rest. Not just six feet under, but more like oceans under.

All of Violet's family is in town now, people who haven't seen her since she was knee-high and whom she doesn't even remember. I've lost track of names because there are just so many of them.

And now, we've completely filled up Papa and Nana's house for a get-to-know-you lunch. I feel like a bug under a microscope as they circle me, patting my back, shaking my hand, and pulling me in for wet kisses to my cheeks as they exclaim in Italian. They might be saying kind things, or they might be discussing how a beauty like Violet could do so much better than a schmuck like me. I'm not sure either way.

"Tell us about your work, Ross."

"How many babies are you planning to have?"

"How soon for the babies?"

"Do you know how lucky you are to catch a woman like Violet?"

"If you hurt her, I will kill you so badly, the polizia will never find your body."

That last one had been said straight-faced and seriously in broken English by a big, beefy wall of a man whose name, I think, is Rafael. I won't dare call him that in case it's wrong, though, because I'm not willing to risk inciting his anger or violence.

It's nice that they're protective of Violet, but they don't need to worry about me. I have no intention of hurting her.

I excuse myself from the group surrounding me and go in search of my bride. I find her in the kitchen, holding an olive in her hand. She's killing me with this egg diet. I want to just feed her and worship her curves. But she's holding strong and seems confident that her fitting with Weston will go fine later this afternoon. I know the olive is just a cover because if there's one thing I've learned, it's that her family will feed you at every opportunity or create one just so that they can spoil you.

I step to her side, sliding my hands around her waist, and eat the olive from her fingers. "For me?"

She smiles and whispers as she leans into me. "Thank you. Nana and Sofia keep trying to get me to taste everything. I finally had to say the olives made everything taste salty, and that got them arguing about how much salt to add to the marinara again."

I laugh. "Evil woman, making them fight just so they'll leave you alone." She shrugs and I press a soft kiss to her cheek.

"Aww, to be in love . . . such is *amore*," a voice says behind us.

I turn to see Gianna . . . no, wait . . . it's Giovianna—those extra syllables are a killer—leaning against the door frame with her hands clasped beneath her chin. She's a cousin, I think, from somewhere on the family tree. I swear I'm going to need a PowerPoint presentation or a flowchart to keep them all straight.

"Violet, I wanted to ask you something," Giovianna says. Her smile looks friendly enough, but I've been in enough board rooms to recognize a shark approaching when I see one.

"Of course," Violet says, unaware of the minefield she's stepping into.

"I wasn't sure you knew this or not, but Michael and Anna have been in several weddings now. Anna does enjoy sprinkling the flowers along the aisle, and Michael is very responsible and would keep the rings safe and sound. They'd be a lovely addition to your bridal party. They're *family*, you know?"

Giovianna wants her kids to be the flower girl and ring bearer? Are these the same kids who are currently running wild in the living room using tubes of wrapping paper as swords and bopping each other over the head like feral Bunny Foo-Foo characters? Why do they even have wrapping paper out? It's not Christmas or a birthday.

And did they just . . . yes, Michael did in fact just launch himself from the chair to the couch in a dive roll to escape Anna's foot kicking out at the chair legs.

No way are they flower girl and ring bearer material. We're not even doing that. Are we?

I turn to Violet, who looks like a horrified deer in the headlights, and decide to take the oncoming bullet myself. I squeeze her side, letting her know that I've got this.

"That is so kind of you to offer, Giovianna. But we truly are trying to keep things as small as possible, given the size of Violet's family and my family's business associates. I'm sure you understand that when an event like this is pulled together so quickly, it has to be as streamlined as possible to prevent anything from going awry. But thank you, truly." I smile, thinking I handled that quite nicely.

The temperature in the room drops to frigid, and I swear, conversations stop all over the house as eyes turn this way. Even Nana is looking at me through narrowed eyes, but I have no idea what's wrong. I thought I was pretty polite about the whole thing because who forces their kids into someone else's wedding party twenty-four hours before we walk down the aisle? Especially hellions like Michael and Anna, who are now smearing *something* on the coffee table. Dear God, let that be chocolate.

Violet suddenly finds her tongue and leans toward Giovianna. "Of course, we'd love to have them."

There's an audible sigh of relief, and conversations begin again. Giovianna glares at me as she walks away, hopefully, to corral her demon spawn.

"What just happened?" I whisper to Violet.

"You can't turn down an offer like that. It's . . . it's just not done," she says, as if that explains everything. It doesn't, not at all.

We both look to the living room. Giovianna has Michael by the ear, which he's struggling against, and Anna is sitting pretty as a picture in the chair, her feet swinging where they don't reach the floor. She looks like one of those girls from The Shining, all sweet and innocent, but it's a cover for the evil beneath.

"So we're up to a news crew, an orchestra, family guest singers, and a forced ring bearer and flower girl. Anything I'm missing?" I ask, shaking my head in disbelief.

Violet grimaces. "If we can pull this off, it's going to be a miracle."

WE'RE LYING ON THE SOFA, VIOLET'S BODY LIMP AFTER THE whirlwind of today. In the last eight hours, we've marked every last detail off the to-do list . . .

* The get together with her family, where I insulted everyone with my lack of understanding about forced wedding party participation being a gift.

* A walkthrough of the ceremony with Father O'Flannigan, during which Violet looked ready to collapse.

* Coffee with my mom, though my Dad was noticeably absent and Mom's excuse that he was at work was painfully thin.

* Violet's final fitting at the bridal shop. I'd heard her whoop of delight at fitting into the dress from the lobby, where I'd been relegated because it's bad luck for the groom to see the bride.

And now, we wait. In less than twenty-four hours, we will have pulled off the biggest prank of our lives . . . together this time, instead of against one another.

"Ross?" she says, her voice a bit scratchy.

I put my arm around her, holding her gently. "Yeah?"

"Did I snap at Father O'Flannigan during practice today?"

I nod, kissing the top of her head. "Just a little. I'm sure he's seen a few nervous brides before. It's okay."

"Really?" she asks, utterly exhausted. "Then why do I feel like everything's going to be a giant mess tomorrow?"

"Because despite every bride's best intentions, and every wedding planner in the world, a wedding is like a football game," I say with a soft laugh. "Everyone's game plan goes right out the door when something smacks you in the mouth."

"Thanks," she complains, punching me weakly in the ribs. "You know, this isn't helping with my pre-wedding jitters."

I wrap both my arms around her and lay her back on the sofa, wiggling until I'm wedged in next to her. Reaching up, I stroke her hair out of her eyes, looking at her in awe and worship.

"You've moved heaven and earth to get this done. Your Papa is going to be so happy," I tell her softly, "and we've gotten through it. Sure, it took a team, but something this big always will. It's going to be fine, honey."

The assurance slips out easily, comfortably. She sighs and relaxes into my arms, finding some solace from the world outside that's going to take over again.

I want to wake up every morning next to you and go to bed every night with you in my arms. I want to feel you from the inside. I want to feel your heartbeat under my fingertips. I want to . . . I want to have a family with you. I want to be your husband.

For real.

The thoughts run through my head in one big continuous wave, and it should terrify me, take me under, but I just feel peace. I look at Violet, unsure whether I should say anything. On one hand, it could make tomorrow so much better. But if she still sees this as something she's doing for Papa only, and our sex as just a bonus, it'll make tomorrow and the next six months awkward as fuck. It's a gamble I'm not willing to take, not because I'm a wuss but because I know how much this means to her and I won't risk messing it up or making it uncomfortable for her.

For now, I decide to bite my tongue and just keep doing

everything I can for her. Maybe one day, she'll grow to feel something for me too.

"I have to go soon," I whisper to her. "I'm supposed to be at Kaede's by eight. We're doing a simple dinner in instead of a bachelor party, I promise."

She smiles, and I know that a bachelor party is the least of her worries right now. I soothe the wrinkle between her brows. "You gonna be okay here tonight? You sure you don't want Abi to come over?"

Her nod is hesitant. "I'm sure. I just want to take a bath and go to bed. But the bed will feel big without you in it with me."

I lean down, meeting her lips with my own. "After tomorrow, you'll never have to sleep alone, Vi. You'll be my wife." It's as close to a confession as I can get.

She melts for me, writhing dreamily beneath me. I feel it. This isn't just sex. Not for me, and I don't think for her, either.

As my hands stroke her body and she caresses me back, there's more to it. My lips write on her skin in passion, but there's no greediness there.

This isn't just 'frenemies with benefits.' It hasn't been for a while.

"Violet," I whisper as my hand slides between her thighs and she lifts her leg to rest it on the back of the sofa, "do you want this?"

I mean so much more than the physical things we are doing to each other, but she doesn't know that. Can't know that . . . yet.

She nods, whimpering in pleasure as my fingers stroke over her panties. My head's already swimming, and even Violet's face looks different, more serious somehow. "No sex until tomorrow, though, remember? We agreed."

Her whine of disagreement almost makes me forget our plan and just bury myself in her, but I hold steady, finding strength I didn't know I had.

"No sex, but I'll make you feel good," I tell her gruffly.

I move between her legs, shoving my shorts down to free my hard cock. Wrapping my fist around it, I press my knuckles along her core. As I stroke myself, I tease her through the soaked fabric of her panties.

It's heaven and hell all at once. I want her so badly, but waiting is the right thing to do.

I kiss her, slow and deep, driving us both higher and hotter.

I make promises with my mouth — that we can do this, that's it's going to be okay, that we're in this together.

My hand speeds up, sending sparks through my body, and I bury my mouth in the curve of her neck. I can feel the racing thump of her heartbeat beneath my lips.

"Vi —" But I stop myself, swallowing down the words that are trying to escape.

The heat builds between us until I explode, my groan rough in my throat until Violet captures my mouth with hers. Her returning moan is soft, and I taste it greedily as she bucks her hips, guiding my knuckles right where she needs me most. Hot stickiness spurts between us, and I feel her cream on my hand, mixing with my own. I look down to see my seed covering her panties, her belly, and feel like a god claiming what's his.

Deep inside me, my heart unlocks, and I collapse onto her as I wrap her in my arms, not wanting to go.

Across the room, her phone begins to play a tune. After a second, I recognize it — *Going to the Chapel*.

I lift up, looking at her questioningly. "That's my alarm. You have to go so you make it to Kaede's on time and I have the evening to relax and get ready."

"That's my girl, always thinking ahead and planning for everything, even this," I say, lifting my chin toward the sexy mess we've made. "Don't move."

I get up and silence her phone before heading to the bathroom. I wet a towel and wipe away the evidence of what we've been up to, then get dressed. I turn the hot water on and fill the tub for her, throwing in some bubble bath that turns the water pink below a froth of bubbles.

In the living room, I pick Violet up from the couch, her body soft and pliant in my arms. I pull her ruined panties down and ease her into the hot water, and she moans out a breathy sigh. "*Dio Mio*, this is perfect."

I press a kiss to her forehead. "Violet, I . . ."

Weak. I am so fucking weak as the words try to sneak out again. She opens her eyes, and beneath her heavy lids, I can see her hopefulness. But I'm too scared that if I say them, I'll be jinxing things.

So I punt. "I'll be the guy at the end of the aisle tomorrow. I'll be your husband."

Once upon a time, those words would've terrified me, sent me running for the hills screaming faster than a defensive lineman chasing me down the field. Tonight, I can't wait for tomorrow.

CHAPTER 22

VIOLET—SATURDAY—WEDDING DAY!

*T*he sound outside the choir room is just short of chaos, a cacophony of voices talking and string music playing. Okay, so the orchestra is here. I guess I'd kind of hoped they'd just forget to show up or something. That probably means the news crew is here too.

I lean against the wall, alone for just a moment after all the hair and makeup fuss I've been pampered with today. I know it makes me sound ungrateful, but I really just wish I could sit down or breathe fully. For some reason, doing some yoga stretches sounds like a brilliant idea, except I've never done yoga in my life and starting doesn't seem prudent when I'm in a dress that fits me like a glove.

So yoga's out, but I think I could actually sit down and not pop a seam or cut off the circulation to my lower half. Maybe it's the lack of food, though I may never eat an egg again in my lifetime, or that I haven't anything but coffee and water since this morning, or that the shapewear's elastic has given up on the losing battle of holding me in. Whatever it is, a chair sounds like bliss, and isn't that the simplest pleasure?

But before I can attempt sitting, the door opens and Abi comes in, looking like she just crawled her way through a frat party. "How's it going out there?"

"Let's see . . . your triplet cousins have been hit on by half a dozen men, two of whom may or may not be your cousins from Europe, your Aunt Sofia is defending the front pew of the church with a rolled up umbrella and a look that makes me think your ancestors fought in the Colosseum, and the camera crew looks scared to even approach her. On my family's side of the church, my father still looks like he'd rather be getting a salt 'n vinegar enema than be here. You've heard a mullet described as business in the front, party in the back?" She grins, the giggle already coming. "It's like that out there too . . . business on the right with Dad's stuffed shirt friends, and party on the left with all of your crazy family. But other than that, your wedding plan's going off just as you wanted, perfectly!"

"Plan," I chuckle ruefully, sighing. "You know, I had the perfect plan? But somehow, all this craziness seems apropos, don't you think? Does the wedding planner need anything?"

Abi shakes her head. "Nope, that's not for you today. She's top-notch, not scared of anyone, my family or yours, and has everything prepped, ready, and decorated. I'll remember her to refer brides to at the flower shop for sure."

There's a knock at the door, and a shaky voice on the other side calls out, "Violet? Are you decent, baby?"

My eyes go wide, and I'm grateful when Abi tosses me a blue choir robe that I can pull on quickly without messing up my hair or makeup. "Come in, Papa!"

Papa opens the door, and his smile when he sees me makes this all worth it. "Oh, my dear, you look beautiful."

I look down at the shapeless blue robe, laughing a little. "Papa, you can't even see my dress."

"No need. You're always beautiful to me," Papa reassures me.

He looks so handsome in his black suit, strong and healthy for the first time in a long time. I know it's the excitement, but he looks . . . alive again. "It's not the dress, or the church, or any of that that makes this day for me. Violet, it's you. To see you happy, the love in your eyes, the honor of walking you down the aisle. Honey, you've given me the gift of a lifetime. Thank you."

I smile, trying to find words, but my throat's closed up, and Papa leans forward, kissing me with feathery light kisses on both cheeks. And suddenly, all the craziness is worth it. I'm this close to making his dream come true. I can handle a little extra fanfare if it's for Papa.

"Now, I'll get out of your way. You need to get ready, and you're going to cry and ruin your makeup if I stay here any longer. Your grandmother would skin me alive if I did that!"

"Oh, Papa, stop!" I laugh, still wanting to cry but smiling through it. "I'll be ready on time."

"You'd better be. As handsome as Ross looks, if you're late, there's going to be a stampede of young women trying to get up there to marry him in your place!" Papa teases as he walks out the door.

In the silence that follows, I look over to see Abi wiping carefully at her eyes. "What?" she asks when she sees me looking. "There's a reason I didn't go for smoky eyes today. I knew I'd end up looking like a raccoon if I did. I went straight for the dramatic fake lashes, so I'm good. Now, let's finish getting you ready before one of your cousins steals Ross right out from underneath you, literally. What's left?"

I laugh and smack her arm at the dirty joke. "Why's it gotta be my cousins?" I ask before realizing the point. "Oh . . . your family. Yeah, that'd be weird."

I go through my checklist, reading down the paper the wedding planner taped to the mirror for me. Hair and veil—check. Makeup and teeth brushed—check. Dress—check. Garter and lingerie—check. One glass of champagne—I decided to skip that one, so check.

"Hey, Abi? There's just one thing left on my list and I'm definitely gonna need some help with it," I say haltingly.

"What?" she says, reading over my shoulder.

"I need to pee," I say.

Like the good friend and trooper she is, Abi straightens her back. "Okay, let's get to it."

I never thought bathroom stalls were particularly small.

Apparently, that's because I've never been inside one with another person plus what seems to be one hundred yards of white fabric. We giggle a lot, I almost pull a hamstring, and ultimately, we end up in some configuration that has me sitting backward on the toilet as I hold the front of the dress and Abi holds the back.

I say a literal prayer of thanks for snap-crotch shapewear, choosing not to think about Abi having to help me re-snap.

We're close, but not that close. Until today apparently.

I close my eyes, trying to pretend that she's not actually looking at my ass and that I don't have an audience so that my shy bladder will do its damn job. But it's not working.

Abi shuffles my dress to one hand and pulls her phone out with the other.

"Are you taking a picture of my butt?" I scream.

Her eye roll is epic. "No, I'm calling in reinforcements. Yeah, it's me. Women's bathroom in the choir room."

A moment later, the door opens, and I flinch, afraid someone else is going to see my ass. I hiss, "Abi, for fuck's sake, cover me up. It might be the videographer!"

Archie sighs dramatically. "If only. That would be hilarious." I don't kill him because he's obviously being sarcastic, and you know, I'm currently stuck on a toilet.

"Turn on the water and you can go," Abi orders him.

I hear all three sinks start gushing water and am struck with inspiration, my bladder finally deciding to perform.

As the door opens once again, I hear Archie call back, "I want a raise, boss lady. A good one, effective two minutes ago."

I think I hum some agreement, but I can't be sure over the sound of all the streaming, both the sinks and me.

THIS IS UTTER MADNESS.

Leaving the choir room, I have to walk around the outside of the church in order to get to the back. Yesterday, I walked it in my jeans in a minute, with half of that being Father O'Flannigan talking through the ceremony and slowing me down. The only creature that saw me was a single chipmunk that chittered at us from the big maple in the middle of the church courtyard and a couple of birds flying overhead. It was peaceful and I'd thought it'd be a nice nature break to catch my breath before the ceremony began.

Today, it's like a prize fighter pushing their way to the ring. Somehow, whether it's the news coverage, social media, or something I just totally don't understand, the entire courtyard is crowded with people. At least a hundred people line the concrete walkway, though I can tell someone has worked to keep them back from the actual sidewalk so I can pass safely. But among the faces in the sea of humanity, I only recognize maybe a quarter of them. Why in the world are these people here? They're not even invited, not going to get inside for the ceremony or the reception. People are so weird sometimes.

The news crew takes the lead, staying several yards ahead and somehow easily walking backward as they film our trek. Of our group, Abi takes the front, plowing her way through the congratulatory hands that want to reach out to touch me, either in genuine affection or to have their momentary brush with temporary celebrity. They call out questions and congratulations and I try to smile, but I'm sure it looks more like I'm baring my teeth.

"Okay, okay, outta the way!" Abi growls as two random strangers pop out to snap photos. "No photos or I'm going to shove that iPhone so deep you'll need some angelic help to get it out!"

Even from behind her, I hear the news group say, "Did you get that?" Great, way to go, Abi. That's going to be on the evening news. Delilah assured us the crew would film for our personal memories only, but I have no faith that anything particularly interesting won't end up on the *Sunday Local Wrap-Up* first thing in the morning.

The foyer of the church is nearly as bad, but at least the

camera crew disappears to go set up in the chapel. Mom is talking to Vanessa, Marissa, and Estella while Archie and Courtney look on uncomfortably. Michael and Anna are sitting off to the side on a small bench, but even from here, I can see that they're poking and pinching each other while simultaneously trying not to get caught misbehaving.

As I walk up with Abi, I can hear Vanessa's too-loud whisper. "Ooh, did you see that redhead? I'm telling you, that was a Harvard ring I saw on his finger!"

"And?" Marissa giggles. "Mine's got a big Marine Corps tattoo on his shoulder."

"Wait, how'd you see John's tattoo?" Courtney asks, sucked into the conversation. "Or do I want to ask?"

"Not in a church you don't," Estella says before blushing as she looks at Father O'Flannigan.

"I'd hand out Hail Marys, but I doubt they'd be useful," Father O'Flannigan says with a smile. "Perhaps you ladies would like to head up to the choir loft and prepare? Ah, Violet, there you are."

"Where's Papa?" I ask worriedly, and Mom waves me down.

"Papa was getting a bit hot, so he's sitting down just inside the sanctuary," Mom says. "He'll take your arm as you step in . . . kinda like Kate Middleton, right?"

I sigh in relief and turn to Abi. "Okay, what now?"

She smiles sweetly, her eyes glassy with unshed tears. "Now, you go marry my brother and have your happily ever after, one way or another. You deserve this, Vi."

I know what she's saying. She's probably known for longer than I have, but I need to say the words to someone, even if I can't say them to Ross. "I love him, Abs."

She nods. "I know you do. You always have. And he loves you too. He's just a bit slow on the uptake. Sorry about that, but no take-backsies. He's your problem now."

If only that were true.

She takes a big breath and switches into boss mode. "Okay, ladies, you heard Father, get upstairs. *Ave Maria* and then the wedding march. Courtney, head around to Ross's room and tell him to line up at the front. Father, you know what to do. Ms. Russo, you'll walk in first, then the kids, Archie, and me. Last, but certainly not least, Violet with Papa." We all nod along after receiving our assignments. "And break! I've always wanted to say that," she says with a chuckle.

I hear the music change, something slow and driving, and through the doors, I hear the crowd die down. I didn't realize how loud it was until it got quiet. "How many people are in there?"

Archie pats my hand. "It'll be fine, Vi. Hold your head up and slow march yourself down there. It doesn't matter if there are five or five hundred. The only one that matters is the hottie at the front."

I laugh a bit. "A tad bit more than five and a lot less than five hundred, I'm sure." He makes a face, but I think he's kidding. Sometimes, it's hard to tell with him.

The wedding planner, Sarah, sticks her head out. "Mother of the bride?"

Over her shoulder, as Mom slips through, I get my first peek of the crowd.

"It's . . . insane," I whisper, fear gripping me tightly as I squeeze my beautiful bouquet when I see the new mass of humanity. The church is designed to hold five hundred, and I figured that would be way more than enough. My family is ridiculously large, but Ross only invited a few college friends, his immediate family, and the people at work.

Now, the church, which was plenty big enough in my plan, is swollen to overflowing. Folding chairs have been set up on the end of every pew, and I get a glance of men standing along the walls in suits of every shade of grey.

"That's not a wedding crowd. That's a convention!"

Abi glances over, smiling a little acidly. "Sorry. Mom invited basically everyone we know from every social club and circle she's ever been in, and no one at the office was willing to piss Dad off with the way he's been acting, according to Courtney, so the entire company is here. From the mailroom to the board. And with your family . . . guess it's gotten pretty big."

"Fire Marshall's gonna shut us down," Archie whispers, but before I can fully freak out, the music changes again and I can hear the triplets singing a beautiful rendition of *Ave Maria* with harmonies that blend perfectly. At least that's going well. "Our turn. Let's go, Abi. She'll be fine." Archie glares at me, daring me to prove him wrong. Abi pats my hand and smiles.

They go in, Michael and Anna leading the way, and leave me alone in the hallway. It's then that I hear it. *The Wedding March.*

My throat tightens up, and as the double doors of the church swing open for me, all the worry drops away. Papa's right where he's supposed to be, standing next to the second pew to take my arm and walk me down the aisle, and as he kisses my hand lovingly, I know this has all been worth it.

Ross stands at the altar, with Kaede and Courtney next to him.

I have a vague impression of lush greenery surrounding the altar, but my eyes are locked on Ross. He's standing tall, like a prince, my knight in saving armor. Except . . . wait . . . is his tuxedo green? I smile, delighted that he'd do something so unique and surprising.

It's perfect.

It's my wedding day.

But I have to keep reminding myself that this isn't what it looks like. This is a charade, a performance . . . it's not real. Except to the man already standing by my side.

I look at Papa, my reason for all of this. He's openly crying, smiling so broadly that I feel better. All of this stress and drama were worth it.

"Violet, my beautiful one, you make this old man happy," Papa whispers as we reach the end of the aisle and I turn to him, exchanging cheek kisses.

Turning to Ross, Papa gives him my hand. "Protect and love her the way I've loved her, young man. And you'll never go wrong."

"I will, sir," Ross says, taking my hand, and Papa steps forward to kiss Ross on both cheeks too. He surprises Ross, and there are a few laughs from the audience, but it's perfect for today, and as Papa sits, I'm struck with how perfect everything's been.

Sure, there's been stress and craziness.

But the orchestra has been lovely so far, the triplets sound beautiful, the video crew is discretely moving about the room, our families are here, and Papa walked me down the aisle just like I wanted.

I'm going to ignore that Giovianna had to drag her kids to the pew to sit them down because I don't want to know what they were doing before I walked in with Papa. It doesn't matter. The only thing that matters is the smile on Papa's face.

But then I see the smile on Ross's face and my own blooms. His smile. That's important too.

Father O'Flannigan clears his throat, and we start the ceremony. After our first hymn, he launches into his opening comments, and I'm shocked at the emotion and power pouring from his words. I can barely keep up with everything he's saying. I'm still in so much shock, but this isn't the cookie cutter speech I was expecting.

"A lot of people think that being a priest for weddings is easy. Stand up here, don't mess up the vows, read from a book, and bam, seal it with a kiss. And my work is done. But it's so much more than that. It's helping couples find their way to the altar in a manner that will create not just a wedding, but a marriage. Creating a life together, a love together, two truly becoming one. Some say that takes time, as if there is some hourglass of sand and a particular number of grains have to fall before you're 'ready', whatever that means. And I could have politely said that this couple standing in front of you today hasn't done enough to 'prove' their relationship to satisfy the church."

"But then I thought a little harder, and I've watched how this young woman and young man have jumped through every hoop the world's put in their way to get to today. I've watched as they've become unwitting celebrities and how they've endured the scrutiny, and yes, the occasional doubt from those around them."

Damn, if that isn't Father O'Flannigan bitch slapping Morgan Andrews, I don't know what is.

"But yet, they've persisted, sacrificed, and shown an utter devotion to each another. Their love has stood steady, resolute against those who would put their union asunder before it is even blessed, as I intend to do today."

"Though stories and movies tell us otherwise, love is not a fire. Sure, it flares up, and yes, it can have passions that don't get talked about a lot within the walls of a church. But there are also tough times, and low times, and sad times. Love is about walking through the fires together, withstanding the rain together, breathing in the present together, and creating a foundation for the future together. And that takes hard work."

"Work that Ross and Violet have already shown they are capable of tackling, and I have faith they will continue to do so. As we begin the ceremony that will unite you in marriage, I praise you both. May your commitment be a shining beacon to everyone about what love actually is."

I blink, stunned by the words from the normally calm Father O'Flannigan. Beside me, Abi sniffs, and I see her wipe away a tear. I can hear people sniffing behind me, but before I can check to see if they're crying or if it's just really, really dusty in the church, O'Flannigan starts in on the ceremony.

I let myself be carried away by the rehearsed words, caught up in my own thoughts. Devotion? My stomach twists as I think about what he just said and how I could be making a mockery of his praise.

My worry increases when Ross reaches out, taking my hand, and I can feel him tremble for the first time. He's nervous too, probably just waiting for someone to jump up and call us out right here and now.

FAKE!

FRAUD!

LIAR!

I expect all of these words to be brought up, but instead, there's nothing but soft, happy murmurs as O'Flannigan says, "If anyone should have reason for these two to not be wed, may they speak now or forever hold their peace."

Nothing. Well, Papa and Nana are now openly crying, and Mom's sniffing like a coke fiend, but nobody objects.

"May we have the rings?"

Giovianna releases Michael, doing the two-finger thing between her eyes and his that says 'I'm watching you, mister,' and he solemnly walks the pillow of rings toward us. Ross unties the rings and hands them to Father O'Flannigan as Michael runs back to sit beside his mother.

The vows feel like bitter sawdust on my lips as I look up into Ross's smiling face. Not because I don't mean them but because I can't shake the feeling that we're lying to everyone.

But I don't want to lie.

I want him.

I want to be his wife.

And maybe that's the biggest lie of all . . . the one I'm telling Ross by not telling him the truth. That I love him. That I mean every word I'm saying, every vow I'm making.

Suddenly, it's time.

"You may kiss the bride."

Ross leans in, and for a moment, I feel my fear rise up. I want to pull back, to plead forgiveness and go running down the aisle, away from all of this madness.

And then I want to walk back down for real and marry Ross. But that's even crazier.

But then his lips touch mine, and magic blooms. In his kiss, I can feel him, his heart, and I respond with my whole heart, kissing him back until Father O'Flannigan has to clear his throat. "Save some for the honeymoon, folks?"

We pull back, both of us chuckling. "Sorry, not sorry," Ross whispers to Father O'Flannigan, who smiles knowingly.

We did it.

As we walk down the aisle and the entire church breaks into applause, each clap is a fresh wave of relief.

But the reason this whole crazy idea even started is wiping

fresh tears from his own eyes. Papa, standing with Nana, gives me a nod, pride and happiness in his teary smile.

It's going to be okay. Nobody knows our secret. Nobody called us out. Nobody is going to wreck this.

It's time to celebrate successfully giving the sweetest, most loving man I've ever known his dying wish. "Thank you," I whisper . . . to Ross, to Papa, to the universe for giving me enough time with him for this dream to come true.

CHAPTER 23

ROSS

"*R*oss, I can't believe you actually went through with shackling that ball and chain on," Vincent Van Johnson, one of the executives from the company says as I wait for Violet to be ready for our entrance. Really, he shouldn't even be out here, but I haven't found a semi-polite way to tell him to head on into the reception. "Though she makes my ex-wife look like dog food, so there's that. Am I right?" he says, laughing and holding up a palm for a high-five, which I merely raise a brow at.

"Calling her dog food might be why you're divorced, VJ," Kaede says, steering Van Johnson away from me and directing him toward the main room of the reception. When he comes back, he's shaking his head. "Don't mean to talk ill of your family—"

"Go ahead, I don't mind."

"But your dad's idea to invite the whole company blows chunks," Kaede finishes. "Devious, but sucky."

He's dead right, but right now, I don't care. I mean, I just had a hell of a wedding, and seeing Violet's smile is all I really need.

The door to her 'refreshing' room opens, and she comes out. I know I just saw her a little bit ago for the ceremony, but now, something's different.

Now, she's my *wife*. And damned if that doesn't mean something real, I think as my heart swells to bursting just from the sight of her.

"Hi," I say softly, the smile breaking across my face instantly.

"Hi," she says back.

Okay, so maybe we're both in a little bit of shock. But she's smiling too, so maybe it's a good kind of shock.

Kaede pats me on the back, grinning. "You two are too cute. I'll be waiting inside."

Kaede leaves, and I lean back, marveling at everything's that's happened today. From the moment Violet walked into the church, looking like a total vision of beauty, to the moment our lips touched and we were officially married, I was nothing but a mass of nerves.

But she was so steady and sure, my rock in the eye of the storm. The craziness continues. The main room of the hotel ballroom we've booked for the reception sounds like Comic Con is going on, but with her by my side, I don't mind. I don't even notice.

I only see her. I only hear her. I only feel her. I just want Violet to be happy.

Because she's *mine*.

Okay, I'm being a bit of a caveman, and maybe it's all fake . . . but the paper in my coat pocket isn't. Yeah, we still have to go down to the county clerk's office to file it to make it legal, but in my heart, I know it's the truth.

"You take my breath away," I murmur, pulling her close and kissing her. In seconds, we're entangled with each other, Violet pushed against the doorway as our tongues twist around each other and her body yields to me.

We're this close to opening the door and making our first dance as man and wife a private affair when there's a cough and soft laugh behind us. "Excuse me, big brother, but if you don't mind . . . Violet, your cousins would like to sing? Like now. They're literally bouncing around, and half the office is watching their boobs jiggle like it's a peep show about to happen in three . . . two . . . one."

I press my forehead to Violet's, catching my breath, and then glance over to see Abi, her arms crossed over her chest, grinning like the Cheshire Cat. "What are you smiling about?"

"You two," she says, her grin growing as she sing-songs. "You know the old adage. First comes love, then comes marriage, then comes Rossy with the baby carriage."

"Abigail," Violet says with a warning in her voice. I rarely hear anyone call my sister by her full name, least of all Violet. She points, directing Abi back into the reception. "We'll be there in a second."

Abi turns and leaves, giving Violet and me a moment of peace. "Violet, about that—"

"We can talk all about it on our honeymoon," Violet says, her eyes promising me so much. Maybe, just maybe, we are thinking the same thing, and the isolation and privacy of Hawaii will help us get past our own doubts and the unusual start to this marriage. "For now, point that thing down your leg if you don't want everyone to comment on the tent you've got in your pants." She raises her brow and grinds against me slightly, torturing me deliciously.

I make a show of adjusting my cock while Violet watches before offering her my arm, and we head into the ballroom. The applause is overwhelming, especially when partnered with the DJ blaring air horns in some pattern that vaguely reminds me of S-O-S in Morse code.

Holy shit, there are so many people, and while I agree with Kaede that Dad's invitation of everyone and their brother is sort of a dick move . . . it has its benefits. This is going to be a party, a celebration of Violet and me, and maybe the start of something greater than either of us had ever dreamed.

On stage, the triplets are ready, and as the DJ throws it over to the orchestra, they kick into their first number. Maybe they're trying to have fun, maybe it's just part of the collaboration, maybe they're trying to respect the fast-paced public nature of our engagement, but as they launch into a jazzed-up version of the eighties classic *Making Love Out of Nothing At All*, I feel a little chill down my spine.

Really, girls? Sure, they change the lyrics, and I'll give them credit for personalizing it, changing lines like "I know just how to fake it, I know just how to lie," to "I know I can't keep fakin' it, I can't keep up this lie," in a way to play up our public story that Violet and I have been in love since childhood and only recently came to our senses.

As I spin Violet around the dance floor, I can't help but think of the original and can only pray that what Estella, Vanessa and Marissa have done to the song will stick with us. I want that happy ending they're singing the hell out of. I want it desperately, with Violet.

The crowd eats it up, ahhing as I dip Violet and giving the girls thunderous applause as they blow us kisses when they're done. "Okay, Ross, now that you've given us this big stage, we wanted one more before we let the DJ take over. If that's okay?"

"Only if you give me a liner credit when your album drops!" I toss back, earning a laugh from everyone. Violet laughs along with them, leaning into me as the music starts and then the triplets start singing in Italian.

"Oh, no, I forgot to warn you! It's the *Tarantella*!" she says suddenly.

I look at her, confused as my brows jump together. Did she say tarantula? No, that's not it, but I have no idea what Italian word sounds like tarantula or what it might mean.

But the Russo family is getting up *en masse* and virtually sprinting for the dance floor, yelling loudly. I have no idea what's going on and have a split-second fear that I'm about to be thrown over someone's shoulder and carted out of here for a ritual initiation into the family.

"Just go with it," Violet calls out to me, but I have no idea what she's talking about until someone catches my elbow with theirs and spins me. As I start to ask what's happening, my other elbow is snared and I'm spinning with someone else.

Soon, we have two circles, the men in one and the women in the other. I'm doing this weird elbow thing that vaguely reminds me of square dancing in elementary school, and then we join hands and march around counterclockwise and then reverse to go clockwise. Every once in a while, by some cue I can't discern, we all shuffle to the middle and back out.

It's a loud, wild celebratory dance.

I look to the other circle and see Violet's face beaming with happiness, which lifts my spirits even more. As we dance, even apart, I can feel her. She's a part of me.

The circles surge and become one, and someone pushes me into the center. I have that middle-school fear of being in the spotlight at the school dance and freeze a bit. But Violet hooks her elbow in mine and spins me, and I relax. This I can do.

Her whole family surrounds us, and even some of the people from my side of the aisle get up to join the fun, all encircling us with joy and love and celebration. The music gets faster and faster, and we spin wildly. Every once in a while, the whole circle comes in close and I can hear their outbursts of congratulations before they spread back out to move around us once again.

It's amazing, and all for us.

The triplets hold a long note, and the music stops with sharp freeze, and the whole group cheers and claps.

"Wow," I say too loudly into Violet's ear, but she smiles anyway.

"So, that's the Tarantella, an Italian wedding dance." Her laughter is bright and bubbly, music even more beautiful to my ears than the triplets' singing. Even when she snorts, and chokes out, "You should've seen your face! What did you think I said?"

I laugh, vowing to never tell her I thought she had seen a tarantula, despite the fact that that's highly unlikely.

The DJ takes over while Violet and I take our seats, catching our breath and watching everyone have some fun. The DJ's good, mixing in songs for every age.

A few minutes later, a sultry guitar riff comes through the speakers and Violet smiles and says, "Oh, here we go again." She's up and pulling me to the floor when I recognize Carlos Santana's *Maria, Maria*. She starts to sway, and I let her hips guide me as the dance floor fills back up with Italians, Italian-Greeks, Italian-Americans, and just everyone who feels the groove moving their feet and asses.

"I guess everyone caught their breath?" I whisper in her ear. We're not exactly dirty dancing, but it's as close as we can get with her in the poof of her wedding dress. *Why does there have to be so much fabric?*

Violet smiles as she looks up at me through her lashes. "This is Mom's absolute favorite. She's been obsessed with Santana since she was a kid, and when this song came out, she always joked it was about her. I think she watched interviews where Santana talked about the song just so she could hear him say her name.

"Your mom's a super fan? Good to know if I ever need to get out of the doghouse with her." I'm just joking, of course, but knowing something personal about Maria and dancing around the floor with the family makes me feel welcomed and accepted into their crazy family. It's a good feeling, even if it's under false pretenses.

Later, Nana and Papa Russo get lots of 'awws' and a few tears as they slowly sway together to Sinatra, while laughs erupt when Archie and Aunt Sofia decide to do an impromptu dance off.

"I can out boogie your skinny butt any day of the week!" Sofia declares as she pops a few nifty steps that I have to admit are impressive for an old woman with a bad hip. "Challenge, honey!"

"Oh, it's on now, lady!" Archie declares, doing a few shuffle steps before spinning and dropping into a half-split. I don't know how he doesn't split his pants or pull a muscle. "Now match that!"

It goes back and forth, everyone getting into the act as Archie busts out everything from the Roger Rabbit to the Dougie, while Sofia more than holds her own, doing the best septuagenarian floss I've ever seen.

Finally, both of them collapse into laughter, Archie sweeping Sofia up in a big hug and carrying her in his arms off the dance floor to set her carefully in her chair. "I give up. You're too much for me."

"Too bad you play for the other team because I'd love to

show you just how 'too much' I am!" Sofia jokes back loudly, earning even more laughter.

The DJ directs everyone to their tables and the wait staff begins delivering dinner. It's delicious, fresh salads for our first course, followed by a tasting menu of chicken parmigiana, steak, and fresh pasta in cream sauce. It's so good that not even Nana and Sofia argue about the salt content and instead just dig in like everyone else does.

It's time for speeches, and as they set up the microphone, I glance over at Violet, who looks so beautiful and happy that I feel the powerful emotions and words bubble up inside me again and I can't hold back any longer. "Violet?"

"Yeah?" she asks, looking over. She slurps a little bit, grinning at the yummy pasta. I'm glad to see her enjoying some real food at this point, but there's a tiny dribble of sauce by the corner of her mouth.

I press my lips to hers, letting my tongue peek out to taste her sweetness and the richness of the cream. "I just wanted to say . . . I wanted to say that I —"

"Congratulations!" Abi calls from the microphone, cutting me off, and we look up to see her grinning hugely. I decide the words can wait because though I know I want to say them, it probably would be better when it's just the two of us. "God, it feels like I've waited for this day since . . . well, forever!"

A ripple of laughter goes through the crowd, and Abi continues. "Ross and Violet, what can I say? I knew from about two minutes after Violet met Ross that she was enamored with him, even though she tried to hide it by calling him names. My brother, though . . . let's just say he was a bit blind to Violet's charms."

She glares at me with a raised brow, but it's softened by a sly smirk, and I shrug. "I never said I was the smart sibling . . . that's Courtney." I look over to see my youngest sister smiling triumphantly.

"Regardless, caught somewhere between the both of you, I felt like I was the only one who could see what the two of you refused to see. Ross, you're a pain in the ass, but you've got the biggest heart I've ever seen. You fight for what you believe in, and you've protected me more than once from . . . lots of stuff. And you kept my secrets, like the time I snuck out of the house so that Violet and I could go to the club, *shh*."

I glance over at Mom and Dad, who both exchange surprised looks, but I'm grinning because that was probably the only time Abi pulled something like that. And not only had I covered for her, but unbeknownst to them, I'd followed her and Violet to make sure they were safe.

"And Violet, you are the sweetest, most loyal friend a girl could have. I would not be the confident risk-taker I am today without you—and your notes in statistics. Actually, I'd probably be taking that class for the tenth time without your getting me through it."

She chokes up a bit and fans her face, looking up to the ceiling to stop the tears from falling. "In some ways, I'm jealous of Ross because he's going to take away some of the times we get to share. He's going to be the one you confide in, the one you tell your dreams to . . . but at the same time, I'm happy about it. I want you both to hold on to each other, to let your love keep growing. And twenty years from now, when you're both at your kid's high school graduation—"

Someone in the back yells out, "Their twins' graduation!" and a chuckle resonates through the room again.

Abi nods. "Wouldn't that be awesome? But just remember who set you two up. I get the credit for this little match made in heaven." She points from me to Violet and smiles.

For all her scheming, she's not half bad. I could definitely do worse for a sister.

I laugh, and Violet joins in, both of us hugging Abi when she comes over. "I love you, Abs," I whisper to her, and she hugs me harder. "Thank you."

"I'm serious about that twenty-year thing," Abi whispers. "Your little sister sees all." She wiggles her fingers in the air, like she's casting a witchy spell over us, but I don't need one to be in love with Violet.

"Yeah, well—"

"Excuse me."

The voice is unfamiliar, but as soon as it comes over the speakers, Violet goes pale and looks toward the stage. "No—" she quietly says in horror.

I follow her gaze and see Colin Radcliffe holding the microphone that Abi just abandoned. He's sharply dressed in a suit, but his face is twisted in smug satisfaction. "What is he doing up there?" I ask out loud to no one in particular.

"Sorry to interrupt, folks, but I figured before this . . . *farce* went on any longer," Colin says to the stunned crowd who are looking at each other with questions in their eyes, "well, I wanted to put my two cents in. I'd have spoken at the wedding, but a certain maid of honor saw me and made sure a couple of the bride's cousins escorted me out." He glares at Abi, and even from here, I can see a couple of guys getting up to make their way toward Colin. I'm pretty sure the one in the front is Rafael, and I'm glad he's putting his muscle to good use today.

"Get off the stage!" I call out, standing to lend Violet's family a hand.

Colin must sense that his time is running out because he begins talking faster, his face turning red with impotent fury.

"What's the problem, Ross?" Colin taunts with an ugly sneer. "Afraid everyone's going to learn the truth? That this wedding, this whole romance, is nothing but a lie? It's all fake."

Shit. Fuck. That motherfucker.

I move toward the stage, but out of the corner of my eye, I see the camera crew moving, and a sick dropping feeling hits me. If I go after him, I'm damned. If I don't, he talks, and I'm damned.

I try to remember what Violet told me about this guy, which admittedly isn't much because we'd spent most of our time talking about each other and the future. But she said he's all about image, so I play to that weakness with an insult, hoping to put questions in folks' minds about whatever he's going to say.

"Sour grapes are so tacky. You're insane, Colin."

"Jilted lovers often are," Radcliffe replies, his voice not shaky at all, though he's feigning sadness as he looks at Violet.

"For those of you who don't know me, I'm Violet's previous fiancé, or *one of them, at least,* because it does seem like she's collecting them." He laughs harshly into the microphone like he told a joke with his salacious suggestion. People murmur and look to one another in confusion.

"You broke up with me, Colin. What are you doing? Why are you doing this?" Violet yells hysterically, standing up but staying behind the table when Abi puts a hand on her arm, keeping her in place.

Colin whirls on Violet, "I did, but I made a mistake. This was supposed to be our wedding—our venue, our ceremony, our day. You should have fought for us. But nooo, Violet Russo's too good for that. Hell, I even tried to get you back and you turned your back on me. *No one does that to Colin Radcliffe.*"

The furious proclamation has weight, floating dangerously in the air. That he's talking about himself in third person only amplifies how crazy he sounds, which I hope works in our favor.

"But you'll pay," he threatens darkly.

He pulls out his phone and clicks the screen. A video begins playing, too small to see from where I am, but he holds it up to the microphone, and I recognize Violet's voice at the same time everyone else does. It's muffled, like she's on a speakerphone, but it's obviously her.

"I'm scared, Abs," Violet says on the recording. *"I'm scared every-one's going to find out this is all fake and it's all going to fall apart in flames of glory. I'll be the laughingstock of the city, and Ross will be a pariah, any hopes he has of improving his reputation at work dashed by our secret arrangement."*

Then we hear Abi's answer. *"No one is going to find out that it's a fake marriage so you can both save face. You're going to walk down that aisle and make your Papa proud for his last days, and Ross is going to get Dad off his back and kick ass at work. And—"*

It's like a bomb just dropped on the whole reception.

Abi and Violet are pale and look like they're going to be sick. Out of the corner of my eye, I see Maria Russo burst into tears, and suddenly, everyone's talking over one another, yelling and gesturing and just trying to figure out in two different languages what the fuck's going on.

On my side of the room, Mom also looks horrified while Courtney looks betrayed. Dad, for his part, is turning a pinkish purple of rage, and I can read the 'I knew it' in his glittery eyes.

"So congratulations to the whore and groom on a well-done performance." He gives a light golf-style clap against the microphone with a satisfied smile. "May your fake marriage be as real as your fake romance," Colin says, standing up and dropping the mic on stage.

"What's he talking about?"

"How could you!"

"Violet!"

"Ross!"

I can't put voices to faces. There are too many people yelling at once and too many of the same questions being asked. I look at Violet, who's got tears running down her cheeks, and I know what I need to do.

Pushing through the crowd, I beat Rafael to the stage and jump up next to Colin. I'm already murderous, but Colin looks so self-satisfied, it angers me even more. "You're welcome. She's such a cold bitch, right?"

His switch from heated, spoiled entitlement to bro-casual chatter is disgusting. He's ruined everything, for Papa, for Violet, for me, and doesn't care in the least.

My fist flies even before I know it, catching him under the chin and sending him tumbling into the DJ's equipment. I can hear and see the flashing lights as the news cameras catch it all, but I don't care.

I've got one chance to fix this. Reaching down, I pick up Colin's dropped microphone. "Everyone, please, this isn't—"

Colin's punch catches me blind, and I go stumbling back a few steps before he swings on me again. Suddenly, we're in a full-on fight, falling to the stage and rolling back and forth as we exchange punches and elbows.

I don't want to hurt him . . . well, at least that's not my number-one priority. All I want is to get on the microphone to explain to everyone how what started as one thing has changed into another.

Violet's scream pierces the haze just as I blast Colin in the nose with a sharp elbow that sends his head smacking backward into the stage. I look over, but she's forgotten me as she kneels in front of Stefano.

"Papa!" she screams again as he slumps to the side, his hand on his chest and his eyes rolling backward. "Papa!"

Dimly, I hear someone else pick up the cry and another voice screaming for an ambulance.

And for the first time in my life, I have no answers at all.

CHAPTER 24

VIOLET

*T*he waiting room feels like an interrogation room. Not that I've ever been in one, but I've seen enough on television to know this is what the bad guy feels like when he knows he's been busted.

The triplets are staring at me with utter hatred in their eyes, and a few of my other cousins all look like they'd kick me out of the family if they had the option. I'm sitting in a chair, surrounded by my family, but I've never felt more alone.

It's because of me that Papa's here in the hospital.

If he dies, the coroner can put whatever he wants on the paperwork, but the truth is he's going to die of a broken heart . . . and I'm the one who broke it.

Finally, Mom speaks. "Do you feel any shame at all about what you've done?"

"Mom, I—"

"Quiet!" Mom thunders, getting out of her chair to tower over me. She's not that tall, but right now, I feel like I'm five years old again and she's a giant that I have to crane my neck to look up to. "Just shut your mouth, Violet! You . . . you lied to us! You lied to your family, you lied to *me*, your own mother! Why? What reason could you have for this . . . this *charade?* What could be so important to you that you'd bring shame on yourself and on your family—"

"Maria."

"You've disgraced yourself, Violet Antonia Carlotta Russo," she spits out.

"Maria Valentina!"

Nana's voice cuts through Mom's yelling, and she takes a step back, tears coursing down her cheeks. "Never," Mom whispers, "never have I been so . . . *disappointed* in you."

Mom sits down, and I swallow my tears, looking down at my hands in my lap. I'm still wearing my wedding dress, the white silk stained reddish-purple in spots where wine spilled on me as I rushed to Papa's side.

"Mom, I—" I start, choking back my tears to try and be mature and adult. I can't change what I've done, but I can be the woman that she and Papa raised me to be from here on out.

"I don't want to hear it, Violet. Not right now."

"You asked me why, and—"

"You've heard of a rhetorical question, haven't you?" Mom snarls.

"Maria!" Nana snaps, her voice brooking no argument. "I raised *you* better than that."

Mom looks like she's about to snap at Nana, and I whimper at the thought. Nana and Mom fighting? And Aunt Sofia sitting calmly next to her sister, being a supportive rock because she's been through this already?

It's too much, and I feel like I'm about to crawl out of my skin.

The waiting room door opens and Ross comes in, his hand wrapped in an elastic bandage and another large bandage covering his eyebrow. After he and Colin finished beating the shit out of each other, he'd gotten a nasty gash that the emergency room doc insisted on treating, probably to keep the crowd down.

"Get out!" Mom yells at him, starting to get back up again, but Aunt Sofia grabs her and holds her back. From her seat, she waves her hands. "Get out. You are not family, not really. Look what you have done, what you have both done. Stupid children!"

Ross starts to speak, but a doctor comes in. "Mrs. Russo?"

I can hear it in her voice, everyone can, but Nana's a rock. She stands with all the dignity of a queen, her voice barely quavering. "Yes, I'm Angela Russo."

Ross comes to my side, and this time, at least, Mom doesn't say anything because all of us are laser-locked on the doctor and what news she might bring.

"Mrs. Russo, we're doing the best we can, but I want to warn you that there's a real chance he might not make it through the night. If there's a priest or other spiritual advisor you'd like to contact, now is the time."

Her words shatter me, and the tears that I've struggled to hold back since I saw Papa collapse pour forth.

This was supposed to be the best day of my life. I'd tried to give Papa that last happy memory, to make his dying wish come true.

Instead, it's become my worst nightmare, and as Sofia supports her sister, I feel worse than I've ever felt before.

Nana, though, as much as she must be breaking on the inside, draws upon that well of strength she has.

"May I see him?"

The doctor nods, leading Nana and Mom to the back but stopping everyone else with a shake of her head. In the silence that follows the door swinging closed, I want to scream in anguish, but I can't. Not after the strength Nana just showed.

"I think there's a conversation you need to have," Aunt Sofia says, lifting her chin at Ross.

I can't do this, not now. My brain is too fried, my heart too filled with fear, but she's right. "Let's step out," I tell Ross, wanting to get away from the glares of my family. They're frigid with me, but they look like they're plotting Ross's murder.

He nods woodenly and then winces, and I think he must have a hell of a headache from the fight and the blow he took to the head.

In the hallway, I close the door behind me, separating us from my family, not that anything's secret now.

"Violet, I—"

"No, Ross," I whisper, the anger building within me. I want

to rage at the world, bemoan the unfairness of it all, go back and wipe the last little while from existence. I'd do anything to have Papa healthy beside me once again.

The guilt gnaws at me. Oh, there's enough to go around, but most of it lies on my shoulders. But Ross is the one standing here with me while everyone else either hates me, is disgusted with me, or is just avoiding me.

So Ross is the target, and he's going to catch the full blast of everything I've got.

"What the fuck just happened?" I ask, stepping up to him. "How did Colin even get in? Why didn't you stop him before he ruined everything? What if Papa doesn't make it?"

The questions I've been asking myself blurt from my lips. I've been replaying the scene in my head on a loop, changing small details and trying to figure out how that would've affected the outcome. If anything could have prevented Papa from being here like this.

Ross tries to put his arms around me, to hug me to him, but I shake him off. "No. Don't you get it? It's over . . . our lie, our relationship, our . . . everything. Everyone knows it's all fake. It's all fake, and because of us, Papa's here! You and I, we did this!"

I fall apart, ugly, snotty tears making my puffy face slick with sadness and fear again.

"We didn't mean to," Ross says lamely, trying to find some sort of justification for what we've done.

I shake my head. "It doesn't matter now. Just leave. Please."

Ross looks like he's about ready to cry now, his throat working. "Vi—"

"Leave," I whisper. "This fairy tale's over."

Ross looks like he wants to argue but instead, after a moment, nods, leaving me alone in the suddenly empty hallway.

I'm alone.

All alone.

The tile seems so comforting, and I sag to it, finally able to sob the way my heart demands.

CHAPTER 25

ROSS—SUNDAY—1 DAY AFTER THE WEDDING

*S*unday's supposed to be a day of rest.

This specific Sunday should have been a day of celebration. Violet and I were going to wake up late after a long night of making love, enjoy a leisurely brunch somewhere around two or three in the afternoon, then get on a private plane to fly off on our honeymoon, maybe joining the Mile-High Club in the process.

That was the plan. A start of a new life and an opportunity to tell Violet that things have changed. That even though it's been only two weeks, this isn't fake anymore. Not to me.

I planned to tell her that I've developed feeling for her, ones that run deeper than I'd ever imagined. I planned to tell her that I love her and want to spend not just some short blip of time with her, but I truly want to be with her forever. I planned to tell her everything.

What's that saying about the best-laid plans?

Something about them so often going awry. Well, they have done that, for sure. In a big ball of spectacularly destructive flames from which there might be no recovering.

Now, those future plans lie in utter ruins.

Papa is desperately ill. Violet sent me away, her family glaring at me only marginally harder than they frowned at her. My mother crying as she asked where she went wrong that I would do something like this to a nice girl like Violet. Courtney's eyes full of hurt as she said, "I asked you straight out and you lied to my face." And my father. I'd almost feared he was going to end up in the hospital next to Papa with the way the vein in his forehead was throbbing. Red-faced and furious, he'd told me that he had to go clean up my mess, like I was nothing but an unruly child.

"That was another call," Kaede says as he gets off the phone. He's been doing damage control with me all day. "Another of the shareholder groups says they're going to dump all of their stock. You know, it was a lot easier to pull this shit back in the days before online trading. Someone has the world's biggest fuckup of a wedding on Saturday, you still had all day Sunday to calm down before markets opened on Monday. Damn shame how the world's speeding up."

I know Kaede's trying to keep things light, trying to keep my spirits up, but it's not working very well. I'm not going to jump on his ass over it. He's still being professional.

I'm just not in the mood.

Reaching up, I start to run my hand over my stubble when I wince and pull back, both my bruised face and my wrist reminding me of yesterday's debacle. I guess I wasn't quite prepared for how hard Colin Radcliffe's skull could be.

The cut over my eye hurts more, simply because of how I got it. I don't think Violet even realizes that she's the one who sliced me open as I gathered her in my arms, forcing her away from Papa so the EMTs could help him. The pain in her eyes and the anguish in her cry hurt more than her ring ripping my skin, and I refused the doctor's desire to stitch it closed. I want it to scar, want the reminder of the day that started with such happiness and that, because of my misguided actions, ended so terribly.

"Have you heard from Abi?" I ask Kaede. After Violet threw me out, the staff said it'd be better if I didn't return, that it'd cause the family stress. But Abi sent a text late last night that she was with Violet, supporting her because her family is treating her like a pariah. It'd pained me so much to know that Vi's hurting, but I can't do anything to help other than stay away. I have to be thankful that Abi is there, though.

"Nothing new," Kaede says, his voice reflective of the situation. "Is there anything you'd like me to do?"

"Just . . . just . . ." I start before my mind just blanks out. There's nothing left, nothing inside me. I just don't care.

"I can think of something you can do, Kaede," Courtney says, coming in. "Start drafting up an apology letter for Ross."

"Apology letter?" I ask, shaking myself back to the situation at hand. "Who else wants an apology? I feel like all I've done is say 'I'm sorry.'"

"Actually, Dad wants another apology, preferably a real one and not just lip service this time, but that's a totally different matter," Courtney says, her voice still heavy with the hurt she obviously feels over this whole matter. "We all want one. But this is a corporate one, and it's my idea to save your undeserving ass."

"Undeserving . . ."

"Yes, undeserving!" Courtney fumes at my murmured word. "Dammit, Ross, you'd have been better off keeping on doing what you were doing before. *Ross Andrews, the manwhore of the city.*" She sneers the words, and though we all know they're not true, it is the foundation of what the media was publishing all too often. "At least then, we could write it off as immature ways to let loose from the stresses of your corporate responsibilities. This is a lot fucking worse. There are even people saying Dad was complicit in this scam to make it look like you were finally going to follow corporate policies instead of flitting about with a pastor's wife. Who knows where this is headed if we don't get out in front of it!"

"The company will survive," I murmur, not really caring. All I can focus on is Violet and Stefano and what I've done to them. Compared to that, dollar signs mean nothing.

Courtney crosses her arms, looking at me carefully before hooking her thumb at Kaede, who pulls a fade, closing the door behind him. Courtney sits down and sighs. "On a more personal note, Colin Radcliffe's lawyer called. I handled it, but the long and short of it is, he's going to sue you. And his dad's pressuring the cops to arrest you for assault because you threw the first punch."

"Don't care."

Courtney rubs at her forehead, staring at me, but I'm done with this conversation. "I can see that. Actually, I wish Dad could see what I see right now. Maybe then he wouldn't be verging on an explosion." She mimes his head blowing up from his temples. "I know you've been through this with Mom and Dad, but can you tell me what the hell you were thinking?"

I bury my head in my hands, my elbows on my desk. "Court, it was supposed to be for convenience. Dad was putting all of this pressure on me to settle down, and for some stupid reason, I thought a steady plus-one would be enough to get him off my back. But Violet needed more, for Papa. She needed the whole fairy tale wedding thing. It was his dying wish to walk her down the aisle and see her happily married." A humorless huff escapes. "Fucked that up, didn't I?"

Courtney's mouth falls open, her eyes scanning me, analyzing me. I can't take any more. I spin in my chair, giving her my back and facing the wall of windows. Her voice is soft, gentle as she asks, "When did it become real to you, Ross?"

I can hear that she's not the corporate up and comer right now but just my little sister who's worried about me. I don't bother trying to deny it because I would shout it from mountaintops if I thought it would help anything. "I don't know," I tell her honestly, looking over my shoulder at her. "Too late to prevent what happened, I guess."

She nods. "You guess right. The important thing now is, what are you going to do? Does Violet know?" Her eyes widen. "Does she feel the same way you do?" She brings up so many good questions, ones I have no answers to.

I turn back to the windows, staring over the city but not seeing anything, my vision blurred by images, memories of Violet. "I don't know what to do. Violet doesn't know how I feel. I was going to tell her, but it seemed like too much of a risk before the wedding. I wanted to give her what she wanted and thought we'd have time afterward. I thought I'd have time to make her love me too."

I can hear Courtney tapping on her phone, and I turn to look at her incredulously. Angrily, I demand, "I'm pouring my heart out over here and you're working? You really are Dad's daughter, aren't you?"

She literally snaps her fingers at me, and despite myself, I freeze in shock at the rudeness. She gets up, walking around my desk to stand at my side, looming over me. "I am my father's daughter, which means that when new information presents itself, I make adjustments accordingly. For the good of all involved. He's not the monster you seem to think he is. I told you that he was pressuring you for your own good. Surely, you can see that in the last two weeks, even if it started as some scheme, you've changed in positive ways. You're finally growing up and putting someone else's wants and needs over your own, and that's all Dad wanted for you. A future, a family. He didn't want some fake convenience woman on your arm for a hot minute for appearances. He wants you to have what he has, a family he loves and takes pride in."

Her words are sharp barbs, poisoned for maximum pain, because she's right. So many times, I've butted heads with my father, thinking him old-fashioned or feeling like he was forcing me in directions I didn't want to go. But maybe it's because he was happy with that path, and since it's all he knows, he's guided me that way too.

"Maybe," I concede.

"Progress," she proclaims with the barest hint of a smile, but I'm unable to return it, which makes her lips fall again. "Look, I just want you to know that I love you, and whatever you've done, that doesn't change. Especially knowing what I know now. You're my big brother, and though I'm just your annoying little sister, I love you."

"Thank you," I mouth before finding my voice and repeating myself. "Thank you."

Courtney holds her arms out in invitation, and I find the strength to stand up and hug her tightly. She hugs me back, and in her arms, I find the ability to release. The tears start slowly, and I never devolve into full on sobbing, but with each hot tear, Courtney hugs me tighter. For the first time in our lives, she's the one supporting me and I'm the one needing strength and comfort.

It's a short storm, a summer squall of the agony I'm in, but it helps. When I'm done, Courtney wipes her thumb under my eyes like Mom used to before standing on her tiptoes to kiss my forehead, again, just like Mom.

"Thanks. I think. Though let's never discuss this again," I say awkwardly. I sigh and straighten my spine, falling back into my comfortable role. "Can you do me a favor?"

"Anything."

"Work with Kaede on the damage control letter. I'm going to talk with Dad."

"You sure?" Courtney asks.

I nod, adjusting my tie a little. "Yeah. The sooner, the better. No use in prolonging this and letting others control my destiny. I did that for too long."

I leave Courtney and Kaede and head upstairs to my father's office. He's here too, of course. Most of the senior management's dealing with the PR fallout of yesterday's insanity. They all want to be here, both for the good of the company and because everyone loves to see the prince taken down a notch. I can feel their watchful eyes—curious, amused, shocked, angry.

But yet, they work to minimize the impact, even if the majority of the responsibility is sitting on my shoulders, and everyone is waiting for Dad to decide what he's going to do.

But professionally, I still don't care. Yeah, I don't want Kaede, or Courtney, or anyone in the company to be hurt or lose their jobs because of this, but as for me?

I don't care. This corporation's in good hands with Dad in charge, and if the future of this place doesn't involve me . . . I can live with that. I don't want it to come to that, but it's not the most important thing in my life right now.

Violet is. She's all I care about.

Dad's sitting behind his desk when I walk in, his face still thundery. "Dad?"

"I assume Courtney found you?" Dad says, his voice so tight that I'm afraid he'll snap a tooth if he bites his words off any harder.

"She did. I wanted to say I'm sorry."

"So you've said. But sorry won't cut it this time. Do you even realize what you've done?" he growls, slamming his hand to his desk as he rises to his feet, pacing about the room.

"I've got board members yelling about stock prices, which have dropped by eighteen percent in the last twenty-four hours. That's people's lives, Ross! Their life savings shot because of your shenanigans. The shareholders are bitching about morality clauses, demanding my own son's dismissal from the company I started from nothing. I've got lawyers calling, police calling, and the media . . ." He shakes his head. "The fucking media! Showing that sniveling shit Radcliffe on the news first thing this morning. And it's trending on social media too. Congrats, you've gone viral," he says sarcastically.

"Dad—" I say, trying to get a word in edgewise, but he's on a roll.

"What is it your mother calls them? Culture vultures? They smell blood in the water and they're hunting like sharks, hunting *you*, Son. And what am I to do about it?"

"Nothing," I say sharply. "Let me fix this. I'm the one who fucked up. Let me fix it. At least I can drown myself in work and be useful for something."

Dads laughs tersely. "You? Fix this? This whole thing is your mess, as always."

I grit my teeth. "It's never my mess! It's you believing those parasites and the tales they make up over your own son. So what if I wasn't ready to settle down and get married? It wasn't your place to force me to do it, regardless of why you did it and whether your reasons were well-intentioned or not." It's the smallest give that I have, based on what Courtney told me about Dad's thinking process and what he wants for my future.

LAUREN LANDISH

"I didn't force you to lie to everyone. You did that all on your own, didn't you?" he booms.

It's on the tip of my tongue to say that it was Abi's idea, just to show him that I'm not the only one who thinks he's gone too far. But I can't. I won't throw my sister under the bus that way.

But Dad heard the video and knows that conversation was between Violet and Abi. I can see the moment he remembers that.

"And you got your sister involved in this too!"

Fine, if that's how we're doing this, then so be it.

"You know as well as I do that no one mixes Abi up in anything she doesn't want to get mixed up in. She's as hard-headed as you are." It's not a compliment, but he smiles slightly as if it is. "She knew you were pressuring me, she knew Violet needed this, and she put one and one together."

"Except she came up with three, and we're all paying the price."

"No one is paying the price more than Violet," I remind him, which sobers us both from the war of words we're engaging in.

It's a dash of cold water on both of our tempers. "We are never going to see eye to eye on this, so what do you want me to do? How do we move forward from where we are now?"

He sits down in his chair, his face stoic as he returns to the all-business mode he's known for. "The company is putting out a press release, you will write an apology letter, the lawyers will do what we pay them to do, and the company will ride this out."

"And us?" I say.

He sighs, turning in his chair to look out the window, so similar to what I did to Courtney just moments ago. "You should go visit your mother."

I know a dismissal when I hear one. I swallow thickly and turn on my heel, leaving Dad to deal with the company he loves, to repair the image he cares about. He wants me to settle down, have a family, be the two-dot-oh version of him, but right now, I feel like his family is the last thing Dad cares about.

A tiny voice in the back of my head tries to remind me of all the times Dad was there for me, teaching me about the company

300

I begrudge him for loving, throwing spirals in the yard when I was just a pee-wee football player, and showing me how to love by treating Mom well. But I can't, not now when we've been ripped apart at the seams that used to hold us together.

I do a quick check-in with Kaede and Courtney, who are working on the apology draft, to tell them where I'm headed. Courtney wishes me luck, saying that as mad as Dad is, Mom is more hurt.

"She really believed you and was so happy for you. She was already thinking about what she wanted your kids to call her. I think she'd settled on Lolly but was still talking Dad into going for Pop."

Guilt blooms afresh.

I climb into my Camaro and drive out to the estate. There's media both just outside the parking garage of the office and at the gate to the house, but a pair of sunglasses and a cranked-up radio help me ignore them.

Karl greets me at the front door, his face tense but professional. "You doing okay, Karl?"

"They are respecting the property lines, sir. I wish they'd respect a few more lines, but that's beyond my powers," he says. "Your mother is in her library."

Mom's library is the equivalent of Dad's study. It's her 'cave', the place she gets to do whatever she wants and express her tastes however she wants. You'd expect a library to be all dark woods and expensive tomes, but you'd be so very wrong. She's turned it into the epitome of old-school femininity, with patterned lace wallpaper, pale rose-colored crown moldings, and a bunch of books with covers I'd rather not think about my mother reading. It's safe to say this my least favorite room in the house.

I find Mom sitting on her white loveseat in loungewear, even though it's late afternoon, which is unlike her. She's staring out the window that faces the garden, a cup of tea on a saucer next to her. As I close the door, she turns around, and I stop, shocked.

Somehow, my mother's aged ten years overnight. Normally, she looks a good decade younger than she actually is.

Now, though, the woman looking up at me is a wreck. She looks shattered, her face lined with wrinkles that weren't there yesterday, her eyes puffy and red, and I have to blink to convince myself that the gray I see in her hair is sunlight and not gray.

"Why?"

Only one word, but it breaks me more than all of Dad's ranting and Courtney's browbeating. Her voice is a cracked, paper-thin parody of the soft voice that I grew up listening to, the cool balm to Dad's bluster.

"I wish I had a good reason," I finally admit, unable to hold up to Mom's pleading eyes. "We never meant for it to happen like this. We didn't mean to hurt anyone."

Mom's soft smile says that even the consequences we don't intend are ours to bear.

"When you came to me saying you were marrying Violet, I remembered an old dream I had," Mom says vacantly, looking out the window again. "It was soon after Abigail and Violet became friends, and she'd invited Violet over for a sleepover."

"Which time? She was always over here." The attempt at lightness falls flat as Mom cuts her eyes back to me.

Mom takes another sip of her tea and nods. "She was. But this time, you spent all day being the most annoying pain in the ass a big brother could be. When the girls wanted to swim, you complained they were splashing too much. When they played inside, you complained they were too loud and disrupting your homework. You, of all people, complaining about being able to do homework."

"If I remember right, you said I could sleep outside then."

Mom nods. "And that night, when you'd gotten your sleeping bag arranged in Abigail's treehouse, I noticed something. From this window, I could see both your and Abi's rooms, and you were looking up there at Violet. And I just had this vision, a dream. I brushed it off at the time, though I did wonder when you two would fight so fiercely through high school. Love and hate are such a thin line, and you lost interest in everyone else so readily, but never Violet. And the engagement brought it back around."

"I'm sorry, Mom. Truly, but I'm going to make this right."

"How?" Mom asks, her eyes starting to water. "How can you make it right?"

"I don't know," I admit honestly, "but I'm going to." I reach out and take her hand, "Mom, it started out because I was trying to get Dad off my back and because Violet wanted to do right by Papa. But over the last two weeks, or maybe you're right and it started long ago . . . but when I stood up there yesterday, I meant every word I said to Violet."

Mom looks at me hopefully, swallowing. "You mean . . . ?"

"I mean I've got some things to do, some people to talk to . . . maybe some asses to kick, and a few lumps to take."

Mom smiles and stands up. "Then go take care of them."

CHAPTER 26

VIOLET—SUNDAY—1 DAY AFTER THE WEDDING

*T*he dawn breaks bright through the hospital's waiting room window, waking me up from the fitful sleep I finally found about three in the morning.

My spine feels like someone's filled it with glass and then beaten it with a rolling pin and my neck, especially, is cricked in a way that makes me wonder if I'm going to need a chiropractor *stat*. I can barely feel my toes, and my left wrist hurts from cradling my head while I slept.

But nothing hurts worse than my chest, where my heart thuds hollowly. The one kindness is that Abi brought me some clothes and helped me change out of my wedding dress late last night before she went home to get some sleep. She promised to be back today, though, which I'm glad for because I feel so alone and so scared.

My family fills the entirety of the hospital's waiting room, sprawled over every chair and piled up in the corners, leaning on each other. But only Nana and Aunt Sofia are willing to sit on this side of the room. Mom and the triplets sit across from me, glaring at every opportunity. And my cousins mostly just look confused and concerned, but they understand the basics of what I've done and choose to go the safe route of the majority and ignore me.

Nobody sits within three seats of me, and I fidget to try and

LAUREN LANDISH

get back to some feeling in my right foot because my bladder's screaming at me that it was a really, really stupid idea to drink that last coffee at two o'clock this morning.

Finally, I can't hold it any longer and go waddling out of the waiting room, wincing with every step until I'm all the way to the ladies' room. After I'm done, I wash my face, looking down at the streaky mess that comes away in my hands, the stubborn remnants of yesterday's makeup that withstood the tears of the night. Using the harsh soap by the sink, I scrub at my face, wishing I could wash away the last twelve hours as easily.

When I come back to the waiting room, a few more people are awake, and a doctor is talking with Nana. She nods, then points toward me. I can read her lips even from the doorway. "There she is."

Oh, great, what did I do now?

"Miss Russo?" the doctor says, giving me a supportive smile. It's the first one I can remember seeing since yesterday, and I feel myself tearing up again before I can blink them back.

"Yes?"

"We're allowing a few people in to see him. You should prepare yourself. He's on machines, so we have him heavily sedated, but he's made it through the night. Angela said you should go first."

I swallow and look over at Nana. "Are you sure?" I ask, feeling like she should be the first to go in, or Mom, maybe. Not me, when this whole thing is my fault.

Nana nods. "Stefano and I have had many conversations about his health, his life, and yes, even his passing. There is nothing I need to say to him that I haven't already said many times over. But I don't think that's true for you. Go to him, open your heart, and be at peace, Violet."

Though her words are a balm to my soul, I can hear that she's exhausted. I doubt she slept at all, instead staying awake to be the rock of our family and provide comfort to everyone else, just like she's doing for me. I love her so much.

I follow the doctor to Papa's room, where I find him hooked up to not just one machine but to a whole plethora of them.

306

There are beeps, squiggly lines on monitors, tubes running from his arms . . . everything. Even though the doctor tried to prepare me for this, I don't think anything he'd said would've made me ready to see Papa like this, weak, a shell of his usual self, and so pale and frail looking.

I nod, and the doctor leaves, probably to fetch more of my family. In the few moments I have before someone else comes in, I cross over to his bedside, taking his hand. He looks so small under the white sheet, his head tilted back and his eyes closed. His mouth's a little open around the tube that's taped in place, and if it weren't for the mechanically steady rise and fall of his chest, I'd be even more afraid.

"Papa," I whisper, looking into his face. "Papa, please . . . please come back to us. I'm sorry. I just wanted us to have that good memory of walking down the aisle. I know how much it meant to you to see me married, and I just . . . I couldn't see any other way. Oh, God, I'm so sorry. Please, I love you so much, and I'm not ready to let go of you. I need you to be here, to give me advice because I don't know how to fix this. I want you to know that I do love him. Ross, I mean. It was fake, and I'm so sorry for lying, but it was real too. Oh, I messed up everything, Papa!"

The words tumble out of my mouth, one on top of the other as tears track down my face in rivers. It's the same roundabout loop my mind's been stuck in all night but the first time to give the words voice because no one wants to hear anything from me.

The door behind me opens and Mom comes in, her hand entwined with Aunt Sofia's. It looks like she's holding on for strength, but it's probably at least a little bit to keep Mom under control. Sofia gives me a supportive look, but Mom's still so upset I can feel it coming off her in waves.

'I raised you better than this, Violet Antonia Carlotta Russo,' she'd said last night before clamming back up, tearing a fresh jagged wound open. Disappointing my mom is something I've strived to never do. She's done so much for me, raising me, sacrificing for me, and I've always wanted to show her that I was worth it.

And then she'd pointedly directed the conversation away from me and my sham of a wedding to Papa. Everyone had sat around until late in the night, and even early this morning, sharing stories of his life like he was already gone, even though he's still here, fighting for his life. I'd kept my mouth shut, not wanting to bring any attention back to myself, and thought of happy memories with Papa alone in my mind and heart.

"Daddy," Mom says as she comes up, and I know how much she's been shaken. Though Mom used to call her father 'Daddy' when she was a girl, I've only ever heard Mom call Papa 'Daddy' twice in my life. The first time was when Mom had a uterine cancer scare that turned out to be a benign tumor, and the other time was when Papa was diagnosed with his heart condition. She'd rushed in shortly after Dr. Lee had told me his prognosis, afraid she wasn't going to make it in time.

Now, she just holds Papa's hand, whispering against it in prayer, as Aunt Sofia switches to holding me up. Mom rises silently and kisses Papa on the forehead.

"He's going to get better," I whisper, clenching Aunt Sofia's shirt in my fist. "He has to."

Mom looks at me so grimly that Sofia squeezes me protectively. "Come on, Violet," she says. "Let's give your mom a few moments alone with Stefano."

It's another of Sofia's dodges, but she's right. This isn't the place for Mom and me to have this conversation. It's also not the place for Mom and me to reevaluate our relationship. Our emotions are too raw, too fresh.

In the hallway, Nana is waiting for us. My heart drops. I don't think I can withstand an attack from her after Mom's harsh words from last night are still so fresh and the result of my actions, Papa lying unconscious in bed, stared me in the face just moments ago. But she hugs me and I melt into her arms.

"I'm so sorry, Nana," I cry, sobbing against her small shoulder.

She pats my back, rubbing soothing circles between my shoulder blades. "I know, baby. I'm not here to pile guilt at your feet. I wanted to let you know that Dr. Lee came by just now. You remember his cardiologist?" I nod, thinking back to that first big spell and Dr. Lee's direct but kind manner. "He looked over all the tests and reports from last night and this morning. He wants to do surgery on Stefano."

I gasp, and Aunt Sofia switches her support once again, taking Nana by the arm. "Is he sure Stefano can handle that? Can you handle that?"

Nana's sad smile is hopeful but resigned. "No, and no. But it's his best chance. Before, he didn't want to risk it, but now the risk-reward ratio, as he called it, has shifted. With the surgery, Stefano might have a chance, a small one. Without it, he . . ."

Her words break off as the strongest woman I've ever known breaks down. It's not a crumbling, dramatic scene. Angela Russo would never. But tears slip through the soft lines of her face and she hugs Aunt Sofia tightly. I feel like an intruder on their moment of sisterly support and quietly slip away to give them some privacy.

A little bit later, Aunt Sofia plops into the chair next to me in the waiting room, handing over a steaming cup of coffee. "Your uncle, my husband, was an idiot," Sofia whispers to me. I have no idea what she's talking about or why she's talking about it now as they're preparing Papa for surgery.

"I loved him more than is healthy, but Giuseppe was one of those men who always had an angle, always a scheme . . . and more often than not ended up the sucker. I blame us for living in New York, that city . . . eh, it is what it is. But 'Seppe . . . I can't tell you the number of times he'd come home having lost five hundred dollars here, a thousand there. That is a lot of money today, but back then it was months of wages. One time, he even lost five thousand dollars from our retirement account because of some 'plan' he had."

I look over, surprised. "I didn't know that." Apparently, hearing about my Uncle's poor choices is supposed to make me feel better about my own, but losing money and what I've done to Papa are nothing alike.

Sofia nods, chuckling. "I tore the hide off Giuseppe's back more than once when he screwed up, and he slept on the couch more days than our children probably remember. But the reason I stayed with him . . . well, two reasons. One, Giuseppe might have been a sucker, but he was also a man who'd do whatever it took to fix things. That five thousand dollars? It took him six months of working a second job at night to replace it, but he did it. He made us right again. Second, I loved him. And love is sometimes crazy, Violet."

My voice is small, quiet enough to keep it just between the two of us. "I would do anything to make this right because I love Papa so much. You're right, love is crazy, and maybe what I did was ridiculous, but it was because I wanted to give him that memory. I wanted to give *us* that moment."

Aunt Sofia tilts her head, looking at me with soft eyes. "That is true, Violet. But I think you're missing the point of my story. I'm not talking about Stefano. I'm talking about your Ross."

I protest, "I can't do that right now. It was all for Papa, and I have to focus on him."

She hums noncommittally and pats my hand, letting me disappear into my mind. Thoughts of Ross and the wedding try to sneak in, but I push them out, not able to handle thinking of that when my grandfather is lying on a table with his chest open and we're praying for a miracle.

Sometime later, Archie comes in with lunch. He's subdued too, not his usual big and brash self, which only reiterates how dire the situation is. But at least he's on my side and not judging me for the fake wedding. "You couldn't have known this was going to happen. If anything, this is that sniveling rat, Colin's, fault."

He's trying to make me feel better, but we both know this is on me.

Dr. Lee comes through the double doors down the hall that we've been staring at, and we all stand, his few steps down the hall to the waiting room taking way too long. "Angela," he says, taking her hands, and my heart stops.

No! No, no, no, no. Please!

"The surgery was rough, but it was a success." A sigh of relief goes through the room and then a few whoops of joy sound out. Dr. Lee smiles, but it's that detached professional one that doctors have. Distantly, I wonder if they practice that in the mirror during medical school.

"But that was the first step of *many*. He has a long way to go, so I want you to be prepared for that. He's in the recovery room, and we'll get him into ICU tonight. At some point, we'll wean him off the medications keeping him unconscious and see how he does, how his heart reacts. He's going to be a hospital guest for a while."

Dr. Lee looks around the room. "Please, everyone, go home, get some rest," he urges us. "There's nothing you can do for him sitting here."

A few of my cousins glance at each other and nod, getting up to kiss Nana on the cheek and promising they'll be back if needed. Nana kisses them back, giving them all a little bit of comfort before they walk out. As they pass me, though, more than a few give me dirty looks, and I doubt that I'm going to be invited to any more family gatherings anytime soon.

Finally, it's just Nana, Sofia, Mom, and me, and the doctor clears his throat. "Mrs. Russo, you really—"

"No."

She doesn't raise her voice, she doesn't sound shrill or hysterical. She simply is stating the truth. The only way she's leaving this hospital is if she's physically carried out.

Dr. Lee doesn't know Nana the way our family does, though, and tries to talk to her. "Mrs. Russo, you need to rest, and eat, and—"

"And I'm sure that my husband is being provided with a hospital meal. I can eat that," Nana says matter-of-factly. "As for sleep . . . at my age, sleeping is something I can do sitting in a chair by my husband's bedside just as well as I can in a regular bed. Now leave me alone."

Dr. Lee turns to us, knowing when he's been beaten. "I'll stay with Mama," Mom says. "Someone needs to go to the house and wrangle the family."

"We'll go," Sofia says quietly, taking my hand and hauling me up with unexpected strength.

I swallow but go over to Nana and kiss her on the cheek. "Nana, I—"

"I know, dearie," Nana says, patting my cheek. "And Stefano knows too."

I kiss her again, leaving before I start crying again. In the hallway, Sofia takes my arm and pats my hand. "You heard the doctor. He's going to be okay." That's not what he said, but it's what I need to believe. "Come on, let's get back to Angela's and feed everyone. It's what we Italians do . . . feed a fever, feed a cold, feed to celebrate, feed to mourn, feed our families at every chance we get." She's trying to distract me with silly prattles, but the thought of going to Nana and Papa's house and seeing his favorite chair empty as everyone studiously ignores me, is more than I can take.

"Aunt Sofia, I think I'm going to go home for a bit. I haven't been there in . . . weeks," I say with a swallow, remembering that most of my things are at Ross's, but I don't want to go there. I want to go to my little apartment, with the tiny tub I have to bend my knees to fit in, and just hide away from everyone and everything. "I'll get Archie to take me." I'm already pulling out my phone to text him before he leaves the hospital. I swipe away the dozens of missed calls and texts, some from Ross, some from Abi, some from unknown numbers.

My phone dings in my hand. "Archie says he'll come around and meet me out front," I tell her. After asking if I'm sure, she kisses my cheek and walks me in that direction.

The front sliding doors to the hospital open and suddenly, I'm blinded by a flash.

"There she is!" someone yells, and it's like blood in the Amazon river. Instead of piranha, though, I'm surrounded by journalists, paparazzi, and more cameramen than were at the wedding.

"How's your grandfather?" one asks, but it's the only halfway sympathetic question yelled at me.

Every other question I can make out is insane.

How do I feel about my fraud? Am I a gold digger or a sugar baby? How much did Ross pay me? Did Colin pay me? What kind of magic pussy tricks do I have to get two of the city's hottest bachelors fighting over me?

"What?" I cry out at that last one, horrified at his crudeness. "Excuse me," I say, pushing my way through.

Behind me, I hear Aunt Sofia. "Just go, honey! I'll get the cousins!"

I'm not sure if she means that she'll get them to beat the shit out of the reporters, which while that sounds good, is definitely a bad idea, or if she means she'll ride with them to Nana's and to just leave her.

I pray she means the second one and dive into Archie's car as he pulls up. He peels out of the lot, looking in his rearview mirror. "Sorry, Vi! I came up through the parking garage and had no idea they were out there." He looks pale, and for his dark complexion, that's saying something. He was scared back there too.

They think I did this for money because of who Ross is or because I'm some sort of kept-woman whore. Regardless of the questions, they all say the same thing. I've ruined my life and the lives of a bunch of other people, too.

ARCHIE IS HESITANT TO LEAVE ME AND EVEN FILLS MY RINKY-dink tub for me, but that just reminds me of Ross and the tears start to flow again.

Archie tries to joke lightly, testing the waters. "Oh, no, she's leaking." But even his overexaggerated look of 'what do I do' doesn't change my dull expression.

"I'm sorry, Arch. I just can't. You can leave me alone to wallow in my own pity party. I'm okay, I promise."

He eyes me thoughtfully and then does what he always does, takes care of me. "Okay, sweetie. I'll grab you a glass of wine . . . hmm, make that the bottle. And I'll get your softest PJs and set them on the counter. You hop in the tub and cry it all out. I'll have food delivered later, so answer the door, but look out the peephole first because I wouldn't put it past those sharks to impersonate a delivery guy. You . . . bath, eat, sleep. Got it?"

I nod, not having heard most of what he said. But he leaves after a few minutes and finally . . . finally, I'm truly alone to fall apart.

Papa.

Ross.

What have I done?

CHAPTER 27

ROSS—THURSDAY—5 DAYS AFTER THE WEDDING

*D*espite my promise to my mother that I would fix this, as Thursday morning dawns, I've been doing a lot more talking than fixing. I've talked to the hospital, I've talked to doctors, I've talked to the media, and I've talked to executives around the company.

But I haven't been able to talk to Violet. She hasn't returned my calls or texts, and when I've called her office, all Archie tells me is that yes, he told her I called. I tried again yesterday when the couch she ordered for my office was delivered, but Archie said that the movers knew what to do. He'd apologized and said he'd be in touch soon, but it'd been his professional voice, not the friendliness I've come to expect from him.

Abi hasn't been able to help either. The only time she's been able to talk to Violet, she told Abi that right now, she's focusing on her grandfather and that she'll reach out when the time's right.

So as I sit in my office, trying to prepare myself for what's next, I feel like shit.

This isn't what I want to be doing or where I want to be. I want to be doing whatever it takes to help Violet, to help Stefano. But I know that if I go in there, kicking down doors and forcing myself into the mix, it's only going to make things worse.

I can't drive myself into Violet's life . . . but I can damn sure drive my way out of it.

"Hey," Kaede says, knocking on my door frame. "Five-minute warning."

"Thanks," I reply, standing up and buttoning my suit jacket. "How do I look?"

Kaede looks me up and down and smirks. "You want the truth or for me to kiss your ass?"

"The truth," I reply, not going for his joke. He's been doing his best to keep things lighthearted while attacking this clusterfuck from every angle by my side. He's been my savior, the one holding me back and making me think, not just react.

I hate to say it, but he's been right. In the last forty-eight hours, I've never thought so much. About what I'm doing, what I want, what my dreams are. I'm a damn psychology book of best-friend-supervised pseudo-therapy.

Even so, I'm doing what I'm doing today without his full support. He wants me to wait it out a bit longer, ride the storm and then make steps when things settle a bit. But I'm done waiting, done letting life take me wherever it sees fit.

I'm ready to captain the ship of my life. Finally, I realize, I'm ready.

And isn't that the shit? Dad wanted me to grow up and follow in his footsteps. Well, I'm feeling pretty fucking grown right about now. It's been a long time coming.

"You look like well-dressed shit," Kaede replies, coming over and brushing off my shoulders. "The suit's fresh . . . you're welcome for that. But your shave sucks, and you've got bags under your eyes that'd qualify as checked suitcases. But other than that, you're ready."

I nod in appreciation of his honesty.

"You sure about this?" he asks for the tenth time this morning.

"I am." I pause in the doorway. "Before we go in . . . I wanted to tell you that I'm sorry if I've hurt you or held you back. If there's anything I can do for you later on, if anyone gives you any shit about what we did—"

"Don't sweat it," Kaede says, clapping me on the shoulder. "I'll just tell them that my boss was an absolute psycho, which everyone will believe after the stuff they've been publishing, and I was but a loyal soldier who tried his best to stop the debauchery." He throws his voice, almost into a woefully piss-poor imitation of a British accent.

I laugh finally, the first in days, and though it's slight, Kaede takes the win. I offer him my hand. We shake, and he falls into step behind me as we take the elevator downstairs to the conference room. Two soldiers approaching the firing squad. We've been here before, a rag-tag team of two brothers facing down the other team on the football field, and later, the rest of the world, but now, we're facing down our future.

It's crowded in here today, because not only am I making my speech to the board, but there's a TV camera to livestream this throughout the company and for the PR department to send out to the media just in case they want to chew on this case even more.

If I have any advantage in all of this, it's that I've kept my speech to myself.

Dad, Courtney, the board . . . nobody knows what I'm about to say. Even Kaede doesn't know all the particulars, although he knows the gist of it and helped me work out the framework of my speech. It wouldn't have been fair to him otherwise.

The podium looks overwhelming, and as I set my tablet down on the metal surface, I have to take a few deep breaths in order to calm myself. As I do, I think about the one thing that matters the most, and as her face fills my mind, I find the strength to look up.

"Members of the board," I say, looking over the accumulated stern-faced suits in the room, and then I glance to the camera. "And my fellow co-workers. Over the past week, I've been embroiled in a scandal that has reached much, much further than I ever thought possible. That scandal has brought embarrassment to this company and to my family, and for that, I am sorry."

Bare-boned apologies while looking contrite, the start of any 'oops, got caught' press release . . . check. Time for a little personalization to make me seem human.

Is it bad that there's a formula for this? Probably, but with everyone from presidents to corporate giants having to apologize for various things over the years, there's actual science to back up the best way to save face when the shit hits the fan.

"I have spent my life as a representative of the Andrews name and this company. With that comes scrutiny and even lies. I'm sure you've all seen the headlines about my behavior, and certainly, the majority of those have been exaggerated, twisted, or flat-out made-up." I pause, letting that sink in.

"Truthfully, I have always tried to do the right thing, act in what I felt was the best interest of the company, and I've never, ever intended to harm anyone else with my choices." I swallow. "But the reality is, regardless of my good intentions, I have hurt the company and my family, and I will carry that burden with me for the rest of my life."

I lean over the podium with practiced ease, making it seem like it's only me and a small group of people speaking intimately. "May I speak frankly?"

There are a few raised eyebrows at my sudden change of tone and words, and down at the end of the front row, Dad tenses, looking like he's about to jump up and cut me off if I push the line.

Thing is, I'm not going to push the line. I plan on obliterating the fucking thing.

"A few weeks ago, it was suggested to me by people in this room and in shareholder groups that I needed to settle down. They chose to believe the lies printed about me over the truth, and their worries about image and stock prices seemed more important than my own integrity. I 'took one for the team', as it's said. I wanted to show that I was fit to run this company one day, willing to do whatever was needed to see that happen. I worried that without me, this company that my family built would suffer, that it would lose the path that it's followed for decades now. Ironically, I see now that my plan was nothing more than the ultimate expression of my unfitness."

I can see people looking to one another uncomfortably. They certainly didn't push me to do what I did, exactly—that's all on me—but they did put pressure on me.

"So that's the 'why' from me about why I did this." I intentionally don't say that we got married as a farce because I'm doing my damnedest to be as honest as I can be. "As for Ms. Russo? She had much more honorable reasons. Again, the media is painting her as everything from a gold-digger to a scam artist. She is none of those things. She is a kind, beautiful soul who wanted only one thing out of all of this. She wanted to give her dying grandfather a final memory, a thank you for everything he sacrificed to raise her. She wanted to give him the opportunity to walk her down the aisle and give her away in a fairy tale wedding before he meets his maker."

"That's it. Nothing in her mind ever thought of money, or social climbing, or scamming anyone or anything. She did what she did because she loves her grandfather with all her heart."

"And now, as Stefano Russo lies in a hospital bed, possibly dying due to our actions, I can only pray that he forgives us."

"But as Violet's scream pierced the chaos of our reception and I saw what we'd done to Stefano Russo, I realized the truth. Anyone who's willing to engage in such a sham to appease a group of shareholders, who was willing to lie to his own family and more, is not ready to lead this company."

There are gasps and murmurs through the room at the confession. This is something I've been groomed for since birth, and I'm admitting to an inadequacy in front of the whole world.

"So I've thought, and as I thought, I realized that there is an Andrews ready to lead this company when my father decides to step down many years from now. She stands at his shoulder every day at work and puts up with . . . well, more than I could. She's smart, she's capable, and she's the true next generation of leadership for this company. Of course, I'm talking about my sister, Courtney Andrews."

I look over to where she sits at Dad's side. Her jaw drops open for a split second before she composes herself and smiles politely, dipping her chin at the people who look her way. See?

She's already ready for this—professional, strategic, thoughtful, analytical. With several more years at Dad's side and his admittedly excellent mentorship, she'll be a fantastic leader.

"As for me . . . well, in all honesty, as I wrote this speech, a lightness came to my heart. Because I realize that there's something more important to me." I don't say her name, but it's readily apparent who, not what, I'm talking about. Dad blinks rapidly a few times before his eyes narrow as his lips twitch. I wonder what Mom's told him about my conversation with her. Does he know that he was right, after all? That his 'suggestion' that I settle down might have gone so shockingly wrong, but also so amazingly right?

"So effective immediately, I'm resigning from both the board of this company and as a vice president. I thank all of you for your years working with me and wish this company success in all its future endeavors. I am looking forward to setting out on my own and directing my own future where I see fit."

Without taking any questions from the board, most of whom look more than a little shocked, I walk out and go back to my office. I'm surprised to see Abi in my seat, her feet up on the wood and her lips pursed.

"Falling on your sword?" Abi asks, taking her feet down. "Didn't think that was your style."

"Guess you watched it, huh?" I reply, sitting down on the couch Violet ordered. She was right, of course. Even unfinished, the casual seating area does make my office feel more welcoming. Too bad it's coming right as I'm leaving. "What'd you think?"

She shrugs evasively and gets up to pour two glasses of scotch. She hands one over and sits down beside me. "It's eleven o'clock in the morning, Abs. A little early for scotch, don't you think?" Even as I argue, I take a small sip and swirl the liquid, looking for answers in its amber depths.

She takes a sip too, though she winces, and I remember that she's not much of a drinker to start with, so straight scotch has got to be downright disgusting to her. She's doing it for me.

"It's to celebrate," she says, lifting the glass to clink with mine. She looks for someplace to set the drink down. "You need a table."

I huff. "Violet ordered one. I think it'll be here next week, not that it matters. Celebrate what?"

She side-eyes me. "You finally stood up to Dad. It's about damn time."

"What the fuck are you talking about, Abs? I argue with Dad all the time. It's literally what we do most here, lately. I'm just taking my ball and leaving the playground." I shake my head, sure I'm doing the right thing by leaving the company but in shock that I actually did it.

"God, you are so blind sometimes. Please promise me that you won't go open some hot-shot venture capital day trading multi-marketing pyramid scheme. You're not cut out for it." She rolls her eyes, and forgetting, takes another sip of scotch. She hisses out loud this time.

I don't have a chance to argue because Courtney pops into the doorway. "Celebrating or commiserating?" she asks, lifting her chin toward our drinks.

"I'm not sure," I say honestly.

Courtney pulls a chair over to sit across from Abi and me. The new ones haven't been delivered yet. "I think you probably gave me the biggest endorsement ever," Courtney says, her face a mask of confusion. "Why'd you do it? You could have just said fuck this place, popped a peace sign, and walked out without a single fuck given."

"I could have," I admit, "but I do care about this place, and about Dad and you, Court. And I meant every word I said. I would have even said more, but I didn't want to spend ten minutes kissing your ass in front of the board. A big brother's got to have his line in the sand. Simple truth . . . this company's in damn good hands when Dad steps down."

"Weren't you just saying you were taking your ball and leaving?" It doesn't sound like it to me," Abi says, inserting herself into the 'Courtney's the best' lovefest.

Court looks at me, fury in her eyes. "Is that what you think you're doing? For the love of fuck, Ross. How stupid are you?"

Okay, there are things in life that will make you feel like less of a man—screaming like a little girl at a bug, cringing away from a punch, and . . . having your two little sisters call you out back to back.

"What the hell are you two mouthing about? It's not like I'm leaving on good terms or even know exactly what I'm leaving to do. But I just can't stay here. It's not good for any of us, and it's going to end up destroying the company, and more importantly, our family." My voice is getting louder, not in anger but frustration that they don't see what I see.

Courtney claps her hands, accenting my name. "Ross Andrews, you listen to me and you listen good." Even Abi shuts her always-running mouth at Court's don't-fuck-with-me tone.

"You just said some really sweet things about me in that meeting, but you have no idea why Dad works with me the way he does, do you?" She pauses for a nanosecond then dives back in. "News flash. It's not because I'm some yes-man who does what he says at every turn."

I raise a brow sardonically. "Seriously?"

She laughs big and bold. "Dad and I fight like cats and dogs about virtually everything—analyzing angles, negotiating percentages, calculating and strategizing in every way we can. It's what we do for *fun* because we are two peas in a pod. And then, once we reach a resolution behind closed doors, only then do we open the floor to discussion, knowing damn well what direction we're heading. Just because you only see me agree with Dad doesn't mean that I do. It means that I know when and where to argue and when and where to play nice. *He taught me that.*"

I look at Abi, who's looking at Court with thoughtful eyes. "I can see that," Abi says, nodding. "You're good at managing everything but protecting the image that needs to be presented."

"Thank you." Court dips her chin graciously. "Abi, why don't you work for the company?"

I'm spinning at the random direction change after Court drops a bombshell like her and Dad fighting all the time about work stuff. Okay, maybe it's not *fighting*, exactly, but I guess I did think Court went along with Dad most of the time. I guess not. I had no idea, literally none.

Abi grins. "Uhm, because *this*" —she waves her hands around my office— "is not me at all. I don't care about shareholders and making millions. I like losing myself in a beautiful arrangement, seeing someone's face light up when they get flowers, and the small potatoes style of my shop. Janey and I work damn hard, but I feel like I'm in control of my own destiny there. Here, I never would be."

That I knew. I remember Abi telling Dad that she was going to open a boutique flower shop after she graduated from business school. He'd been aghast, but she'd proven him wrong with hard work, dedication, and her own rebellious spirit.

Court smiles like that was exactly the answer she was going for, but I still don't get it. Shit. Could my sisters be right, and I'm an idiot? Evidence is pointing to that being the case with the way they're both looking at me like a bug in a jar, but I'm not sure why.

Abi rolls her eyes. "So, Dad wants what's best for us? Agreed?" I nod slowly, realizing that though he might've gone about it in the wrong way entirely, his intentions were good. Court said the same thing before. "He puts Court at his side, knowing she can hold her own there." I nod again, looking at Court, trying to picture her arguing with Dad.

"I might need proof of that," I suggest.

"He lets me go wild and open a flower shop." I smile, because Abi is a bit wild, but she's smart about it.

"And you . . ." I hold my breath, afraid of what she's going to say, of what failure she's going to point out because she's got several to choose from. "You, he puts in charge, but away from his shadow to let you shine because he knew you needed that space. You have always been the golden child, the one who worked his ass off to make Mom and Dad proud, but Dad wants you to grow up and be your own man. He was trying to help you stand on your own two feet, Ross."

My brows furrow in denial.

LAUREN LANDISH

Court jumps in. "What would've happened if Dad had told Abi or me to 'settle down with a good boy'?"

I scoff. "Well, first off, Abi would've told him to fuck off, and you would've probably said you're too young. And then I would've killed him."

She laughs. "But when he told you to, you marched right out there and got yourself a bride. Fucking overachiever."

Abi and Courtney both laugh, and I'm reminded of the years at home, the two of them having each other's back, but me always watching over them. I feel like those roles are changing. That maybe we're on equal footing now, protecting each other, and their attempt to knock some sense into my head is done with love.

"So, you two think my leaving is a *good* thing?" I'm trying to put pieces together here, but I feel like everyone else had the puzzle finished long ago and I'm just getting the box opened.

"Give the man a cookie," Courtney says.

"Well, that's what I'm doing," I say, throwing my hands up. "Why are you giving me such a hard time if I'm doing what you think I should?"

"Because you need to do it for the right reasons," Abi says, chill as a cucumber.

"Yeah, well, I've been doing all sorts of things for the wrong reasons lately, haven't I?" I say morosely.

They've given me so much to think about—my own personality, my history with Dad, my work here at the company—but I was telling the truth earlier. It's really all about Violet right now. The rest can wait. "She hates me. Look what happened to Papa. That was why she was doing all of this, and I ruined it."

"Pretty sure that was Colin," Abi says drolly. "But she doesn't hate you. She's just struggling right now. Papa had surgery Sunday, and he's still in ICU."

"They're moving him to rehab today," I interject, and she gapes. I shrug. "The hospital talks to the financial guarantor to arrange payments. What insurance didn't pay, I am. It's the least I can do."

Court and Abi both grin. "Good move," Court says with approval.

"Well, it's the only one I have until she talks to me again. I just want to be there for her. I know she's hurting and I don't want her to go through this alone."

"You really do love her, don't you?" Court says, and I nod.

Abi whispers something, looking at the ceiling, and I get the impression she's praying for forgiveness. "Uh, Abs . . . you okay?"

"I'm going to break a cardinal rule of friendship here, and that's something I don't take lightly. I want you to know that." Her build-up is making me nervous, but then I fly with her words. "Violet loves you, Ross. She always has, I think, but more importantly, she really does now. She didn't want to tell you before the wedding, but she's in love with you. Disgustingly so."

I stand up in shock, getting in Abi's face as I grab her shoulders and shake her. "Are you serious? I love her too, but I figured I could make her love me after she'd married me."

She laughs. "Figured a captive audience would be in your favor, did you?"

"Holy shit, I have to go to her. Now. Where is she?" I grab for my phone, already looking for her number. No, Archie's number. Violet won't answer, but I'll get him to tell me where she is.

"Whoa there, cowboy," Court says. "I think this is the time when you don't go rushing off half-cocked—wait . . . some other expression because I can't talk about my brother's cock. Anyway, what you need is a plan."

Abi claps happily. "Ooh, you're speaking my language, Sis."

"Scheming?" I ask, worried. "Isn't that how we got into this mess?"

Abi laughs. "Yeah, but sometimes, the only way to get out of the mess of a scheme . . . is another scheme. This one'll be different, though."

"How so?"

"You're going to make a complete ass of yourself while being totally honest. We combine that with enough romantic over the top gushing and you may have a chance."

I nod and wrap an arm around my sister's shoulders. "Okay, if we're being all honest and shit, I love you guys."

"You're all right sometimes," Court says with a smirk that looks so similar to my own.

Abi hugs my ribs, grinning. "Love you too, big brother."

CHAPTER 28

VIOLET—FRIDAY—6 DAYS AFTER THE
WEDDING

"*P*apa?" I ask as I come into his room. He's awake, which I didn't expect, but also, Nana and Mom are standing next to his bed looking happier than they have been in nearly a week.

"Violet, come here honey," Papa says, waving me over as he pats the bed next to him.

Mom still hasn't said much to me over the last few days, sticking mostly with Papa's medical updates and some orders on what to do at Nana's house, like 'go by and water the plants.' But right now, she seems to be in a better mood because she nods with a smile. She plants a kiss on Papa's cheek and then she and Nana move to give me space next to him.

"Sit down. Your grandmother's been filling me in on a lot of what's been going on while I was taking a nap."

"You weren't taking a nap, Papa," I remind him, worried he's confused about what's been happening. "You were—"

"I know, little one," Papa says with a smile, rubbing my hand. His voice is so soft I can barely hear him, but the light in his eyes means so much to me. He's not giving up, not yet. "But I'm not going just yet. I just wanted to pass along a little bit of advice, an old man to a young lady."

"Papa, I'm so sorry." I look from him to Nana to Mom, pleading with them for forgiveness.

"Don't apologize for anything," he says, patting my arm. "As for my advice . . . live your life, Violet. I love you, honey, but I am an old man. Regardless of whether I live one more day or one more decade, you can't live your life for me. Go and find your happiness. That's what I truly want. That's what I wanted all along. Walking you down the aisle was never about it being the end of my bucket list but about it being the beginning of your life. I just wanted to see my little Violet grown up and happy. That's all."

The words take a lot out of him, and he's wheezing a little at the end. "Stefano?" Nana says carefully.

He smiles and holds up a hand, letting us know he's okay.

"But . . . wait," I reply, starting to argue before something he just said hits me. "What's this about a decade?"

Papa taps his chest, tracing over the scar I know is hidden by his hospital gown. "That's the good news, too. Dr. Lee said that I was a textbook patient on the table. He said that with my new hardware, if I'm good and listen to Angela" —he looks at her lovingly— "I've maybe got a few more years in me. No promises, of course, but we're never promised tomorrow. But it's enough hope that maybe I'll give up a few things, and lead a bland, boring life of ease. Except for lasagna. They can pry that out of my cold, dead hands."

I swat at his arm super-gently. "That's not funny, Papa!"

"I was the one who almost died, so if I want to tell jokes about it, then I will. And no granddaughter of mine is going to stop me." He smiles, and I can't help but return one, even if the reminder still hurts.

Papa lies back and closes his eyes. "Tell me what happened. All of it . . . from that *figlio di puttana* to your Ross."

Mom gasps, "Dad!"

My Italian is excellent and fluent, but that's not an expression I've ever heard Papa say. I look to Mom in confusion and whisper, "What's that mean?"

Nana chuckles. "Mmm, my English curses are not the best, but something like son of a . . ."

Mom interrupts. "Motherfucker. Your grandfather just called Colin a motherfucker."

Nana exclaims happily, "Yes, that's it!"

I can't help but laugh, and it feels good. Papa is awake and going to be okay, my mom and Nana are sitting with me, and we're all smiling. It's everything I wanted . . . almost.

I tell them the whole story—how Ross and I ended up faking an engagement and wedding, how Colin came crawling back and I'd told him to get lost, and how I fell in love with Ross. For real. But now it's all in ruins.

"Oh, Violet," Mom says, tears in her eyes as she hugs me to her. I let myself get wrapped in her arms like when I was younger, even if I'm taller than she is now. "I'm so sorry."

"I'm sorry too, Mom."

Nana throws her arms around us, sobbing out. "I'm sorry too."

I look at her through blurry eyes. "What are you sorry for?"

She smiles. "I don't know, but I didn't want to be left out."

And then we're hugging again, a mess of tears and a blend of Italian and English as we make up.

Papa looks on from his bed with one eye open and a smile until we're done.

"So, what are you going to do about your husband, Vi?" he asks.

"Papa, he's not really my husband. We'll probably just get it annulled." The words catch in my throat painfully.

He motions for Nana to come closer and whispers in her ear. She dips her chin like she's asking if he's sure and he nods. She stands upright and then lays a sucker punch to my upper arm.

"Hey! What was that for?" I say, rubbing the spot even though Nana couldn't hurt a fly with a weak punch like that.

"You'll do no such thing until you tell him the truth of how you feel and see if he feels the same way," Papa decrees. He literally just told me to live my life for myself and not him, but then he turns around and starts making proclamations like he's a king. Not that I'm going to tell the man in the hospital bed with a new hardware-improved heart to hush.

Mama is slightly kinder. "Baby girl, that boy is over the moon for you. I saw that, which is why I was so mad. I thought he was lying to you, you were lying to him, and you were both lying to everyone. And that Colin boy? What were you ever thinking?" She shakes her head, her nose crinkled like she smells something bad.

I twist my lips. "I don't know, Mom. Maybe we were lying. Maybe mostly to ourselves."

"Tell him," Papa says again.

And this time, I nod in agreement. "I will."

"If he is not so sure, maybe remind him how beautiful you looked in your dress. Or remind him of *other things*. The stomach is not the only way to a man's heart," Nana says slyly. "Did I ever tell you how I got Stefano to propose to me?"

"NO!" Mom and I shout at the same time, but we smile when we see Nana and Papa making lovey-dovey eyes at one another. I probably don't want to hear that story, but if that look after fifty years of marriage is what I can have with Ross, I'm willing to do just about anything.

I STEP INTO THE HALLWAY, PULLING MY PHONE FROM MY BAG, and dial Ross. It rings three times and then goes to voicemail. I consider leaving a message but hang up, wanting to talk to him in person.

I call Abi next, thinking maybe she'll know where Ross is.

She answers right away but sounds breathless and her voice is a little too high. "Hey, Vi! Is Papa okay?"

"Yes," I say, nodding even though she can't see me. "Abi? I'm ready. I need to talk to Ross. Do you know where he is?"

She hums. "Uhm, maybe I do. He's had a really rough week at work. I'm sure you understand. Dad's coming down on him pretty hard."

There's a scuffle in the background, and I swear she makes some noise that translates to 'no' in dog language. "You okay, Abi?"

"What? Oh, yeah, *fine*. Just some ornery flowers not wanting to wait to bloom. I tell you what, give me until tomorrow. I'll get Ross and you together. It's what I do, after all!" She sounds breezy and weird, but I'll take it if she can get Ross to talk to me.

"Deal. What time and where?"

"Hmm, how about if I pick you up? That way, if it goes well, you can just go home with my brother."

"Shouldn't my going home to have make-up sex with your brother ick you out?" I say, remembering our earlier conversations about this very subject and finding a bit of my usual sass now that Papa's okay.

"Ew, you're right. I have to go bleach my eyes out. I'll pick you up tomorrow at eight!" And with a click, she's gone.

That was so weird, but that's Abi. And I'm sure her family is going nuclear with the fallout. I've tried to stay away from everything, the news, the papers, social media, because I wanted to focus on Papa. But now I wonder just how bad it's been for Ross.

PULLING INTO THE FAMILIAR PARKING LOT, MY NERVES START jangling all the more. "Abi, where are you taking me?"

"Zip it," she says from the driver's seat, her eyes gleaming. "Let me do what I do best. Put this on," she orders, handing me a swatch of black fabric.

I spread it out and realize, "Uhm, why are you giving me a blindfold? Is this going to be one of those high school nightmare things where everyone makes fun of me?" I smile as I say it, mostly trusting that Abi wouldn't do that to me but not one hundred percent.

"Do it. You know you wanna. Do it, do it, do it . . ." she chants like an after-school special about peer pressure.

I grin and slip the blindfold—okay, it's more a black sleeping mask—over my eyes. "If you're fucking me over, Abigail Andrews, I will never forgive you. And I'm going to tell your parents about every bad thing you ever did—sneaking out,

331

parties, making out with guys." She laughs, knowing there's not much to tell. We were pretty good kids.

The car stops and her door opens. A minute later, mine does too, and I feel Abi's hand as she helps me climb from the car.

"Are you ready for this, Violet? No going back, no take-back-sies. Once he's yours, you're stuck with him—smells, messiness, faults and all."

I laugh but grab at her hand. "You make it sound like he's a stinky teenager still. Trust me, I've seen Ross. He's all man."

Her retching gag noise is exactly the response I was going for. "Come on, before you start telling me all the dirty details. Oh, I'm supposed to remind you that you owe Archie those. Something about dip-dying silk and that you never make good on your promises. He said you'd know."

I grin beneath the mask, remembering how he'd complained about Bitch-ella's silk draperies but ultimately became besties with Mrs. Montgomery.

Abi is slowly stepping me closer and closer. I try to remember where the curbs are, where the steps are, and even where the old cracks in the concrete are. I don't want anything to take me down when I'm so close.

I feel the squishiness of the track under my heeled feet and Abi stops me. "You'll want to take your shoes off. They'll sink in the grass."

She helps hold me steady as I kick off my shoes. I can feel my sundress swishing around my ankles without the added height. She moves me forward a few more steps and then says, "Okay, we're here."

"Breathe for me, Vi. And then take the blindfold off," Abi chirps brightly. I can hear the excitement in her voice and can't wait. I don't bother with the breath and just reach up and take the mask off, my heart in my throat, to find . . .

Nothing.

I mean, I'm in our old high school football stadium. I knew that from the parking lot and the walk in, but it's dark and I can't see anything, even without the mask.

"What?" I ask, looking around, but it's too dark to see anything. "What are we doing here?"

"Close your eyes," Abi says, but it's not fast enough because suddenly, the whole stadium lights up and I'm blinded by the bright white lights. I throw my hands up to cover my face as I cry out, but slowly, I adjust.

I inch my hands away from my eyes, blinking, and that's when I see him. Or at least I think I do.

Ross is standing in the other endzone, literally one hundred yards away from me. I only know that from watching him play in high school and college and have literally never watched a game when Ross wasn't on the field. But he's not wearing a football jersey now. No, he's got on dark jeans and a button-down shirt and is holding a beautiful bouquet that I already know Abi made for him to give to me.

That schemer. God, I love her and her crazy ideas.

"Ross?" I whisper, knowing he can't hear me.

Across the distance, I hear him yelling. "Violet Russo, I love you!"

I gasp and shout back, "I love you too!"

There's a moment of frozen realization, and then I'm running. I have to hitch my skirt up when I almost trip, but I never miss a step. Running, running, running . . .

Straight into his arms. He catches me, spinning as I wrap my legs around him, our mouths devouring each other as we say it over and over again.

"I love you."

"I love you."

And I don't know how we ever thought this wasn't real because it's deep and pure and beautiful.

The lights wink out, drenching us in darkness, and Abi's voice calls out from somewhere. "Well, I'm out. It's on you two from here. The picnic basket's on the home team bench, Old Joe's the new guard and promised to keep any lookie-loos away, and the stadium is yours until morning."

Ross and I look at each other, so close that we can see each other in the dim light from the sliver of moon that's rising in the sky. We laugh and say at the same time, "Abi." She's a force of nature, my best friend. No, my sister-in-law.

He walks over and grabs the basket Abi left for us, dropping it gently to the center of the fifty-yard line. He spreads out the big blanket and we sit down.

"Oh, hey, Ross?"

"Yeah?" he calls out in the direction of Abi's fading voice.

"Can you take my girl Violet home? Seems she needs a *ride*?" She laughs at the thick layer of sexual innuendo she puts on the word *ride*, and I can't help but bite my lip, thinking she's right.

I do need a ride.

"I did have that dream about fucking you under the bleachers, but maybe the fifty-yard line is even better," I tease. "You think Old Joe would mind?"

Ross growls, "I don't give a fuck if he does. Get over here, Violet." He grabs me, pulling me astride his lap before I even get a chance to move. My dress moves easily out of the way, putting my core against the thick ridge of his cock behind his jeans.

"Oh, feeling bossy again, are we?" I say, running my fingers through his hair and down over his shoulders.

"That depends. Are you going to obey or am I going to have to spank you?" he murmurs against the delicate skin of my neck, kisses peppered between the words.

I hum in pleasure and admit, "Both of those sound pretty good."

"Honey, I love you so much, but I don't think I can wait. I need to be inside you. I need to be inside my wife."

I'll have to examine the words later because the blood is rushing south as my pussy soaks instantly. I fumble between my legs, trying to undo his jeans as quickly as possible.

"Ross, fuck me. Right here, right now," I plead.

He shoves my hands out of the way and makes faster progress, undoing his jeans and shoving them down his hips. His cock is rock hard, jutting up proudly between us.

He grips my hips, his fingers denting the supple flesh there as he lifts me. With one smooth motion, he sheathes himself in me to the hilt and I see stars. Not in the sky, but between us as my eyes slide shut in ecstasy.

This. This is what I need, what I am.

At one with Ross Andrews, my husband.

Oh, God, the thought drives me wild.

I buck against him, fucking him as he fucks me back, and I feel dangerously out of control but secure in the knowledge that he's got me. I clench around him, hugging him with my entire body. "Shit, Vi. You feel so good. Do that again," he grits out.

I tense every muscle in my core, and Ross wraps his arms around my back, holding me in place as he rocks his hips. He doesn't let me help now, instead making me take it—him, his love, his cock.

It's all I never knew I wanted.

The new angle rubs my clit against him with every thrust, and I quickly feel my orgasm bearing down on me. "Yes, that's it. Come on me. Come on my cock, wife."

I burst into fiery flames of passion, the electricity jolting through my entire body as I shatter and cry out his name. He follows me into the abyss, jerking against me, and I can feel the hot spurts of his cum filling me.

"I love you, Violet," he groans through his pleasure.

"I love you, Ross," I answer.

We collapse to the blanket, panting for breath. Too soon, he slides out of me and I shift over to lie on my side next to Ross, one leg thrown over his and my head cradled on his shoulder.

We're quiet, lost in our thoughts, but then the giddy little girl in me peeps up. "When did you know?"

"Know what?" he says, not letting me skate by. He wants me to say it, but I don't mind. I'll say it over and over.

I lift up, leaning on my elbow. "When did you know you loved me?"

He smiles that cocky smile that used to make me so furious, but now, I love it. "I think always. I was just too stupid to know it. Abi and Court have recently enlightened me on just how stupid I've always been about so many things."

I push at his chest. "You're not stupid. Don't say that."

"Truly, I didn't know when this started. But as our supposedly fake engagement continued, I woke up every morning feeling more and more like it was real. And when you were walking down the aisle toward me, all I wished for was that we could make it real. That somehow, despite my high school idiocy and all the other insanity, I could be the one to wake up next to you every day, that I could be the one to hold you in my arms every night. I wanted . . . I want to be your husband. Because, Violet Russo, somehow, some way, I've finally realized something that I should have seen years ago. I love you . . . I'm in love with you. So, Violet Russo, will you marry me? For real, this time?"

The words hang in the air, him asking me to marry him for real . . . or is it again? And before I realize it, a silence has stretched out between us.

But I don't want to wait. I know my answer.

Find your happiness.

I've known what that's been since I was a little girl, it seems.

"I love you too. And yes. I knew when I was walking down that aisle, too. I meant it, every word."

We seal the words with a kiss, this one honest and real.

CHAPTER 29

ROSS—TWO WEEKS LATER

"*S*ir, it's good to see you in such a good mood," Karl says as he opens the door for me. "I hear congratulations are in order?"

"For real this time," I reply, shaking his offered hand. "Violet will be here shortly. She's picking up Papa and Nana from his rehab appointment."

Karl smiles. "How is Mr. Russo doing?" Karl and Stefano have played chess a couple of times, and they get along very well. "Is he ready for a rematch?"

I lean forward, whispering conspiratorially, "I think he enjoyed his time at the inpatient rehab maybe a bit too much with all the attention." Karl and I laugh, and I tell him the rest. "He's home with Nana now, and they have a home health nurse coming every morning. In the afternoon, he goes to outpatient rehabilitation and does his exercises. It's wearing him out a bit, so you might go easy on him when you play. Let him win every once in a while, you know?" Karl shakes his head. "So far, he's been a picture-perfect patient, so they're hopeful he's going to be okay. At least for a while, and that's significant, considering his previous prognosis and age."

Karl raises a stern eyebrow. "You wouldn't be commenting that Mr. Russo is old, now would you?" If I were generous, I'd say Karl's in his late sixties, but where Stefano has struggled, Karl is fit and healthy.

"Of course not, Karl. I wouldn't dare or you'd probably kill me," I say with a wink.

He grins, patting me a little too firmly on the shoulder as a show of his still-present strength. "Yes, sir. Your mother is around in the garden."

"Thanks," I say, heading that way.

I find Mom out by the pool, trimming a few flowers and humming happily under her breath. "Mom?"

Mom looks up, her grin spreading to cover her whole face when she sees me. "Ross, honey!"

"Uh, mind setting down the clippers before you stab me?" I ask as she rushes over, causing her to pause and set her tools down before she hugs me hard. "How are you doing?"

"Just promise me that you're serious this time, that this is real?" Mom says, her voice thick with happy tears.

"Totally real," I promise her, hugging her back. "In fact, we decided to make a few changes just to show how serious we're going to be."

"Like what?" Mom asks, leading me over to the outdoor couch on the patio and having me take a seat. "Please don't tell me that you're going to re-invite Violet's entire family. I mean, they're lovely people, but things got a little out of hand last time even without the . . . theatrics."

I laugh. That's Mom. An interrupted reception, a fist fight, and a fake marriage, all caught on camera and played on the evening news . . . theatrics.

"We are thinking that smaller would be the way to go, a lot smaller, actually," I admit. "Now that Papa Stefano is doing better, we were thinking a nice, long engagement . . ."

I let it drag out, purposefully teasing Mom a bit, and she looks at me harshly. But I can read the humor in her eyes and relent. "Okay, long like about six months or so, then a small ceremony, just the close family?"

Mom smiles, nodding excitely. "Oh, you can have it here at the estate, and we can all pitch in. Abi can do the flowers, of course, and maybe Angela and Sofia could make dinner, and Karl would be happy to help Archie set up the altar. That sounds perfect." I can hear the relief in her voice.

I hear footsteps approaching and Dad calls out, "Don't stroke the boy's ego, Kimberly. Lord knows, he's arrogant enough as it is."

I laugh. Dad and I aren't completely repaired, but we've had a couple of long conversations and talked through some of the things Abi and Court brought to my attention. It was uncomfortable as fuck, neither of us particularly adept at discussing things as nebulous as feelings. But we'd muddled through and we're back on solid footing, secure enough to tease each other a bit.

"Well, you must think I'm perfect too, if that's where your mind immediately jumps," I retort, and Dad chucks me under the chin. "Mom was talking about it being perfect to have the wedding here. In six months."

Dad sits down, his lips pursed. "Is that what you want?"

As Abi and Court said, that's *progress*. Dad isn't making suggestions, isn't recommending one course over another, isn't even inviting me to discuss my thoughts on the idea. He's trusting that I've done my due diligence, know my own heart, and have made my own decision. Most importantly, he's trusting that I've made the right one.

"Yes, that's what I suggested to Violet already. I was hoping to ask for your permission, but it seems like Mom's already on board and volunteered the house."

"And the wait?" Dad follows up.

I smile. "We did things all out of order. We fought first, got engaged, moved in with each other, fell in love, and got married. We never really dated. I'm looking forward to doing that with Vi."

Mom's smile is wry. "Is it really dating if you're already living together?"

I chuckle. "Well, it didn't make sense for her to move out because she's already my wife."

Yeah, there's that. We decided to stay married and not seek an annulment. We know what was in our hearts as we walked down that aisle, and that's what matters. When we're ready, we'll do it again, and it will mean just as much. A continuation of our marriage vows, a renewal of our commitment, and another date for me to remember.

Abi threatened to tie me down and have both dates tattooed on my ass so I'd never forget. I think she's still worried that I'm going to fuck this up and ruin her relationship with her best friend. But I'm not that asshole I was in high school, not the cocky bastard I was just a few long weeks ago. And that's mostly because of Violet. Okay, and Abi and Court, though I won't ever tell them how much I appreciate the kick in the ass. And Dad too, but I did tell him that in one of those clumsy conversations.

Dad jokes back, "Okay, so you're living together. Does it make sense to date your wife?"

Mom answers for me. "Yes, Morgan. Yes, it does."

"Oops, walked right into that one. Sorry, dear. Maybe we could go to that restaurant you like this weekend? The one with all the spicy food that gives me heartburn?" He smiles, and I laugh as I figure out where I got my slick moves with the ladies . . . like flirting by putting frogs down their shirts.

She nods, committing him to a weekend of antacids, and I come in like any good wingman, pulling a distraction. "How're things at the office?"

He sighs gratefully. "Actually, Ross, I wanted to talk with you about that. Any chance you'd like to come back and rejoin the board of directors? Not the VP role. I know you want to step away from that, and Courtney is thrilled to step up and take on more responsibilities. She's already doing well with that. But the board position is less time-intensive, so you could do it and whatever else you decide to do."

I think it over, but as I do, what comes to my mind isn't the prestige of being with the company. It's the late nights, the hours that I've spent working, and how I'd much rather spend that time with Violet. My time at the company was never a nine to five.

"Dad, I'm not saying no . . . I'm saying I'm not sure I can give you an answer right now," I admit. "The idea of being part of the family company is nice, but the idea of being with Violet and spending time with her is pretty damn nice too. And this would be something we need to discuss together."

Dad purses his lips, disappointed but respectful. "I understand. It's open to you any time you'd like to have it. What are you thinking you're going to do?"

I appreciate that there's no pressure, no drive to get out there and make something of myself right this minute. "I'm still discussing it with Kaede. There's a part of me that wants to see if I can do what you did, build something of my own too. You taught me a lot, and I think it's time I put all those hours at your side to good use. If you or Courtney ever need me at Andrews, I'll be there, but I'm looking forward to a new challenge."

He smiles proudly and nods. "I'm sure you'll do whatever you put your mind to, Son."

THE WARM EVENING'S PERFECT FOR DINNER AS WE LIGHT UP the patio and set everything up for dinner. While I wish Marissa, Estella, and Vanessa could join us, along with the rest of Violet's family, they all had to leave town and return to their own lives. Apparently, the triplets' performance at our reception earned them some positive notoriety, and there's talk of their doing some recordings when they're on break from school. That was a silver lining to that particular dark cloud, at least.

"Good news, everyone," I report as we settle in and Nana starts passing around a huge tray of lasagna. "I got a call from Colin Radcliffe's lawyer. He's agreed to drop his suit if Abi and Violet are willing to drop the lawsuit over his recording on private property. Seems they got a rather threatening call from someone at Andrews?"

Courtney smiles like she's some sweet, innocent thing, but I know it was her. It was a stroke of genius, and all Courtney's idea, but a little bit of research by our lawyer found that Colin violated quite a few laws with recording Abi and Violet's conversation. It seems video recording on private property without the owner's permission is a huge no-no, and partner that with the audio recording, which is a separate offense, and Colin was looking at potential jail time. That was before we tacked on the civil suit with solid cases against Colin for defamation and trespassing at the wedding and reception with ill intentions.

Around the table, my news is greeted with smiles, except from Aunt Sofia. "I would have liked to have had a few minutes with that . . . excuse me, I must watch my tongue," she says, her lips pinching shut. "Father O'Flannigan says I inspired him to learn a little Italian, and I already owe him enough Hail Marys as it is. He's learning a new language. I'm learning to bite my tongue." She holds her hands up to the sky. "*Dio Mio!*"

Violet, who looks amazing as always sitting next to me, laughs. "I give it a week before you're back to your normal self."

Sofia laughs, shrugging. "Someone has to keep you all in line! And nobody's better than an Italian aunt!"

"Whoa, there, Aunt Sofia," I plead, holding up my hands. "I'm new around here, but I already know not to mess with you."

"Well, as long as you're scared of a little old lady," Abi teases as she reaches across me, "I'm gonna grab the garlic bread."

We get everything passed out, all of the dishes coming around family style. Plates are filled, and the conversation's loud and boisterous. If anyone looks upset, it has to be Stefano.

"What is it, Papa?" Violet asks after Nana's said grace and everyone starts to dig in. Stefano's got a pained expression in his face, and I swear he looks emotional. "Are you okay? Is it your heart?"

"Yes and no," Stefano says, sighing miserably. "All this wonderful food, but those doctors, they want me to eat less!"

"Well, you know, Stefano," Mom says, trying to be helpful, "tomatoes are very rich in lycopene and vitamins. They're actually great for your heart. You might just need to adjust the recipes . . ." Mom pauses, feeling the glares from Nana and Sofia. "I'm just saying."

"Kimberly," Maria says, patting her on the arm, "stop before Nana invokes Susan Lucci on you. Just trust me, it's not worth it."

Mom looks very confused but does indeed drop her suggestions about how to make Nana's Italian food healthier for Stefano.

Stefano, though, has one more complaint. "And worst of all, no more of my cigars!"

"Thank *Madre Maria!*" Nana declares. "It'll still be years before I get that stink out of my house!"

"Your house?" Stefano growls, and out of the corner of my eye, I see Violet covering her mouth as she tries to hide the smile. "Woman, I worked for forty-five years to—"

"I have an idea," Dad says, not used to their bickering. "Stefano, after dinner, would you care to join me in my study for some fine bourbon?"

Stefano immediately stops bickering with Nana and turns to Dad, grinning. "If you've got a good scotch . . . I think I might find your study even more enjoyable than my own bedroom."

"Where you won't be sleeping tonight if you keep up with your mouthing, man," Nana sasses back. "The couch is calling your name."

I can't help but laugh, and everyone else busts out too. Maria tries to reign her mother in. "Mom, could you maybe not discuss your sleeping arrangements in front of Violet's new family? You're going to scare them off because you're acting *pazza*."

I lean over and whisper in Violet's ear as everyone teases and jokes around us. "I think I can see where you got your smart mouth from."

She licks her lips and my eyes follow the movement. "Yeah, we're all pretty much ball-busters. Some people can handle it, some can't," she whispers back with a shrug like she hasn't decided if I can handle her or not.

Sassy minx. She knows exactly what she's doing.

"Keep talking about handling my balls, Vi, and I'll give you everything in them. Where do you want it tonight?" My voice is low and dark, full of promise.

"Wherever you want to give it to me, husband. You know how much I like to *obey*." She drawls the last word out, a dare and challenge all at once because we both know that there's not a

LAUREN LANDISH

damn thing in this world that could make Violet Antonia Carlotta Russo obey an order she doesn't want to. But oh, when she wants to, she is glorious in her utter wanton surrender.

And I'm the only man who gets to see her that way, her husband.

EPILOGUE

VIOLET—TWO MONTHS LATER

So what if it's not six months?

Simply put, two months was enough time.

Not for us to fall deeper in love, although that's happened. Every moment Ross and I spend together, we find a new reason to love each other even more deeply.

And not because we needed to gain the understanding of our families. If anything, Nana's repeated suggestions that we 'get down to the baby making' seems to have ignited a desire in both families for us to speed things up.

Including us, which is why we've been ready for this for weeks already.

In the end, the only thing that's held us up was Father O'Flannigan. After we went back to him and explained everything, especially what was in our hearts as we said our vows, he said he needed to talk to the archbishop. Our situation wasn't something the church normally dealt with, after all.

Regardless of the particulars, everything's perfect now. Father O'Flannigan is blessing our union and giving us a chance to speak our own thoughts as a reaffirmation of our vows. Since we're already officially married and this is more of a casual thing for our family, Father O'Flannigan even agreed to do it at the Andrews estate instead of the church. That alone took two conversations to make sure we could do that.

But finally, here we are.

The air's cooler than before, and the leaves are starting to change, making everything even more beautiful, in my opinion. There are lots of reds and oranges in the trees around us, and as Papa slowly and carefully walks me down the grassy aisle, I'm ecstatic.

It's only our immediate families, plus Archie and Kaede. No company executives, no fourth cousins from Sardinia or Crete, nothing but a baker's dozen of chairs lined up, a simple altar in Kimberly's garden, and us. I've even ditched the fancy dress for a simple white silk slip dress, which is much more comfortable since it's my actual size.

"You look beautiful, Violet," Papa says as we walk. "So happy, which is all I've ever wanted for you, dear."

"I am, Papa," I tell him quietly so I don't overshadow the soft music pumping through the home stereo system. No DJ this time, no orchestra, just a fancy sound system. It's better that way. "I'm marrying for the right reasons, and I've found my happiness."

Papa hums and kisses my cheek at the end of the aisle. "That's my girl."

The ceremony is simple, with none of the craziness that marred our last wedding. Father O'Flannigan talks about the specialness of love and living with an open heart and then performs the blessing over our interlocked hands.

This time, when I say my vows, I remember every word because I wrote them myself. Ross did the same.

"Sometimes, there are events in your life that are like big, flashing signs that things are going to change," Ross says as he holds my hands. "Sometimes, though, those life-changing events happen so quickly, or so subtly, you don't even notice them. For me, that event was the first day my little sister invited you over to play at our house. My life changed that day. And while it took me a long time to figure it out, I realize now that I want one thing in my life. You. To love you, to honor you . . . to be your husband. Forever."

Kimberly's openly crying, and I have to blink back tears as I reply. "I hated you. For so long, I thought you were my tormentor, the boy to haunt my dreams and make my school days a living nightmare. But then I saw through the teasing, the hard words, and saw the real you. The man you've become, the man I love with all my heart. Today, forever and always, I want to be yours. Your love, your woman, your wife. Forever."

A minute later, we kiss, and as our family surrounds us, Father O'Flannigan gets a joke in. "So . . . about the marriage license. Should I sign it this time?"

Morgan is the quickest response. "You'd better have already done that months ago. That's my daughter-in-law right there." He tosses me a wink, and I remember how Ross said that Morgan didn't want me to get hurt. That all along, he truly wanted what was best for everyone. He might've been a bit bumbling about it, but he was right in the end.

Ross was ready to settle down. I was too. And thanks to Abi's scheming, we've actually got a true happily ever after of a marriage, not just a big, fat, fake wedding.

Ross

THE BRIDAL SUITE'S NOWHERE NEAR AS BIG AS MY penthouse . . . excuse me, *our* penthouse. Then again, the penthouse doesn't have a view that can even hold a candle to the view outside our hut. With an unspoiled view of the beach and the ocean on one side and the Hawaiian jungle on the other, I can forgive the relative lack of bells and whistles.

Besides, the most beautiful vision I've ever seen stands in the doorway right now, her red slip clinging to every curve as she hungrily traces my naked body with her eyes. I'll admit that I flex a bit for her.

"You're gorgeous," I murmur as Violet climbs onto the bed, the hem riding high enough on her hip to show me that she's not wearing any panties underneath. I don't know what it is about my girl going commando, but knowing that she's not wearing panties now, and in fact hasn't worn any panties since we left for our honeymoon, certainly had me hard as a rock on the entire flight across the Pacific.

"You're just saying that because you want to have sex with me," Violet purrs, leaning down to dangle her dark hair around our faces and envelope us in a shadowy cave. "Admit it."

I wrap my arms around her, flipping her over in the soft bed and making Violet squeal in surprise. "I'll admit one thing. I love everything about you," I growl before showering her neck with kisses. "I especially love the way your pussy feels when you cream all over my cock." I thrust against her, sliding along her slippery seam but not entering her yet, teasing us both with what we want.

Violet purrs underneath me, our hands touching and exploring each other as we celebrate our marriage. It's been a long, twisty road, and in the future, I'm not looking forward to Aunt Abi and Aunt Courtney explaining to our children just how we got together.

But that's for later. Much later.

Right now, I'm thankful to be feasting on Violet's voluptuous, luxurious body. Soft swells of breasts capped with delicious nipples pebble at my touch as I slip the straps off her shoulders, exposing her skin to my lips and tongue.

As I taste her, Violet arches her back, her hands running through my hair. Her core presses against my rock-hard cock, precum oozing from its tip. I ride her, my cockhead dancing over her clit as I suck and nibble her breasts, moaning as she slips from side to side, encouraging me.

Violet moans as my hips speed up. Reluctantly, I pull back, trembling as I kiss down her stomach to the softness of her pussy. I dip my tongue deep inside her cleft, scooping her honey out into my hungry mouth, so sweet and tangy all at once.

I look up while lapping at her, my cock leaking between my legs at the sight of Violet watching me, squeezing and massaging her breasts and pinching her nipples. She lifts her hips, offering herself fully to me and letting my hands have access to her ass. We've both explored and discovered so much about each other over the past two months, and as my tongue flicks over her clit, I use my little finger to circle her asshole, the two combining to drive her wild.

"Fuck, Ross!" she screams as she falls apart on my tongue, grinding against my mouth and covering my face in her juices. She bucks and quivers, her hips driving up until she collapses and she pushes me onto my back. It's something that we've just learned about Violet . . . when she's double-stimulated, the orgasm doesn't drain her but supercharges her, something we both enjoy.

I lie back, letting her have her way with me and happily giving her control the way she just trusted me with it. Violet places my steely hard shaft between her tits, moving in a sexy massaging wave that leaves me breathless. With each stroke of my cock between her soft mounds, she voraciously sucks on the head of my cock, leaving me trembling on the edge of coming.

But Violet knows me as much as I know her now, and she pulls back, panting as she quickly climbs on top of me and impales herself on my cock. Both of us freeze, the feeling of being together with no doubts, no questions, no lies, and having been blessed anew stopping time as we adjust to the powerful sensations in our hearts, minds, and bodies.

"Mmm . . . I like married sex, Mr. Andrews," Violet purrs when she's ready, kissing my chin.

"I like married sex too, Mrs. Andrews," I reply, reaching down and cupping her ass. Violet lifts up, riding me slowly, her slip a puddle of silk around her belly button as she slides up and down my cock.

We take our time, letting the heat build within her body, her breasts rising and falling until she reaches down and I capture her fingers in a tight grip, our hands intertwined.

Faster and faster we go, my hips thrusting up to meet her tight pussy, sheathing deep inside her with each slap of our skin. Violet throws her head back, her hair a cascade of curls and her skin flushed pink as she nears the edge again. Her pussy squeezes and tightens around my cock, driving me right to my limits.

She drops down hard, taking all of me and shattering herself as she cries out, her voice pure and joyous on the warm tropical air.

'Say it,' I growl through gritted teeth.

"I love you, Ross. My husband." Her words are breathless and stilted but what I need to hear to trigger my own orgasm.

I join her, my balls tightening and exploding, filling her with my seed as deep as I can as I grunt out, "I love you too. Wife."

Finally, the world spins and I pull her to me, holding her tight until everything comes back together.

In the calm following the storm, Violet sighs happily on my chest. "Two whole weeks of this, huh?"

"That's the plan."

Violet laughs and kisses my chin again. "Keep it up, mister, and we're going to have a stowaway on the trip home." Violet rubs her belly down low, and I wonder if Nana's baby chatter is getting to her the way it has to everyone else.

"Sounds good to me," I say seriously.

Violet looks up at me, her eyes searching mine in question even as she jokes. "You do remember that twins and triplets run in my family, right?"

I snuggle her to my chest again. She relaxes, thinking I was just kidding and that she scared me off. But there's no way. The only thing better than the thought of her by my side every day for the rest of our lives is the idea that she would be there holding our child.

"Bring it on, Chickie," I whisper, and she balks loudly. Until I flip her over and slip my fingers in her messy pussy and press my lips along those shapely legs she's trying to wrap around me. Amazing how she settles quite quickly and starts chanting my name when I do that.

By the time she comes, she'll have agreed to think about babies. We'll get there, when we're both ready. Just like we got to this point, happily married, when the time was right. Even if it did take a big, fat, fake wedding.

Thank you for reading! I hope you enjoyed the book. If you did, please take a moment and leave a review!

Don't want to miss any of my new books or special sales?

Join my mailing list here. I typically only send two or three emails a month.

Continue reading for a preview of the first book in my *Get Dirty* series, Dirty Talk. It's naughty, but it's sooo sweet! Derrick King is the ultimate book boyfriend.

ABOUT THE AUTHOR

Bennett Boys Ranch:
Buck Wild || Riding Hard || Racing Hearts

Dirty Fairy Tales:
Beauty and the Billionaire || Not So Prince Charming || Happily
Never After

Get Dirty:
Dirty Talk || Dirty Laundry || Dirty Deeds || Dirty Secrets

*Irresistible Bachelor*s:
Anaconda || Mr. Fiance || Heartstopper
Stud Muffin || Mr. Fixit || Matchmaker
Motorhead || Baby Daddy || Untamed

Connect with Lauren Landish
www.laurenlandish.com
admin@laurenlandish.com
www.facebook.com/lauren.landish

Made in the USA
Coppell, TX
22 March 2020